Kirin Rise
The Shadows Unleashed

To Isabelle,
Always B U,

To Isabelle.
Thanks.

Kirin Rise
The Shadows Unleashed

Ed Cruz

Illustrated by Ron Langtiw

Preface

*I*mpossible. The single word was burned into the minds of millions of fans by the United Federation of Mixed Fighting (UFMF). Long ago, the UFMF had established the precedent that no one should ever dare challenge its power. To do so was unimaginable. However, human nature is a force that is difficult to contain. A handful of the mightiest had tried and failed. Yet, like a fairytale, it was not a hulking fighter that destroyed this fan belief. Instead, an unsuspecting hero, small in stature and meek in voice, rose to the challenge and ignited a movement against the UFMF greater than anyone could imagine.

Kirin Rise became the first woman and unranked rookie contender to win the UFMF Dome Championship. After she overcame nearly insurmountable odds to defeat Diesel, the number one contender, her final act was a reminder that compassion and humanity still existed. Kirin had shown that an indomitable spirit could be a force to stand up to anything. Her actions shook the UFMF to its core and showed the masses that the all-powerful Federation had been handed a major setback. Kirin's victory had unified a nation in disarray, and her voice now carried more weight than those of the corrupt government and greedy corporations combined.

Naturally, Kirin's actions have not gone unnoticed by those in power, and her victory celebration with family and friends may be very short-lived.

Deep within the UFMF, a powerful force has surfaced: Youshiro Watanabe, the owner and CEO of the UFMF. Emerging from the shadows, he stands poised to unleash his master plan—a plan that will call into question if indeed Kirin's victory was nothing more than a single piece of the puzzle.

The challenges facing Kirin are more than most twenty-year-olds can handle. Her decisions will drastically affect those around her, family and friends alike. Her closest friends, Gwen and Sage, have always been a wellspring of support for Kirin and her actions. Now more than ever, she needs the wisdom of her Gung Fu teacher, Sifu, to guide her through her most difficult times. Complicating everything, Kirin must now tackle her feelings toward two rivals for her affection: Hunter, the boy who fell for her at first sight, and Tobias, the tough guy who is too afraid to express his feelings.

Kirin Rise must learn a new lesson: for every decision and every action set into motion, there will be a price to pay. Only Kirin can know if her convictions are worth the sacrifice she must make to achieve her goal.

This book is dedicated to all the teachers out there who continue doing their job even though they may be unappreciated and underpaid. Please continue to endure, even if it seems students don't understand. I, for one, am a clear example that the lesson will eventually be learned.

To Mrs. Carlisle, my seventh-grade English teacher, little did I know your fifteen minutes of freestyle writing would aid me on my journey into writing. To my Sifu, Augustine Fong, the debt I owe you is unrepayable. Your knowledge and teachings go above and beyond description. To Junko Sumogye, Michiko Lilly, and Yuko Kawashima, my Japanese teachers, thank you for your patience and understand. To my parents, who have guided me, you set me on the right path from the very start.

Finally, a special thanks to all the individuals who helped bring this project to life. Here's to our Kickstarter supporters for believing in us.

Mario & Cora Afable	Kristen Goad	Snacky Pete
William L. Allen	Oscar & Lolita Gramata	Rejane Pierre
John Alvizuri	Danish Haque	Phillip Pooler
Alphonse Arias	Cody Hasty	Alan Prentice
Ray Arias	Harlan Heiber	Teocarlo Pulgar
Burn In Designs	Mark Howard	Anthony Pinto
Mike Brettle	Winifred Hu	Trina Ro
Philip Cairns	Mary Jack	John Roiniotis
Rolan & Wanda Capua	Kusagaya Ryocel Joshua	Joseph Salazar
Ryan Carandang	Amm Kay	Luis R Santiago Jr
Manny & Mila Caspillan	Clarence Keener	Jessica Sarzynski
Eric Chen	Mireya Ledesma	Malte Momme Schmidt
Mark Colbert	Robert Lee	Medy Silva
Jennifer Colvin	Chun Li	Neal Sipkovsky
Ryan Concepcion	Frank Li	Miss Snep
J.R. Dadivas	Karen Lim	Dicko Mas Soebekti
Audrey De la Cruz	Christopher Louis	David Thompson
Flor de la cruz	Lance E Loving	Touacheng
Paulette de la Cruz-Johnson	Enrico Luna	Austin Tseu
Cynthia Ruiz-DelaCruz	Thomas Mac	Heather Jenelle Ulangca
J. de la Cruz	Victor Medina	Joseph Von-Dortch

Contents

Character Information

	**Name:** Youshiro Watanabe **Family:** Single, one son **Profession:** Majority shareholder of the UFMF corporation. **Interest:** Bringing balance to humanity **Tidbits:** Has a board game in his main office. Always carries a lighter, but does not smoke. Has not been seen in the public eye since Thorne took over.
	**Name:** Kristen Lawless **Family:** Single **Profession:** Youshiro Watanabe's right-hand "man" **Interest:** Taking over Thorne's job **Tidbits:** Graduated at the top of her class. Is a workaholic. She hates Fawn even more than she despises Thorne. Is an expert at guns, and in her free time she cooks.
	**Name:** Justice William Dye **Family:** Unknown **Profession:** Thorne's personal bodyguard **Interest:** Unknown **Tidbits:** Highly skilled in fighting. He is antisocial and his only form of interacting with the outside world is playing MMORPG.
	**Name:** Bryce Adams **Family:** Wife and one daughter **Profession:** Political activist **Interest:** Conservation **Tidbits:** Is a vegetarian and grows his own vegetables and raises his own chickens. Enjoys watching the UFMF. If he didn't' live in the city, he would be a farmer.

Name: Ripley Hawkins, aka Whiskey
Interest: Being popular and shopping
Tidbits: Has a secret that no one knows. She has heterochromia iridis, as one eye is green and the other is blue. Only wears name brand shoes and clothes. Always has an entourage of two girls with her.

Name: Quinn Michaels
Profession: Works for the UFMF in accounting
Interest: Plays several instruments
Tidbits: He was born blind. Is a terrible painter but is exceptional at sculpting. Really loves music and on occasion will DJ. He drinks only one kind of alcohol.

Name: Tyrone Walker, aka Big T
Interest: Carpentry
Tidbits: Always steals chopsticks at every Asian restaurant. He collects old electronics. Is terrible at sports, but enjoys reading more. Big T and Danny always gamble with one another. Works part times with at a barber shop.

Name: Ryan Bautista, aka Peanut Boy
Interest: Loves anime and video games
Tidbits: Holds the record with his group for most marshmallows stuffed in his mouth. He wants to be a professional eater. Immune to brain freeze and dresses in layers. Allergic to peanuts. Has no luck with the ladies.

Name: Danny Torez, aka The Rabbit
Interest: Coffee and troubled women
Tidbits: Is an askhole—someone who asks for advice and does the complete opposite. Goes to confession 18 times a year. Has a Puerto Rican frog tattooed on his arm. Shirks from responsibility.

Name: Kenneth Fischer, aka El Blanco
Interest: Huge sports fan and burger expert
Tidbits: Talks comics with Robert nonstop. Is a sweets addict. Thinks he can draw. Unlike Ryan he can get a girlfriend, but can't hold on to them. Wants to be a firefighter and secretly enjoys watching love stories.

Name: Danish Chaudhary (D0c), aka The Professor
Interest: Flying drones
Tidbits: He's the brains of the group and for good reason. He is the voice of reason and is the first one everyone confides in. He has a dark side to him, as he likes to be a troublemaker to balance things out. He secretly dates the girls that Tobias dumps. He also has a crush on Kirin, but for some reason never acts on it.

Name: Robert Ho, aka K-pop
Interest: Plays the trumpet
Tidbits: He won't date his own kind and says he's not racist. He has a type A personality—"A" meaning asshole. He dresses like a K-pop star and avoids tasteless American food by carrying a tiny sriracha bottle with him all the time. He always rags on Danny and Ryan.

CHAPTER 1

The Meeting

Late December 2032

Two sets of footsteps could be heard strolling down the lengthy hallway. Odd, considering there were four people approaching the entrance. As Thorne's footsteps echoed their own beat, the three secretaries walking directly in front of him somehow managed a singular sound. Thorne's normally razor-sharp focus was put to the test. He was lost in the mesmerizing motion of their swaying hips instead of the moment at hand. Despite the situation, he appreciated this quirky oddity before him. He pondered briefly whether this was coincidence or somehow a symbiotic bond between the three women.

Thorne leaned slightly to the side to see what lay ahead. He winced at the sight, but remained silent for the time being. In the distance, he could see a large half-u-shaped table made entirely of glass, split into three sections. Behind each table were three chairs, thin and shaped like wine glasses in design. He questioned how comfortable one would be to sit on, but quickly dismissed its importance. Thorne was always very aware of his surroundings. He began to piece things together. The theme of the entire floor seemed to parallel the three secretaries. Strange, yet beautiful, things were done in threes. As they drew nearer, the three large TV screens set horizontally on the wall turned on. Each one was playing an identical silent ad with the stars of the UFMF. An image of Kirin flashed. Thorne cringed.

Thorne and the secretaries finally reached the end of the hallway, and the sound of their collective footsteps came to a halt. To Thorne's left stood a grand double door. Colored in charcoal black and crafted from mahogany, it made for an impressive display. The three secretaries lined up next to each other and turned around—again in unison.

Thorne froze in place, adjusted his tie, and waited. He tried to make eye contact with each of them, but they all stared directly into nothingness. Their beauty was captivating, but something about them seemed almost too perfect.

The lead secretary finally made eye contact with Thorne and spoke. With an artificial smile and a robotic voice, she said, "Mr. Thorne, would you please wait a moment?" She bowed, stepped back into place, and synced her endless robotic stare along with the other two secretaries.

Thorne nodded and waited with both hands behind his back. He stood there remaining cool, but deep down he felt on edge. For a man who was always several steps ahead of the game, his discomfort lay in the unknown. He cut his eyes to the secretaries, trying to force some interaction, but none bit. All three stood still modeling a pose and seemingly waiting for a photographer to say, "Cut." Thorne looked away, as his earlier appreciation for this oddity was quickly turning to annoyance.

Moments later, the door swung open. Each secretary's head turned one after the other like a set of dominos. There at the door entrance she stood, Kristen Lawless. A beam of light showered her from behind, showcasing her Barbie-shaped figure along with her bleached-blonde hair. It was tied back in a bun like a librarian's; she adjusted her glasses to look at Thorne. She did her best to tone down her looks and let her brains be the center of attention. However, even with her dull business suit and tie outfit, there was no denying that there was something special about her. Her gaze toward Thorne was like a laser, as he could feel the hate. The hairs on the back of his neck began to rise.

It was apparent that neither one liked the other, but respect was equally given. They smiled at each other to appear civilized and approached for the usual formalities. A firm hand shake was followed by a brief, no-contact kiss to the cheek. All superficial, but it was the appearance that counted.

Thorne often found Kristen's last name comical. From his past conversations with her, he knew she would swear it was her real name. It was one of many things that Thorne was kept in the dark about her. Thorne's past relationship with Ms. Lawless was … complicated, to say the least. Both had carried the same ambition and excellent pedigree to rise to the top of the UFMF company, but when the final decision was made, Thorne had been chosen over Kristen to serve as president of the UFMF. Thorne found it suspicious that, instead of leaving the company, she had taken the position of being a personal assistant, much like Fawn. However, he had quickly deduced that Kristen was positioning herself to take over if any mistakes were made under his watch.

Kristen turned around so that her backside was facing Thorne. She said, "Please follow me, *Jacob*." The way she said his name had just the right amount of Southern twang.

It irked Thorne slightly that his proper title wasn't given. He was sure that Kristen did it on purpose. He peeked at the curves of her hips, which brought a quick run down memory lane. He recalled the bad along with the good and remembered why she was not worth the trouble. That one moment of weakness had taught him not to make decisions with that part of his anatomy.

Thorne straightened his jacket and hastened his pace so that he walked slightly ahead of Kristen. She noticed this as they continued to jockey for position. Kristen was notorious for playing amusing little games with him.

They turned down another hallway, slightly shorter than the first, this time going in a completely opposite direction. It seemed redundant, but whoever had been put in charge of design had been told to do so.

"You're looking good, as always, Kristen," said Thorne. That was his dig back at her. Thorne knew that she hated that her looks were the first thing she was judged on. But, beautiful women all live with that same curse—the truth no ugly person would ever want to hear them complain about.

Kristen stared straight ahead. "Thank you … *Jacob!*" Kristen emphasized his name again, as the two played a round of childish games with one another. It was hard to imagine that two high-level executives could regress to acting as teenagers in high school dealing with a lovers' spat.

Just as words were launched, silence quickly ensued. Now, neither one wanted to make the first move, but Thorne was at the disadvantage. He had been summoned. Unlike the first hallway he had walked down which flowed in threes, the layout of this one was more suited to Kristen's personality. It felt cold and lifeless, shimmering a plain white from the marble floor. This was the perfect lair for Kristen: a palace befitting the Ice-Bitch-Queen of the South.

He said coyly as he turned to Kristen, "Any ideas why I was called in?"

Kristen's demeanor remained unchanged as she replied, "Honestly, Jacob, if I knew, I would tell you. This is the one time that he's left me out of the loop."

Thorne listened intently as he calculated her words. Surprisingly, he believed her as they continued walking. She remained cold to his presence and kept the conversation to a minimum. He decided to throw her another line and see if she would bite.

"The ratings were astronomical for the fight, and UFMF stock was up about another 5%."

Kristen stopped walking, and Thorne paused and followed her lead. She looked at him and laid the sarcasm on thick. "That would be great, Jacob, if the UFMF were geared toward making money over fighting matches."

They stood silently at each other, staring one another down, neither willing to blink.

Kristen took the initiative and said, "Hurry. We shouldn't keep him waiting.... You know how he hates to wait." She began walking briskly, this time with more intent, and Thorne followed. Moments later, they reached the other end of the hallway where a desk stood. Thorne faced another door on his right side.

Kristen knocked on the double doors, and the sound flooded the hallway. She did not wait for a response. She grabbed hold of both handles and opened them for Thorne. Thorne stepped to the side, giving her room to maneuver. Without speaking another word, she waved her hand, directing Thorne to enter.

Thorne began to walk past Kristen, who wore a smirk on her face. As he passed by, she whispered, "Good luck, *Jacob*."

Her words passed through Thorne unnoticed. He was too focused on the moment. He walked by her without a word or a glance, and she turned away, discouraged like a little child being ignored.

His zig-zag walk through stretched-out hallways finally revealed a peculiarly designed triangle-shaped office. Thorne took a quick scan of his surroundings. Not much had changed in the look of the room; in fact, it was almost the same. However, a strange new table sat on the opposite end of Watanabe's samurai display. Thorne tried to catch a glimpse of what was on it, but could not make it out. The two outer walls made of glass stretched far and met at the tip of the room. That was the only thing that their offices had in common, for the rest was a stark contrast to his own. While Thorne's office felt like the inside of a museum, this room was virtually empty. The white marble floor made it look like a hospital ward; the only things missing were the patients waiting. The room had a minimalist look, which wasn't quite to Thorne's taste.

Upon entering the room, flashbacks of a celebratory time brought back some of Thorne's emotions. He remembered the very day he had been chosen to head the UFMF. That was a distant memory and a different time. Thorne wondered if things had come full circle and the spot where he had stood while beginning his reign would also mark the end.

The doors slammed behind Thorne and caused a slight breeze, confirming his entrance. He stood still for a moment and then began his walk toward the glass desk that stood at the triangle tip of the room. Behind the desk was a black leather chair, with its back turned toward him. The desk was clean, supporting only a single clear container placed neatly on the side. The only other object in the room was a finely crafted samurai suit, along with two swords near its base. If not for these three items, the room would have been plain and boring.

He glanced toward the window, finding it odd that it was raining heavily outside. However, no words were uttered as Thorne continued his walk. The sounds of his footsteps echoed through the room. Soon, the footsteps began to match the beat of his heart as Thorne neared his destination. He began to recall everything he could about Youshiro Watanabe. Thorne felt he was above most individuals, and he rarely looked up to anyone—yet, Watanabe was unlike any leader he had ever encountered. He did not demand respect; instead, his demeanor and personality led to many individuals admiring him. It was a mutual giving and more powerful than that which could be bestowed due to someone's position.

Watanabe was full-blooded Japanese. He had been raised most of his life in his hometown of Kyoto, Japan. His great-great-grandfather was a Kamikaze fighter in World War II. He was an only child, brought up by tradition with a very strict and unforgiving father. His résumé was much different from Thorne's elite pedigree, as he had learned from the school of hard knocks. Over the years, Watanabe had become more reclusive, handing the reins of his company to Thorne and playing a more silent role. It had been years since he had been seen by anyone in public.

Thorne did not wait for a greeting from Watanabe and spoke in Japanese. "*Kono tabino kotowa subete watashi no sekini desu....*" Roughly translated, he humbly apologized for his actions. He immediately followed his words with a bow, but before he could utter another word, a hand raised from the side of the chair, gesturing for him to stop. Thorne remained still, waiting to see what Watanabe would do next.

Seconds passed, and the chair slowly spun around. Thorne finally caught sight of Watanabe. He was dressed in a humble outfit, not matching the expectations of someone with his net worth. It had been several years since Thorne had last seen him, but Watanabe's face remained untainted by time.

"It's good to see you ... my old friend," said Watanabe, with a slight smile on his face.

Thorne said politely, "*Kinishinakute ii desu yo. Kore ga watshino shigoto desu kara.*"The pleasure is all mine.

Watanabe nodded in agreement and stood up. Watanabe said, with a pinch of accent, "English, Thorne, English … your Japanese is as good as ever, but I, on the other hand, need to practice my English. It's my own fault for always speaking in Japanese, even while living in the States."

Thorne bowed and spoke. "Sir, you're being too modest. Your English is very good."

Watanabe chuckled and said, "Kind words, my old friend … kind indeed." He began walking toward the window and stared outside at the beautiful yet damp city of New York. Below, he could see the city alive, millions before him and each with a different goal in mind. Even with the dreary weather, he smiled and enjoyed that brief moment.

The sound of the rain continued to pelt the window as the dark sky shaded the entire room. With his back turned to Thorne, Watanabe spoke, "I'm curious. Why was the first thing you said to me an apology, Thorne?"

Thorne hesitated for a moment and said, "I believe it was the right thing to do, in light of the situation regarding the fight."

Watanabe pondered Thorne's statement and then nodded. He turned around and looked at Thorne. He said, "Today is a day for celebration, not apologies, my friend." As the rain dripped down the window, Watanabe pressed his finger on the glass. The sound of the rain pouring down froze still like a picture. The entire room stood silent, and one by one each window cleared to reveal a bright and sunny day.

Thorne's face reacted to the change as well as Watanabe's words. "I'm confused, sir," Thorne admitted bluntly. Watanabe was a master at disguising his emotions; even Thorne felt lost at times when speaking with him. From the outside, Watanabe seemed like a regular guy from the street. But he was far from that. He was a unique breed, the kind that stories were made from—stories where individuals could start from nothing and accomplish much.

"Be careful, my friend. Sometimes we look upon situations and have a quick emotional response to the moment. Human beings are susceptible to this kind of reaction. Emotion rules them and makes them like wild animals. Yet, a dog can be trained to control its own desires, at times more impressively than man himself." Watanabe stayed stern-faced and continued speaking. "It is a rare skill to be able to see things from both sides.... With that ability, you can see the truth."

"My apologies again, sir. I admit, the outcome was not what I had expected," said Thorne.

Watanabe laughed. "I know you all too well, Thorne. That is one of your greatest assets, which I admire about you. If uncontrolled, it can easily become a handicap. Sometimes you can over-think a situation. We can believe it to be perfect. There is no such thing as perfect, merely the illusion of perfection. Correct me if I am wrong, but this is what I believe has happened."

"I did, sir. I believed I had everything covered."

Watanabe walked over and put his hand on Thorne's shoulder. He stared at Thorne directly and smiled. "Like I said, old friend, no need to apologize." His words brought a sense of comfort to Thorne, who finally relaxed.

Watanabe walked away and said, "You're a history buff, aren't you, Thorne?"

"Yes, sir."

"Tell me, what is it about history that you find so fascinating?"

"I believe, for me, studying the chosen actions of people at key moments in history is fascinating," said Thorne.

"Hmm, interesting. You are more well-versed in history than I am, Thorne. I am curious, though.... If I ask you the one constant in the history of mankind, what would that be?" asked Watanabe.

Thorne thought for a moment before responding. "I'd have to say ... that history tends to repeat itself."

"Ah ... good, good. I concur with your answer. Do you think I am wrong by saying that this repetition, these things we see over and over again ... in the end, it's all about the struggle ... the struggle for ... hmm, control?" Watanabe leaned forward slightly, waiting for Thorne to respond.

Thorne nodded and said, "It's always about control ... and history has shown that every rise has a fall. The fall happens when the leaders at the time fail to control the situation."

"Hmm," said Watanabe. "So, the question to end all questions is how to break a trend that has existed for thousands of years. A trend that appears to be almost ingrained in the very fabric of our DNA. Is total control an obtainable goal? If you squeeze the masses too hard, they fight back. So, we know that, while intimidation is a quick solution, revolution is a forgone conclusion. Over the last fifty years, we've given the masses the illusion of having control—internet, voting, reality TV … yet, it's still not enough. Thus, there's always the handful that challenge the system. Those renegades, misfits, those idealistic do-gooders who believe that they have a better way of running the world."

Thorne was captivated by Watanabe's speech and was unsure where he was headed. Watanabe began strolling toward his samurai display. "Thorne, please come over here for a moment," said Watanabe.

Thorne stood beside his mentor, admiring Watanabe's display. The suit was a full set of body armor from head to toe. Red was the main color with an array of other colors highlighting the suit. Below, nestled near the bottom of the stand, were two swords. Set properly with the katana laid over the top with the wakizashi, the weapons sparkled from the reflection of the light.

Watanabe said, "Did you know this is the oldest known O-yoroi and daisho in existence?"

Thorne continued to stare at it. "I had assumed it was rare, but I was unaware of its prestige."

Watanabe asked, "Do you want to take a guess at its value?"

Thorne snickered and responded, "I would think this is priceless?"

"Actually, you are correct. This is considered uninsurable because of its value." Watanabe chuckled at the thought.

Thorne continued to stare at the display.

"Would you be surprised if I told you that it's possible for anyone to walk out with this suit and sword from my office?" Watanabe turned to look at Thorne, who was wearing a puzzled expression.

"That would, in fact, catch me by surprise," said Thorne. "Something of this value, I would think would be heavily protected with alarms if not guards."

"Go ahead. Touch it. See for yourself if there are any alarms, Thorne."

Thorne hesitated before reaching out to touch the sword. His eyes widened when he finally lay his hand on it and no alarm sounded. He gripped it tightly as he shook his head in disbelief. "I can't believe there's no alarm."

He turned to Watanabe and asked, "May I?"

Watanabe bowed slightly. "Please."

Thorne slowly removed the sword from the scabbard. Inch by inch, more of the steel came into the light. "Incredible," said Thorne. The blade was true and reflected his image. "I can feel it…. This is death," said Thorne, as the skills of the swordsmith were imbedded into the sword.

"Do you know that thieves have broken into this office twice, and not once did the robbers attempt to steal this display?" said Watanabe. "Surveillance tape showed that, in both incidents, they approached the suit and sword and were about to grab them, but decided not to touch them."

Thorne continued to listen but was in awe of the sword. The blade seemed to speak to Thorne as he held history in his own hand.

"You see, Thorne, the greatest cage you can create is the one that has no walls." Watanabe smiled.

His last statement grabbed Thorne's attention. As he put the sword back into its scabbard, Thorne asked, "So, how does one create such a thing?"

Watanabe said, "Cage a man, and he will naturally find a way to escape. It requires manpower, time, and resources to contain his will. But, if you give him hope and each time destroy it, slowly you'll notice a change. In time, you can leave the cage open, and his very own will can contain him.

"You apologized earlier because you believed that Kirin, by winning, shook the foundation of this company. I believe this played perfectly into our hands. She is the hope. We should allow her to rise, and with it bring along as many of the masses as possible."

Thorne asked, "Will that be enough to achieve total control?"

With a secretive smile, Watanabe said, "That is part of our plan. To ensure it, we must break through with the new hope for tomorrow." Watanabe had a smirk of confidence glimmering on his face as he glanced toward the top of his desk. There it stood, a simple glass container. At first glance, it appeared to be empty, but upon closer inspection, Thorne noticed something inside. He had been too distracted earlier and lost sight of what was right in front of him.

Thorne's eyes widened in surprise. "I don't believe it. Is that what I think it is?"

"Like I said, old friend, this is a day for celebration, not apologies." A grin formed on Watanabe's face. He made a gesture for them to walk toward his desk.

"May I...?"

Watanabe nodded his head.

Thorne reached for the container and plucked out a translucent white pill. He held it between his fingers and raised it up toward the light to get a better look.

Watanabe said, "It doesn't look like much, does it?"

Thorne nodded his head in agreement.

"It's always surprising how the littlest things can have the greatest effect." Watanabe opened his hand as Thorne placed the clear pill onto it.

Staring at it in awe, Thorne said, "So, this is the latest one?"

"That's correct. What Williams was given for the fight dampens the pain receptors of the body.... While effective, the subject's will is still his own."

"And this allows what?"

"The answer, my friend ... total control." Watanabe smiled.

"How about the duration?"

Watanabe replied, "That's still being worked on and is dependent on the personality of the individual. But, for now, it is ranging anywhere from one minute to a maximum of ten minutes."

"Incredible," said Thorne as he realized the UFMF's ultimate goal was getting so much closer.

"Well, staring at it doesn't really do anything," said Watanabe. "Do you think a demonstration is needed?" As Watanabe stood at Thorne's side, he called in a voice that echoed through the room, "Kristen, can you have the girls escort him to my office?"

Kristen's voice came through the hidden speakers. "At once, sir."

Several minutes passed as neither man spoke a word. They stood by Watanabe's desk, waiting for whomever it was he requested. Suddenly, the doors swung open, revealing Justice, who waited for his invitation.

Watanabe called, "Please come in," as he made a slight gesture for him to enter.

Thorne kept his cool, not showing a hint of emotion, even though inside he was surprised to see that it was his bodyguard, Justice. He took a deep breath to calm his emotions.

Justice began walking toward them. As usual, he didn't speak but did as he was told. He stopped a few feet from them and waited.

"It's good to see you, Justice.... It's been a while," said Watanabe.

Finally, a kink in his armor—Thorne was caught off guard but quickly regained his composure. He did not want Watanabe to notice his surprise; he hadn't known the two had ever met before. Justice acknowledged Watanabe's comment and bowed before him.

Watanabe asked, "Thorne, do you think your man is up for a quick demonstration?"

Thorne nodded and said, "He's always ready." Justice looked at Thorne and confirmed his comments.

Watanabe shouted, "Kristen, can you please let them in?"

"At once, sir."

A few seconds passed before the doors again swung open. Three men stood side by side, waiting. They all stared at Kristen, who then signaled it was okay to enter. They began walking toward the center of the room. All three had a rough look about them, and each one appeared to be a physical specimen of awe.

To Watanabe, Thorne said, "Only three?"

Watanabe snickered. "Justice, I'm wondering if you can take out these fine gentlemen in less than … hmm, let's say fifteen seconds."

Justice never turned around to look at who had entered the room. He stood still facing both Watanabe and Thorne.

Justice said with confidence, "Easily."

The three men heard his snide and overconfident comment and became irate. Each one became motivated to make Justice eat his words.

Watanabe said, "If you will do us the honor. Whenever you are ready."

Justice began removing his tie along with his jacket. He folded them nicely and laid them on the ground. He then began un-cuffing his sleeves and rolled them up. He finally turned around and saw all three men for the first time. Without hesitation, he began walking toward them.

The three men dwarfed Justice in size and build. But, to Justice, everyone looked the same. Size and shape did not matter to him. He cared for only one thing in a fight.

The guy in the center spoke with a deep, loud voice. "You got a lot of nerve to think you can beat us in fifteen seconds."

Justice stared at all three and, out of character, said, "I would have said the same thing had he said five seconds."

This really pissed off all three guys, each one wanting to get their hands on Justice and make him pay the price for his snide comment. Only the command from Watanabe was holding them back; they were prepared to dish out some pain.

Watanabe called, "At your discretion, gentlemen."

Justice stood there in a casual stance, with no guard, waiting for them, daring them to begin the attack. He stood passively, waiting for a sign, and then he felt it: their intent. It screamed, signaling Justice. As all three were about to move in, Justice beat them to the punch and closed the gap furiously.

His rush forward caused all three to hesitate, and that delay was their undoing. Justice targeted the one in the center, since he was the closest. His opponent tried to cover his upper body, but Justice laid a swift kick to the groin. He cowered, holding his groin as he crumpled to the ground, groveling in pain.

Justice smiled, seemingly enjoying the process as the other two finally reacted and moved in. The opponent to the right took a hard swing as Justice ducked. The swing was wild and uncontrolled as he had gone for the knockout and missed. He stumbled over himself.

Justice was not concerned about him and decided to deal with the third opponent. He went for a roundhouse kick toward Justice, who countered immediately and moved in. Like a flash, Justice was out of the danger zone of the kick and delivered a quick combo that dropped his opponent.

The last opponent finally regained his balance. He glanced at his companions who were lying on the ground. He roared, hoping to instill courage as he charged in like an animal. He threw a punch with all his might but was thwarted by a block and counter. The hit wobbled him to a daze, and Justice didn't hesitate to finish him with a punch. He fell to the ground, and Justice quickly turned his head as an exclamation and then waited for a response.

Thorne shouted, "Four-point-eight seconds!" He smiled, proud of Justice's work.

Watanabe began clapping his hands. "Good … good."

The three men began gathering themselves. Each one staggered to his feet, trying to shake off the pain. Justice watched them struggle but felt no empathy for what had happened. A minute passed as they finally recovered from their beating, each one having a newfound respect for Justice.

Watanabe called for them. "Please come here when you can."

Clutching their aches and pains, the three struggled. Embarrassed and wounded, they headed toward Watanabe's desk. Studying them, he said, "I think we need to even the odds a bit." He reached for the transparent container on his desk that held at least a dozen clear pills. He pulled out three and held them gently in his hand.

The men looked at each other and then became hesitant. One asked, "What does this do?"

"Let's just say … it's an equalizer." Watanabe gave a disarming smile.

They were all hesitant, wondering how this little pill could possibly do what Watanabe claimed.

Watanabe said, "If you want to defeat him, as well as receive a hefty monetary reward, I suggest you take it."

It didn't take much for the barriers of doubt to crumble. Money with revenge as the topper was all that was needed for all three to say yes.

Watanabe said, "Please, take this now!"

The men nodded as he handed each one a clear pill. One by one, they swallowed the pill, no longer questioning the cost, only dreaming of the possibilities. Everyone waited for a minute as the room remained silent.

Watanabe turned to Thorne and asked, "That's been about a minute, has it not?"

Thorne nodded. "It has, sir."

"Part of the beauty, Thorne," Watanabe said, "is the speed at which it takes effect."

Watanabe stared at the three gentlemen again and said, "If you will please do us the honors again."

Exchanging glances, the men got into position in front of Justice. It was déjà vu, as they all stood on the same spot. The question was: would there be a different outcome?

Justice stared at each in turn, wondering what difference the pill would make. He shook it off, disregarded its importance, and got ready to fight.

Thorne asked, "Even I'd be curious if Justice could do better than under four-point-eight seconds."

Watanabe put his hand on Thorne's shoulder and began walking toward the center of the room. Once there, he turned to face Justice. "That was definitely most impressive…. I doubt in my youth I could have bested that." He then stared deeply into Justice's eyes and whispered, "Justice, you are going to need to kill these men if you want to walk out of this room alive."

Justice looked confused by Watanabe's statement, but remained silent.

Watanabe spun around and approached the three men. He looked at each of them intently. They all leaned forward, giving him their full attention.

Each one of them had a glazed looked in his eyes. It was the sign that the drug had taken its full effect. Watanabe smiled and said, "Follow my orders. Don't stop till this man is dead. I want you to move in without hesitation.... Do you understand me?" Watanabe had no reservation about giving such an order. His request for taking a human life was like asking someone to bring him a coffee.

Each one nodded and focused his attention on Justice. Watanabe began a casual walk back toward the desk with one last look at Justice. The anticipation began to build and fill the room.

Justice was still pondering what Watanabe meant. He looked back at Thorne, who seemed confident. He then checked out his opponents, noting the difference. Each now had a crazed look in his eyes. They had just received a decisive ass beating, yet they looked eager for a second one.

This time Watanabe shouted, "Begin!" His word echoed through the room, pounding the fighters' ears with his command.

Unlike their first encounter, all three moved in and targeted Justice. He had to position himself so that he wouldn't be surrounded. A quick shift in his center placed him at an advantageous spot as he struck quickly, again targeting the nearest one. He delivered a flurry of three attacks to the first opponent. He circled around and used him as a shield, switching to the remaining opponents. Flowing with the force, Justice's attack was direct and powerful. Each blow made it to his desired target. Within a blink, he had delivered multiple attacks on all three of his opponents. However, this time, each man absorbed the blow and just rocked backward. Justice's eyes widened as all three failed to crumple from the hits. That hesitation cost Justice as one of the men grabbed him and picked him up over his head.

Justice's body automatically relaxed, which caused his opponent to lose a solid grip on him. He threw Justice across the room, but Justice rolled with the toss and found himself on one knee, staring down all three opponents. There was no harm done from his slight miscalculation. Again, a clash was going to happen, as Justice and his three opponents charged in.

Attacks and counters were happening from all angles. Justice's hits were not having the same results as before. All three men continued their savage attacks on Justice. His defense began to crumble. A hit here, a block there, and then suddenly a mistake from Justice caused him to fly across the room. He grabbed his ribs and looked up. The three continued to charge in relentlessly. He stared up, wondering what was going on.

From the other side of the room, Thorne watched the fight in disbelief. Watanabe was all smiles, enjoying what was unfolding before him. Thorne had never seen Justice get bested and was unsure if he would win the fight.

Justice sucked in a deep breath and engaged again. There was no denying his skill as he maneuvered between three fighters attacking from all angles—it was a sight to see. Two of the fighters attacked him simultaneously. Justice took advantage of that and went for a double leg sweep. They flew backward and were stunned for a second on the ground. The maneuver left Justice exposed, as the third one went for a take-down and caught him by surprise.

Justice rolled with him and took several shots that would have downed any normal man. However, like all his attacks, they were not doing any damage to his opponent. Instead, the man continued to bear down on him, pinning Justice to the floor. Like a snake trying to strangle its victim, he was going for a choke.

Justice caught a glimpse of the two opponents on the ground who were beginning to get up. He tried several hits with his back to the floor, but his opponent did not respond to the attacks. He just pressed further with both his arms wrapped behind Justice, squeezing the breath out of him. Both time and air were running out for Justice.

"Fuu—!" Justice's curse was empty and powerless.

His hands were not in position to counter anything as he saw the other two men begin their charge at him. He went with the only option that was open for him.

Justice bit his opponent's neck, and blood squirted out profusely. He tore the flesh and spat it out. His opponent fell limp, but he managed to push him off just in time. Justice wasn't given a second of rest, as the barrage of attacks continued to rain from his two standing enemies.

He blocked and countered, but his hits were ineffective. He was not used to this kind of opponent reaction and recalled what he had seen in Kirin's match. His opponent went for a wild swing, and this time Justice went for a break. The arm snapped like a twig, but the pain didn't affect the injured man. He flowed to another attack that connected and caused Justice's head to snap back. A cut appeared over Justice's eye as he pressed further to deal with his enemies. Even with the broken arm, his opponent's savagery continued.

As Justice was beginning to take on more hits, he went for another break and missed. Justice found himself exposed and took a heavy hit. Stunned, he tried to shake off the blur.

Someone seized him from behind. Before he could counter, the other opponent began pounding Justice in the stomach. Several hits to the gut and he began coughing up blood.

He had to think. He found an opening and went for a head butt. His opponent bounced back, and Justice went for a kick that sent the man flying across the room. Justice quickly countered the grab from behind, freeing his hands for a second as he threw a thumb, stabbing his enemy in the eye socket. This time, Justice heard a scream, a horrified cry that would make anyone with a conscience cringe. Justice pulled his hand back and saw it was covered in blood and dripping with the remains of human flesh.

He was bloody and breathing heavily, something Justice was unaccustomed to. He took a moment to gather himself. From across the room, his last enemy started charging. Without any thought, he ran toward Justice, who stayed still. Finally, he let out a roar. Once he was within range, Justice went for a kick to the knee, snapping it like a twig. His opponent stumbled forward as Justice grabbed him. Buckling slightly, he braced himself from the force and put his opponent in a headlock. His opponent was strong and tried to struggle, but his center was off balance as Justice toyed with it.

With a quick move, Justice spun his opponent around. Facing Thorne and Watanabe, he held his opponent in a reverse headlock, as they were back to back to one another. Justice took a deep breath, still holding his opponent from behind and resting his enemy's neck on his shoulder. Suddenly, he dropped to his knee. The fall snapped his attacker's neck, and his body lay limp, still in Justice's arm. He tossed the body to the side but remained on his knee. He looked down to the floor as sweat poured from his head and blood dripped from his eye, bathing his face. He coughed out more blood, gasping for air and grateful that he had survived. Justice remained silent as he saw the pool of blood forming around him.

Thorne watched in shock, staring at his bodyguard kneeling on the floor and struggling to stay upright.

Watanabe started clapping. "Good ... good." Turning to a stunned Thorne, he added, "Like I said, my old friend, it is a day for celebrating."

"It is man's fears and shortcomings that let him be subjected to the rules of others."—Watanabe

SECTION 1

Short Stories #1—Kirin's P.O.V.

Four Years Prior: June 22, 2028

<u>Family Vacation—Day 1</u>

I n my wildest dreams, I never thought I would be experiencing this, considering that I started from such impoverished beginnings. Yet, there I was, staring outside the window, seeing a part of the world so different from mine. I smiled and giggled, almost wanting to pinch myself and see if I was dreaming. Not only did I feel I was extremely lucky, but vacations for many in the States have become rare due to the current state of the economy.

It was day two into our family vacation before I finally felt like myself. The eleven-hour time difference had everyone's biological clock screwed up. This year, my parents had wanted to do something special, so they went big. We were going to celebrate their anniversary and travel to the Far East. Mom and Dad asked me if I wanted to go visit South Korea, not exactly my old home, but the closest thing possible for me. I lied and told them I wasn't interested, but deep down the memories of the past continued to haunt me. For now, it was easier to deal with things from a distance.

We were on a tour bus headed for another excursion. I sat by myself, gazing at the scenery in awe. It was amazing how one part of the world could look so different from another. If not for the bus, the only hint of modern technology, it was hard to imagine that these were modern times.

With a quick peek to the other side of the bus, I saw my parents enjoying one another's company. Watching them reminded me of Sifu and Simo, as the look of love was very distinctive. I sat back and wondered if one day I would be fortunate enough to find that special someone.

I glanced behind me to see what my stepbrothers were doing. As I suspected, all three—Steve, Mark, and Kyle—were glued to their phones.

It was unfortunate that Jim was missing this trip, but serving overseas didn't afford him the time off.

I shook my head and sighed. Annoyed and frustrated, I decided to lose myself in the beauty of the outdoor view. I found it baffling that we could travel so far and visit a place they'd never seen before, yet they paid more attention to their electronics. I thought, *Why even travel when they can do that at home?*

Most people would see the stoic countryside as an endless road of dust and greenery, but I appreciate the simple things in life and marveled at it. As the minutes passed, however, my brothers' attitude became an unreachable itch that kept gnawing at me. I couldn't contain it anymore, so I turned around and sat up in my chair. I barked, "Guys, you should look outside! There're some really cool things to see."

Kyle's head began to move slowly up, but his eyes were glued to his phone. "Kirin, we're a good thirty minutes from the main tourist attraction. It's just dirty roads from here on, and besides...." I waited for him to complete his sentence, but his focus was clearly on his game. I was just an annoyance.

The thought saddened me. My cute little stepbrother who kept me company when I had nightmares was lost in technology.

My pout quickly turned to a frown as I switched my attention toward Mark and Steven. I crossed my fingers, hoping their maturity would show. However, not only did that lead to further disappointment, but they totally disregarded any comments. They were both entranced with the sounds and flashing lights. I honestly wondered if anything could break them from this spell.

Mark yelled, "Dammit, Steven, cover me on my blind side!"

Steven shouted back, "I am covering you, but I can only handle one guy at a time."

Mark rubbed the edge of his brow and said, "This game sucks."

Steven replied, "Tell me about it."

I looked at them, realizing that they represented the future.

We are so doomed.

Frustrated, I sat back in my seat and realized that I'd have to enjoy this view on my own. *Again, alone*, I thought. I got lost in the miles of countryside and my thoughts of the future. Staring outside, I mused that there was one thing that every place had in common, regardless of where you traveled. Poor is poor, no matter what part of the world you visit. I watched as little kids played with sticks or just ran around, tagging one another. Somehow, with so little, they still found a way to smile. They didn't need expensive technology to keep them amused. It's funny how perspective can easily change, that those with so much can complain about things that others would be grateful for.

After thirty minutes had passed, we finally got to our destination. I was excited for this trip because this would be my first time to use my camera on foreign grounds. It was time to put my skills to the test. Since Hunter had gotten me started in photography, my days were spent mainly training in Wing Chun and shooting pictures. Finally, I had an opportunity to shoot something other than friends, family, and stuff around the neighborhood. This was my chance to get some unique and unbelievable shots.

I had done my research before I left the bus. Bayon Temple was known for its majestic towered faces that appeared throughout its construction. The number of acres dedicated to such phenomenal work was mindboggling. As both my feet landed gently on the ground, I knew at once that the pictures I'd seen previewing this area did it no justice. I sensed something very special, and I immediately switched my camera's power on.

Other tour buses stopped alongside ours, and more tourists disembarked. The guide was speaking and keeping our group in check. Although I heard his voice through my headpiece, I missed most of his chatter, as my focus was on getting that perfect shot. A click here and there and a request for family to pose was how the next hour went flying by. I was having a ton of fun and getting some incredible shots of the temple.

I was busy focusing on a flower when suddenly I heard my mom from behind. "Hey, sweetie … sorry to bother you, but are you having fun?"

I took the shot and turned around. "Mom, this is so beyond … uh, uh …, incredible." My excitement was impossible to contain.

"I'm glad you like it, Kirin."

"You should see all the great pictures I've taken."

Mom smiled at me and said, "I will, sweetie. How many have you taken?"

"A ton, Mom. I can't wait to get back to edit them." I began scrolling through the pictures on my camera, admiring my work. Finally, I found one that really stood out. "Mom, take a look at this picture of the temple!"

I handed my mom my camera. Looking at the picture, she said, "You're right, sweetie. You've really got a knack for taking incredible pictures, but I want you to do something right now for me … will you?"

"What is it, Mom? Is there something I missed that I need to shoot?"

Mom smiled and put her arms around me. "No, it's not that. Do me a favor and just put your camera away. I want us to go over this same area that you just snapped."

I was a bit confused by my mom's request, but I did as she asked. "Uh, okay, Mom." Turning off my camera, I put it back into my bag. Mom and I went walking down the same area that I had photographed, and she told me to look at certain spots, touch parts of the temple, and smell the area around me. It was strange. I had walked by this same area and taken a ton of pictures, but the experience felt totally different. I came upon the face of the temple that I had captured with my camera, but this time I saw it with my own eyes. When I touched it, I could feel the surface's age, its unique texture.

My mom said, "This was all carved by hand. All of this."

I continued to touch it, and I just couldn't imagine the dedication required to be able to create this with one's own hands.

I shouted, "Mom … come here and look at this!"

I pointed to something I hadn't spotted before. While the picture I had taken was unique from the angles and the lighting, seeing it up close and using my own senses to truly experience the temple was unforgettable. I closed my eyes and leaned against the face of the statue as I took a moment just to dream.

"You see, Kirin? Don't get me wrong; the pictures are great memories. At the same time, you don't want to miss the very experience itself."

"You're right, Mom. That was really something very special."

Mom smiled at me and gave me a little hug. "Feel the moment, Kirin. Enjoy it."

I asked, "Do we still have more time to go over the same spot again?"

"We do, sweetie. Do you want to retrace your steps?"

"I sure do, Mom. Will you come with me?"

"Of course, sweetie."

⋏ ⋏ ⋏

We spent several hours enjoying the sights and sounds of Bayon Temple before we finally arrived at the last leg of the tour. The bus pulled to a stop, and we were all let out. There, the guide began taking us through a little village nestled in a rural area of Cambodia. Inside the village, we could see the everyday lives of the local villagers and what they had to do to put food on the table. This was not unfamiliar surroundings for me, as I had lived this before. Surprisingly, my brothers put down their phones and paid attention to what was happening. As much as I was annoyed by them earlier, I appreciated the fact that they finally took the time to see reality.

As we made our way through the village, I wasn't quite sure if we were observing the villagers or if it was the other way around.

Mark came up to me and said, "Man, I've never seen anything like this." I saw that he was taken aback by the living conditions of the locals.

I looked at him, but didn't say a word.

Steve and Kyle soon joined us as we continued to walk through the area.

After several minutes, we passed by a little girl who was pumping water from a well. She was no older than I had been when I fled North Korea, but she was strong as an ox. She carried the responsibility of getting water and was also keeping an eye on her younger siblings.

Kyle shook his head and said, "I can't imagine having to do that just to get water."

Steve said, "Me, either."

I said, "Now ask yourself: how clean do you think that water is?"

They all looked at one another and cringed.

Mark said, "Sometimes you need a reminder as to how good you have it."

I stopped in my tracks and said to the guys, "You know, where I came from, it was even worse."

They stopped, as my words sent daggers through their hearts. They all looked at me with sad eyes and hung their heads. I could tell at that very moment we all understood one another without a single word being spoken. I broke the silence and said, "It's all right, guys. I have you now for my family." They surrounded me, hugging me as I smiled to myself, enjoying the brief moment of bonding.

That evening on the way back to our hotel, the day's events left me exhausted. Kyle was already slouched over me, sound asleep, and I was about to do the same. I began to doze off, but I still heard bits of what the guide was saying. He began by saying he was just going to talk briefly since he realized everyone looked exhausted, but he wanted to talk about Cambodia's dark past. I listened, frozen, to the stories of the atrocities that had been committed.

Most would be shocked that history continued to repeat itself, but I was numb to it all. The cycle seemed to be never-ending, as men of power and wealth continued to use it for evil.

He spoke passionately for the love of his country and the potential greatness that existed. I found myself engrossed in his speech, as I felt connected to his words. He mentioned the stories his grandparents would tell him as a child, making sure that he would never forget. They were survivors who had lived a nightmare very few could understand.

I raised my hand and asked him, "Why don't you do something about it?"

He responded, "I'm not alone. Many of my countrymen feel the same way and want to act, but you have to think where your priorities lie."

"What do you mean?" I asked.

"I know what changes need to be made and the actions that have to be taken … yet, I have to ask myself: does this take precedence over feeding my family?"

I stared at him and knew exactly what he meant.

"How can I help my country when I can't help my family first?"

In the end, it got me thinking. How many were like this man, not just in his country but in the entire world? How many felt the same way, but were bogged down with the same problems that plagued all of mankind? How could we move past humanity when we were struggling just to be humans? Or was there a greater force stopping man's progress to a greater world?

He finally finished his lecture, and the bus of tired tourists remained silent. I sat there wondering what the future held as I looked at Kyle.

"To enjoy the moment, be part of it."—Sifu

The South Side—24 Days

Big T was driving me in his car as we were by his neck of the woods, the South Side of Chicago. He had a project for summer school that he needed help on, and I said I'd be more than happy to do so.

The South Side of Chicago wasn't a place I visited often. It was on the news constantly and not for a good reason.

Big T said, "You never been down here before, have you?"

"Can't say I have," I murmured as I continued to stare outside. It looked so different from the neighborhood I was living in, but it was not strange territory for me. Poverty carried that same feeling whether I was on the South Side of Chicago or my impoverished town back in North Korea.

"Don't worry. You'll be all right with me," said Big T.

"I'm not worried at all." Even as I spoke, I sank a little lower in my seat and checked to see if the doors were locked.

"Kirin?"

"What's up, Big T?"

"Sorry about the neighborhood."

"You don't have to apologize, T." I could tell Big T felt embarrassed about the situation.

"Yeah...," he said in a depressed voice. "But, look on the bright side. Before, it was just the South Side that was run down. Now even the good neighborhoods are torn up. Come to think of it, we outlasted that yuppie neighborhood, Southport."

I thought about what T was saying. He was right. The bad economy affected everyone who wasn't part of the 1%. There was no stopping the bleeding because this death spiral had no end in sight.

"Hey, T ... can I ask you something?"

"Sure, little mama."

"How come you always help after class and clean up around Sifu's place?" I looked at T, who seemed to be struggling for an answer.

Big T looked cautiously around, even though it was just the two of us in his car. "Okay, if I tell you, promise not to mention it to the guys?"

"Your secret's safe with me. I promise."

"Well, Sifu doesn't ask me to clean. I do it coz he gives me a hookup with classes."

"Why's that?" I asked.

"My extra side jobs I have ... I'm busy giving it to my folks to help them out."

"Well, that's cool. So, how big of a hookup is he giving you?"

Big T paused and said, "He's been letting me train for free since I told him my situation."

"Wow!" My eyes widened. The news shocked me at first, but after thinking about it some more, I knew it wasn't all that surprising for Sifu to be so generous.

"Yeah, Sifu's real cool. He just wants us to learn. So, when I can, I try my best to help around in the school or anything else he needs."

"Hey, wait a second." A thought had just entered my mind. "You and Danny always bet against each other. I see you guys gambling all the time."

Big T burst out laughing.

"What? What's so funny?"

Big T said, "Gambling? The same damn credits been going back and forth forever. Longest win streak from me or my homie is three. Ain't nobody making dinero out that."

"Oh ... is that so?"

"Besides, Wing Chun men don't play."

I nodded. He was right, but the thought had me boggled for a bit. "Wait a second, don't play what?"

"Gamble, little mama."

"So all this time, it's the same credits?"

"Yup."

When I didn't speak, Big T glanced at me and cleared his throat, flexing his hands nervously on the steering wheel. "Seriously, not a word. Sifu and you are the only ones who know my struggles."

"I promised you already that I wouldn't," I said.

We laughed together before Big T's face suddenly became concerned. He looked at the side and rear mirror of his car and placed both hands firmly on the steering wheel.

"What's wrong?'

He sighed and shook his head. "Stay cool, little sista. It's gonna turn...."

"Why? What's happening?"

Just as Big T finished his words, a siren went off behind us. My head snapped around to look at the officer who had his lights flashing from behind. The glare of bright lights got my heart racing. We were just several blocks away from Big T's place. Big T pulled his car over to the side immediately.

Big T looked at me and said, "Kirin, stop. Move very slowly. Don't do anything to piss him off. Just smile to officer friendly."

I did as Big T said and just sat and waited. A few seconds later, the officer knocked on Big T's side window. The officer, wearing sunglasses, leaned forward and flashed a light directly into T's face.

Big T smiled and said, "Is there a problem, officer?"

"Turn off the car, now," said the officer in a stern voice.

I watched as T moved slowly and did as he was told.

"You in a hurry? You seemed to be going a little fast there."

Big T replied calmly, "Sir, I thought the speed limit was thirty-five in this area."

The officer said, "Well, I got you clocked over that amount by at least fifteen miles per hour."

I could see the annoyance in T's face.

Big T said, "Would you mind if I saw what you clocked me at?"

"Listen, boy … you looking to start trouble?"

Big T took a deep breath and said, "No officer, I was pretty sure I was way under the speed limit. I just wanted to confirm."

The officer said, "Are you calling me a liar?"

Big T replied, "Not at all."

"Maybe you want me to inspect the rest of the car and see if you're doing anything else illegal." The officer raised his voice.

I knew that Big T wasn't speeding at all; in fact, a bicycle had passed us by.

"My apologies, sir. You're right," said Big T. "I was speeding."

"Well, that's more like it. I'm gonna need a few minutes to write up your ticket." The officer looked inside again and then walked away.

"I don't get it. What's happening, T? You weren't speeding at all!"

Big T clenched the steering wheel tightly and said, "This is the fourth time this year they pulled me over, just because I'm a big black guy in a car."

"What?"

He pointed across the street. "You see over there, Kirin, at the end of the street? Those are drug dealers. Everyone in the neighborhood knows that; the cop knows that. But, he's busy giving tickets to me for something I didn't even do."

"What?" As I watched, I saw Big T was right. They were drug dealers and not even shy about what they were doing. They were a mere twenty feet away from the car, and the officer either was oblivious to it or didn't care.

"I don't get it. Why?"

Big T sighed and looked away. "This has been going on forever. The news plays the death each week in my neighborhood, and society's gotten numb. If the numbers spike up too much, the mayor does a press conference with the police chief on the upcoming changes. The neighborhood rallies for a protest, and then we end up back at square one."

Big T was right. I'd seen evidence on the news at least once a year.

"Anyway, the economy is so bad that people have given up hope. The South Side is a ghost town of economic activity. But now, it's not a case of just us feeling it…. Now all of middle class America or whatever's left of it finally know what we've been feeling for years."

As we continued to talk and face the harsh realities of life, the officer finally came back.

"You got your phone?"

Big T seemed to have gone through this routine before. When he held it up, the officer waved his phone by T's, and it beeped.

The officer said, "All the information is on your phone. Just pay the fine, and everything will be okay."

I couldn't believe what I was seeing. I looked to the other side and saw that the drug dealer had a line formed, which was clearly in the officer's line of sight. I started to feel enraged and was about to say something when Big T grabbed my arm.

The officer leaned over and asked, "Are you okay, miss?"

I took a deep breath and nodded. "Yes, officer, everything's good."

The officer said, "You here of your own free will, miss?"

I said, "Yes, officer, this is a longtime friend of mine."

The officer gave a look of surprise, as if that was uncommon. He pulled away and looked directly across the street. He leaned back and said, "Okay, next time, just obey the law, and you won't have any problems."

Big T said in a calm voice. "I'll be more careful next time."

The officer said, "Sir."

Big T gritted his teeth and took a deep breath. "Yes, sir."

Big T sat in his car, and the officer drove by as I watched. I was livid. I'd gone through this before from a dictatorship standpoint, but his oppression was the first time I had experienced what T was going through from a racial standpoint. What the news showed didn't come close to matching the reality I'd just seen. It was almost as if they wanted this part of the neighborhood to implode.

"I can't believe what I just saw!" I shouted.

"Believe it. This is the everyday happenings on the South Side. Strangely enough, it's not as bad as it used to be since more areas besides the South

Side have gone bad. Police are less bothered to hassle us. My dad said, back in the day, he would be pulled over seven or eight times a year. I guess things are improving coz I'm down to three or four now."

I turned toward Big T, who laughed, but I could tell there was a pinch of sadness in his chuckle. Somehow he did what he could to deal with that pain.

For the first time, I felt a real bond with Big T. He knew what it was like to experience the oppression I'd felt back in North Korea, even if our experiences were separated by thousands of miles.

"Do not be the fuel to ignite the flames of fools."—Sifu

Robert's Korean Lunch—52 Days

"I'm not sure what's worse, waiting to be seated or finding a breathing soul after being seated in this Korean restaurant," said Ken. He was pleading his case to our group, trying to muster support in his favor.

Robert said, "Oh, come on. You can't possibly be comparing our two-hour wait at your infamous burger joint to just twenty minutes."

"Oh, yeah. I most definitely am." He nodded with a smug look on his face and snapped his fingers. The table froze and stared at Ken, and he blushed and looked side to side.

"Was that a bit too white?" asked Ken.

We nodded in unison, and the flow of the conversation continued.

I did my best to hide my silent snicker. It wasn't unusual for Ken to take the brunt of criticism from our group. In some ways, it had me wondering if we were all being racist, since he was the only white guy in our school. Ken had a big heart, and he never let the other guys' digs bother him. That's the one thing that always stuck out about Ken. My nickname for him was Mr. Nice Guy.

Over the last several years, I'd grown to enjoy the little quirks and quarrels that the group constantly had. The usual seven—Tobias, Doc, Danny, Big T, Ken, Robert, Ryan and I, along with Sifu—were the core. On occasion, we'd have our stragglers of new faces coming and going from our school. This was my Wing Chun family, and I accepted them for who they were.

It was Robert's turn to recommend a place to eat, and he had high praise for his favorite Korean restaurant. San Soo was all he ever talked about. He made sure everyone knew he despised all the fast food American fusion joints that were around.

Robert said, "Ken, be prepared to finally taste real food."

Ken said, "That'd be great, if we ever get a chance to order."

Robert scratched his forehead with his middle finger. He was never one to hold back his feelings. Out of our group, he was the best dressed, and he often reminded me of a wannabe K-pop star who couldn't sing. Robert kept our group on edge and made sure that it was never boring.

Doc chimed into the quibbling. "I don't know about you, but hearing Danny's love life for the last fifteen minutes is more painful than waiting." Doc looked around and asked, "Who's with me on this?"

One by one, everyone raised their hands. All eyes turned to Sifu, but he didn't raise his. Danny's eyes glowed with excitement and pride that Sifu didn't join in with the rest of the group.

"Grandioso. You see Sifu. Sifu's a romantic! He doesn't believe my love life is so bad to listen to. Gracias, Sifu. That really means a lot."

It was hard to believe I was the youngest of the group. If you asked anyone, they would've surely said Danny. He dropped Spanish whenever he was trying to cover up his insecurities. He was an over thinker who needed to do more than speak. The guys always hazed him the most, but it was more to help him out than to punish him.

Robert asked, "You're kidding, right, Sifu? Danny's love life doesn't bother you at all?"

"No. Not at all. In fact, I find it quite, uh … interesting."

Danny shouted. "You see that? Interesting!"

Sifu said, "Besides … if I ever wrote a book, I'd use his stories to fill up half of it."

Everyone around started howling in laughter, but Danny had a confused look as to whether that was a compliment.

"Danny, why is it when I hang out with you, it feels like I'm studying your creature habits and logging them in for study?" said Doc.

"See? It's because I'm interesting."

Doc shook his head and said, "I swear my IQ is dropping."

I giggled at that thought. Doc was the brains of the group. He was the logic that somehow existed in our group of pure testosterone. Without him, we would still be in caves trying to figure out how to make fire. Out of all the guys, I always felt that Doc was the nicest to me.

Ken stood up and said, "I'm gonna hit the bathroom. Robert, if there happens to be someone breathing in this joint, do you think you can handle ordering for me?"

Robert smiled and pointed his middle finger to his nose before he quickly bowed. He said, "I'm telling you, guys, I know Korean food service isn't the best, but it's definitely worth the wait. I can't personally think of anything better than this food."

Looking depressed, Danny said, "It can't be better than love."

I chuckled at his pathetic expression.

Seconds after Ken disappeared into the bathroom, the waitress appeared. She exchanged quick formalities with Robert as he ordered in Korean. He went down the list of what everyone wanted as she listened carefully. Finally, she repeated the order, and Robert ended with a big smile and a look of crazed anticipation.

Moments later, Ken finally came back from the bathroom. He stopped just before sitting and looked around. He turned to Robert and made a flippant remark. "Figures!" Shaking his head, he pleaded his case to the group once again, hoping we'd feel the same plight that he was suffering. "There's still no one here to take the order?"

Robert said, "Mr. Snow."

Danny said, "I prefer El Blanco."

Tobias shouted, "One and done!"

Ryan added, "My vote is for white privilege."

I chuckled and quickly swallowed it to silence. All the nicknames given to Ken were just too funny.

After all the voices fell silent, Robert replied back to Ken. "Uh, what are you talking about? I just put in the order for all the food."

"Yeah, right," Ken scoffed, doubting every word coming out of Robert's mouth.

"No, seriously, ask anyone." Robert was determined to convince Ken.

I said, "Yeah, Ken. The waitress did come, and Robert put in the order for everyone."

Ken looked somewhat suspicious as he sat down. "Sifu, did Robert really put in an order?"

I asked Ken, "What gives? You don't believe me?"

Ken said, "I don't know. You two are always in cahoots."

"Is that because he's South Korean and I'm North Korean?"

Ken paused, looking around. "Uh, no comment."

Danny said, "I'm sitting in the middle of both of them. I must be the DMZ."

Robert and I shook our heads, and he sunk quietly back into his seat.

Sifu finally got an opening to answer Ken and said, "Yes. Exactly what Kirin said; food should be coming in a bit."

Big T's stomach rumbled. "God, I hope it doesn't take forever for the food to come."

Danny perked up and took the opportunity. "T? Do you want to bet?"

Like clockwork, they began finalizing details on when the food would arrive. I giggled as I watched the two bet, reassured after Big T had finally revealed the details behind their gambling.

Ryan said, "I can tell you this … I think I have only fifteen minutes of sympathy credits available to listen to Danny's love life." With that, Ryan pulled out his phone and began killing time by playing on it.

Robert said, "You sure it's not 10 minutes?"

I watched, as I noticed some inside joke going on between the two of them. With a small frown, I said, "You seem a bit edgy, Ryan."

Still fixated on his game, he said, "Uh, that's because I'd rather have turmoil in love than nothing at all."

I felt bad for Ryan. I was always closest to him, like a little kid who couldn't let go of a big teddy bear. He was a kind spirit who loved good food as much as I did, maybe a little too much. In the end, I had a special place for him, and I loved him like a brother. Actually, now that I think about it, he was more like a little sister to me.

Tobias said, "Danny, you're making it too complicated."

Danny finished the details of his side bet with T and asked, "How so?"

"Love isn't complicated," said Tobias.

Danny laughed. "Wait a second. You're giving me advice on love? We're talking about love, Tobias—not what you normally do. Wait. Why am I talking to you about this? I've been with this girl forever, and I want to fight to make it work." Danny snapped his fingers and said, "You know what? I should ask Sifu."

Sifu said, "I'm all ears."

"Yah see, Sifu, all the guys think I should just end this and break up with her."

I interrupted, "You didn't ask me for my input."

Danny replied, "Kirin, I said 'all the guys,' and you're part of that group."

I sat back and didn't respond. I was pretty sure I'd just been insulted.

Danny said, "Uh, where was I...? Anyway, I've been with her for quite a while now. I know we have our occasional scuffle, but I think we can work things out. Don't you think you should fight for love?"

Robert said, "I got an idea. Maybe you should get a dog and save the relationship."

I said, "Robert, stop being a ... never mind."

Ryan jumped in and said, "I think Kirin was gonna say, 'Stop being a dick, Robert.'"

Robert replied, "I can't help it, Kirin. I'm thoughtful like that."

"What do you think, Sifu?" Danny pressed, still unsure.

Sifu said, "Sounds good ... fight the force, and go for it."

Danny felt confident after Sifu encouraged him. Then he paused as a thought struck him. "Wait a second, Sifu.... Sometimes I have the feeling you're just saying this so I can entertain you."

Sifu laughed and said, "I'm not sure what's worse: your dating problems or me having to remember the names of all of Ken's girlfriends."

Ken jumped in. "At least I know all the names of my girlfriends. Tobias doesn't even call them anything."

Tobias said, "It would be a lot easier if you dated a Chinese girl named Yu."

Ken replied, "A girl named you or Yu?"

Tobias said, "Either way. All of us would simply say, 'Hey you.'"

Danny said, "That's totally racist."

Tobias said, "It's not racist if her name is in fact Yu."

I couldn't help giggling. Tobias did have a funny side that made me laugh often.

Ken waved at the waitress, who ignored him. "What gives? I'm positive she sees me. She's ignoring me." Ken looked at us and wondered why we didn't seem bothered by it. "Dammit, do I have to shout out 'Agua'?"

Danny said, "That's Spanish, you know."

Ken shouted, "Whatever! That's universally understood."

Big T said, "Agua don't mean water?"

I laughed again; the guys always cracked me up in their own ways. I sometimes wondered if Big T was just playing us all. He towered over everyone and seemed the least likely of our group to even need to know Wing Chun.

Several minutes passed as we were waiting for the waitress to give us water. I said, "You know what? Maybe it's you, Ken."

Ken said, "What do you mean?"

I said, "Just an experiment. Go outside for a minute or two. Pretend that you're making a phone call."

"Fine. I'm so thirsty, I'm game for anything."

Ken got up and went outside. As soon as the door swung closed, the Korean waitress came by and smiled, giving us all water. I couldn't help but laugh. We began laughing out loud as Ken came running back in.

"Don't tell me! She came when I left?"

"Purely coincidence," I assured him. "Besides, she got us water."

Ken sat down, looking frustrated. He shook his head.

I asked, "What's wrong?"

Ken pointed at his glass, which was the only one not filled.

I laughed so hard I almost spit out my water.

Danny said, "Guys, stop interrupting me. I really need to sort this out. Seriously, Sifu, do you have any girl advice?"

Sifu said, "The thing is, guys and gal, if you understand Wing Chun, if you believe in what I've taught you, you can't do it part time. Do you understand what I'm saying?"

Danny said, "I think so."

"Whenever I hear 'I think so,' I know that means you absolutely don't get it. Wing Chun is life, the strategy, the training … all of it applies to everything that you do. You can't just switch it off when you think it's convenient to do so."

Danny sat there with a blank look on his face, but the rest of the guys suddenly were leaning forward just a pinch more to hear what Sifu said.

"Look. Love is not difficult if you know who you are and what you want. But in the bigger scheme of things, why would you force someone who doesn't want to be with you?"

"Well, I figure we should try to make it work, right?" asked Danny.

"Try, yes. Struggle from the start, probably no," said Sifu. He rolled his eyes and said, "Isn't that fighting the force?" He coughed in a bad-acting kind of way just to make his point.

"But we have so much in common," pleaded Danny.

"In common … hmm, I tell you that's overrated. Liking the same things is a minor part of a relationship, but seeing eye to eye leads to fewer headaches."

"Hmm, I just don't know, Sifu."

Robert said, "Danny, stop being an askhole."

"This is what I'm talking about. Wing Chun needs to be practiced in all that you do. One, you're fighting the force. Two, you don't know what you're targeting. Three, you can't control your own ego. If this was a fight, the chances of you winning are slim to none."

Ryan said, "Well, you know what Sifu always says … sometimes you have to touch the fire to know it's hot."

Ken chimed in, "I'd be happy just getting service."

Everyone laughed as Ken shook his head.

Sifu reached out and said, "Ken, give me your empty glass."

Ken looked confused but did as Sifu asked.

Sifu grabbed the empty cup and placed it right in front of him. We were all staring at Sifu, as he was oddly just sitting there.

I leaned over to Ryan who was next to me and asked, "What's Sifu doing?"

Ryan whispered, "I have no idea."

A minute passed as we sat silently, and suddenly a waitress appeared out of nowhere. She came walking by and, without a word spoken, filled Sifu's cup with water. We were all looking at one another with blank expressions.

I said, "What just happened?"

Sifu smiled, picked up the glass, and handed it to Ken.

Sifu said, "Nothing. I just got my water filled."

Ken said, "Thank you," and stared at his water.

I was just as baffled as the rest of the group. "No, seriously, what just happened?"

Ryan said, "It's magic, right?"

Sifu laughed. "The same energy draws and attracts other people. I did nothing special. I just wanted a drink."

I scratched my head and shrugged.

Robert asked, "So, how does this relate to FE?"

Sifu choked on a cough. "Let's save that for another time when, uh, Kirin's not here."

"The only flaw in Wing Chun is when the practitioner fails to use it all the time."—Sifu

SECTION 2

Sifu's Journey Entry #1—Straight to the Source

Late January 2030

Sifu and Lance sat across from each other, eyeing a bowl of soup centered on the table. Dawn had quickly changed to dusk, as the day had been spent sweating over a stove and meticulously preparing a bowl of ramen. Each one looked determined as a single beam from the light above highlighted their day's effort. The sound of their breathing was the only thing penetrating the silence of the room. Neither one wanted to make the first move.

At stake, lying before them, was a quantifiable amount of work they had invested in for the last several months. Perfection was the goal: lofty as well as impossible in theory. They had nevertheless made a pact that they would try to achieve it. Today's efforts reflected that work in a single dish, which would either validate them or send them back to the drawing board.

Sifu finally took the initiative and broke the stalemate. He rustled in his chair and leaned forward, and the creaking sound added to the tension. He cleared his throat and said to Lance, "You go first and taste it." He grabbed the bowl by its side and pushed it toward Lance, reinforcing his words with this gesture and finally selling it with a smile.

Lance was hunched over with a single palm supporting his head. He looked at the bowl and then at Sifu. "You should go first. Besides, I'm cursed with American taste buds." Lance took the bowl and pushed it back in the center, returning it to its original spot. Now both men were no better than they had been several minutes ago, as the process seemed to replay itself.

Sifu thought for a moment about Lance's response. While the argument was valid, Sifu had already determined who was going to taste it first. "No, you should really go first … I insist. Besides, you might be swayed by my reaction." Again, Sifu grabbed the bowl and shoved it closer to Lance. The steam rising from the ramen now cast a transparent wall in front of Lance's face.

The bowl of ramen was again on Lance's side, accompanied by Sifu's counter argument. As the saying goes, the ball was in his court. Lance thought about it briefly and winced. He said, "Why would you say that?" He avoided eye contact with Sifu, but he hoped his decisive voice would be enough.

Sifu sat up, held a little gap between his thumb and index finger, and said, "Because you and I know that I'm just a wee bit more detached than you."

Lance sneered at Sifu's comment and was about to counter it. "Well, I don't know about that...." He paused, deep in thought as he stared at the soup. He then looked Sifu square in the eyes, his confidence withering away. Lance thought, *He's either training me in Wing Chun or after all these months he's finally brainwashed me.* Lance shook his head and said, "Forget it; you're right," throwing his hands up in the air, surrendering.

Sifu smiled and hinted at Lance to get to work. Lance took the hint and grabbed a napkin, placing it on his lap. He leaned forward and hugged the bowl, slowly mixing the soup with his spoon. The steam from the bowl continued to rise as he blew on it. Just as he was about to take a sip, he looked back up at Sifu and said, "You know ... one of these days, I'm gonna win an argument."

"That's the problem."

"What is?"

"You're trying to win."

Lance rolled his eyes, chuckled, and slumped back into his chair. "I'm too exhausted for any more Wing Chun lessons.... I'll save my question to that statement for another day."

Lance took one last peek at Sifu and blew on the ramen once more. Sifu squirmed in his chair and leaned forward, watching intently so he could read the slightest reaction from Lance's face.

Lance closed his eyes, blocked out all sound, and diverted all his senses to the taste of the broth. He placed his lips at the very tip of the spoon and hesitated. In Lance's mind, this was payback. Making Sifu wait was the only battle he could win. Finally, he sipped it, cautiously making sure he did not spill a single drop. A few seconds passed as he swirled the broth in his mouth before swallowing it. It wasn't the normal way one would eat ramen, but he was there to judge it.

He opened his eyes to find Sifu staring directly at him. He said in a stern and hoarse voice, "If this was my ex-wife wanting me to take her back, guess what? I would. Best damn soup we've made. Period!"

Sifu frowned, hung his shoulders, and the look of disappointment was written all over his face.

"What ... what's wrong? I just said this was the best damn soup we've ever made," said Lance.

Sifu grabbed his chin and was quickly lost in thought. He mumbled, "Maybe I read it wrong. Something I missed?"

Lance replied, "We didn't miss anything."

Sifu said, "Something not written on the recipe. I don't know."

Lance said, "I don't get it. How do ya know it's not right? Seriously, this is damn good soup, Sifu!" Lance grabbed the bowl and pushed it toward Sifu to try. "Will you at least just try it? Come on. Humor me."

"I don't need to."

Lance waved down Sifu and any future excuses he could muster. "I'm asking yah, Sifu, friend to friend, give it a try."

Lance's last request finally brought down Sifu's wall. He gave in and tasted the soup. Lance was right that the soup was good—very good, in fact—but it wasn't exactly how he remembered it. Still wearing a look of disappointment, he said, "You're right; it is good, but it's just a pinch off. I can't seem to duplicate that taste, that feeling." His last words hit like reality, as it sobered his mood even further.

Lance hesitated before asking in a softer voice, "I hate to bring it up, Sifu, but is it possible you're not reading it right?"

Sifu looked at Lance and nodded. "I'm telling you, I'm reading it right. Look." He quickly pulled out his wife's recipe and showed it to Lance.

"Uh, it's in Japanese." Lance smiled.

"Never mind. Trust me, it's not that."

"So, what is it? What's missing?" asked Lance.

Sifu sighed and then chuckled slightly.

"What is it? What's so funny?"

Sifu said, "Isn't it obvious? Lance, it's no different from trying to learn Wing Chun from a book. There are limitations to learning from reading as opposed to learning it hands on, you know."

Lance said, "Hmm, maybe one day you'll write a book about the complete art of Wing Chun."

"Yeah, that's a good one. Even better if I make it a story based on my students."

Lance broke the flow of the conversation and asked, "I know the timing of this might be bad, but are you gonna finish that?" He eyed the soup, hoping that it would find a home in his belly.

Sifu smiled and passed the bowl of ramen to Lance. "Please, by all means. Save me from the calories."

With a satisfied expression, Lance began eating the ramen, and the room was drowned with the slurping sound of noodles. As Lance continued eating, he saw that Sifu was lost in thought, wrestling for an answer.

Lance was in mid-slurp with a noodle hanging from his mouth when Sifu said with certainty, "I know exactly what to do."

Lance paused and stared up at Sifu. Wary of his answer, he sat silent and frozen. Whatever it was, the look on Sifu's face showed that he had already decided. Then he watched as Sifu poured a glass of water and placed it in front of Lance.

Lance looked curiously at the water that Sifu gave him. However, he remained silent, shifting his focus back to Sifu.

With a serious and determined look on his face, Sifu said, "I'm going to go. I'm going to go back to the very source."

Immediately, Lance choked and struggled to finish the food remaining in his mouth. Even before he could finish swallowing, he began to speak. "What do you mean go back to the source? You mean...?"

The moment of exhilaration was quickly followed by a sigh and a look of regret. "I have to go back to Japan. I have to go back to the source where Megumi learned to cook ramen."

Lance gagged on his food as he tried to clear his throat. Sifu pointed to the glass of water, and Lance reached for it.

Lance said, "You're kidding me!" as he continued to forget his manners and speak with food in his mouth.

Lance knew that this was a difficult decision for Sifu to make. He wanted to leave it at that, but curiosity got the better of him. He bombarded Sifu with questions. "When? How long do you plan on being there? Are you sure this is what you want to do?"

Sifu waited for every last question to come out from Lance as he watched his friend finally gasp for air, exhausted from speaking. He studied Lance almost as if he were answering him telepathically. Finally, before the silence became too unbearable, he said, "I'll leave immediately. As for how long, until I get this recipe right, I guess.... And yes, this absolutely needs to be done." He sighed, almost unsure of the last answer, which brought a heavy heart.

Lance could see the decision was troubling, and he wanted to help his teacher, who also had become his close friend. He stroked his beard and blurted, "Maybe I should go with you?" Lance watched and waited for an answer, unable to read Sifu.

Suddenly Sifu smiled, stood up, and came around the table, placing his hand on Lance's shoulder. "The gesture is much appreciated, my friend, but this is one journey I'm going to have to do on my own. Besides, someone has to hold down the fort."

Lance felt the weight of Sifu's words and made a joke to lighten the moment. "What am I going to do while you're gone?"

Sifu giggled and said, "I saw your first form the other day."

Lance looked up, waiting for Sifu to finish his thought. He then hung his head, expecting to hear Sifu's usual comment, and whispered, "Yeah, I know. Not bad, not bad."

"Actually, I wasn't even going to say that," said Sifu. "I was going to say it's good at your level."

Lance had decoded nearly all Sifu's phrases, but this was a new one. "Wait a second. If it isn't 'not bad, not bad,' then that's even worse, isn't it?"

Sifu walked away and just started laughing.

"No, seriously. 'Not bad, not bad' means average, but what does 'good at your level' mean?" Lance watched Sifu fade away into the next room, still unsure of the true meaning.

"Sometimes, to go forward, one must be willing to start back from the very beginning."—Sifu

CHAPTER 2

Cosplay

Mid-February 2033

K irin sat and stared, befuddled by the mirror image of herself standing several feet away. She snapped out of her trance and waved her fan forward.

"Hi ... and your name is?" asked Kirin.

"Um ... um ... Gah, Gavin. That's Gavin, Ms. Rise." The teenager beamed and twitched with nervous excitement.

"Oh! Uh, hi, Gavin." The male voice caught Kirin by surprise. *It's a guy?* she thought. "That's, uh, a nice name. She smiled to cover her shock and added, "I don't believe I've ever ran into a Gavin before."

Gavin pulled an item from his backpack and said, "Can you please sign this, Ms. Rise?"

There Kirin sat and pondered for a moment in what could be considered an extremely bizarre situation. She was holding an action figure of herself while a guy who was dressed up to look exactly like her asked her to sign it.

Gavin clapped his hands, nearly salivating while Kirin signed it. She appreciated his enthusiasm, even though it was a pinch over the top, and handed the signed item back to him. He snatched it from Kirin, spun around, and jumped into the air. He was elated, acting as if he had been given a million credits.

Gavin hugged his prize as Kirin kindly watched and waited. He finally snapped back into reality and stared directly at Kirin without saying another word. Kirin did the same and wondered if there was something else he wanted.

Kirin asked, "Gavin, um ... is there something else you need?"

"Uh, yeah ... if you don't mind, can we get a picture together?"

"Sure thing."

The flamboyant male version of Kirin snapped his heels together and shuffled around the table. He got to Kirin's side as he pulled a camera from his pocket to take the shot.

Click.

"One more ... just in case," said Gavin.

Kirin thought, *Always take two,* as her photography experience kicked in.

Click.

"I have to admit, Gavin, you're the first guy I've seen dressed up in my ring outfit ... and I honestly think you look better in it than I do."

He shrieked with excitement, piercing the air around him, after hearing Kirin's compliment. He blurted with pride, "Ms. Rise, I can't tell you how big a fan I am! It took me hours just getting your hair right."

"Really? All I usually do is just shampoo it and put it in a ponytail. You're gonna have to teach me your secrets to getting your hair so vibrant and bouncy."

Gavin flicked his hair around, and it sparkled from the light. He struggled to speak around his braces. "Sure thing, Ms. Rise. I can tell you the breakdown if you want. You see, the vast majority of your hair is made out of protein, so there's a direct proportion between your intake level and—"

"Tell yah what, would you mind emailing it to me? I promise to definitely try it." Kirin did her best to cut him off from his long-winded explanation.

"Anything for you, Ms. Rise," Gavin gushed as he adjusted his hair in a mannerism like Kirin's.

"One more thing, Gavin…."

Gavin waited, eager to see what Kirin had to say.

"Please, just call me Kirin. 'Ms. Rise' makes me seem like I'm … you know … old."

Hearing that personal touch put Gavin on cloud nine. He muttered to himself, "I can't believe it! I can call her Kirin." He kept repeating it as he spun around and tiptoed away. The crowd was growing feverish with excitement. Everyone there was chanting Kirin's name as they eagerly waited for their opportunity to meet her.

Kirin stared straight into the sea of fans waiting in line just to spend a moment with her. This was nothing new for Kirin, but it had taken her a while to grow comfortable with the fact that her every step was always being watched. This was the first time she'd ever attended a costume convention. Like everything else she did these days, this one was the largest in the world. She played with her three strands of hair and took a deep breath, as that little hint of insecurity always seemed to linger.

Angelo tapped Kirin on the shoulder, snapping her out of her daze. "Kirin, are you ready for the next person?"

"Sure thing, Angelo. I'm ready."

Angelo snapped his fingers and set down a fresh cup of her favorite coffee on the table.

"Oh, thanks, Angelo." Kirin smiled as she caught a whiff of the coffee.

Angelo leaned over and whispered, "Thirty more minutes and you'll have a break, okay?"

Kirin nodded and took a sip, and her eyes widened. "Oh wow, my favorite! How'd you get it?"

Angelo said, "It's my job, Kirin, to be a step ahead of you. Besides, you're a big-time celebrity now. These are just the perks." Angelo began straightening out Kirin's table, making sure everything was in fine order.

Kirin thought, *Perks ... ah, the perks, but there's always a price that comes with that.* Kirin knew that Angelo meant well, but it still took time getting used to having someone fuss over you.

"Okay, okay, Angelo ... enough, already," said Kirin.

"I'm just making sure everything is in perfect order for you."

"Whatever, Mom," Kirin joked.

"Can I at least comb your hair?"

"No! Now, go away ... please." Kirin pointed to the corner for Angelo to go. He frowned and, like a little puppy being punished, tucked himself behind her.

Life after the tournament for Kirin was crazier than ever. Upon entering the UFMF, her status had vaulted from unknown rookie fighter to the UFMF Dome Champion. Kirin had struggled early on to come to grips with her new-found fame. But now, after having won the tournament, she reached the pinnacle status that only a handful ever achieved. She had become the voice of the people and appeared almost god-like to many of her fans.

Not a second passed where the name "Kirin Rise" wasn't spoken in some form by the media. Life for her could never return to normal. So, to keep her daily routine from falling into complete chaos, her parents had suggested she get a personal assistant. After spending a month searching for one, blind luck happened to cross her path. Of all the places to find an assistant, Kirin had run into Angelo at her favorite coffee shop. He had the three Cs that she had been looking for: charismatic, charming, and, uh, controversial, as he so kindly stated when he interviewed for the position.

Angelo clapped his hands, and Kirin was again lost in her own world. Thirty minutes quickly passed, and the sounds of the fans' cheers were far from fading. However, the look of disappointment set in on many fans' faces when they realized that they would have to wait for the next session to meet up with Kirin.

Angelo decided it was time for Kirin's break, and the next person in line would be Kirin's last fan. He stood firmly in place and stared at the fortunate soul.

He said, "Today's your lucky day. You shall be the last." He spun around on his heels and faced the other way. "Now follow me."

Kirin watched as Angelo began prancing straight toward her. However, she noticed he was walking by himself. Even when she leaned to the side, she couldn't see anyone.

"Your last fan before your break, Kirin," said Angelo.

"I don't see anyone."

"Oh, my bad," said Angelo. He stepped aside, and behind him popped out a little girl dressed in Kirin's typical red hoodie. Angelo grabbed the little girl by her cheeks and squeezed. "She's the last. Isn't she the most adorable little creature?"

Kirin smiled and waved her forward. The little girl was nervous as Angelo eased her toward Kirin with the girl's mom snapping picture after picture from a distance.

"Hey, what's your name?" Kirin asked as she leaned over, seeing only the top of her head.

Angelo turned toward the mom and asked, "Do you mind?" The mom nodded, giving the green light to lift her on top of the table. She was cute as a button, dressed up from head to toe in Kirin's red hoodie outfit, light brown khakis, and Converse mid-cut shoes.

"So … what's your name?" Kirin spoke softly to put the little girl at ease.

"My name is Annie." Her voice was soft and soothing.

"That's a beautiful name. How old are you, Annie?"

"I'm seven years old."

"Wow! You look amazing. You know what? You look a lot better in that outfit than I do." Kirin adjusted her hoodie to fit better. Kirin paused for a second and thought, *It's not really an outfit…. It's just what I like to wear normally.*

Annie smiled from ear to ear, as Kirin's words gave her a new sense of confidence. Suddenly, Annie's mom jumped in.

"Oh Kirin, Annie wants to be just like you! She watches all your fights and wants to be a fighter in the UFMF. I've got her signed up for several classes at these UFMF gyms. She's gonna be the next big thing." Annie's mom spoke confidently, as if they had been friends for years.

Kirin faked a smile, trying to match the mom's level of excitement. Annie seemed less than thrilled after hearing her mom's plan.

"I'm sorry," said Kirin. "What's your name?"

"Oh, it's Carol Sultan. That's S-U-L-T-A-N. You know, like how a genie has his sultan." She reached for Kirin's hand and shook it vigorously. Kirin's arm waved like a wet noodle as she thought, *Thank God my mom was never like this.*

"Tell yah what, Mrs. Sultan, my assistant Angelo here has some extra goodies for you, if you would just follow him."

Carol jumped up and rushed toward Angelo. She had no awareness of personal space, and Angelo took several steps back in fear he would be crushed. That did nothing to hinder the overzealous mom. She barked into Angelo's ear, asking what goodies he had for her. Angelo gave Kirin a look of fear, and she returned it with a small giggle.

Kirin watched and confirmed the mom was fully distracted. "Okay, Annie. It's just you and me now. So, I want you to be you and talk to me."

Annie bit her lip, unsure what to think.

Kirin asked, "So, do you really want to be a UFMF fighter?"

The little girl peeked around the corner to see her mom busy fussing with Angelo. She began to open her mouth, but quickly closed it. Doubt still seemed to hover around her.

"Hmm." Kirin turned around to take a peek, playing along with Annie. "Mom's a little preoccupied, Annie.... It'll be just between you and me, I promise."

Annie smiled, and a look of relief finally settled over her face.

"Let's say you didn't like fighting and could do anything you wanted. What would that be?"

She looked up and thought hard. "I like baking cookies." She sighed, releasing a breath of relief.

"Wow, that's great! I love cookies." *Except oatmeal cookies,* thought Kirin. "What's your favorite kind to bake?"

"Peanut butter!" she yelled and then quickly covered her mouth, fearing her mom might have heard.

Both Kirin and Annie turned slowly to check and noticed Carol was digging through the gift items that Angelo was showing her.

Annie looked at Kirin, and they shared a giggle.

"Do you think one day you can make me some?" asked Kirin.

"Sure thing!" Annie got all excited and began going over the details of the recipe.

As Kirin listened, the thought of food caused her stomach to clench. "That sounds great, Annie. Anyway, you're still so young, and your interests can change."

Looking up at Kirin, Annie asked, "When did you know what you wanted to be when you grow up?"

Kirin paused, her face thoughtful as she fought for the right words. "The truth is, I'm still growing up, and I don't have everything figured out. But I can give you a tip that my teacher told me."

"What is it?"

"See, my teacher is a very wise old man." Kirin thought for a minute of mentioning Sifu's other traits, but she bit her tongue. She shook her head and continued, "He said when you are true to yourself, the world will balance itself out."

As Kirin studied Annie's face, she could see without a word spoken that the girl understood what she meant. She leaned forward and whispered in her ear, "Always be you."

With those last words uttered, Annie leaped forward and gave Kirin a tight embrace. Cameras immediately flashed around them to capture that moment.

30 Minutes Later Back Stage

Kirin was back stage with Angelo as she paced nervously back and forth. The clamor of noise behind the curtain made Kirin tense as reality set in.

"I can't believe you talked me into doing this, Angelo." Kirin frowned as she rubbed her hands and looked around erratically.

"You had to do this, Kirin." Angelo spoke with an endearing voice, hoping to calm Kirin's nerves. "Every year, the convention selects the year's three biggest people, and guess what, Kirin? News flash: you happen to be *the* biggest."

Kirin turned her back and shook her head.

Angelo continued to plead his case. "What did you want me to say ... no?"

Kirin spun around and shouted, "Yes. No is good to say. No means no; haven't you heard that before?"

Angelo said, "I seem to recall hearing it more than saying it."

Kirin rolled her eyes as she felt her stomach turn into knots.

"Excuse me," said a strange voice. Both Kirin and Angelo turned around to see who was speaking.

Kirin looked up at a handsome gentleman in a suit. He was tall, thin, and clean cut. His jaw line was defined, and his nose had some character. She recognized the face, but couldn't put a name to it, as her nerves seemed to get the better of her.

"Sorry to bother you, Ms. Rise. I just wanted to introduce myself personally.... I'm Bryce Adams."

Kirin was caught off guard and snapped a smile. "Oh, nice to meet you, Mr. Adams." Kirin thought, *Of course, that's his name, duh.*

Bryce extended his hand for a shake and said, "Please, call me Bryce. The pleasure's all mine. I'm a huge fan." Kirin shook his hand as his strong grip made an impact. He was charming, and his warm smile somehow put her at ease.

"Well, if you'll excuse me ... I think they're introducing me first." Bryce chuckled and adjusted his tie.

Kirin nodded and watched as he walked away.

Kirin leaned over and murmured, "Wow, so that's Bryce Adams...."

As they both stared, Angelo said, "Yup, Bryce Adams is one of the biggest political movements of 2032. Some say he rode your coattails into popularity, mixing your message with his attacks on the government and his views on corporate corruption."

Kirin said, "I've seen him on TV, but didn't realize he was that, uh ... tall."

Angelo snapped back, "He's not tall. You're just short."

"Hey!" Kirin gave Angelo a look.

Angelo smirked. "Anyway ... you have a good excuse for not knowing who the biggest is when you happened to be it, right!"

Kirin waved off his compliment and said, "Hmm, he seems like a good guy. Hopefully he's not the typical politician."

The crowd erupted as the noise shook Kirin back to reality. She grimaced at Angelo. "So, you said this was a panel of three.... Who else is up?"

Angelo pulled out his pad and said, "Ah, yeah, one of the biggest pop stars of 2032...."

Kirin snapped her fingers as she tried to remember that new group. "You're kidding me. Are you telling me Generation...?"

Suddenly, a commotion drew the attention of everyone in the back of the room. Kirin's eyes opened wide as her face turned pale. She said, "Pluck a duck." Kirin hung her head and began to shake it in frustration. "Why's he here?"

"Why? Who's here?" replied Angelo as he tried to see what had Kirin so distressed.

Kirin didn't bother to look up and just pointed in the general direction.

Angelo stared and asked, "Uh, who's that? Should I know him?" He scrambled and looked on his pad, frantically searching for an answer. "I have no idea who that is. I always know who everyone is."

Kirin mumbled, "I thought you said it was some pop star group."

Angelo placed his pad just below Kirin for her to see. "See, right here? That's what it said! That's what it told me, I swear."

Kirin looked up with a sliver of hope she might be wrong. *Please be wrong,* she thought. *Please be wrong.*

Fawn caught sight of Kirin. They exchanged glances, and he began to approach her with a devilish grin on his face.

Angelo continued to plead his case. "It must've been a last-minute change; you know I'm on top of everything. It's not my fault. It's not my fault."

Kirin closed her eyes and mumbled, "Good lord, he's coming over here."

"I'm in the dark, Kirin. Who is he?" pleaded Angelo.

"He's Thorne's PR guy for the UFMF. His name is Fawn." Kirin did her best ventriloquist act and tried to keep a straight face while looking at Fawn.

"That's a bad thing?" asked Angelo.

Fawn and his entourage approached Kirin. His hands were occupied, as he was petting a cat.

Kirin stared at the cat. Something about it looked odd.

Fawn shouted for his assistant, who stumbled running to get there as quick as possible. He motioned to grab Fawn's cat, but Fawn shouted, "No one ever touches Ms. Yum Yum! Do you understand?"

Fawn's assistant apologized and hung his head down.

Fawn said, "Where is her cage?"

Fawn's assistant said, "Right here, sir." He opened the cage and held it for Fawn.

Fawn awkwardly held his cat as he shielded it from everyone's view. He placed Ms. Yum Yum in the cage and immediately shut the gate.

Fawn said, "Daddy will be with you right after the show." He snapped his fingers, and his assistant walked away.

"Take care of her. Otherwise, your ass is mine," said Fawn. "And, don't you dare open that cage."

The assistant looked fearful as he hoped the statement wasn't literal.

"Pleasure seeing you here, Kirin. I guess I'm always playing second fiddle … since I'm a backup guest."

Kirin avoided direct eye contact and said, "Uh, yeah … that's great. Now you must know how Cinderella's stepsisters feel." Kirin got a little dig in.

Fawn chuckled at the comment, and then something caught his eye. He began to check out Angelo. "Hmm, so who do we have here? Is this one of your new accessories for 2033?"

Kirin sighed and said, "Fawn, this is Angelo, my assistant. Angelo, this is Fawn with the UFMF."

Angelo extended his hand for a shake.

"Pleasure meeting you?" Fawn said, a hint of question in his voice. "And, Kirin, the proper title is UFMF Lead President of Public Relations for Assisting Social Segments."

Kirin fired back, "Sorry, Angelo, my bad. This is Fawn, he's the PR of ASS."

"What the…?" Fawn removed his glasses.

"You said yourself … you're the PR of Assisting Social Segments, otherwise known as ASS."

Fawn looked confused before he thought about it. "Hmm, never realized it. I'm the head of ASS." He snickered and said, "Giving or taking…? Never mind." Fawn bit his lip, easily amused.

Kirin rolled her eyes and shook her head.

Fawn leaned forward and started circling Angelo, who stood still as he wasn't quite sure what to do. Fawn grabbed Angelo's hand and kissed the top of it. In a seductive voice, Fawn murmured, "Yes, indeed … that was a pleasure."

Kirin furrowed her brow and didn't utter a word.

"Anyway, if you'll excuse me, I think I'm up next for introductions," said Fawn.

Fawn walked away with a slight skip as Angelo watched.

"So, what's the problem with him? He's kinda cute."

Kirin punched Angelo in the arm. "Good lord. Focus, Angelo."

"Ow! You know I'm delicate," said Angelo as he rubbed his arm and continued to stare at Fawn.

Kirin said, "How can you stare so long at him? His suit sparkles so much it makes me squint."

Angelo replied, "Making you look more Asian."

"Hmm, I guess I've used that joke too much."

"Don't worry, Kirin. I laugh every time, but now mostly on the inside."

Kirin watched from a distance as the stage turned pitch black. Fawn stood eagerly waiting for his cue. Several handlers surrounded him, checking his makeup and fidgeting with his microphone. He finally shooed them away, and he stood confidently leaning on his walking stick.

From a distance, Kirin waited as the introduction of Fawn began. In some ways, it was a good thing, as it distracted her momentarily.

The announcer said, "Now for our second star of the panel, a man who needs no introduction, yet requested that I make one. He is dark, mysterious, and beloved by all. He is the face of the UFMF public relations ... he is H.T. ... Faaawwnn!"

The crowd erupted, shaking the very ground beneath Kirin as she covered her ears. She continued to watch, wondering what Fawn had in mind for an entrance. Suddenly, Fawn jumped on stage and did something completely unexpected.

Fawn began singing as the spotlight stalked him from one side to the other. Kirin watched as the crowd was enjoying every minute of his antics. He really knew how to work them, and they began clapping to the beat of his song.

Caught off guard, Kirin watched Fawn hamming it up on stage. Next to her, Angelo was snapping his fingers, trying his best to restrain himself from doing a full dance.

"What are you doing?" asked Kirin.

"I can't help it. It's a catchy beat," said Angelo.

Kirin thought, *Great, there's no way I'm gonna be able to top that entrance.*

Angelo leaned toward Kirin and whispered, "It's gonna be tough to follow that entrance." Kirin gave Angelo a dirty look. Her assistant shrugged his shoulders and said, "I'm just saying."

Kirin listened as the music reached its crescendo. Finally, Fawn leaped into the air and slid to the front of the stage.

Fawn caught his breath and screamed to the crowd. "Yes, yes ... I know you love me! I know you really, really love me." He stood up and began blowing kisses to the audience. The crowd responded by shouting even louder as the mass of humanity was driven to a frenzy. It was just an entrance, but Fawn had managed to get the crowd into a standing ovation.

Fawn pulled out a handkerchief and wiped the sweat from his brow. He began walking to his chair, waving to the crowd. Bryce stood up and extended his hand for a shake, but Fawn bypassed his greeting and decided to give him a kiss on his cheek. Caught off guard, Bryce stood there frozen in place as Fawn blew it off like it was no big deal.

Kirin took a deep breath, realizing it was her turn to be called. She fidgeted with her hair and closed her eyes.

"Relax Kirin, this is just a simple Q&A, nothing difficult. Fans will be asking you questions like your favorite food, TV shows, all the simple stuff," said Angelo as he patted her on the back and began to rub her shoulders to comfort her.

"Yeah, you're right. This should be simple." She smiled, hoping she could somehow lie to herself. Kirin thought, *Top ten places I'd rather be than here at this moment.*

Angelo said, "Keep it simple, Kirin. Don't get into politics, and you'll be just fine."

As Kirin stood next to Angelo, the announcer hyped up her entrance and called her toward the stage. Kirin was Kirin, and she walked nonchalantly onto the stage. At first, nothing seemed like it could top Fawn's extravagant entrance. The room was dead silent, and she was just halfway to her seat. Suddenly, from behind, a montage of her fight clips from the previous year was blasted on the screen, mesmerizing the audience. Kirin stopped and watched; she'd had no idea that this was even created for her. A minute passed as the audience remained waiting for the clip to finally end. When it did, Kirin faced the crowd and simply smiled and waved.

The crowd went wild, and security had to make sure no one would jump onto the stage. They cheered for her as the audience shook the entire auditorium. Somehow her entrance ended up being even louder than Fawn's. She took her spot next to Fawn and Bryce.

The host, Chad Sinclair, began talking to all three guests, and he was doing his best to dig for interesting topics. Kirin sat quietly for the most part, as he seemed to be focusing mainly on Bryce and Fawn. Kirin thought, *Well, this isn't so bad.*

Ten minutes into the interview, Chad Sinclair said, "So, Kirin you are *the* biggest thing in 2032. You've achieved a celebrity status that millions could only dream of. I have to know—in fact, everyone here wants to know: how does it feel to be a superstar?" Chad along with all those watching leaned forward to hear her response.

Kirin waved to the crowd humbly as they shouted encouragement. She tried her best to settle them down before responding to Chad's question. She looked away for a moment and gathered her thoughts. Feeling ill at ease, Kirin said, "I don't think I'll ever be comfortable taking that title or any title, and that's just me personally." She touched her chest and made a humble gesture to the crowd.

Chad stepped in and said, "But you are. You are a superstar! Search engines, advertising, the latest polls track you as the number one trend of 2032, and nothing is even remotely close." He then turned toward the crowd and said, "Am I right?"

The crowd replied with a boisterous cheer, solidifying his question with a definitive statement.

Kirin shook her head and grimaced after hearing him say it again. This time, she barked back, "If you define 'superstar' as someone many people recognize, then yes I can accept that. But, unfortunately, the way I believe people perceive that term is one that elevates that person into being better than everyone else. And, if that's the case, I will never see myself that way. The fact is, I'm just hesitant to create such a hierarchy. To me, this labeling of kings, servants, workers, and commoners has existed forever and has defined nothing but servitude."

"That's a very humble way of looking at things, Kirin," said Chad.

He started to change the subject, but his question got Kirin talking.

"I honestly don't think so," Kirin said. "The problem is when we start labeling and giving people a higher status, for some reason or another, it seems to go to their head. I believe that humans, regardless of socioeconomic status, are all equal and not in just name but in how we should treat our fellow human beings."

Kirin stood up, feeling impassioned. "My role in the universe is to inspire people to be better and to find their true calling. I may have won the Dome last year, but I don't think that is even close to what I am meant to do. It's a lifelong learning process that everyone needs to find. To say I'm a superstar means I'm more important than the bus driver, or garbage man, or soldier.... All these individuals play a functioning role in society ... in fact, a vital role. I feel that we've lost our way, and the value we give for just being famous is overblown."

Kirin's rant had the crowd excited, and their applause and cheers fueled her fire.

"I fought in the ring and won 25 million credits, but you see a soldier fight for this country and barely make 25,000 credits a year. Can't we stop for a second and ask ourselves which one is more important? Does that even make sense?"

The crowd surged, people jumping to their feet as they applauded. They began cheering Kirin's name.

"Kirin! Kirin! Kirin!"

Sinclair waved the crowd down and decided to dig even further. "But you have to admit the fame and fortune has to be a plus.... Don't you think so?"

Kirin seemed to be growing more annoyed with Chad's questioning. "You know, Chad, I'm one of the fortunate ones who had a steady income from my photography business. You could say I was happy before all this began. I think the biggest thing we need to understand is that happiness begins with yourself, and no amount of money or fame is gonna change that."

The crowd cheered. Her words lifted everyone's spirits, as she symbolized how it was still possible for anyone to be successful. Kirin got a glance of Bryce as he smiled in her direction and began clapping as well.

Chad took a sip of his drink and turned toward the audience. "Well, that's the last segment of our discussion. We're going to open it up to the fans, and each one will be given a chance to ask someone on the panel a question."

Fawn leaned over to Kirin's ear, but she pulled away. He said in a sneaky voice, "Psst, Kirin ... this is when the fun begins." Kirin could feel her skin crawl. She despised the top brass of the UFMF.

Kirin tried her best to keep a neutral face and looked back toward Chad.

A line began to form by the mic that was placed in the middle of the crowd. Chad had his assistant directing the audience members who wanted to participate.

"This question is for Fawn; they say the UFMF was disappointed that Diesel lost. Is that true?"

Fawn stood up. Always the attention hog, he approached Kirin from the rear of her chair and surprised her by hugging her tightly. She froze in horror, as she wasn't sure what to do. Fawn said, "We favor no one since all the fighters represent what the UFMF stands for. Thus, we hope every one of our fighters does their best to be a champ. We are proud to call Kirin the Dome Champion of the world."

Kirin forced an awkward smile and thought, *First thing I do is shower when I get home.*

A teenage boy approached the mic and asked, "This is for Kirin. I was wondering if you're dating anyone, and if not … would you be interested in me?" The audience cheered him on as everyone got a good laugh.

Kirin blushed and responded, "You know, I'm a little too busy to have a boyfriend right now, and I wouldn't want you to feel neglected. But, I am willing to give you a hug." The boy raised his fist, and the crowd went wild.

When Kirin waved him forward, he began dashing through the crowd. He paused just as he approached Kirin, his inexperience unnerving him. Kirin was no expert on the matter of boys, but she knew a good heart when she saw one, or so she thought. She looked into his eyes and wrapped her arms around him. He melted on his feet with Kirin's touch.

A female audience member approached and waited for all the cheers to subside. She asked, "Mr. Adams do you feel you've run on the coattails of Kirin's message?"

Bryce smiled and was unfazed by the negative insinuation of the question. "It's great Ms. Rise and I share similar views on many things, and I applaud the future generation for getting involved in making a change. Now, while I don't want to speak for her, I'm sure she's busy with her own training and the start of the new UFMF season."

Kirin didn't speak, and his words resonated in her head. Even she was unaware of what the future held for her.

Bryce continued his speech, "The difference, young lady, is I have devoted my life, my focus, to fixing this great country of ours. Anything and everything that I do—let me be clear to all those with ears—is for current and future generations to experience what America used to be, what it used to stand for."

The crowd grew excited as Bryce's presence and his words drew their emotions.

Bryce said, "Now, I'm not one to avoid a question, but as for riding her coattails, I think it's just good timing on my part. I'm sure many in the audience share her views as well. Don't you think?"

The female audience member was smitten with his remark. She began applauding as the rest of the crowd followed suit.

Chad stepped in and took control of the question. "Okay, we've got time for only a couple more questions." Chad pointed at the next audience member. "You, sir. Please ask your question."

A man stepped up and tapped on the mic several times. "Kirin, you've made no mention of re-entering the league for this year. Do you plan on coming back?"

Fawn smiled, sat up from his seat, and paid close attention to this particular line of questioning.

Kirin thought for a moment, unsure how to answer. "I honestly don't know. I mean, I'm not sure if I have anything else to prove."

He followed up, "The reason I ask, Kirin, is some think you cheated. What's your thought on that?"

Kirin took exception to that statement. She said, "What do you mean cheated?" She snuck a glance toward Fawn, suddenly suspicious of both the person and the line of questioning.

"I mean … some say no human could take the damage that you withstood in the ring."

Kirin shouted back, "Are you kidding me?"

Chad stepped forward and tried to settle her down.

"I mean … how does one explain a five-foot-three-inch, hundred-and-five-pound girl defeating a highly proficient killing machine like Diesel without cheating?"

Kirin stood up and said, "It's called skill."

The audience was silenced as Kirin's tone quickly changed. Her emotions were getting the better of her.

"You know how you're busy watching reality shows, texting, and playing fart games with your buddies? I'm focused on being the best that I can be in the art. That's what Gung Fu is all about."

Chad said, "Don't you mean Kung Fu?"

Kirin looked at Chad and said, "No, it's Gung Fu, and the meaning has nothing to do with martial arts. The meaning has everything to do with hard work and the dedication to focus all your attention on a single task to be great at it. That's how I won. Trying to be faster or stronger than those guys would be impossible…. I had to do it with skill."

"Or cheating," the audience member pressed on. "Well, it just doesn't seem possible."

Fawn stepped in and commented. "I just want to point out that every fighter goes through stringent testing before and after the fight. Ms. Rise along with everyone who entered the Dome tournament tested clean. And mind you, this was done by the UFMF and confirmed by an outside independent third party company. That's how thorough we are."

Chad motioned toward another person to ask their question. "This is for Kirin and kinda expands on the previous question. I'm a huge UFMF fan, just like many who are here. Do you feel like you are disrespecting the organization by trying to instill your belief that Wing Chun is the best martial art?"

Kirin took a deep breath and clenched her fist. "I'm not sure why this is even an issue. At what point did society decide it's wrong to have your own opinion? It's almost like, if I say Wing Chun is the best martial art .... I somehow have to apologize for how I feel, just because I might insult some sector of society. Personally, this a waste of time. Why can't I like what I like? Why is it, if our opinions differ, there has to be a wrong or a right?"

Instead of responding, the man said, "So, Ms. Rise, you don't feel that your behavior was inappropriate toward the other fighters?"

Kirin gritted her teeth and said, "I guess I'm not getting my point across. I think Wing Chun is the best martial art for me. FOR ME! I love it. I'm not here to convince people otherwise, coz personally I don't care. And I think you guys are the ones confused. Wing Chun is a universal art. If I say you don't fight the force, every martial art says that same thing. But, the difference is how we approach things. That's all! As for the other fighters, I don't tell them how to train, so why should they care what I do?"

"That seems kind of selfish, don't you think, Ms. Rise?"

Kirin just couldn't get through to him. She finally thought of something that might get through to him. "Look! You have a phone on you?"

At first, he was thrown off by the question and said, "Yeah, of course I do."

"Show it to me."

He looked around, wondering if this was a test of some kind. Eventually, he reached into his pocket and pulled out his phone.

"Do you love your phone?" asked Kirin.

"Uh, yeah, it's one of the latest phones." He shrugged his shoulders, seemingly more confused.

Kirin reached into her pocket and pulled out a little sock. Inside the casing was her phone. "This is my phone. I like it also. Do you think I should change my phone to yours?"

"Well, yeah, your phone is, like, over five years old." He giggled, and the crowd began to chuckle as Kirin held her phone up high.

"Like I said before ... I'm happy with my phone; you're happy with your phone. Why does it matter?"

Someone shouted from the crowd, "I still love you, Kirin, even with your crappy phone!"

Kirin shook her head and cracked a smile, as everyone laughed at the outburst. Kirin was about to speak again but was cut off by Chad.

Chad directed the next audience member to proceed and ask a question. "Okay, let's make this the last question from the audience?"

Fawn leaned over to Kirin and said, "Saving the best for last."

Kirin shook her head, wondering what he meant.

A girl stood up from the crowd. She adjusted her glasses and corrected her posture. She cleared her throat and spoke directly into the microphone. "Hi, I'm Jane. Mr. Bryce, earlier you said your platform and Kirin's message had many similarities. Have you ever thought of approaching her for your campaign in the future?"

Bryce smiled and then looked toward Kirin. "That's a great question, Jane ... and, yes, some of what I've spoken about does reflect many of Ms. Rise's views. I'd love to see the next generation be more involved and restore us to the greatness we can be."

Turning her attention to Kirin, Jane said, "You always speak of the injustices in the country, but rumor has it that you've never even voted. Is that true?"

Kirin looked at Fawn and then didn't hesitate at all to answer. "Yes, it is true."

A gasp from the audience filled the auditorium as whispers and snickers spread throughout. This was definitely one tidbit of knowledge that people weren't aware of.

Jane followed up her question. "I'd like to know how you can be a voice of millions when you've never done the most basic God-given right this country has to offer and vote?"

Feeling a rush of anger, Kirin responded, "I'm not sure why my not voting is such a shock. You're spitting out what's being sold to you—that if you don't vote, you don't have a right to complain. But I'm asking you to think long and hard and look around with your own eyes. Your vote should make a difference, right? Yet, we talk of this change for the better, year in and out, but with our own naked eye we see nothing's happened, and that's the truth. This illusion that we see is just that. It's great to call America a democracy and the land of the free, but the truth says otherwise. We've become the country that loves the image or story, but deep down it fears facing reality and dealing with the truth."

"Well, it sounds very ignorant and uneducated not to vote—or maybe it's just coz you didn't go to college," was Jane's snide comment.

"You want to go there? You want to base this on education? Fine, let's go there. Can you raise your hand if you got a full scholarship offer to attend Stanford University?" Kirin raised her hand and waited. "It's not about intelligence. There are a ton of intelligent people, but unfortunately what they are doing is finding the holes in the system and taking advantage of it. I chose not to go to college, but that doesn't mean I chose to be ignorant. Bottom line, I have a PhD in common sense, and you probably have a mere BS degree."

People were swaying back and forth, laughing at the burn.

"Oh, no, she didn't!"

"Dang...."

The girl stood there dumbfounded and muzzled from the remark.

"If you don't mind my asking, who'd you vote for?" asked Kirin.

"Well, I voted for Johnson," replied the girl.

"Can you give me the main reason you voted for him?"

"Well, I'm a Democrat, so that's one of the reasons."

"Interesting. I'm the one getting criticized for not voting, but can anyone else see the problem here?"

"What do you mean?" Chad inquired.

"Democrat, Republican, whatever, it's all the same thing. They purposely sell you that garbage to divide you from one another."

"That's not true!" replied Jane.

"It's not? How much effort did you put into knowing Johnson before you voted?"

"Well, I did watch most of the debate."

"Well, that's great. Vote for someone based on who has the coolest ads and an hour and a half of a debate. To top it all off, let's just base it off the fact that he's," Kirin gestured quotation marks, 'running as a Democrat'.... Seriously, I'm surprised you didn't factor race or sex into that highly detailed thought process of yours.

"You know why I didn't vote for Johnson, your so-called champion who stands for the Democratic ideals? Well, did you know how many times he voted against tax cuts for the middle class? Four times over the last two years. There were several bills designed to help ease the tax burden, but instead he voted for the middle-class disintegration. But, what does that matter? He's a Democrat.

"Do you know how many times he stood aside for corporations to ease their taxation? Three times. Did you also know he'd only been a Democrat for the last five years and was a Republican fifteen years prior? But he made the shift when the demographics showed he had a better chance of becoming president if he switched.

"Did you also know he was for the X4Z1 gun bill ruling that passed several years ago, stripping American citizens of their right to bear arms? And mind you, this isn't me going on Wikipedia getting these facts off the internet. You see, I didn't vote, not because I was being apathetic, but because I was beyond educated as to the choices that were given to me. And keep in mind, this isn't a slam on a single party because I have just the same amount of grievances for Dickson's Republican card.

"People are electing leaders from ads without knowing anything about what these individuals have done. They watch an hour debate here and there and quote sound bites of their BS speeches that are looped over again by the media. You're entrusting these people in power who make such vital decisions while you know so little about them. That's like saying, 'I do' to the next date that goes well and lasts longer than two hours.

"This is everything I've been talking about, the illusion of choice. But, if the choice is between two people you don't like and you justify it as the lesser of two evils ... how do you call that freedom? How do you really call that your decision? We're all in the situation that we are facing because we're doing the same thing. The system isn't designed for change. It's designed for control, and that's exactly what you've done by voting."

Kirin had been outspoken before about the UFMF and the situation of the country, but seeing her in action left people in shock. The audience wasn't sure whether to applaud or boo as a hush silence reigned over everyone.

Kirin spoke into the silence. "Raise your hand if you believe the situation of this country continues to get worse?"

The hands slowly raised, and everyone showed their frustration in unison, as not a single hand remained lowered.

Chad jumped in as the tensions began to rise. "I hear what you're saying, Kirin, but it looks like what you're calling for is a … revolution!"

"The power is to the people, not the corporations. We've come to the point where the government is nothing more than a puppet of the corporations. How can the people have power when the gap between rich and poor continues to grow every day? There's no need for people to suffer like this when so few have so much and so many have so little. The fix is simple and right in front of us. There is power within us to really make a change and not just be stuck in the game they want us to play. I know everyone's familiar with where I came from and the things they were doing back in my home country. Our government is implementing some of those things now. Let's face it: you don't play a game that doesn't allow you to win."

The thought of revolution and the comparison of North Korea to the United States were difficult truths for many to face. Everyone felt uneasy, and mumbles and talk began spreading through the audience. It would be difficult even though the masses finally were inspired to venture into foreign territory and rise up.

Fawn sat up and crossed his legs, nodding slightly with a grin.

Suddenly an audience member shouted, "Boo! Go back to North Korea, Kirin! This is 'Merica, the land of the free. If you don't love this country, then go back home."

He then started chanting, "USA! USA! USA!" and the crowd began following his lead.

Fawn stepped in as Kirin was shocked from the reaction and sat down with a blank look. Fawn stepped in and pulled out two miniature flags and began waving them. He then looked to the side and gestured with his hand. A video began to play.

Kirin turned around as a favorite American song began pouring through the speakers: "You coming to America."

She pinched her brow and shook her head as she thought, *This can't possibly be happening. They can't possibly be swallowing this BS.*

Fawn grabbed a mic and began singing with the video. "I vote every chance I get because I love this country." The crowd cheered, chanting as they quickly turned against Kirin after her remarks.

Kirin tried to speak and said, "This is exactly what I'm talking about!"

The boos began to get louder as there was no swaying the crowd.

Chad stepped in and said, "Okay, we've gone over the time, and I'd like to thank our guests." Chad struggled as the crowd continued chanting, "USA!" He smiled, trying to normalize an awkward situation. He then motioned to the guests to step off the stage.

As Kirin followed Bryce and Fawn to the back, she thought she was finally going to get away from this mess. But once behind the curtains, she was blinded by the flashes of cameras. Reporters were bombarding her with questions from every angle regarding her comments.

"Kirin, why don't you love this country?"

"Is it true you've never voted?"

"Do you really believe we need a revolution for change?"

Kirin was beginning to feel the squeeze, and it seemed exactly like Chum Night from a year ago. Suddenly Bryce grabbed her arm and said, "Come on. Follow me."

He found an area that separated them from the reporters as they both ducked away and shut the door behind them. They both leaned back to catch their breath. Kirin looked at Bryce and shook her head in disappointment.

"Thanks," said Kirin.

"It's not a problem. I'm glad I could help."

The noise behind the doors was still there, but at least they had control of the situation. Bryce leaned forward and looked her in the eye. "Everything you said, I believe in, Kirin. It's just that you can't force feed the American public an idea so raw and expect them to accept it right away."

Kirin thought about it and nodded, knowing all too well that this would not easily blow over.

"A lie can be forged into the truth, if it's repeated enough times."—Watanabe

SECTION 1

Short Stories #2—Kirin's P.O.V.

<u>New Uniforms—76 Days</u>

T he first day of class junior year was different for not only us, but for every public school in the United States. Schools were desperate for funding and were looking for ways to raise money. In their need to continue everyday operations, they turned to corporations to help bail them out. Throughout the country, under-funded schools got a boost from the corporations, but everything always comes with a catch. The UFMF offered to help every public school if they met certain requirements: one, all students wear official UFMF-branded uniforms, and two, they begin implementing a new UFMF training program for gym, deemed "for the students' protection." From the outside, it looked like a win-win for both sides. But, as Sifu pointed out to me, it seemed like a maneuver to create a fan base for the future and a greater hold upon all of society. Everywhere one looked, the UFMF had its claws imbedded in the world.

From a distance, I could see Sage and Gwen approaching me. Sage was pushing Gwen in her wheelchair as we met at our normal place. Just like we'd done for the last two years, we were going to begin the new school year with our ten-minute walk. It was silent as all three of us were checking each other out, exchanging weird glances, like this was the very first time we'd ever met.

Sage broke the silence and said, "I don't know about you, but I kinda like that we have to wear uniforms now."

Gwen gave Sage the look, but didn't utter a word.

Sage continued to justify his point. "No, seriously, think about it. Before, I'd wake up and have to worry about what to wear for five days. Now, every pair of pants, shirt, and tie look exactly alike."

Gwen frowned and rolled her eyes, shifting in her chair. "This has got to be the worst day ever."

"No! This is a good thing. Now that my mom's forcing me to do laundry, no one will ever know if I'm wearing the same outfit or not. Frankly, I could get away with the same outfit for five days in a row," chuckled Sage.

Gwen whined. "This really blows. And, for some reason, you seem to forget the fifth sense is known as smell ... Mr. Stinky. They may not see the change, but I guarantee you they'll smell it."

Sage looked like he'd been caught off guard as he took a whiff of his armpit and shrugged his shoulders.

I stood there with my schoolgirl outfit on, thinking, *I really miss my red hoodie.* I sighed.

Gwen seemed to take the news the hardest. Fashion was her escape from the daily grind of hacking and tech gear and now she was restricted to a singular look. I recalled her screaming on the phone in the middle of the night when she found out.

We all stood silently and continued to stare at one another.

"Okay, no point arguing about it. It's not like we can change things," sighed Gwen.

"Come on ... we better head out. We're gonna be late on the first day of school," said Sage.

We started our trek to school, but a comment Gwen had made kept lingering in my head.

"You shouldn't talk like that, Gwen."

"What are you taking about?"

"What you just said, 'it's not like we can change things.'"

"It's true, Kirin. Just look around. Look at what's happened around us. All the protesting, rallies, you name it, have done nothing. The country's worse than ever," said Gwen.

"I hear what you're trying to say, Kirin," interjected Sage, "but I gotta agree with Gwen. Let's face it: money is what makes the world go around. You just have to follow where the cash is to see what's gonna be done and what's got no chance in hell."

I felt saddened by my friends' comments, but at the same time their sense of hopelessness was not unusual. From watching the news and my daily reads, I knew the masses had grown more apathetic. The catch phrase "It is what it is" was their battle cry.

"Guys, you can't think like that. We're supposed to be the next generation—a new hope," I argued.

Gwen replied, "Look, Kirin, I don't want to think like that, but let's face it. It's not like the movies, where there's gonna be one person to rise and change the entire world. That stuff just never happens … well, not anymore, that is."

Sage said, "Yes, yes. The chosen one." Sage began to change his voice to a creepy sound, "That would be precious, my precious."

Gwen shook her head, "Oh my god! Do you have to start school with your nerd status at an all-time high?"

Sage turned toward Gwen. "Do you think I'm peaking too soon?"

Gwen thought for a moment and replied, "No. Definitely not. Knowing you, you're just warming up."

The two giggled, but her words continued to haunt me.

"Look, guys, when people sit around and let wrong happen, you know what you get?" I said.

Gwen replied, "I know what you get, 24% interest on your credit card. That's what you get."

I rolled my eyes and shook my head. I replied, "That's your fault, Gwen. Half of the stuff you buy you don't even use."

"It's not my fault, Kirin! It's those advertisers. They're doing a really good job convincing me that life would be better if I had more of their stuff," said Gwen.

"Holy crap!" shouted Sage.

We both looked at him. I asked, "What? What's wrong?"

Sage replied, "I'm paying 29% on my card! What a rip."

I began rubbing my eyes as my best friends were giving me a headache.

"Guys, did it ever occur to you … that buying more stuff won't make you happier?" I argued.

"Ha, this is one argument you're not going to win, Kirin," said Gwen. "I definitely feel better when I buy something."

I gave Gwen a look. "It's a quick fix. You're happy for about five minutes, and then afterward you don't even care."

Gwen turned her nose up to me and said, "Unless you can give me a better solution, Kirin … I'm not listening."

Sage began to speak. "Scientifically speaking, the best thing for us to do is just watch out for ourselves. The old days of believing we can change the world are just a fantasy." Sage adjusted his glasses and added, "Don't you know there's no such thing as heroes?"

Gwen rubbed her eyes. "I swear, Sage … did you spend your entire summer vacation memorizing more quotes?"

Sage straightened up and said loudly, "Why, yes, Gwen. Why, yes, I did."

I replied to Sage, "God, that's really depressing. How can you say that, Sage? And how is that scientific?"

Sage laughed. "You know when you say 'scientific' in front of a sentence, most people don't question it."

Several minutes passed, and our conversation was going nowhere. We finally arrived at our high school, which, at first glance, looked exactly the same. There we stood as other students began to enter the school all perfectly dressed in their uniforms. Sage and Gwen began moving toward the entrance while I stared straight ahead.

Sage turned around and said, "Kirin, hurry up. We're in for one hell of a year." Gwen moaned from Sage's barrage of quotes and moved ahead of us to avoid any more.

I played with my hair to make sure it covered my scar and wondered just how right Sage might be. As I walked toward the entrance, I turned to read the sign by the door, and there I saw it: the UFMF title neatly tucked next to the name of the school.

Drawing Blood—84 Days

Tobias was busy helping me finish my second form. I was excited to finally complete it.

"Kirin, now just watch me finish the last motions," said Tobias.

I stood and watched him. He did a half turn with a jut punch, then a full turn and a jut punch on the other side, ending up with his last punch being fully squared. He chambered both hands and closed out the form.

"That's it," said Tobias. "That's all of Chum Kiu."

I clapped and hopped in excitement. Tobias looked at me, shaking his head.

"Why don't you work on it for the next ten minutes? If you have any questions, just ask me."

"Not a problem." I smiled and got right to work.

I spent several minutes trying to finish out the form, and suddenly the doors flew open. I looked toward the door with a frown. I said, "Of all the times, not now." I thought, *Not again, I have to practice this so I don't forget the form.*

Two guys entered, one of them holding a scroll. The challenge matches were becoming such a regular event that they had become disruptive to our learning process. It annoyed me even more since they had found a loophole in the law. Even though the loser had to shut down, the UFMF was funding brand new schools to open. So, if one of their franchises did close down, in only a short time, the same instructor and group of students would just end up opening another school with a different name. I was worried as to what ends they would go to to close down our school.

Sifu walked toward the challengers and went through the regular formalities. He turned around and yawned, heading toward his office. He stopped for a moment awkwardly and stared at the challengers again, but a second later retreated to his original path.

I thought, *Well, that was kinda weird.*

Sifu looked at me and said, "Wake me up, if anything interesting happens." He walked away chuckling as I shook my head. I had never gotten used to how nonchalantly Sifu took these challenges. Soon he was in the back room doing what he normally did during these matches: sorting. I often wondered if it was just a way for him to get his mind of the stress of losing the school or if he was just confident that Tobias would always win. I took a quick peek into his office and saw that it was, in fact, in shambles.

The gang got into their regular routine. A quick glance showed me Big T and Danny were busy outlining the details of the newest bet. Robert and Ken were having a discussion about some comic book heroes that left me totally clueless. Ryan was on his phone killing some time by playing some online game. Knowing him, he was leveling up some character. Doc was on his phone, too, but doing something constructive: reading. I'd grown to know their habits so well; I thought, *Guys are so predictable.* Several minutes passed, and the fight was about to begin.

Tobias walked toward me and handed me his phone.

I rolled my eyes and said, "Yeah, yeah ... I know. Tell you if anyone's texted."

Tobias gave me a weird look.

"What? Am I wrong?" I said.

"Yeah, you're way off. My mom's sporting a fever, and I'm waiting for a call from the pharmacy to pick up her prescription."

"What about your side action?" I asked.

"I don't care about them. Mom's the number one priority ... yah got that, Kirin?"

I nodded, caught off guard. I thought, *Maybe he's not as shallow as I imagined him to be.*

Tobias stood in the center with no guard as usual. His opponent squared up in a fighting stance. He was hopping back and forth, looking energized.

I leaned over to Doc and said, "This guy needs to kick down the caffeine."

Doc coughed and laughed. "You sure you're not talking about yourself?"

I nudged Doc on the arm, but realized he was right.

Tobias didn't waste time. As soon as it was a go, he closed the gap. He went for a straight punch to the face and easily connected, but what transpired next shocked the entire room. Instead of going down from the hit, the challenger countered with a hook punch that caught Tobias off guard.

Robert shouted, "Holy shit!" It was what the rest of us were thinking.

I looked around, and everyone was stunned. We'd never seen Tobias take a hit before, but his hit failing to knock out his opponent was what really caught everyone off guard.

Tobias acted quickly and regained his center. He smiled almost as if he enjoyed taking that hit. He rushed in and, this time, delivered several attacks to his opponent. Each one connected, and his opponent dropped to the ground.

Simultaneously everyone jumped up and cheered. I could almost hear a big sigh of relief, as we witnessed something we hadn't expected.

Danny shouted, "Frick yeah!" He quickly high-fived Big T, who was all excited from the win. For once, they weren't so concerned who won the credits from the fight. We had grown accustomed to quick and easy fights. Even this victory breathed life into all of us.

After the challengers left, I stepped closer to Tobias to see if he was all right. I wasn't sure why I was so concerned, but I touched his face and examined it. He had an awkward reaction to this, but I said, "You know, it's a little red. Maybe you should ice it."

Tobias, ever the macho guy, replied, "Think of it as me over tanning."

"You don't tan," I replied.

"Like I said, think of it...."

I frowned at him.

Big T said, "Damn, man, how'd you get hit?"

Even Tobias looked puzzled. He said, "Not really sure, maybe the guy knows how to take a hit."

Sifu was listening in on the conversation and began to chuckle.

Tobias asked, "What's so funny, Sifu?"

"You kids crack me up ... learning to take a hit," laughed Sifu. He was actually tearing up, as he couldn't stop laughing.

I listened in as Tobias continued to talk to the other guys.

He said, "I know I won, but I swear, that first hit connected, and he didn't even flinch from it."

Doc and Ken nodded.

Ken said, "I saw it clearly. Dude, you totally got the hit to plant on the center, and he somehow didn't react."

Doc leaned over and said, "Tobias, maybe you should ice your face. Kirin's right; it is kinda red."

Tobias replied, "I'm not gonna ice it. Besides, I'm not a puss like Danny."

Danny shouted, "Hey!"

Ryan said, "For all you know, this guy has super powers."

Robert said, "Ryan, that's so stupid.... That's the kind of thing Danny usually says."

Ryan said, "I know that, but Tobias already called him a—"

Danny shouted again, "Hey, don't you dare say it!"

Ryan said, "Anyway, I saw it, too. You did connect with that hit, but it didn't even stun him."

I walked up, trying to join in on the conversation. "Well, maybe it's possible that you thought it hit, but it didn't," I said.

Tobias glared at me. He didn't appreciate that comment.

"Look, I'm just trying to give you possible explanations. I'm not saying that happened." I could tell that peeved Tobias a bit, and I quickly thought of something to change the mood. I asked, "So, we all ready to go out to eat?"

Sifu nodded. "Yup, I'm ready. Maybe we can discuss the art of taking a hit."

Robert chimed in with his last two cents. "Maybe it's just karma paying him back for kicking a ton of people's asses." The gang all looked at one another and shook their heads.

Tobias said, "Fine with me. Let's go with the good ol' 'karma's a bitch' theory."

Just Be Good—92 Days

Since I'd come to the States, our family followed the same ritual every Sunday. I found myself sitting in the pew with my family alongside our fellow parishioners. I looked around mid-sermon and saw that, while the majority were there physically, mentally they were adrift from what was happening.

Over the years, part of the fun was seeing the different ways people would pretend to be paying attention. I felt empty most of the time when I came to church. With my background, most would think I'd find a greater sense of meaning being able to practice religion freely.

It wasn't uncommon for me to see my classmates there. From a distance, I could see Sage, trying not to get whiplash as he struggled to keep from falling asleep. Every so often, I would see his head slowly tilt to the side, shocking him awake as his eyes flew wide while he pretended to listen.

Hunter had made it an art form, and I eventually figured out his pattern. Seating was strategically done so that he would be buried as much as possible by heavily set individuals covering him from sight. Hunter always sat near the front, and while he looked wide awake, he had mastered a frozen face stare.

Gwen was the unfortunate one of the bunch. Always forced to sit in the front, in the handicapped space, she had no options to hide.

Hmm, I thought. If there was ever one thing I believed a church should do, it was to bring peace. But that wasn't the case. Every week, the girl I most despised, Ripley Hawkins, would be dead center seated in the mass. Everyone knew Ripley, inside and outside of school, as she was the most popular girl. *Blonde, beautiful, bold* is how many would describe her, but if you asked me there was one *B* missing that encompassed everything. Ripley was the picture-perfect girl that had the guys drooling to do anything for her. It always amazed me that a girl who seemingly had everything going for her could also be the meanest person I had ever met.

For the most part, I'd had only brief encounters with her, either through passing in the hall or a couple classes. But, anytime I was near her, the hair on the back of my neck would raise. Ripley was never alone; she was always surrounded by her groupies, Trina and Jessica. Wherever Ripley went, you could bet those two were close behind. To be part of her group, you had to meet Ripley's standards: shallow, sexy, and stupid. Ripley treated them like pets, and they were more than happy to wag their tails just to be near her.

Jessica was a natural blonde, but since Ripley wanted to be the only one in the group to have that status, she forced Jessica to color her hair brown. Trina was more of Ripley's voice; you had to talk to her first before you could speak to Ripley.

They were her shadows and remained so, because Ripley wanted the spotlight.

Somehow, Father Duncan's sermon snapped me out of my stare. He had been the regular priest delivering the mass for the last five years. He was like my teachers in school, repeating the same lesson year in and year out. Even with years of repetition, I doubt I was the only one wondering what the heck he was talking about. Until recently, I had slowly drifted to oblivion like many, as the sounds went in and out. So, to keep myself occupied for that hour, I began practicing the hand movements of the first form and thinking about the inner details behind it.

I sat there, thinking, *Tan sau, feel the elbow in and sunk, shoulder stretch, index finger in the center, stay in your triangle and stay square. The balance of the entire arm should feel the same.*

Kyle nudged me and whispered, "What are you doing?"

I panicked and responded, "Uh, hand exercises for band. It helps keep my fingers relaxed."

Kyle wasn't the most inquisitive, so he accepted the answer and didn't investigate any further.

Where was I...?

I began moving my hands again, and this time did wu sau. I thought, *Palm at an angle, changing it slightly as I pull back, elbow adjusting slightly out.... Once I feel like my hand is going to sink, then it's time to stop pulling it back to my chest.*

I heard Mark cough, and I looked at him. He shook his head, indicating to stop what I was doing. So I did. It was difficult for me not to do this, as it was the only thing keeping me awake.

But, as the monotonic voice of Father Duncan continued, I fell back into a trance.

I began doing fok sau. *Don't drop the wrist. Allow the entire forearm to fall slightly, make sure the tension is even throughout, and pinch the thumb and index fingers together.* I stared down at my hand, which ended up being exactly where it should be.

20 Minutes Later

Mass finally ended, and that was the best part. This was officially the longest time until we had to do it all over again. We finally headed back to our car, and Mom and Dad lagged behind. I was listening to Kyle, Steve, and Mark as they were talking about an upcoming UFMF fight. I was up front leading the pace when suddenly things turned horrific.

I cringed and fixed the several strands of hair by my bangs as Ripley stood in front of me confidently. "Wasn't that such a moving sermon, Kirin?"

I thought, *If by 'moving,' she means I want to get away from you as quick as possible, then the answer is yes.* Unfortunately, what I thought and what came out of my mouth were two different things. "Uh, yeah, Ripley, it was very moving."

After I answered, both Jessica and Trina cackled to confirm.

Jessica said, "It was totally the best sermon ever."

Trina smirked. "My only regret was that I wish it was longer."

Ripley smiled and motioned for her two friends to be quiet. She glided closer and walked right past me. Her perfume and her Sunday outfit, which was less than appropriate, caused all three of my brothers to stop talking about fighting as they quickly said, "Hi," and glanced in her direction.

Ripley approached my parents and said, "Mr. and Mrs. Rise, it's a pleasure seeing you again. It's so unfortunate that it's only once a week."

I rolled my eyes, but somehow this diva had hypnotized my entire family.

My mom and dad both said, "Hi Ripley, it's good to see you."

After several minutes of the emptiest words coming out of her mouth, she finally said her goodbye. Inside the car, I felt relief—and like I needed a shower after listening to Ripley. Dad started the car, but getting out was slow because of traffic. I was all ready to lie back and relax when my mom turned around and said, "Kirin, what exactly were you doing in church?"

"Uh, what do you mean, Mom?"

She said, "I'm not sure, but you were doing these weird hand motions."

I sat up. "Oh! Yeah, that … I, uh, hurt my hand. It was warmup exercise I learned from band so it doesn't tighten up."

"Hmm," my mom replied. "Well, it didn't seem like you were paying attention in there. You should be more like Ripley; she really loves going to mass."

I had no idea why that got me going, but it did. "Mom, I'll just come out and say it … I don't get it. I don't get why we go to church!"

A silence fell over the car, even more so than the silence that occurred when we were in church.

The guys turned around slightly, their faces pale. Mark shook his head just enough to gesture not to take this any further.

"You've been taking me to church for the last eight years, and it's the same sermon each time. And guess what? Eight years later, I still have no idea what he's talking about."

My brothers' expressions were priceless, and even my mom did a neck spin, but remained perfectly quiet.

My rationalization was, if my feet were already dirty, what's the big deal if I just dove all the way in? So I continued to spill my guts out, and I felt a lot braver since I was sitting way back in the minivan.

"The way I see it, Mom, is that religion serves a basic purpose. Is it not there to help you become a better person?" I figured I would attack this argument from a common-sense point of view. I had to admit that my training had made me see things differently lately, and had helped me break out of my shell. Unfortunately, I was going to find out if this was gonna be a case of my foot going right into my mouth.

My mom finally responded, "Yes, that's one function of religion. To help you become a better person."

"Okay, if that's the case, then why is it failing so badly? I mean, I see a good chunk of my classmates in that very mass we came from. And, come Monday when school starts, these are some of the biggest jerks and asses you can imagine…. I mean, what's the point then?"

My mom looked surprised. "Kirin, I can't believe you said that about your classmates!"

"I'm saying it only because it's true, Mom."

"What do you mean, Kirin? Who are you referring to?" she asked.

"Since you asked, I'll give you a perfect example: Ripley Hawkins. She is, without a doubt, the meanest girl in the entire school," I said.

"Sweet Ripley? Are you sure about that, Kirin? You know, maybe you're just going by word of mouth." I rolled my eyes as my mom tried to defend someone she had no idea about.

"No, Mom, I'm not quick to judge, and normally I don't care. But, yes, Ripley is a really mean girl. She's very mean, indeed, and keeps a fake front with people that don't know her." I paused and added, "There's one word in the English dictionary that really describes her, and that's—"

Kyle jumped in, "Smoking hot!"

"Kyle!" I yelled at him.

Mark got into the conversation and said, "You dumb ass," as he punched Kyle in the shoulder.

I said, "Thank you, Mark."

Mark replied, "Besides, that's two words. You could've just said, 'HOT!'"

I rolled my eyes at my brother.

Steve added, "I second that.... Oh, wait a second. Is it 'I third that'?"

I shot Steven a withering look. "Are you sure you're not skipping your classes?"

My dad intervened then. "Yeah, I'm concurring with the guys ... but, of course, this is if I was the same age as all you guys."

"Good lord, Dad." I giggled, thinking this was my dad's rare raw humor. My mom turned toward him and gave him a look that spoke volumes in silence.

My dad said, "Hey, I'm just saying."

"We'll be talking later about that comment, Kevin."

"Mom, if you trust me," I began, "then trust me on this. She's totally, uh ... uh, what word rhymes with 'witch'?"

"Kirin Rise!" my mom snapped.

"She really is," I stated, "and that's my entire point. Isn't religion simple? Just like life. Don't all the rules and commandments just boil down to simply being a good person?"

My mom thought about it as our car crawled through the traffic of the parking lot. "Well, you know ... there are rules we should abide by that help us to follow a good path."

"Okay, if that's the case, why not eat beef this Friday? What's the purpose of that?"

Mom said, "That's just something we've done forever, Kirin. Think of it as a sacrifice."

"Mom, that's all great ... and sure, sure, I get it. But at the same time, I'd rather have Ripley eat a piece of beef this coming Friday and not be such a—"

"Don't swear, Kirin," she interrupted.

"I never swear, Mom. But, do you see my point? If they invested the same effort into not being a dick to your fellow man as they did into forgoing beef on Friday, I think they'd achieve a lot more."

"Kirin Rise, language!" snapped my mom.

"Mom, all I'm saying is things don't add up. You have people sit in church for an hour, and the entire week they end up doing nothing but being an ass."

"Language, Kirin."

"I just said 'ass,' Mom."

Mark cut in, "Are we talking about Ripley's—?"

Mom and I said simultaneously, "Quiet, Mark!"

Mom heaved a sigh. "Kirin, you're still young, and you're being too quick to judge what religion can offer. There's a deeper meaning that you are missing. Besides, I thought you'd like that we go to church."

"I appreciate it, Mom. I appreciate the freedom of choice. I appreciate the time we spend together. But, when we started doing this, I thought I would get so much more from it, and I'm not. I mean, are people being good so they can end up in a better place when they die? If that's the case, it seems almost hypocritical of them. To do something for the sake of getting something in return. What I want to know is if they would behave the same way, if they believed there was no such thing. That, to me, is the greater test. Don't you think?"

I looked at my mom, and I could tell she was getting flustered with my comments, but something just made me say what I wanted.

Her voice rose as she began giving her speech. "Kirin—"

Suddenly, two cars honked at us, one from behind and the other from the side.

My mom turned quickly and shouted at the top of her lungs, "Oh, for the love of God, stop honking you assholes. We just came from Goddamn church!"

My mom covered her mouth with her hands, and we all stared at her.

My eyes bulged, and suddenly it was dead silent in the car. Not a single person moved as I bit my lip, trying my hardest not to crack up.

Mark said, "Dang, Mom! Didn't you break a commandment or something?"

"Mark, you're grounded for today."

"What did I say?" Mark complained. "It was Kirin who wasn't paying attention!"

"Kirin, you're grounded as well."

I knew better than to make another sound. I had gone well beyond the buttons I could push. I thought, *Just eat the cake, Kirin. Don't say a word.*

The next ten minutes to our house were the longest ten minutes of my life. It was going to be a long Sunday, as I didn't think anyone would escape the doghouse that day.

"Refining the heart has nothing to do with going to church. It is a choice and a decision that one makes to simply be a good person."—Sifu

SECTION 2

Sifu's Journey Entry #2—Universal Harmony/ First Encounter, Part 1

January 31, 2030

Sifu leaned back and stretched his legs. He looked down and was surprised that he could fully extend them. *Spacious* and *comfy* were two words that one rarely used to describe economy seating. Enjoying his moment of newfound comfort, he tilted his head to the side and looked out the window. A quick glance revealed an infinite amount of clouds, each one shaped differently with no discernible pattern. Sifu became lost in a stare.

A sharp grunt on the opposite side caught his attention. There, sitting next to him, was a man half his age. He was in deep sleep, armed with a headset along with a wad of drool slowly working its way down his chin. Sifu cringed at the sight and thought, *At least he's not a snorer.*

Sifu sighed and reached into his aged fanny pack, which he wore all the time by his side. He pulled out his cell phone and checked the time. Another sigh came about, and an unexpected yawn caught him by surprise. He thought, *Eleven more hours to go. No wonder I hate flying so much.*

Ten minutes passed, and the continuous humming sound of the air blowing in along with the monotonous look of the back of a seat finally did the trick. His eyes grew heavy, his breathing slowed, and before he knew it, he hunched deep into his chair and was sound asleep.

▲ ▲ ▲

Dreaming (2001)

It was a Wednesday night, and class strangely ended exactly on time, 9:00. The usual after-class chitchat was nowhere to be found as students scattered quickly. Sifu closed up his school and rushed to make it to his favorite eating spot. The warm summer air swirled around him, doing very little to cool him off. His brisk walk was the closest thing to a run that Sifu ever did. Several minutes passed before he finally got to the front door. There, he pulled his phone from his pocket and checked it. *Perfect*, he thought. "Right on time," he said, his voice slightly strained from his activity.

Sifu got there roughly an hour before closing. He justified it as perfect timing, since anything later usually got some rude stares from those working that shift.

Inside, the restaurant was a long rectangular room, decorated in your typical Japanese décor. It had a look screaming that it was outdated. To the side were several other rooms, hidden behind sliding doors with paper walls that were used by larger parties, but a quick look in revealed only a handful of customers tonight. He glanced over to the corner spot where he usually sat and saw that it was empty. Seconds later, he sat himself down and pulled out a Japanese study book. Sifu had finally made the decision to take some time to study. He had always been a huge fan of watching anime, the only other thing he set aside time for besides Wing Chun, but he grew tired of reading the subtitles. At the table, he began memorizing verbs and sentence patterns as he waited for his usual waiter to come take his order.

Suddenly he heard a different voice, but was too focused on his own work to allow the change to register.

"Excuse me, can I take your order?" said a soft and pleasant voice.

"Yes, I'll have the usual," said Sifu. He thought, *Masu form … te form, why the heck is this so complicated?* He continued to be lost in his studies as he mumbled more words to himself.

"I'm sorry, sir," said the kind voice, "but I don't know what your usual is."

Sifu snapped out of his study and realized he was talking to someone different. "I'm sorry. My apologies." Sifu pointed to the menu and said, "Can I have ramen number…?" As he was about to finish his sentence, he looked up. His mouth cracked open, and his eyes widened in surprise. There standing above him was a beautiful Japanese girl ready to take his order. Her hair was black like the night sky as it fell perfectly in place, touching her smooth, clear skin. She tossed it slightly and then combed it to the side of her ear as she continued to smile. He stared for a brief second into her eyes and felt the kindness of her soul.

Sifu stuttered slightly and said, "Oh, uh … you're, ah … definitely not Steven."

The waitress smiled and waited as she held her pad and pencil. She spoke with a hint of an accent and said, "Steven called in sick, so I'm helping out."

"Oh, okay." Sifu awkwardly stared and found himself lost in her gaze. He shook his head and snapped out of his trance, fearing it would be rude. "Oh, I'm sorry. Uh, I'll have ramen number C. . . . Yeah, that's it, C," he said as he pointed to the writing on the menu.

Sifu frowned at his behavior and blushed. He tried to cover it up by saying, "I usually come here every week, and I'm pretty much a regular. Um, I don't believe we've ever met. If you don't mind my asking, are you new here?" Sifu's face looked puzzled as he was trying to recall if he'd seen her before.

"I've worked here for about three months now. Maybe you haven't seen me because I usually work in the back and help prepare the meals," she said.

"Oh, that explains it." Sifu smiled as he continued to get lost in her eyes. "By the way, my name is Bing ... uh, excuse me, I mean Gordon. Yeah, that's it, Gordon." He flushed at finding himself somewhat tongue-tied.

She slipped him a curious glance. "Are you sure that's your name?" she teased as she covered up her smile with her hand.

Sifu shook his head. Embarrassed, he replied, "Actually, most people call me Sifu. Long story short, Bing is my Chinese name, Gordon is my American name, but most of the time my students call me Sifu." He scratched his head and innocently looked up at her, wondering if she believed what he'd just said.

"Well, now I'm more confused," replied the waitress with a smile. "Tell you what, when I come back with your meal, I'll pick one of the three, okay?" She began walking away as Sifu hung his head, somewhat flustered at himself. She turned around and said softly, "By the way, you can call me Megumi."

The sound of Megumi's voice brought a smile to Sifu's face as he nodded and watched her walk all the way to the kitchen. Sifu continued to repeat it to himself multiple times, so it would be etched in his memory forever. It was unusual for Sifu to feel such an emotional swing, as he was jumping from one end of the spectrum to another. There was something about her, and it wasn't just a case of being a pretty face.

The room began thinning out while he waited for his meal. He was working on learning his Japanese, but spent most of the time waiting to see when Megumi would come out again. Sifu's focus was broken, as Megumi's voice and smile were the only things he could think of. Finally, she popped out of the kitchen, but remained empty-handed.

Sifu didn't care as he was glad to lay eyes on her again as she approached him.

Megumi said, "About five more minutes and your soup will be ready."

Sifu smiled and stalled before spitting out his next words. He decided to put his Japanese to the test. "Uh, sumimasen ... mizo wa kudasai."

Hearing Sifu speak in Japanese brought a big smile to her face. "Wow, you speak Japanese?"

Sifu floundered in embarrassment and held up his book. "I think trying to learn to speak is a better description of what I'm doing."

Megumi laughed and asked, "Do you mind?"

"No, please, by all means ... I need all the help I can get."

"It's mizo wo kudasai.... The *wa* should be a *wo*, but that was really close," she said, trying to encourage him.

"Arigatou gozaimashita." Sifu continued to show off his limited Japanese.

"Do itashimashite," said Megumi. She added, "I'm sorry. I totally forgot to ask you if you needed something to drink. Like I said, I normally don't wait tables."

"No worries."

Megumi scurried back as Sifu looked through his book and tried to brush up on some last-minute Japanese. He was hoping the effort would impress Megumi. Several minutes passed, and she finally came back with a bowl of piping hot ramen.

"Here you go," she said. "Is there anything else I can get for you?"

Sifu paused for a second, trying to think of something to prolong the conversation before he replied, "No thanks. I think I'm good."

Megumi looked somewhat disappointed that he didn't want anything else. She said, "Oh ... uh ... okay. Just call me if you need anything." She turned around and headed back toward the kitchen. Sifu sighed, realizing that he had wasted an opportunity.

For the next five minutes, he sulked while trying his best to enjoy his favorite ramen dish. During this time, he noticed that he was the lone customer in the restaurant. Only the sound of his slurping followed by brief periods of silence filled the dining area. Sifu wondered if hump day along with a hot summer night contributed to the low turnout at the restaurant.

Suddenly, the doors swung open, and Megumi reappeared from the kitchen. She smiled at Sifu as she approached his table.

"So, how's the ramen?"

"Delicious, as always. The best in Chicago," said Sifu.

"I'm glad," said Megumi.

Sifu stared and read Megumi's facial reaction when she said that. He smiled tentatively, but couldn't resist saying it. "Uh … mmm, uh, you don't like the ramen, do you?"

Megumi looked surprised and politely replied, "I didn't say that."

"I'm sorry. I don't know why I just blurted that out." Sifu hung his head and pretended to eat his ramen, hoping that Megumi wasn't offended.

Megumi headed back to the kitchen and then suddenly froze. She took a quick peek around and came back to Sifu's table. She stared at Sifu, who continued to eat his ramen without paying attention to her standing there.

"How did you know that I don't like the ramen?" she said in a sharp voice.

Sifu looked around and scratched his head. "It was just a lucky guess."

Megumi looked away and thought for a moment. She was about to accept the answer when she jerked back toward Sifu and said, "No … no, that was no guess." She waited patiently for a response as the silence made Sifu feel uncomfortable.

He tried to delay the inevitable with another taste of his ramen, but finally decided to come clean. He went for the direct approach, the Wing Chun way, and said, "I'm sorry about that, but you could say I'm pretty good at reading people."

Megumi had a curious look on her face as she found Sifu's comment fascinating. "Earlier, you said your students call you Sifu. Students … so, I'd assume that would make you a teacher, right? So … what do you teach?"

"Just Gung Fu."

"Gung Fu?

"Oh, sorry. Uh, it's a Chinese martial art."

"Ah, okay. Interesting … are you any good?"

"My Gung Fu is a lot better than my Japanese, if that means anything," chuckled Sifu.

Megumi replied, "Well, I don't know. You are learning from a book."

Sifu laughed. "Hey, it's not my fault. You know finding the time to study is hard, but it's even more difficult task to find a good teacher."

"My father had an old saying. He believed that, when the student is ready, a teacher will come," said Megumi.

"Well, your father sounds like a wise man," said Sifu.

Megumi smiled as Sifu continued to gaze upon her, but this time she noticed something. "You're doing it again. This time I saw you," said Megumi.

Sifu raised his hands up defensively and said, "I'm not doing anything. I don't know a thing about your relationship with your father."

"You do. You read something or felt something. Okay, now I'm curious, uh, Sifu.... What can you tell me about my relationship with my father?"

"Seriously, I haven't the slightest clue." Sifu dove back in and continued to eat his ramen.

Megumi crossed her arms and just stared at Sifu silently. Feeling the pressure of a woman's stare can make any man break, and Sifu finally succumbed to her will. Sifu put his spoon down, wiped his face, and blurted out, "It's just a guess, but...." Sifu inhaled deeply and spoke rapidly on a single breath, "You love your father, but you're here in the States because of him. He's probably trying to show you a path that you're not interested in. So, you're trying to buy some time so you don't have to confront him on that issue." Sifu bowed his head and remained silent. He began sipping on the soup, pretending that his focus was elsewhere.

Megumi was in shock as she flinched backward at his words and the surprising accuracy of his statement.

Sifu looked up slowly and saw Megumi's piercing eyes on him. With a humble voice, he said, "Am I right?" She didn't respond right away, and he avoided eye contact and went back to his soup for safety.

Megumi's eyes began to squint, trying to figure out who this stranger was she'd encountered. As she watched Sifu pretend to eat, she said, "You are right, but I believe that was a lucky guess."

Sifu mumbled, "Well, I am usually right."

"Well, you're way off with the ramen." Megumi took a swipe at Sifu's ego.

"Ouch! Was that necessary?"

"Well, since you can read me so well, what do you think?" said Megumi.

Sifu rubbed his chin, as he was enjoying his conversation with Megumi. He decided to change the subject and said, "You know that saying your father had about a student and a teacher....? Out of curiosity, you wouldn't by chance be teaching ... would you?"

Megumi thought about his words and said, "It all depends. I'd be willing to teach someone ... someone who's teachable," Megumi emphasized the last word as she stared at Sifu.

"You don't think I'm teachable?" Sifu said in his most innocent voice.

"What do you think?"

"I think you believe that I'm not teachable."

"But you think otherwise?"

"I believe a good teacher is also a student. So, I do think otherwise," said Sifu.

"Do you mind if I do a little reading myself?" asked Megumi.

"By all means … I'd love to know more about myself."

"I think you definitely do know something. And, whatever this Gung Fu stuff is, you're probably extremely good at it. But, at the same time, you're afraid to go outside the box and venture into new things. It's like how you're stuck thinking this is actually good ramen."

Megumi was dead on with Sifu's description, but he didn't take it as an insult, as he relished in the fact that Megumi was so aware. He was about to say something whimsical, but suddenly took notice of his surroundings. A quick scan around the room revealed only the two of them were left. His internal clock told him it was probably closing time. He asked, "Shouldn't you be in the back room closing up now?"

"Don't worry. If anything, my boss is getting drunk in the back or is already passed out," sighed Megumi. "I'm pretty sure I'll have to do the full closing … so it doesn't matter."

For the next hour, Sifu and Megumi talked and enjoyed one another's company. The universe had made a connection and, for that moment, everything was just right. It was the beginning of something special that each of them would always remember.

"That moment when someone captures your heart and never gives it back, is something everyone should experience."—Sifu

CHAPTER 3

The First Time

The Next Day, Monday Morning

The TV was blaring as Kirin paced her living room, trying to get ready. In the midst of all this chaos, her friends Sage and Gwen were sitting on her sofa watching both the TV and Kirin. Neither one could decide which was more interesting to view. Bacon was on the floor half-asleep, and Gwen was petting him to keep him company.

Sage said, "Kirin, they're talking about you on the news."

Kirin's voice was fading in the distance as she shouted, "Uh ... I'm always on the news."

Sage replied, "But this time, it's not good news."

Kirin called back, "When is it ever?"

Despite Kirin's disinterest, Sage and Gwen watched what was transpiring on the news. "This is Danny de la Cruise reporting for *VRAI* magazine. It seems that Kirin Rise sparked some controversy at the recent con show. Here she is in a three-person panel, being asked a question that seemed to get the superstar all revved up and led to the heated debate. Let's play a clip of what transpired this weekend that got everyone talking about her...."

Both Gwen and Sage watched and listened to the remarks as they grimaced at each other. Sage shook his head, "Oh boy."

Bacon's ears perked as he quickly sat up, wondering what all the excitement was about. Gwen began rubbing his belly to calm him down as they all continued to listen to the news report.

The reporter said, "So, to Kirin, this is just my two cents ... but even the most beloved celebrity isn't immune to taboo topics." The TV faded into a commercial as Sage, Gwen, and Bacon stared at each other.

Kirin struggled to the side of her TV, hopping on one foot as she tried desperately to put on her sock.

Sage said, "For someone who beat the best UFMF fighter, you don't look particularly skilled this morning."

Kirin replied, "Okay, sorry about that. I had to get ready." Kirin finally bested her sock, spun around in a circle, and spread her arms, waiting for an honest critique.

Kirin asked, "So, what do you think?"

Gwen looked at her and said, "Kirin, you look horrible."

The truth was she did look horrible. Kirin was never a slave to fashion, but in some ways, maybe she shouldn't be freed. Her messy hair looked like it had never seen the light of a comb. Her shirt was unevenly buttoned, and her socks weren't even close to matching.

Gwen said, "Now I *know* you're a superstar."

Kirin asked, "What's that?"

"You're so big a star, you don't even care what you look like."

Kirin snapped, "Some best friend you are. Just because I'm handicapped in fashion."

Gwen rolled her eyes.

Kirin caught her mistake and apologized. "Sorry...."

Sage added, "Uh, don't forget technology."

Kirin pouted and looked at them. "Why are you both still my friends?"

Gwen replied, "Because we're honest with you."

Kirin said, "Good point." Kirin began to spin around, looking at herself, like a dog chasing her tail to see what Gwen meant. After realizing the folly in such effort, she snuck a peek at a mirror near her. At first glance, she was startled by the person staring back at her. She then stuck out her tongue and said, "Ahh."

Sage said, "So what gives, Kirin? Even for you, this is a bit more slothy than usual."

Kirin replied, "Sorry, today I'm just preoccupied with stuff. Actually, I shouldn't say that. These last couple of days have been somewhat stressful.... Who am I kidding? This past year has been Prozac city."

Gwen said, "Would you mind filling your BFF in on the details of your sudden unknown tension?"

Sage said, "Well, it has to be this past weekend's con, right?"

Kirin shook her head. "If it was just that, I could live with it. Putting my foot in my mouth on the news usually blows over in a couple of days."

Sage and Gwen stared at each other, wondering what the issue could be then.

Gwen said, "So if it isn't this weekend's fumble, what is it?"

Kirin replied, "I'm supposed to have both Hunter and Tobias come over today, and—"

"Today?" Sage said.

Gwen gaped in surprise. "You invited them both over at the same time?"

Kirin said, "Yes."

Sage yelled, "Here!"

"Yes, I know. At the time, I thought it was going to be a good idea. You know me. Wing Chun is efficient. Why do two moves when you can get the job done in one?"

Gwen said, "I can tell you right now, just hearing it for the first time, not one part of it sounds like a good idea."

"Now you're blowing it out of proportion, Gwen. Besides, those two seem to be getting along well with one another."

Gwen said, "Kirin, can you give me the rainbow-colored glasses you're using to see this BS?"

"Rainbow-colored what?" as Kirin stood in front of Gwen and Sage looking clueless.

Gwen said, "Wait a second. Why are you going to meet up with both of them?"

Sage said, "That seems highly illogical." He made a strange gesture with his hand, splitting his fingers and forming a V-shape with them.

"Oh, I don't know. They said they had something that they needed to talk to me about … uhm, I think. I'm sure it's nothing important. Anyway, shouldn't you guys be going soon? I mean, I'm glad you both stopped by this morning, but I need you to skedaddle from here in the next ten minutes."

Sage leaned over and whispered to Gwen, "She really has no clue why they want to talk to her?"

Gwen whispered back, "She doesn't even notice that I colored my hair."

Sage said, "Maybe she's colorblind."

Gwen grabbed a lock of her hair and said, "It's purple."

Sage shook his head and replied, "Point taken."

Gwen just shook her head, wondering how someone so smart and so aware could be so clueless about love.

Kirin finally came back to the living room area where both Sage and Gwen sat. She said, "Okay, this time I got things right."

Gwen looked her over and gave her a thumbs-up.

Sage said, "Any chance we can stay to watch how all this unfolds? Because I'm pretty sure there's a storm coming…."

Kirin walked toward Sage and said, "You know how that one superhero—I can't remember his name—who can create a force field?"

"Yeah, I know of whom you speak."

Kirin then punched Sage in the arm. "Guess what? It's not you."

Sage rubbed his arm as Gwen laughed. He said, "What was that for?"

Kirin said, "That's for creating trouble where it doesn't exist."

Sage said, "I don't need to create trouble. I just need to be in your vicinity, and somehow it finds you."

"Kirin, as your BFF, I demand front-row seats to these kinds of events," begged Gwen.

Kirin replied, "As your BFF, I'm gonna make sure you're well out of here even before those two ring the doorbell."

"Come on, Kirin. This is better than any Korean drama I could pull up on the net. Please, please …. please, I'm begging you, just let me watch this."

Kirin ran to her closest and tossed them their coats.

"You know, I love you both, but seriously … go and do what couples normally do."

Sage smiled, "I'm all for that."

Gwen looked at Sage, "Are we both thinking online gaming?"

Sage winked at Gwen and replied, "If that's what you want to call it. I'm all for gaming…."

Gwen looked at him strangely and said, "Uh, this isn't going to be multiplayer."

Kirin giggled, and she was insistent that the two leave now.

Sage walked out and said, "Good luck."

Gwen wheeled past Kirin and said, "Call me afterward. I want to know everything."

Kirin stood silent and was hesitant to reply.

Gwen gave her the puppy dog look and said, "Promise you'll call me, Kirin. That's the least you can do."

Kirin finally gave in and said, "Fine. I promise. Now, go!"

Gwen extended her arms and hugged Kirin. "Oh, I wish my life was as exciting as yours." Gwen began heading toward the door when she paused. "I can't believe I forgot to tell you."

"What … what is it?" asked Kirin.

Gwen smiled and said, "Guess?"

Kirin paused to think and then a big grin formed on her face. "Oh my gosh. Did you get approved?"

Gwen nodded. "You are correct, Ms. Rise. My number was bumped up and now I'm on the official waiting list."

"That's incredible news." Kirin hugged her best friend again. "Why didn't you mention this right away, silly?"

Gwen said, "It's not hard to get lost in the exciting world of Kirin Rise." Gwen's eyes began to water as she said, "I know it's still a long shot, but if I can get this treatment and it works ... who knows, maybe I can walk again."

Kirin kissed her best friend on top of her forehead and said, "Regardless, I'll love you no matter what."

One last hug was exchanged between the two as Gwen signaled to Kirin with a phone gesture.

Kirin nodded her head and whispered "Uh, 3, 2, 1 ... go!"

Sage got behind Gwen's wheelchair and helped her out. Kirin closed the door immediately and began cleaning her loft. Kirin thought, *Gotta clean the house so I don't look like a slob.*

She scampered from one end of her loft to the other, tossing things in the closet and tucking others away in unusual places. Bacon had gone through this routine with Kirin many times. He headed to her bedroom and found the little steps that would lead to the top of Kirin's bed. He managed his way to the center and plopped down in between the sheets for a quick nap.

Several minutes passed with Kirin busily vacuuming before she heard the door buzzer. She dropped what she was doing and then rushed to buzz whoever that was in. *Wait a second,* she thought, frowning. *Did Gwen have purple hair?*

Kirin asked, "Who is it?"

"It's me, Hunter."

"Okay, come on up."

Kirin ran to the mirror and did a last-minute check. "Why am I doing this? It's not like house cleaning makes you prettier."

A minute later, the door pounded as Kirin shouted, "Just give me a second!"

Kirin brushed her hair one last time, tested her breath, and then pretended to casually walk toward the front door, as if it was not a big deal. When she opened the door, she saw Hunter was covered with snow, and he was trying his best to dust it off.

Kirin said, "I'm glad you made it." She approached Hunter and gave him a firm hug.

As the two shared that moment of a kind embrace, the door buzzer went off again. Hunter, knowing all too well that the timing was as horrible, as it always was, rolled his eyes.

Kirin pulled away and said, "Sorry, I need to get that."

Kirin shouted, "Who is it?"

Tobias replied, "It's 10:30 am. It's not the pizza guy."

Kirin buzzed in Tobias and waited by the door.

A minute passed before Kirin saw Tobias covered in snow as well.

Kirin asked, "Aren't you gonna dust off the snow?"

Tobias replied, "I don't dust things. It melts off me."

Kirin rolled her eyes and said, "Let me guess. Is it coz you're hot?"

Tobias laughed and said, "Hey, you said it, not me."

Kirin shouted, "Oh, will you get in already?" She began patting the snow off Tobias.

Tobias said, "Hey … could you pick a worse day for travel, Kirin?"

Kirin said, "I'm sorry" and continued to dust the snow off Tobias. After removing his coat, she gave him a hug. "Come on in."

Hunter watched, not too pleased and definitely jealous of the hug. Tobias had squeezed hard and stared at Hunter in the process.

Strangely, Bacon had gotten out of bed, probably the result of the second buzzer waking him up from a deep sleep. He began barking at Tobias.

Tobias looked at Bacon and said, "How come when I come over you always bark at me?" He looked at Hunter and asked, "Does he bark at you?"

Hunter shook his head and said, "No…."

Kirin laughed, "Maybe he's racist."

Tobias began to laugh as well and then had a dead serious look on his face.

Kirin said, "What?"

"Nothing. There just might be some truth to that."

"Well, I like you, and that's all that matters." Kirin apologized right away. "Sorry, guys, I know the place is a mess, but I haven't had a chance to clean it."

Tobias said, "Had you kept some of that money, maybe you could've hired a maid."

Kirin replied, "Are we gonna talk about that again? Don't you think that's a little over the top?"

Tobias said, "Over the top is donating 25 million credits to a charitable organization."

Kirin gave Tobias the look.

Hunter said, "So you called us both here."

Kirin snapped her fingers and said, "Oh, yeah, that's right. Why don't we sit down over there and talk?"

All four of them navigated through Kirin's loft to the living room area. Kirin sat on the loveseat by herself, and Bacon rested by her feet. Hunter found a spot on the larger sofa, and Tobias followed the one-space guy rule and sat on the far end.

Kirin said, "Okay, so Sifu told me to talk to both of you guys."

Kirin's remarks caught both Tobias and Hunter by surprise. Neither one suspected that those would be the first thing they'd hear out of Kirin's mouth.

"Anyway, I'm not really sure what you guys wanted to discuss, but I am all ears," said Kirin.

Hunter scratched the side of his head, wondering how this subject could be eased in without shocking her. Tobias took this time to recalculate a new strategy.

Suddenly, Bacon got up and nudged Kirin's leg. Kirin extended one out, trying to accommodate Bacon's request. He then clamped onto her leg and began thrusting against her.

Tobias and Hunter looked at each other and then stared at Kirin.

Kirin asked, "Well, guys, what did you want to talk about? I'm all ears."

Tobias asked, "Uh, what's Bacon doing?"

Kirin said, "Oh, he's just humping." The guys stared at this act strangely.

Hunter said, "He's neutered, right?"

"Oh, yeah. Of course he is!" Bacon continued to gyrate on Kirin's leg. "I guess it's just a way for him to relieve stress or something. Isn't it cute?"

Tobias and Hunter watched in silent horror as Bacon continued his act. Tobias said, "Okay, I can't talk about this here with your dog humping your leg."

Hunter said, "Yeah, I agree."

Kirin shook her head, wondering what the big deal was. "Fine, let's head to the table and sit over there."

Both Hunter and Tobias sat at the table as Kirin made a quick dash toward the kitchen. "I'm such a bad host. Did you guys want something to drink or eat?"

Tobias replied, "Kirin, knowing you, the fridge is empty."

Kirin leaned back to see if both boys were at the table. Then she took a quick peek into her fridge. Unfortunately, Tobias was correct.

Hunter said, "If it's no problem, can you just give me a glass of water?"

"Got it," said Kirin. "That I can do."

A few minutes passed before Kirin sat opposite Hunter and Tobias at her dinner table.

"So, you both wanted to talk to me about something, right?"

Hunter made a funny face and said, "I wanted to talk to you, but I thought I was going to do it without a third wheel involved."

Tobias said, "That was the plan, but I think I know you well enough that nothing ever goes exactly as you plan."

Kirin was nervous as she looked at them in relationship to where she sat. She thought, *Odd, I think technically the position we are in is a triangle.*

When neither spoke, she prompted, "So, Sifu told me that you both needed to talk to me."

Tobias shook his head. "What exactly did he tell you?

Hunter rubbed his eyes and said, "Seriously, this is not how I envisioned this."

Kirin replied, "He said that both of you had something very important that you wanted to discuss with me. Sorry I've been putting it off, but I've been so busy since the tournament and…."

Tobias and Hunter exchanged a glance and then turned their attention to Kirin. Hunter said, "You have no idea what Sifu was talking about?"

Kirin made a funny face and said, "Uh, should I have an idea?"

Tobias mumbled to himself. "I swear he purposely does these things just for his own amusement."

Hunter looked at Tobias and said, "Okay, I'll start it off, if you don't mind."

Tobias shrugged. "Go for it."

Kirin leaned forward and stared at Hunter with wide-open eyes and a huge smile.

Hunter looked nervous and stumbled when speaking. "So, I was wondering, if you're free this Saturday, if you want to go and grab—"

Tobias said, "Dude."

Hunter looked at him. "What?"

"Seriously?"

"What? It's just my style."

Tobias said, "Okay, you owe me … and one more thing: that is not a style."

Kirin turned toward Tobias and stared at him.

Tobias cleared his throat. "Okay, I'm gonna be direct and just say it. Kirin, I like you, and Hunter over there likes you as well."

Kirin replied, "Oh, that's so sweet! You guys know I like you, too. You both mean the world to me."

Tobias let out a sigh. "All right, let me be a bit clearer. We both like you, but like you more than a friend."

Kirin looked puzzled and just stared at them.

Tobias started to get frustrated, and he rubbed his head.

Hunter jumped in. "Kirin, what Tobias is trying to say is … whether it's Tobias or me, either one of us would really want to be your friend, but … add the word 'boy' right in front of that 'friend.'"

Tobias said flatly, "Really?"

"Hey, the picture you painted wasn't any clearer than mine."

Kirin bit her lip and sat silent as Hunter and Tobias continued to squabble. A few seconds passed as the situation slowly began to piece itself together.

She thought, *Boy in front of friend. Boy in front of friend. Wait….*

Kirin's eyes widened, leaving her looking like a deer in the headlights.

Hunter and Tobias quieted, turning to face Kirin.

"Oh … oh! That's why you both came here this morning. Oh … my."

Kirin stood up, blinked several times, and began pacing back and forth. She muttered to herself as both Tobias and Hunter began wondering what was going on.

Kirin finally froze where she stood and opened her mouth to speak just as her phone rang. She ignored it initially, but the sound eventually overwhelmed her attention.

"Sorry, guys. Give me a second." Deep down, Kirin felt relief at dodging the bullet, at least temporarily, in dealing with this situation.

Both guys rolled their eyes, knowing these ill-timed moments were synonymous with Kirin.

Kirin answered the phone. "Hey, Sifu. Yes … I know. Okay … uh, okay." She looked at the guys and faked a smile. "Wait, you want to see me now, in the next fifteen minutes?" She glanced over to the clock just above her stove. "Uh, no … no, it's not a problem. I can leave immediately and make it. Okay, I'll see you soon. Bye."

Kirin looked at the men sitting at her table. "Guys, I'm sorry that I don't have an answer for you both ... but I need to meet Sifu in the next fifteen minutes. I thought it wasn't going to be until later, but he really wanted to see me now. You can stay here if you want. Just lock up if you decide to leave.... Okay."

Kirin gave an awkward wave and grabbed her coat on the way out. She again struggled to put on her shoes as the guys watched her. She breezed through the front door, slamming it behind her.

Tobias and Hunter sat still for a moment before turning to one another.

Tobias said, "Did we just get friend-zoned?"

Hunter said, "I don't think so ... and I know what friend-zoned feels like. This wasn't it."

"So, are we in some kind of dating limbo?"

"I'm not quite sure."

They both sat there in a confused state as Bacon watched.

▲ ▲ ▲

15 Minutes Later

On very rare occasions, Kirin would find it easier to sneak out alone. Still disguised to avoid the crowd, she attributed her luck either to her controversial weekend or to the unexpected heavy snow that was hitting Chicago.

Kirin found herself all wrapped up, still cold inside her cabbie's well-heated car, thoughts racing through her head. She knew she was running away from the mess she'd left in her apartment, but this was easier for now. At hand was a more important matter that needed to be dealt with.

"We're here," said the cabbie.

Looking dazed, Kirin didn't even realize that she had arrived. The cabbie was kind enough to drop her off at the entrance. She got out and handed over some credits.

"Keep the change," she said through her muffler.

The cabbie took the credits and then realized who she was. "Hey, aren't you...?" Kirin politely timed it so she closed the door before he could complete the question.

She stood outside as the snow continued to come down. She hugged herself, trying to stay warm as she battled her chills. Several minutes passed, and she checked her phone to see if she had arrived early. She was on time, but Sifu was running late, which was unusual for him.

Kirin took a deep breath, knowing that this would be difficult for him. She looked around and decided to be a little patient. She thought, *Just give him a little more time. He'll be here.* Finally, in the distance, she saw a lone figure approaching. Kirin squinted and stared, eventually confirming that it was Sifu.

Whew, she thought. "He's here," she said aloud, the heat from her breath forming around her. She stood in place as Sifu finally approached her. Kirin did her best to try to read him, but it was always impossible to tell how he felt. Sifu didn't say a word and just stared back.

Sifu finally broke the moment of silence. "So, how'd the con show go?"

As usual, Kirin was caught off guard by Sifu's line of questioning. "Uh, maybe we can talk about that another time ... if that kinda gives you a hint."

"Oh," said Sifu.

Kirin began walking and then stopped in her tracks. She turned around and said, "Seriously, Sifu. You didn't hear anything about my con on the news?"

"No. I haven't listened to the news in a while."

"Oh, uh ... okay." With that, Kirin started walking again.

Sifu glanced at Kirin. "That bad, huh?"

Kirin stopped without turning around. She said, "I hate when you do that."

Sifu said, "It's not my fault. You're like a book turned inside out for everyone to read."

Kirin said, "Well, not everyone can do what you do."

"Hmm, that's true, but you need to work on controlling your emotions."

"There's a lot that I need to work on."

"Practice, of course, Kirin."

"Must you always remind me?"

Sifu chuckled a short laugh.

Silence ensued as they stood at the entrance. There before them towered a huge iron gate; part of it was rusted while most of it was covered in snow.

Kirin looked to the side and silently read the sign. Turning to Sifu, she said, "Are we too early?"

Sifu stood there without answering.

Suddenly the groundskeeper came from the side and began to unlock the gates. He pulled one side first. It creaked open as the two of them waited for him to complete his task.

"Thank you," said Kirin. The groundskeeper didn't respond, as he was more concerned about getting back into his office where it was warm.

Kirin said, "You know we could do this another time, if you're not up for this."

"No, it's been far too long," said Sifu in a monotone voice. He looked around the area he had avoided for so long. The pain still felt fresh, but he could control his emotions, for now. For such a sad place, the freshly coated snow made it feel peaceful and new. He stared straight from the entrance and took another deep breath.

Kirin said, "Ready?"

"Sure."

Kirin took the initiative and grabbed Sifu's hand. "Come with me, Sifu. I'll lead the way." Kirin pulled, but Sifu stood like a rock. Sifu's eyes spoke to Kirin as he remained silent.

Kirin said, "It'll be okay." She pulled once more, and this time they began to move.

Kirin had been here many times before as she often took care of the area when Sifu was gone. However, last year's craziness had prevented her from doing her task, so she'd hired someone to maintain it.

The snow continued to pour heavily, but it didn't seem to make a difference to either of them. They began carving a new path of footprints with each step. The area was picture-perfect as they approached their destination. After a few minutes, they arrived at the spot arm in arm.

"We're here," said Kirin.

"I know," said Sifu as he looked straight ahead and struggled to hold back the tears.

Kirin was surprised at what she saw and muttered, "Wow, it's grown so quickly." She snapped out of her trance and kneeled to remove the snow. Sifu stood silently in place; only the hint of his shadow reminded Kirin that he was there. Not a single word was spoken during this time.

Several minutes passed before Kirin was done clearing everything, as she tried buy some time to figure out what to do next. Kirin could feel what Sifu was going through, leaving her uneasy. The silent tension finally broke Kirin, and she said, "I know you haven't been here since…." She caught herself before she spoke any more. "Uh, so I … I hope you didn't mind, but I planted a tree. I just thought it would…."

"I know," said Sifu. He was still deep in emotion, and small words were all he could muster. It was easier for him to deal with the subject offhand than what was right in front of him.

"You knew?" asked Kirin.

"A couple of years ago, I thought I had the strength to pay a visit. I was so close to doing it, but then I saw you from a distance. I hid over there and watched you." Sifu pointed to an area shielded by brush.

Kirin asked, "Really?" There was so much Kirin still wanted to ask Sifu, but she knew how difficult it must've been for him to speak about it.

Kirin reflected back and asked, "Sifu, there was one day, I was here cleaning, and I remember I felt something odd. It was a really windy day, cold and snowing much like today, and...."

Sifu said, "Yes. That was the day I saw you here."

Kirin covered her mouth with her hand, surprised by Sifu's words. "I knew it, and I remember it so well. I often came by to take care of the area, but it was just like today ... and I swear I could feel you nearby. I remember looking all around, hoping you'd be there and thinking, 'Is he here?' Yet I didn't see you."

Sifu said, "I've never been able to thank you for tending to this area."

Kirin said, "There's never a need to thank me, Sifu."

Sifu reached into his pocket and pulled out a sheet of paper. He opened it and looked at it. As tears slowly ran down his face, he began to open his mouth, but no words came out as it quivered uncontrollably. His hands trembled as he tried his best to keep control of the situation. He took a deep breath, again trying to keep his thoughts singular.

Kirin said, "It's okay, Sifu. Do you want me to read it for you?"

Sifu felt ashamed that he was not strong enough to do what he had set out to do. "No, it's okay. I'll have to read it. I'm sorry, Kirin. Is it okay if we just stand here for a while?"

Kirin squeezed Sifu's arm, hoping her touch would bring an ounce of comfort. "It's okay, Sifu. When you're ready ... when you're ready."

"People don't want the truth; they want to be lied to. I know this to be fact because they fear looking at themselves."—Watanabe

SECTION 1

Short Stories #3—Kirin's P.O.V.

<u>10,000 Punches—126 Days</u>

S ifu looked around at the class and glanced at the clock overhead. I did the same and noticed only the core group was around.

Sifu clapped his hands and said, "Let's get started. Everyone, open up your basic stance." He gave us a second as we lined up in a four by two formation, arm's length from one another.

"Everyone, face toward the mirror," he said.

I found it a somewhat odd request, since we always faced in the direction he was instructing. I thought, *He's up to something.*

"Do you guys mind if I ask … does everyone have an extra thirty minutes to spare for class today?" Everyone glanced at one another and nodded.

"Perfect." He smiled and turned his back to us. "Danny, if you will please count up to one hundred punches."

"Yes, Sifu."

Danny did as he was instructed and started counting, "One, two, three …"

The rest of the group began punching in unison with Danny as I noticed Sifu scurrying to the back room. A few seconds later, he returned just as Danny finished counting up to one hundred.

"Good job, Danny," said Sifu. "All right, everyone, if you noticed one hundred punches at regular speed and power took about one minute. What I want to do is set the timer for two hours."

"Yah cooking something, Sifu?" asked Big T.

"Uh, not really." Sifu gave Big T a strange look. "I don't want you guys to bother with counting the punches, so I got you this timer."

Everyone—including me—stared in confusion.

Danny was still clueless. "No seriously, Sifu. You're not cooking anything?"

"No," said Sifu with more conviction.

With his usual perplexed look, Danny mumbled something in Spanish.

"Once I say, 'Begin,' I want you to punch till this timer stops."

Ken jumped in and asked, "For two hours straight?"

Everyone stared at Sifu with anticipation as he said, "Yes, for two hours straight. If my math is correct—and it should be coz I'm Asian—that should be about 10,000 punches."

A sense of shock and some murmurs echoed throughout the room. Before everyone could get a grasp of what was going on, Sifu clapped his hands and said, "Let's get ready."

I was unsure what to expect, since Sifu had never requested us to practice this before. I wasn't alone, as the guys looked befuddled as well.

Sifu grabbed his timer as we got set in our basic stance. He met everyone's gaze, one at a time, and then raised his hand and said, "And, here ... we ... go."

He said it oddly, something that Sage had mimicked before but I couldn't quite put my finger on it.

I stood at the back left corner, and to my right were Doc, Big T, and Ryan. In front of me were Ken, Danny, Robert, and Tobias at the head of the class.

As we began punching, Sifu said, "Good luck," in a nonchalant way. He walked to the back office like he usually did to sort and clean. He would always do that whenever he gave us a drill that was repetitive. Sifu turned around and said, "If you end up stopping at all, just sit down in the spot where you're standing.

Danny said, "Two hours of punching? Well, that's longer than Tobias ever stayed with any one girl."

Tobias replied, "Two hours, huh? That's one hour longer than it takes for you to fall in love."

I looked at Ryan, who was already not enjoying the process as he said, "Does anyone know if Sifu is treating us out for lunch afterward?"

Robert joked, "Maybe he's treating the guy who can last two hours punching?"

"Hey! Why'd you say 'guy' only?" I exclaimed.

Robert turned back and replied, "Oh, Kirin, give it up. You've been here the shortest amongst the group."

Big T joined in, "Come on, guys, don't be so hard on Kirin. She's improved a lot. If nothing else, she'll last longer than Danny."

Danny shouted, "Hey!"

Big T smiled and said, "You want to bet?"

Danny nodded. "Twenty credits?"

"You know it.

Doc chimed in. "Guys, focus. Two hours punching is not going to be easy for any of us, regardless of how long we've been practicing."

Ken shouted, "Did he say *straight*? What if we need a bathroom break?"

I looked at each one of the guys briefly, wondering who amongst them would stick it out and do all two hours of punching.

Danny looked determined, with the look that he would be the one to complete the task. Although, I was positive he'd be the first one to yield. He was always quick to pick up a new technique from Sifu, but his problem was his lack of focus on refining things further. Basically, he lacked the mental discipline to endure the training, and it wasn't a physical demand, but a mental one.

Only ten minutes later, I heard him scream. "Frick! My arms are burning." He was the first to stop, like I had predicted. He began rubbing his arms and stopped short of crying. I thought, *Action means so much more than words.*

Five minutes later, Ryan was huffing as he shouted, "This is impossible! There's no way you can do 10,000 punches without warming up. It's like asking a person to do a marathon from scratch."

Tobias added, "Maybe it's because you didn't wear your kicking jeans."

I looked at Ryan, surprised that he folded. Ryan was second only to Tobias in skill. He had the smoothest flow of anyone and surprisingly was the quickest to close the gap, regardless of his slightly stout build. But there he was, leaning both his hands on his knees in defeat. Sifu had always said, *The mind is powerful. Once you think you can't … you can't.*

Thirty minutes into punching, at around 3,000 punches, Ken bowed out. Ken didn't bitch out loud. He was always looked upon as the all-around practitioner. Everything he did was solid, but not spectacular. He crossed his legs, joining both Ryan and Danny on the floor.

Ken said, "Man, I run all the time, but this is worse than running." He shook his head. "I don't think I could do one more punch. My arms felt like they were gonna fall off."

Forty minutes into the punching, both Doc and Big T looked at each other and then stopped at the same time. Doc was the theorist of the group; he knew as much as anyone could about the details of the art. When I had a question and Sifu wasn't around, he was the guy to go to. He could explain things inside out.

Big T, on the other hand, had the softest touch. One would think that a guy who dwarfed me—and everyone else in the room—in size would have heavy hands, yet working with him was like working with air.

Neither of them said a word as they joined the other guys on the floor.

Only three of us remained with a good hour and fifteen minutes of punching ahead of us.

Robert said, "Damn, Kirin. I'm surprised you're still punching."

I ignored Robert and focused on what I was doing. Robert was an ass most of the time, but his perfectionist attitude toward the art was something that could be admired. However, he couldn't separate that desire for perfection with that of being natural. Thus, his self-critical state was probably more taxing on him than on others.

One hour fully into it and Robert screamed, "Ugh! No more, that's all I got."

I didn't take any pleasure in his failure as he looked at me and I continued to punch.

"Dammit!" He swore again in Korean, and I was the only one to understand it. He sat down, slamming his hand on the floor.

Then there were two of us left, Tobias and me. We were both sweating and were a long way from taking that break. Sifu walked by dusting as he gave a quick glance at everyone.

Danny asked, "Sifu, should we just sit here?"

Sifu replied, "Did you take a break?"

"Yes," replied Danny.

"Then, yes, just sit there."

Tobias was the last one standing just several feet away from me. He could see me in the mirror, and I pretended not to look at him. Tobias's skill in Wing Chun was just pure domination. He was the enforcer of the group for a reason; a single hit from his hands would lead to sleep time.

But as we both continued punching, I noticed him staring more at me. Fifteen minutes later, I noticed him wincing as he finally gave in.

"What the fu—!" he shouted. He caught himself and stopped short of swearing.

The group looked at him, surprised, as both his arms hung by his side. He looked exhausted. He shook his head and sat down, and all eyes were on me.

I thought, *I could stop right here. I proved my point and outlasted everyone.* There was a good forty-five minutes of punching left. Even my feet could feel the ache of punching for this long. But, suddenly, I just decided. I wanted to do two hours of punches, so I would do two hours of punches, regardless. I focused on just the punching and no longer the goal. I picked a target and continued.

My arms were exhausted and I could feel the burn, but I wanted to make a point. I was the youngest, the least experienced in the art, but I wanted to be the best. I was the least physically gifted, but above all things else, I knew what I wanted and why. I didn't care about my limitations or what others thought. I just knew what I had to do.

I heard the murmurs from the rest of the guys.

Doc said, "Come on, Kirin, fifteen minutes left."

The guys were cheering me on, as even Sifu came out and watched the remaining time.

I could hear Big T and Danny form another bet, but I zoned out, ignoring their conversation.

All eyes were on me with five minutes left. Instead of just doing regular punches, I started unleashing the full power of the punches for the last five minutes at an even faster pace.

"Holy shit," said Ken.

"Damn," said Ryan.

I forgot the amount of time remaining and suddenly zoned back in as the guys were counting it down for me: "Five ... four ... three ... two ... one!"

The alarm went off as I continued to punch. I felt energized even past the two-hour mark. I didn't want to stop. Suddenly, I felt a tap on my shoulder.

Sifu shouted, "Enough, Kirin! Enough. You did it."

I was covered in sweat from head to toe as my socks felt extra moist. All the guys came around me and patted me on the back.

Sifu said, "Not bad, Kirin. You let the will dominate over the skill."

"One's will can overcome the greatest of challenges."—Sifu

<u>Are You Gonna Eat That?—143 Days</u>

I took a deep breath and sat down. I wasn't quite sure if we could label this as a first date or not. The fact that Hunter was bringing his little sister, Bella, helped to ease some of my nerves as well as the tension.

Hunter said, "Okay, I've never eaten here before, Kirin, and you seem to know all the good places to eat. Do you want to order for all of us?"

"Uh, sure thing," I said.

Bella looked around, almost as if she were somewhere foreign.

"Wow, this is different!" Bella scratched her head.

I smiled at Bella and then looked at Hunter. "So, I know the menu by heart here. Does Bella have any food restrictions?"

Hunter asked, "You mean like allergies?"

"Yeah."

Hunter frowned and said, "No, she's not allergic to anything, other than … food."

"She's a picky eater?" I asked.

"Picky is an understatement." Hunter looked down at Bella and rubbed her head hard until she smacked his hand away. "If it wasn't for mac 'n cheese and nuggets, she'd starve. Just order anything, Kirin, and I'll try to force her to eat."

Several minutes passed before the waitress came by to take our order. It was a very Asian menu—well, Asian for Hunter and Bella—but I was starved.

Hunter looked at me and said, "Sorry, I had to bring Bella to this. It was a last-minute babysitting duty that my dad thrusted upon me. Either I brought her, or I would have had to cancel."

"No, it's all good. And, besides I love hanging with Bella."

The waitress arrived and started laying down the food. I had ordered several meals family style. Bella grimaced as she stared at the food.

I took a moment to explain a bit about each dish, but Bella looked unmoved.

"Wow. Never tried this before, but I can't wait to taste it," said Hunter.

I began eating as Hunter was busy trying to see if there was anything that Bella would eat. Five minutes went by as I continued eating and Hunter's frustration grew. Bella only wanted the water.

With food still slightly in my mouth, I said, "Hunter, can you give Bella and me about ten minutes alone?"

Hunter looked a little confused, as I winked and took another bite.

"Seriously, Kirin for someone who eats that much, I don't know how you don't gain a pound." He began to walk away and then turned around. "Make sure you leave me some food."

I smiled, my mouth still full, and waved him off.

I continued to eat as Bella just watched for the next several minutes.

"Uh, Kirin," asked Bella, "aren't you going to try to get me to eat some of your food?"

I grabbed another wrap and started preparing it. "Nope ... not at all."

Bella looked surprised as I continued with my meal.

I smiled at her.

"Then why'd you ask my brother to leave?" asked Bella.

"Well, since you're not eating anything, I figure I can eat more of the food with your brother away."

"What about Hunter?" she asked.

I leaned forward and said, "I guess we can always order again." With a sadistic laugh, I kinda choked on the food. A few seconds later, I was back to my goal, the food.

Bella was even more confused as she looked at me. "Really, Kirin, you aren't going to make me try the food?"

I thought she finally deserved an answer, and I grabbed a napkin to wipe my face.

"Okay, Bella, the truth is: the reason you can be picky with your food is because you've never starved."

Bella looked confused. "Well, I'm kinda hungry right now."

I changed my demeanor. "Bella, being hungry and starving are as different as night and day. I know you are young, but imagine if you had to go several days wondering where your next meal was coming from. I've experienced that. I know what that feels like. I tell you there's no such thing as a kid being a picky eater. So, when there's food, regardless of what kind it is, I don't take it for granted."

"But I don't like the taste, and the food looks weird," said Bella.

"Everything is learned. Just like knowing what is and isn't good food. You think this food looks weird? Those nuggets you love to eat are the farthest thing from food. Have you ever seen how they make them?" I thought, *Come to think of it, is it even chicken?*

She shook her head.

"Give me a minute." I retrieved my phone from its sock holder and pulled up a video on the creation of nuggets. "Here, Bella, watch this."

Bella grabbed my phone and started viewing it. I saw Hunter starting to approach, but I waved him off and signaled I needed another five minutes.

He grabbed his stomach and gave a puppy dog look. I ignored him and focused my attention on Bella.

Bella's eyes opened as she was staring at the screen funny. "What is this, Kirin?"

"Wait for it," I said. I grabbed another lettuce leaf and began to prepare another Korean wrap.

"Oh my gosh! That's how they make nuggets?" said Bella.

"Yup." I continued my rude manners, talking and eating at the same time. "So, you see, when you say that the food is weird … well, at least I'm eating food. I have no idea what all these other people are eating or think they're eating."

"Kirin, what if I try it but don't like it?" asked Bella.

"Well, at least you tried. Most people look at it and make a judgement by its appearance. But bottom line, Bella: to know good food, you have to experience it. 'Why limit yourself?' I always say."

A few minutes passed as I could see Hunter from a distance. He rubbed his belly as I waved him back, indicating I was far from done. He hung his head and walked away again.

"Okay, Kirin, can I try what you're trying?" asked Bella.

"Hmm, I don't know, Bella. What if I give it to you and you take a bite and you don't like it? I'd rather not waste the food." I chowed down another wrap and was preparing one more.

"I promise, Kirin, I'll try at least two bites," said Bella.

"I don't know, Bella. That means I'd have to share." I began laughing as food started falling from my mouth.

"Kirin, really, I'll try it," said Bella.

"Fine," I said hesitantly. I began preparing a wrap for Bella and left it on her plate.

Bella grabbed the wrap and smelled it first. "It smells kinda different."

I didn't bother responding and continued eating. I was kinda hoping she didn't eat it, so I could have more.

I pretended not to watch but saw every move she was doing. She finally closed her eyes and took a bite.

"I don't like it." She frowned and spit it back out on the plate.

I grabbed the wrap from her plate and put it on mine.

"What are you doing? Why'd you take my wrap?" she asked.

"You said you didn't like it."

"I know, but I did as you said and tried one bite," she replied.

"Trying? I don't know if I'd call that trying. Maybe you're just not hungry enough," I said.

"I think you're being mean."

"It wasn't just one time I was hungry. There were several times I didn't eat anything all day. If I'd found food from the garbage can, I would've eaten it. That's life being mean—and real mean, at that. Besides, you promised to really try it. Trying to me is at least chewing the food ten times and swallowing it."

The next minute was silent as Bella thought of her options.

"Okay, give it back to me. I said I promised to try it, and I will."

I gave her wrap back and watched as she was determined to prove me wrong. She took a bite and started counting with her fingers the number of chews until she eventually swallowed her first bite.

She looked somewhat surprised. Without me saying another word, she took another bite. We were silent, both eating our wraps, as I smiled across the table at Hunter when he returned.

"Holy crap, you're eating, Bella!" said Hunter.

"Can't talk," said Bella, with food still in her mouth. "Busy eating."

When Hunter met my gaze, I smiled again.

"Wait a second. Where'd all the food go?" Hunter frowned.

"Oh, don't worry," I said. "We can always order more."

Bella wiped her face and said, "Kirin, can I have the last piece?"

"Sure thing, Bella."

Looking confused, Hunter complained, "I'm still hungry."

Bella and I looked at each other and began to giggle.

"There are endless possibilities to experience new things. Only one's prejudice prevents you from the adventure."—Sifu

Black Friday Deals—156 Days

It had been about two hours, and both Sage and Gwen were trying their best to stay warm. It made no difference, marching up and down and trying to do any form of movement to deal with typical Chicago weather.

I said, "Okay, what is it you are looking for, Gwen, that you don't already have?"

Gwen replied, "I know you don't get all the customs here in America, Kirin, but this fifty-inch TV is half-off at this store."

I scratched my head and countered, "I still don't get it. Don't you have a one-hundred-inch TV at your home now?"

"You're right, but this is brand new and is half-off. How can you possibly beat that deal?" argued Gwen.

"Uh, so you're getting it just because it's half-off."

"Exactly! So, does it make sense now?"

"So, American custom is to get something that you don't need just because it's cheaper."

"Kirin, Kirin, Kirin … it's not so much buying it, but the excitement of chasing something down and getting it," said Gwen.

I frowned, shaking my head. "Let me get this straight: you're saving money because you're getting a new TV, which you don't need, from an unknown company called Kindehworks Television."

"Bingo!" She pointed to her nose.

I looked at Sage and asked, "What's your excuse?"

Sage said, "They got some gaming stuff I need that's on sale as well."

"I'm afraid to ask if you really need it or not."

"You know, Kirin, we go through this argument every year," said Gwen.

"That's because, each year, waiting in line with you guys makes absolutely no sense at all, but you're my friends so we always stick together," I replied.

Gwen asked, "Well, you went through the ads. I thought I heard you say that you were dying to get something."

"Well, yeah, but…."

Gwen said, "Well, then, you're being hypocritical, aren't you?"

"I am not."

Suddenly one of the employees stepped out of the door with a megaphone. We were at least number ten in line, and the people behind us lined up as far as the naked eye could see.

"Okay, everyone, please … just walk in casually and don't rush in, please! There's more than enough stuff for everybody to buy."

Sage said, "I got Gwen, if that's okay with you."

Gwen nodded and said, "Thanks, Sage."

"Besides, I could use her as a battling ram."

Gwen swiped at Sage and said, "You jerk."

After waiting a few minutes more, the crowd grew anxious. I could see the fear in the store employees' eyes, that they wouldn't be able to handle the rush.

Gwen said, "Sage, you know the layout and the direction for the stuff, right?"

Sage said, "I got it fully memorized."

"I'll just follow behind you guys and make sure I don't get in the way," I said.

We all looked at each other and nodded.

We stood in anticipation as the store employees inside began opening the door. At first glance, everything went normal and in an orderly fashion. Gwen, Sage, and I were inside the first entrance, with the main entrance several feet away. But, suddenly, I felt a huge surge from behind as the crowd in the back was forcing a stampede.

I ducked out of the surge as soon as I felt my stance off balance, but I noticed that Sage was thrown to the side and Gwen was immediately knocked out of her wheelchair to the ground.

Everyone stampeded, blinded by greed, forgetting what being human was all about.

Sage maneuvered Gwen's wheelchair in front of them, but that was quickly swallowed away by the crowd. Sage fell over right in front of Gwen.

As I saw Gwen and Sage on the floor, I jumped in front of the swarm and put my guard hands up. Sage got on top of Gwen and shielded her from hits. Gwen was in a fetal position, trying to protect herself from the mob who continued to devour everything in their path.

I shouted, "Sage, stay behind me and try to drag Gwen to the side."

Sage shouted, "Someone's on the ground. Don't push. Don't push! What's wrong with you people?"

But his voice fell upon deaf ears as the value of saving over 50% was more important than human life.

The crowd continued the charge, and nothing anyone could say would stop their rush. I couldn't believe what I was seeing or their lack of humanity. So, I decided right then and there, I couldn't hurt them, but I could sure as heck throw them off balance.

I screamed at Sage, "I'm gonna try to clear a path to the side entrance to let these idiots through."

One by one, no matter who it was, I threw people to the side. Even when I was screaming at them, they wouldn't listen. "Stop pushing! You're going to trample my friend." But, they didn't care, and I had to restrain myself from losing my temper and possibly throwing a punch.

I formed my triangle and was guiding people off the straight path from Sage and Gwen. Any time someone pushed, I used their force and tossed them away. Even after they fell to the ground, they staggered up and continued toward the entrance as if nothing had happened. A handful of them were getting impatient, and then one of them took a swing at me. I ducked his punch as he clocked another guy from behind. The two ended up scuffling with one another but continued with the flow of the crowd.

I thought, *What's wrong with these people? All this chaos just for money.*

It seemed like an eternity passed as I finally made my way to the side and out of the flow of humanity that was ready to ravage anything in its path.

I pressed my hands over my knees and leaned forward to catch my breath.

Gwen looked up to me and said, "Thanks, Kirin. I owe you one."

"No, you don't. You're my best friend. You'll never have to owe me."

Sage said, "Well, I helped, too."

"I know you did, Sage. I know you did." I patted him on the head to thank him.

We both help setup Gwen's wheelchair again as Sage and Gwen took a moment to see if it was still intact.

Gwen said, "I think it looks okay."

Sage nodded and pushed the wheels back and forth. "Just a few scratches, but it seems to be working."

I saw Gwen was depressed, and I asked, "What's wrong? Are you hurt?"

"I'm not hurt. I'm just disappointed that I won't get my stuff anymore."

Sage had the same frown. "Yeah, same here. If you're not the first twenty people in line, all the good stuff is gone. And, I'm sure all the electronic stuff has been torn from the shelves already."

We waited several more minutes by the side as the swarm finally subsided and we could exit out through the front.

Gwen said, "Wait a second, Kirin. You never got what you wanted here."

Sage said, "That's right. What electronic gizmo, pray tell, were you looking to buy?"

I said, "Actually, if you guys don't mind, I think my item might still be there."

Both Gwen and Sage looked at each other in confusion.

"Come on, guys, follow me."

They trekked behind me to a part of the store with no one around.

Sage asked, "Why are we in this section?"

Gwen said, "Yeah, I don't get it. Nobody shops in this area for Black Friday."

Suddenly, I screamed. "It's here!"

"What's here?" they both asked.

I ran as quickly as I could and grabbed the pair of socks I'd seen in the ad.

"Yes!" I exclaimed and jumped for joy.

I hugged the socks and lifted them up into the air.

"Are you kidding me?" asked Gwen.

"If this is a joke, I'm not laughing," said Sage.

I paused during my moment of celebration and asked them, "What's wrong?"

Gwen said, "You're telling me the main thing you wanted for Black Friday was a pair of socks."

I bit my lip and said, "Uh, yeah. I was really eyeballing these socks when I saw them in the ad."

Sage said, "Who the hell buys socks on Black Friday?"

I said, "I thought they looked really nice, and I badly needed a pair." With that, I took off my shoe and showed the massive hole by my toe.

Sage screamed, "Put it away! Put it away! I've seen something that can never be unseen."

I said, "Come on, guys, let's hit the register so I can bring this baby home."

I was so happy I got my socks I started skipping through the store. I turned around as both Gwen and Sage just look baffled.

"If you think about it, all you really need in life is to be loved and to love somebody. Everything else is just a distraction."—Sifu

SECTION 2

Sifu's Journey Entry #3—Universal Harmony/ The Dance, Part 2

Dream Continued (Summer 2001)

From across the street, Sifu could see a stir of activity outside the building. He pulled out his phone to check the time. *Hmm, there's still forty-five minutes left,* he thought. He stood by himself and wondered what he was doing there just after midnight. A summer breeze came from behind, and Sifu took it as a sign that the universe had spoken. He inhaled deeply and walked hastily across the street.

As he approached the building, people continued to pass through the doors. Most were fashionably dressed for the occasion, and Sifu felt quite the opposite. Again, he asked himself, *Seriously … what am I doing here?*

Even with all the excuses he could muster up, he continued to head toward the building. There was an energy somewhere inside drawing him closer, and he knew better than to go against the force. Seconds later, he stood outside the door to the building. He paused and began to reach toward it. The door swung open, jolting Sifu for a second, as a couple exited, bursting in laughter. Sifu said apologetically, "Excuse me," and smiled. They ignored his apology, as they were lost in each other's company.

Sifu took no offense as he finally grabbed hold of the door and forced himself into the building. Immediately, the sound of music surrounded him. He felt like he was drowning in it, as he was clearly out of his comfort zone. Usually on a Saturday night, he would be asleep alone in his apartment at this time.

He continued to walk through the maze of humanity and followed the music to the very center of the room, dominated by a dance floor designed in a wooden checkered pattern. The floor was packed with couples twisting and shaking to the beat of the music. Surrounding the dance floor were several tables for people to rest, place their drinks on, and converse. Somehow, within this chaos of activity, people were smoothly interacting with one another, all from the source of a single beat.

Sifu scanned the dance floor, while the beat of the song seemed to go with the moment. He shook his head in frustration as he thought, *What am I doing here?* Suddenly, he spotted her; despite the distance, her energy made her stand out from the crowd. Megumi was there like she had promised, and Sifu had the answer to his question.

Megumi was already dancing with someone when Sifu spotted her. He watched her move gracefully to the beat of the song. With each spin, her long hair flowed and her supple body moved in a graceful arch around her partner. Sifu was mesmerized as he continued to stare at Megumi dancing. Time seemed to be moving in slow motion. Sifu's heart raced, and his stomach twisted into a knot when he realized that he felt nervous for the first time in a long time.

The music finally ended, and the crowd cheered. Megumi smiled and began chatting with her partner. Sifu saw no one else in the room, his gaze centered on her. Megumi spotted Sifu and waved from a distance. Sifu returned her wave and smiled back awkwardly.

Sifu stood in place and played passive as Megumi made the first move toward him. Her smile never wavered as she began her approach across the dance floor. With each step, the crowd blocking her path parted magically as she neared Sifu. Megumi stopped just short of handshake distance and said, "Well, I must say … I am surprised."

Sifu was coy in his reply. "Now, why would you say that?"

"From our last talks, I was pretty sure that I had you pegged as someone who didn't venture outside the box."

"I'm a difficult person to read," said Sifu as he gave her a hint of a smile.

"The night's still young. I'm pretty sure my other feelings about you are correct," she replied.

Sifu smiled and said, "I've been known to prove a lot of people wrong."

Megumi felt that Sifu was bluffing and wanted to see how far he would go with it. "So, when are you gonna admit that you're afraid to go outside the box? That dancing is definitely out of your comfort zone?"

"You know it's dangerous to assume," said Sifu.

"I think it's time you prove it then," said Megumi.

Sifu said, "I just got here. Mind if grab a drink first and catch you on the dance floor in a bit?"

"Is that a drink for courage?"

"Nope, it's a drink because I'm thirsty."

Megumi's friend approached and grabbed her by the hand. He didn't even bother to introduce himself as he said, "Come on, let's dance."

Megumi turned around and said, "Just admit it! It's almost closing time. You're gonna have to admit I'm right sooner or later." She jerked away from Sifu as her partner began dragging her away.

Sifu stood as Megumi went back to the center of the dance floor and began to dance. It irked Sifu to see her being held by this stranger, but he was clearly at a disadvantage. He was skilled in fighting, not dancing. Sifu thought, *It'd be so much easier if I just knocked him out.*

The DJ spoke and broke Sifu's jealousy as he shouted, "The last thirty minutes before closing will all be dedicated to rumba … the dance of looove." The crowd cheered at the announcement, and the energy continued to fill the room.

Sifu had never danced before. He'd never had a chance to attend his prom. His time had been devoted to learning the art of Wing Chun. On this night, though, it did not matter. He was dead set on trying to prove Megumi wrong.

He looked to the dance floor and began watching other guys do their dance. He thought to himself, *Dance is nothing more than motion and feeling the music. …You move to the force. That's just Wing Chun.* He knew exactly what to look for, the dancer who looked the most natural in their movement. This was the one he would study and copy. Time was not on his side, and he was banking on his skills to pull off the impossible.

One gentleman was garnering the attention of many onlookers, as he tried feverishly to dominate his partner's attention. Sifu snickered and thought, *Okay … I don't want to look like that.*

Finally, he spotted another gentleman dancing with his partner. He moved smoothly across the dance floor, and Sifu began studying his motions. He watched for the basic foundation of his steps. Minutes passed as he tapped his foot, trying to understand the rhythm of the music. He was mentally dancing in his head, slightly shifting his weight to each beat to mimic the motion of the dancer. He made sure he kept his movement to a minimum just in case Megumi were to take a peek.

He thought, *Hmm, interesting, he moves to showcase the motion of his partner. He's the foundation for her to move about.* Every so often, he would glance at Megumi, who continued to dance with her partner. He would occasionally catch her staring back at him. He would nod his head, and she would bashfully smile back. His heart would melt with each of her looks, and he was finally driven to action.

Always go for it, thought Sifu. With that last thought, he began walking toward the dance floor. It had a been awhile since he had found anything that caused his nerves to be unsettled. His heart was beating heavily, so he focused on his breathing to calm his nerves. He switched his focus to the goal at hand, and that was standing right in front of him: Megumi. She continued to dance with her partner, but Sifu had seen enough of that.

Sifu took the initiative and said in a definitive voice, "I'm gonna cut in."

Megumi looked at Sifu and then toward her partner. She nodded as she pulled away from him. He glared at Sifu and bumped into him, but Sifu's stance was a rock. He looked shocked, but Sifu never gave him the time of day. His focus was clearly on Megumi.

The music stopped briefly, and the timing seemed almost too perfect. The DJ made another announcement as the crowd turned toward him. He waited for all eyes to be on him as he said, "Okay, everyone, it's closing time. This will be the last song of the night." The crowd jeered back, disappointed with his words. Many were hoping the night would never end and the fun would continue.

The DJ shouted, "Let's end the night with a bang ... so let's 'Save the Last Dance for Me.'" Megumi looked immediately at Sifu, as his sparkling eyes never left her.

Sifu took a deep breath and made his move for Megumi. He thought, *Don't hesitate. Close the gap.* He grabbed her firmly, confidently faking that he had done this before, bringing her close to him as their bodies touched.

Megumi looked up to him and said, "So, how long are you gonna keep this up that you've danced before?"

Sifu didn't say a word, and the music began to play. He stood still, holding Megumi tightly as everyone else was moving around them. Megumi said, "You know the music started already? Just admit it, that—"

Sifu took the lead, interrupting her talk, and began dancing with her. Megumi's face was bewildered as Sifu was moving gracefully to the beat. He smiled confidently, trusting his skill in Wing Chun and his ability to feel the flow. With each step and beat, the bond between the two grew. Sifu continued to move through the dance floor with Megumi, as no one else around them mattered. He made her his complete focus, and she knew it and loved it.

Megumi said, "You were right. I admit I was wrong.... You definitely are full of surprises."

Sifu bashfully smiled and continued to dance. Guilt crept in as he finally had to tell her the truth. "I have a confession," he spun her around, "this is the first time I've ever danced. Ever!"

Megumi looked somewhat upset and said, "Please, don't lie to me."

Sifu continued to dance, holding Megumi. "First, I never lie. Second ... I definitely would never lie to you."

Megumi didn't speak right away, suspicious of his words. She stared into Sifu's eyes to find the truth. However, the longer she gazed into his eyes, the more she saw something that she had never seen before in another man. She hesitated briefly, knowing that words weren't needed to tell him what she was thinking. Timidly, she whispered, "You are telling the truth."

Sifu nodded and continued to whisk her around the dance floor. "For the last twenty minutes, I've been studying and watching the moves of the dancer over there," he said, gesturing toward his unsuspecting teacher.

Megumi continued to dance with Sifu. As she glanced over at the dancer Sifu had pointed out, she noticed that his moves were in fact similar to Sifu's moves.

With an embarrassed look on her face, she said, "I guess I'm still wrong.... You definitely are full of surprises."

Sifu said, "It's not that I never go outside the box. It's that, when I find something I like, I focus all my attention and effort toward that."

The two continued to dance as the song seemed to last forever. The energy between them continued to grow, as the intensity of the moment was about to erupt.

Megumi looked up to Sifu and asked, "So, now that you know you can dance ... do you think you'll be dancing again?"

Sifu didn't respond right away as he was looking for the courage to let it all out. It was a moment of complete vulnerability where his feelings were exposed, a leap of faith where he had to risk it all, hoping his heart would be returned in one piece. He stopped cold in his tracks, as the music continued playing and people around them danced. He held Megumi tightly and stared into her eyes, laying it all out for her. He said, "I don't think I'll ever be dancing again."

Megumi frowned with a look of disappointment on her face. "Why ... why wouldn't you dance again?"

He looked deeply into her eyes and waited until he finally could see into her soul. He leaned forward closer to her face and said, "I don't think I'll ever dance again … unless it's only with you."

Her face flushed as she smiled gingerly and looked away. Her tough wall had crumbled, and she feared to reveal any more of her feelings. Sifu did not say a word, leaving it all for her to absorb. The silence made Sifu feel awkward. After fully exposing himself and revealing the truth, he felt unsure what to do next.

"I, uh…," said Sifu.

Megumi looked up and pressed her lips gently upon Sifu, cutting off his words and catching him by surprise. A few seconds passed before she pulled away from Sifu and they both smiled. She felt lost in the moment, almost out of her character for taking such initiative. Now she was the one unsure what was to happen next.

"Oh, I…," muttered Megumi.

Sifu leaned toward Megumi, interrupting her words as he kissed her intensely on the dance floor. She broke down from his kiss and returned the favor with the same vigor, as a powerful and emotional bond had just been created. They were locked away in each other's arms as the music continued to play and people around them danced.

CHAPTER 4

Controlled

Several Hours After the Meeting

Watanabe was staring at a picture as he sat silently by himself in his office. He was old school when he could be; unlike most today, the picture wasn't in a digital format. There in his hand was a standard frame with a slightly faded image that captured all his attention. Watanabe curled his hand into a fist and clenched it tight. Just behind the frame, catching his eye, was the jar containing several clear pills. He mumbled something under his breath and let out a big sigh.

Knock. Knock.

It was Kristen at the door, breaking Watanabe's concentration. He grabbed his picture and sneaked one last peek before stashing it inside his desk.

Watanabe said, "Come in. Please."

The doors swung open as Kristen appeared from behind. She had a long walk before she would reach Watanabe's desk.

"Morning, sir. Here are the latest results on the test." Kristen pressed her tablet, and it immediately shot to Watanabe's computer.

"It's finished already?" asked Watanabe.

"Yes, sir. Last night, to be more precise," said Kristen.

"I didn't realize they'd have test results a week in advance."

Kristen said, "I pressed them hard to get it done sooner than expected."

Watanabe wore a smile on his face. "You're not going to make many friends being that demanding."

Kristen replied, "That's my goal, sir."

"Hmm," said Watanabe.

Kristen could tell that Watanabe was lost in thought, distant from his normal personality.

Watanabe began to stare at the results on his screen impassively.

Kristen said, "Sir, the results are impressive—quite impressive, in fact."

Watanabe continued to examine the results and quickly absorbed the information. He leaned back in his seat and looked to be occupied. He let out a deep breath, stood up, and approached the window, staring outside. There below him in his view were millions of people going about their everyday life.

Keeping his back to Kristen, he spoke. "Do you think what I'm planning to do makes me a monster, Kristen?"

"Sir?"

"Before us is the answer that I believe mankind has been searching for … the answer to the question that has plagued us throughout history. Yet, here we are, hiding the fact when we should be out there promoting it."

Kristen answered, "It's difficult to change, sir, even when it's for the better."

"Is it for the better?" He turned slightly, waiting for a response.

"I wouldn't be here if that wasn't the case, sir."

"Hmm. The way I see it—"

"Sir, you don't have to sell me on this…. Oh, I'm sorry for interrupting."

"No … please. Did you have something to say?"

"Every revolutionary change always faces opposition. Like I said before, new may be better, but it is scary for most people."

"Go on," asked Watanabe.

"If you look today where society is, mankind is always clinging onto a belief. We need that, whether it's real or not—we somehow always need that. So, whether that comes from a religion, an idol, or a tiny pill, why not give them exactly what they need?

"Let's face it, sir: people want to be controlled."

"You're certain of that, Kristen?" asked Watanabe.

"They do, sir. I believe they'd be lost if someone didn't lead the way."

Watanabe faced Kristen. As she began to speak, he let out a glimpse of a smile as he appreciated both her intelligence and her honesty.

Kristen's voice rose. "The apathy that you see before us proves it to be correct. Reality TV's popularity shows that people are afraid to face the truth. It's easier for them to go brain dead and waste an hour on nothing than deal with the world around them. The fast food that we supply them, they gobble it up like pigs at a trough. They know it's bad for them, but that doesn't stop them from eating it. The products we sell that they don't need, they line up and stampede one another for it. I can cite one example after another that proves they want this—in fact, they need this. In other words, we give it to them, and they take it.

"I honestly believe what you are doing is the solution that mankind needs to believe in. They're afraid to make tough choices, so it's our job to control them to be better … all for the greater good."

Watanabe turned toward the glass again and stared at the people below. He spent a moment admiring her speech. "Kristen, did I ever tell you the story that impacted my life the most?"

"No, sir … you've never spoken about it."

Watanabe turned around to look at her. "I'm sorry. I'm not sure if your busy schedule has the time to listen to an old man's rant."

"Sir, you will be my top priority … and, sir, you're not that old. Please continue with your story."

Watanabe stared up to the sky and began to recall his past. It was fresh, as if it had occurred just yesterday. He clenched his fist and began to speak as the feelings and emotions surged through his body like blood.

"Hmm, where to begin…?What's that saying again? Ah, yes, I'll make sure to cut the fat out." He chuckled at his own English and began to speak. "I guess, like all things, many people underestimate the effect a single event can have on one's path. When it happens to you as a child, it's multiplied exponentially beyond calculation.

"My parents had sent me to the States to study overseas for one year. I was ten years old, and it was a typical day, hanging with my friends headed home from school. Now, keep in mind that walking home in Japan is an everyday norm for us. However, in the States, that was not the case, especially if you weren't in the best of neighborhoods.

"Well, I was walking home, goofing around, and for whatever reason we decided to take a different path. At the time, it seemed like nothing at all, just that: a decision.

"That decision to go that route changed my life forever. Now, to make this long story short, we came up against a stranger, only a few years older than me. I didn't think it would matter so much since I was with three of my closest friends. He wanted to start trouble, I stood up to him, and suddenly he was on top of me, beating the hell out of me."

Watanabe's voice changed as he continued to look away from Kristen.

"There I was on the ground, crying and bloodied. I looked at my friends, who just stood there and didn't help."

Kristen interrupted, "Why didn't they help you?"

"That, Kristen, is the question that was finally answered many years later. That was the defining moment when I realized, given the ability to choose between right and wrong, human beings will fail … and seemingly always fail at that choice. You see, it's easy to choose right, to do good, when you have nothing on the line. But at that moment, when my friends were asked to make a choice, only then could I see their true colors. For years, I cried when

I realized what I had lost. In that instant, the innocence of childhood was gone forever, as I would never look at things the same way."

"I'm sorry, sir."

"That's when I realized that the free will given to man always leads to wrong choices. That's why we repeat the same mistakes over and over again."

Watanabe sighed and continued with his story. "You might think that's where it ended … and had it ended like that, who knows where I might be today. But I was alone and scared, and he was evil itself ready to send me to my maker. He pulled out a gun and aimed it right at my face. Why, I have no idea. Maybe it was just my path to encounter this, but whatever that reason may be, at that very moment, he created who I am today."

"I see," said Kristen. "So, that's why…."

"Yes, that's the *why* that led the way to abolishing guns in the United States."

Kristen stood surprised to hear it from the source itself.

"Kristen, to get the plan in motion, we needed to do away with the guns. Let's face it: anyone can just pull a trigger."

"Sir, no one could have ever imagined that Amendment would be overturned, but you were able to pull off the impossible," said Kristen.

"To create that change, we needed a dramatic impact. You could say, you either wait for it or create it."

"Sir?"

"Hmm, let me get back to finishing my story. I wasn't quite prepared to go yet. Something in me said to fight. I wanted to live. I wanted to see another day. I had no skill, but the desire was so strong that it outweighed the fear. Even though he was overpowering, my hands were free, and I desperately reached for anything that I could around me. Then I felt it: a rock that was larger than my fist. Without hesitation, I smashed it on the side of his head.

"He fell to the ground instantly, and I stood up. But, to my surprise, I wasn't in shock. Instead, I stared at him, lying lifeless on the ground. I was covered with my own blood as I looked at him, and blood began to run from the side of his head.

"That day changed everything. That moment, I knew I had to depend on myself, that the will with its own flaws could be limited only by its desire."

Kristen said, "You've always been so strong, sir."

Watanabe replied, "In the end, man's failure has nothing to do with money or power, but with free will. It's in human nature to want more, to desire more, never being content with what they have. That's why every civilization until now has failed in the same identical way. We continue to fail to learn from history and duplicate the same mistakes over and over."

Kristen nodded without interrupting.

"Mankind will always be faced with that choice. When asked to choose between right and wrong, he falls susceptible to such power."

They both stood silent, as his words carried much impact.

"Sir?"

"Yes, Kristen?"

"Sir, the numbers are promising. I was wondering if you feel ready to...." Kristen hesitated. She knew the subject was touchy for Watanabe. She decided to push further to see. "Would you be willing to test it again on—"

Watanabe hung his head down. "No, not yet!" he said sternly.

"I'm sorry, sir."

"There is no need to apologize. It is my failure as a.... It's just my failure to maintain balance that has put me in this situation. Only now can I see that for myself."

Watanabe walked back to his desk and sat. There, he folded his hands and said, "Not until we are 100% sure will I try it again on him."

"Understood, sir."

Watanabe said, "I want stage two to be implemented. Thorne has his orders, which I'm sure he will follow through without a hiccup. As for you, I want you to deal with Ms. Rise."

"I'm on it, sir," said Kristen. She began to walk away before hesitating.

"What is it, Kristen?"

"When should I begin it?"

"We need to position her to carry on the movement, so the answer is ... immediately."

"And, sir?"

"Yes, what is it, Kristen?"

"You're okay with keeping Thorne out of the loop?"

"Thorne knows what he needs to know. That's what's most important," said Watanabe.

▲ ▲ ▲

Meanwhile in Chicago

Thorne went immediately to work as soon as he arrived in his office. Fawn trailed behind him like a puppy dog and waited to see what his boss had in mind.

Thorne sat at his desk and stalled by staring at his computer. The silence made Fawn feel uncomfortable, as each second that passed filled the air with tension. Fawn was unsure what was eating at Thorne. Fawn said, "So … um, sir. Um, you haven't seemed the same since we returned from New York."

He left it at that, hoping he would get a response. A minute felt like forever as Fawn squirmed in his spot, but Thorne continued to ignore him.

"Did the meeting not go well, boss?" He leaned back slightly and cowered.

Thorne was engrossed with his work and did not reply.

Fawn looked around with a sense of unease. He wasn't sure if he should stay or if he should go. So, he flipped a mental coin in his head which told him to cautiously move forward to Thorne's desk.

A few minutes passed before Thorne finally spoke. "We have a lot of work ahead of us, Fawn. But, your first priority is to secure all the bosses who are…."Thorne stopped what he was doing and combed his hair with his hand. He suddenly slammed both his fists on his table and took a breath. He had, on this rare occasion, lost his cool.

At first, it shocked Fawn, seeing Thorne like this. "My god! What is it, boss?"

He stared at Fawn and said, "He gave me a direct order, a plan to follow."

Fawn looked confused at the statement. "Well, he is the boss. Isn't that what he's supposed to do?"

Thorne didn't say a word, but he thought, *And therein lies the problem.* He looked away, disgusted at the thought. "He's planning something and keeping me out of the loop."

"How do you know that, boss?"

"Ever since he put me in charge, he's let me have free reign of the company … and now, all of a sudden, he's got me doing something specific, like a trained dog."

"Maybe it means nothing, boss?"

"Fawn, I got to this position because I can see what most people would miss."

"You are brilliant, boss."

"No ass-kissing right now, Fawn."

"Sorry, boss. It's as natural for me as it is to breathe."

Thorne glanced away, looking distraught.

Fawn said, "I don't get it, boss. What's the big deal? You've told me yourself that you've always admired Watanabe."

"I do respect him, Fawn, but that doesn't mean I have to kiss his ass."

Fawn rolled his eyes and looked away, whistling.

Thorne said, "Just like you said, it's as natural for you to breathe as it is within my core to not settle for being second best."

Fawn said, "So, what do you want me to do?"

Thorne adjusted his tie and stood straight up. "We do exactly what he wants. We secure all the mob bosses and make sure they are fully under our control."

"Got it, boss. Do you need me to go visit all four of them?" asked Fawn.

"Yes. Start with the Russian mob who've taken over Jabbiano's territory. As Russians, they need to be put in their place before things get out of control."

"That's fine, boss. I'll have Linda arrange a meeting, and I'll be with them ASAP," replied Fawn. "You know, last year when you made an example of Jabbiano … you'd think that would have kept everyone on a tight leash."

"Remember, Fawn … when you're on top, you always have to make sure everyone is in order. And last year's example might need a pinch more … impact."

"Uh, what about Justice?" Fawn wondered aloud. "He normally comes with me for all these enforcement meetings."

Thorne looked up and finally stared at Fawn directly. "He's still recovering from the fight. Just take several of your best men, and make it clear to them who's running the show."

"And boss, what are you going to be working on?"

"I'm gonna make sure I end up on top."

Fawn began walking away as Thorne said, "Fawn, this is just between you and me. Understood?"

Fawn clapped his hands and zipped his lips, as he made a hand gesture of throwing away the keys. "Total silence, boss."

Thorn said, "You just spoke."

Fawn giggled and said, "My bad … I meant, right now … right now. I'll be totally silent."

▲ ▲ ▲

An Hour Later

Fawn arrived late as usual, entering a dirty bar filled with less than the most upscale of citizens. He didn't go alone. Six of his top guards were with him, but his sense of security was lacking without Justice.

Fawn shouted, "Olov, it's a pleasure to finally meet you! I've heard such great things about you." Fawn was brilliant at keeping a straight face, even when his words never matched his true feelings. He extended his hand, and Olov gripped it like a vise, squeezing it hard. "Oh my, that's one firm grip. What big muscles you must have!"

Olov ignored his remarks and turned away. Fawn, a stickler for cleanliness, removed his glove and slipped it into his pocket. *Mental note: burn this glove.*

Olov spoke English with a thick accent. "I'm so glad to finally meet you, Fawn. I've heard so much about you."

Fawn giggled and said, "I hope they're all good things."

Olov bellowed a laugh and said, "Before we get to work, is there something I can offer you to drink?"

"Hmm, what do Russians drink? Is it vodka? I can never remember. Oh well, just give me one of those drinks with a cute little umbrella in it."

Olov made a strange face and then gestured to his bartender to fix his drink. Olov confidently strolled by a table, pulled a seat out for himself, and kicked his feet up. "Please, let's sit down over here."

Fawn went to sit down, but before planting his bottom on the chair, he pulled out his handkerchief and began to wipe it. He turned to Olov and said, "Sorry, I'm a little OCD when it comes to these things."

Olov laughed. "Please, my friend, sit down, and tell me what's on your mind."

Fawn said, "Let me get right to the point. Since you've taken over that fat slob Jabbiano's territory, I wanted to make sure you understood that you've also locked yourself to the duties under the UFMF."

The bartender brought their drinks. Olov whispered into the bartender's ear as Fawn removed the little umbrella from his drink.

"Now about these duties," said Olov, before stopping abruptly and looking around. "Where's your bodyguard, Justice?"

Fawn rolled his eyes and said, "Would you believe he actually took a vacation day? I can't remember exactly where he went, but I'm sure it's somewhere warm."

Olov was far from interested in the details, as he made a subtle signal to one of his guards.

Fawn continued to jabber away. "And, I was just complaining the other day that I rarely get any vacations anymore."

Olov shook his head and said, "Word on the street is he's actually injured."

Fawn waved his hands and laughed. "Please, word on the street is as reliable as news on the internet." Fawn sipped his drink and giggled at his own words. "Anyway, what does it matter? Besides, what's the point? I never travel alone. I've got six of my best guards with me all the time."

Olov kept his head perfectly still and began making signals just with his eyes. "That's too bad he's not here."

Fawn said, "Why is that?"

Olov began speaking in Russian and slowly stood up. His shadow cast over Fawn, engulfing him in the darkness. Suddenly, a swarm of men jumped at Fawn's bodyguards and subdued all of them to the ground. Fawn looked on in shock and curled into a fetal position in his chair.

"What are you doing?" screamed Fawn.

Olov leaned forward, placing both his hands on the table across from Fawn. In his thick accent, Olov said, "You take me as a fool, Fawn. I know of your tactics, putting the other mobsters in place and strong-arming them like dogs. You think you can come to my own bar and intimidate me and my men?"

Fawn waved him down in a panic. "I have no idea what you are talking about."

Olov was displeased with that response as he pointed to one of his guards. With that, several of them began pummeling one of Fawn's guards relentlessly.

Fawn shrieked at the top of his lungs. "Stop it! Stop, you meanie!"

Olov demanded, "Tell me I'm wrong!"

Fawn peeked through his jacket and said, "You're wrong."

Olov's face turned beet red as he raised both hands in the air. His men took the command to heart and began beating all of Fawn's guards.

Fawn looked around in a panic and said, "Stop. You're right … you're right! I was wrong. Listen to me; we can work this out."

Olov said, "Much better," as he waved his hands across and the men stopped what they were doing.

Fawn was crying in his chair, sobbing like a little child.

Olov said, "You are correct, Fawn. We will work this out when I return you and your men back to Thorne in pieces."

Fawn whimpered. "Please, please, Olov, this isn't necessary. At the very least, can I tell you a story?"

Olov thought about it and drank another shot of vodka. "It's 2:42 in the afternoon. My schedule is clear just so I can torture you guys.... Speak, little man, and amuse me."

Fawn straightened up from his fetal position. He took a second to look around and adjusted his suit. He cleared his throat and inhaled deeply. "When I was a little boy, it was a daily routine for bullies to beat me up in school. 'Fawn, give me your milk money.... Fawn, your wallet fell in the toilet.... Fawn, come here. It's time for your daily wedgie.' For years, this went on, without any help from the teachers or my classmates." Fawn looked away and chuckled as he recalled the anti-bullying campaign they stressed at his school.

Olov looked bored and said, "So far, that doesn't surprise me," as he laughed, and the rest of his men chuckled along.

Fawn said, "Ah yes, I know. I'm the fairy queen of the city. Anyway, I realized that I could work only with the hand I was given. No matter how much I worked out or lifted weights, I would forever remain the skinny Asian guy everyone could pick on. The odds would never be in my favor, but I learned that everything has an equalizer."

Fawn's last statement caught Olov's interest. He shrugged his head and said, "Go on...."

Fawn leaned slightly forward and spoke in a soft voice, "But do you know what I learned from all those years of torture?"

Curiosity got the best of Olov as he leaned forward and placed both hands on the edge of the table. "Nyet, little man. Tell me your idiotic lesson in life."

Olov's men began to advance toward Fawn's seat. Fawn sprang forward and pulled out a butterfly knife in each hand. He spun the knives, the blades hypnotically moving inside and out, and then stabbed both of Olov's hands with authority.

"What the fuck!" screamed Olov. The blood began to pour out of Olov's hands as Fawn's sudden attack took the entire room by surprise. The Russian stood in pain, unable to move, as Fawn had crucified him to the table.

"You see, the lesson of the story ... I needed to find a way to balance the playing field with my own physical limitations." Fawn pressed the knives even deeper into Olov's hands. He cringed in pain and began to shake. Fawn leaned over and whispered into his ear, "Guess what? I found a way...."

As his own guards were frozen from the horror, Olov, who was reeling in pain, shouted, "Kill this son of a bitch!'

Olov's command finally shook the guards out of shock, and they began to run toward Fawn. Fawn smiled devilishly and quickly spun around. He pulled a pair of knives from within his jacket.

Fawn began singing, "I feel pretty, oh so pretty! I feel pretty and witty and gay. And I pity any girl who isn't me today."

Slash here.

Stab there.

Slash and stab everywhere.

The blood was splattering in every direction, forming musical notes in the air. Fawn was slicing up the mobsters like butter as he continued to sing the song until he finished his mission. He pulled a seemingly unlimited array of knives from his coat, stabbing Olov's henchmen without mercy.

Body after body began to drop to the floor as the room quickly changed to a pool of blood. Two guys remained as Fawn stood there, seemingly unarmed. One of the henchmen decided to rush him. Fawn tapped his foot as a blade popped up from the front of his shoe. As the man dove forward, Fawn lifted his leg, stabbing him right in the gut. He dropped immediately, as the piercing was clean and deep.

The last guy panicked and began to run out of the room. Fawn whipped out a throwing knife from within his sleeve like a magician. He spun around and nailed the guy right in the back with his knife. The man dropped to the ground, falling face first with a loud thump.

All this time, Olov was staked onto the table. He was in excruciating pain and continued to swear in Russian.

"You son of a bitch, Fawn, I'm going to kill you!" screamed Olov.

Fawn skipped toward Olov and asked, "If something were to happen to you, who's next in command, Olov?"

"Fuck you, Fawn."

Fawn touched one of the knives that had him pinned to the table. He lifted it slightly to relieve the pressure but then began twisting it within Olov's hand.

The Russian screamed and cracked under the torture. "My cousin! My cousin … Yule is second in command. Yes, yes, Yule."

"Beautiful, can you do me a favor and call him for me?"

Olov nodded toward his pocket, motioning for Fawn to grab the phone.

Fawn reached into his pocket and said, "Olov, is that your phone, or did I just grab a roll of quarters?" After a few seconds of reaching into his pants, he pulled out Olov's phone.

"Now call him," said Fawn.

Olov spoke into the phone. "Give me Yule's phone number." The phone picked up the command and began to dial.

"Hello, this is Yule."

"Do you mind?" Fawn asked Olov sweetly and then held the phone close to his own ear.

"Yule, this is Fawn. I want you to hear something from your cousin Olov." He put the phone by Olov's ear and leaned next to him.

Fawn whispered, "Tell him that he's in command now, and whatever I tell him to do, he does."

"I'm not going to tell him that, you bastard."

Fawn spoke into the phone and said, "Yule, can you hold on for just an itty bitty second?" Fawn placed the phone on the table next to Olov.

"Hmm, that's a shame." Fawn took one of the knives that had Olov pinned down and plucked it out of him. He slammed the knife back into his hand, impaling him again.

"Aaahhhh!" screamed Olov.

Fawn said, "I never ask twice."

Olov said, "Yes, yes … I'll tell him what you said."

Fawn put the phone by Olov's ear again, and he began speaking in Russian. After letting Olov finish his speech, Fawn began to speak with Yule. "Do you understand who's calling the shots, Yule?"

Yule sad, "Yes. Yes, I do."

"Perfect, I'll be in touch. Oh, by the way, Yule, you might want to come down to the bar this afternoon and clean up the mess." Fawn took the phone and threw it away.

"It's been a pleasure doing business with you, Olov. Oh, yes ... that's right."

He slowly drew another knife hidden in his suit. "I feel stunning. And entrancing. Feel like running and dancing for joy. For I'm loved by a pretty wonderful boy!"

As Fawn finished his song, failing miserably to hit the correct note, he spun around with his knife and slit Olov's throat in a blink. The blood squirted all over as he held his pose and lifted his knife in the air. Olov's head dropped to the table, and a mess began to drip all over the wood.

Fawn looked around at his work and smiled, gasping for air. He began walking to the front of the bar and said, "Bitches, get up. What kind of bodyguards are you, for the love of God?" Fawn shook his head, smiled, and began to skip. He was delighted with his handiwork as he hummed the song aloud.

"Mankind can easily justify the atrocities that occur between one another, each one believing that they are right."—Watanabe

SECTION 1

Short Stories #4—Kirin's P.O.V.

The Gift—171 Days

Knock. Knock. Knock.

From behind the door, I could hear the scurrying of feet, and then a familiar voice fought its way through the wooden barrier. "I'm coming!" shouted Sifu. "I'll be right there!"

The door flew open, and a gust of cold air hit Sifu in the face. He said, "Come in, Kirin. Hurry, it's bad outside." He smiled even though he had a somewhat stressed look on his face.

"Wow, Sifu, I don't think I've ever seen you in a suit," I said. I stomped my feet before entering to get the snow off.

"Yeah, I know. I hate it," he muttered as he struggled to adjust his tie properly like a little kid.

"Do you mind if I help you?"

Sifu said, "By all means. The last time I wore this was for a funeral."

I said, "Well, let's hope you don't have too many of those."

Sifu said, "By the way, how'd you learn to tie a tie?"

I giggled and said, "I have four brothers, Sifu. I've helped all of them."

Sifu shook his head. "How is it possible I've mastered Wing Chun, yet I can't put on a simple tie?"

With another giggle, I asked, "So, where are the little ones?"

He rolled his eyes and gestured to look behind him. I leaned over to his side and saw the kids lined up in a single file, tallest to shortest, hiding behind Sifu. Hana smiled her sweet look, and her single tooth beamed out brightly. The twins, Hideo and Akira, stood at attention, all dressed up in their pajamas, giggling and whispering in each other's ear. Suddenly, the twins began to bicker.

Hideo said, "I'm taller than you, Akira."

Akira struggled to keep his position. "No, you are not."

Hideo shouted, "Yes, I am. Mom said I was the first one born."

Akira said, "It doesn't matter. It's tallest first."

Hana turned around and spoke something in Japanese. Both boys stopped in their tracks and begrudgingly got into position.

Sifu said, "Thanks for the last-minute babysitting, Kirin. You sure you can handle this? The twins can be a handful, you know."

I nodded confidently and said, "Sure thing, Sifu. This will be a breeze." I strolled past him and hugged Hana. She squeezed me hard, and I patted both twins on their heads. They were so cute I was about to lean over and pinch their cheeks. However, a spark of glitter caught my eye as Simo came down the stairs in a stunning dress.

"Wow, Simo. You look absolutely incredible," I said. Simo came out wearing an elegant black evening dress. It was simple, but it hugged her well and highlighted all her good features.

"Thanks, Kirin," said Simo. "Now, you have our number if any emergency should occur. Make sure the kids are asleep no later than 9:30, since it's a Saturday."

"Sure thing." I smiled, trying to assure them.

We waved our goodbyes, and I shut the door. I spun around and blurted out, "So, how about some TV?" As I looked around, only Hana was standing in front of me. I peeked over her shoulder, but the twins were nowhere to be found.

Hana shook her head and shrugged her shoulders.

I quickly sprinted to the dining room to see that both the boys were playing with a handful of action figures. I let out a deep sigh of relief. "Hey, guys, do you want to come to the family room and watch TV instead?"

Hideo said, "Kirin, is it okay if we just stay here?" He was grossly captivated playing with his toys.

Akira said, "We promise we will be good, Kirin."

I looked at them, so cute playing with their toys. "Okay. I'll be in the next room watching TV with Hana, okay? So call me if you need anything."

The boys nodded and continued to play with their toys.

I walked in to see Hana lying on the couch, watching TV already. I sat beside her and asked, "What are you watching?"

Hana turned to me with a concerned look on her face. "Uh, Kirin, I don't think it's a good idea to leave the twins by themselves."

"Oh, Hana, don't worry. I can hear them playing right now, and they said they would be good. Besides, they are so cute."

Hana shook her head as she said, "I'm telling you. They behave when my parents are around, but they are literally both demons without them."

I did my best to put Hana at ease as we began getting invested in a silly TV show.

About fifteen minutes later, I realized the TV was all I could hear.

I turned to Hana and asked, "Do you hear that?"

Hana said, "Hear what? It's totally quiet."

"That's what I mean," I replied. I got up and walked over to the dining room with Hana following me. Once there, I saw that their toys were scattered on the table, but the twins weren't there. I wasn't too concerned at first as I called out their names. "Hideo … Akira!"

Hana tugged my shirt and said, "I don't like this."

"Hmm," I said.

"I told you not to leave them behind," said Hana.

"Oh, you're just a worrywart. I'm sure they're just playing hide and go seek."

We searched the living room and then upstairs. I called them several times but still got no response.

Glancing at Hana, I said, "Well, they couldn't have left the house. Where else could they have gone?"

Hana and I both stared at each other and simultaneously said, "The kitchen!"

I dashed down the stairs to see if they were okay. As I turned the corner, I heard a noise that gave me a sense of relief, but suddenly my eyes popped open.

I screeched to a halt, speechless for a moment. Then I screamed, "Oh my God!"

Hana bumped into me and said, "Oh no!"

"What are you doing?" I shouted.

The boys looked up at me with wide eyes. The kitchen was completely covered with flour.

Hideo made puppy dog eyes and said, "I wanted to bake a cake for Dad."

Akira nodded as they both stood innocently looking at me.

I was about to get mad and yell, but it was my fault for not keeping an eye on them. I replied, "Well, were you planning on wearing the cake?"

We spent the next hour cleaning the mess the boys had made. We double checked the kitchen to make sure it was spotless, and I said, "Not bad guys."

The boys looked sad after they had done such a good job cleaning.

"What's wrong?" I asked.

"We didn't get to bake a cake for Dad."

"What's the cake for?"

"We wanted to give it to Dad for Christmas."

I looked around and said, "Well, I think you used all the flour, so it's gonna be difficult to make a cake now."

Hana pulled me aside and said, "Kirin, I have an idea. I'll be right back."

A few minutes later, Hana came back with something in her hand. She proudly presented it to me.

"Uh, what is it?" I asked.

"It's a fanny pack. I saved up to buy it for Dad. I thought it'd be perfect for him to carry all his stuff. Anyway, the twins can help me wrap it and make a card for him."

I looked at the twins, who nodded in excitement.

Hideo said, "That's a great idea!"

Akira said, "Kirin, will you help us wrap it?"

"Sure thing. Just help me find the wrapping paper and tape, and I'll help you with the card."

We spent the next thirty minutes working on our little project. The kids were very proud of all the work they did.

"Kirin, do you want to read what I wrote?" asked Hana.

I said, "Sure, Hana. Read it to me."

UFMF Class—216 Days

There I was, standing on the floor mat with everyone else. Since the UFMF had taken over the school system by bailing it out, little by little they were implementing and selling their classes through our school.

A brand new UFMF class was set up for all students to take. It was humorously entitled the "Voluntary Safety UFMF Self-Defense Course." The moment I heard all this, my eyes rolled like never before—especially since, if you did bypass the class, your grades were affected. Thus, that laughable title couldn't be further from the truth.

Both Sage and I were waiting for our PE teacher to greet us for class, but we were surprised not to see Coach Smith, our regular teacher.

The doors swung open as a well-sculpted, middle-aged man came walking through. He smiled hypnotically; his teeth undeniably white. He said, "Hello, everyone, my name is Coach Stewart. For the next three weeks, I'll be your substitute teacher. I'm a representative of the UFMF, and we hope to get you excited and interested in being part of our organization when you get older. At the very least, we hope you'll be a fan."

I thought, *It's bad enough seeing their ads plastered throughout our school, but this has to be the cherry on top.*

Mr. Stewart said, "Everyone needs to learn how to grapple and fight, so I'll be teaching you the proper techniques of take-downs and choke holds for the first week in Gym. Now a quick show of hands, how many have grappled before?"

I looked around to find almost three-quarters of the room knew some form of grappling. A good chunk of that population were girls.

Sage said, "I'm gonna get my ass handed to me."

For the next several minutes, Mr. Stewart gave us tips on how to deal with a take-down. He was annoyingly pleased, as if by the end of the class we would have to sign over our souls to him. He was demonstrating take-down techniques with one of the students as the rest of us circled to watch.

After doing the demonstration several times, Mr. Stewart turned to the class and asked, "Does anyone have any questions?"

I didn't say anything, and the room remained silent. I was familiar with the technique, having watched both Hunter and my brother during their matches, but it was something I'd never done before.

"Perfect, let's grab a partner and get to work."

After partnering up, I made several lame attempts at doing the sprawl. Mr. Stewart walked up to us and said, "Please show me how you do the sprawl."

"I'm sorry, sir, but it makes absolutely no sense to stand this way and counter his take-down with a sprawl without controlling my own center of gravity."

"I'm sorry. What's your name?"

"Kirin," I said.

"Well, Kirin, it's not too complicated if you listened earlier. This sport is all about leverage and skill."

I replied, "I don't see how this is leverage and skill when I'm using that much muscle."

I could tell my comment didn't sit well with Mr. Stewart, who looked away from me and placed his hands on his hips. He scanned the room briefly and pointed to Tim.

Mr. Stewart said, "Son, what's your name?"

He replied, "Tim."

Mr. Stewart asked, "Aren't you part of the wrestling team here?"

Tim said, "I sure am."

"Well, Kirin here doesn't think the sprawl is an effective technique against the take-down."

I stepped in right away. "I didn't say that."

Tim gave me an evil eye. I only recognized him because he was one of the jerks who had bothered me last year, until Hunter stepped in.

Mr. Stewart said, "Why don't you do a demonstration for the class, so that Kirin can understand?"

Tim said, "I'd be glad to."

Mr. Stewart said, "Now get into position and stop him with the sprawl. See if you can prevent him from pinning you."

I got into position and waited for Tim to move in on me. I did as he said, and because of his size, he quickly took me down and got me to my back. I tried to maneuver out of it, but he began pressing hard, pinning me down.

His weight was pushing against me, making it difficult to breathe, and I looked up to see Mr. Stewart smiling.

He shouted, "Tap out. Tap out!"

I refused to as my partner kept pressing even harder. I started to feel light-headed.

Sage yelled, "You're hurting her!"

Suddenly, Mr. Stewart said, "Okay, stop now, Tim."

I lay on the ground as he got up off me. Sage came rushing to my side to see if I was okay. All the students were laughing at me as Mr. Stewart said, "See, that's what not to do when someone tries to take you down."

I was peeved, to say the least, that he'd used me as the scapegoat for his example.

Mr. Stewart said, "Why don't you partner up with your friend here till you figure this stuff out?"

After School

Annoyed and flustered at what had happened, I didn't even bother to say bye to either Sage or Gwen. I rushed to Sifu's immediately after school.

As soon as I got there, Sifu knew something was wrong.

"Don't even ask, Sifu," I said.

He looked at me and didn't say a word, but his silence was maddening. I had no idea how he did it, but he guilted me into making the first move.

"Ugh, Sifu … I hate it when you do that."

"Do what?" he said.

I shook my head and asked, "I know I'm early. Do you mind if we just chi sao?"

"Not at all."

We began rolling and before a minute had passed, I blurted out, "I got my butt kicked, Sifu, this afternoon grappling."

"Hmm, didn't know you guys had a grappling class."

"Normally we don't, but the UFMF has implemented it into their class schedule, since they've taken over all the public schools."

"So, what happened?"

"Today, we went over take-downs, and they wanted us to work on a sprawl to counter it. Next thing I knew, I was being pinned down, and he tried to force me to tap out. I got into an argument with the UFMF teacher, so he put me with this huge dude to grapple against."

"So, he basically pinned you down right away."

"At first, he couldn't take me down, but then the teacher asked what the heck I was doing, and I tried to explain the basic concept."

"He laughed, didn't he?"

"Yeah, how'd you know?"

"Because what I've taught you makes no sense to others."

I thought, *Well, that's great.*

"So, what are the rules?" asked Sifu.

"Well, there's no kicking or hitting the opponent. For whatever reason, they just want you to grab."

Sifu said, "Perfect. Let me show you something for your next, uh, grappling class."

The Next Day

Mr. Stewart barked, "Do we have any volunteers for today's demonstration?"

The first guy who raised his hands was Tim Miles, the same guy who'd kept pinning me and made me look really bad. He stepped into the middle of the mat and was already trying to stare down anyone who dared enter the ring. The alpha male demonstration was on.

I raised my hand and said, "I'll volunteer."

Sage leaned toward me and whispered, "Uh, Kirin, what are you doing? Remember what happened yesterday?"

"Of course I do. That's exactly why I'm going for seconds."

"You know you didn't have to volunteer for tribute," said Sage.

I whispered, "God, that movie was terrible."

Sage replied, "It's not always the movie, but the quote that counts."

I giggled and punched Sage in the arm. "Funny, just watch and learn, Sage."

Mr. Stewart said, "Ah, good, Ms. Rise is volunteering. Hopefully you've learned from your rebellious attitude from yesterday."

I looked at Mr. Stewart and said, "Yeah, I've learned my lesson, sir!"

Mr. Stewart started mumbling over the lesson again. "Now, keep in mind, when Tim comes in for the take-down, I want a sprawl and for you to be on top of him. And the hips … shoot them out of his grasp, and you'll be able to counter it easily."

Tim got in his grappling pose as I stood several feet away from him. I didn't care what Mr. Stewart was saying, and I just stood naturally and waited for Tim to go in.

From the corner of my eye, I saw Mr. Stewart shake his head.

"What are you doing, Kirin?"

"I'm getting ready to deal with meathead over here … uh, I mean Tim."

The class laughed at my remark, but I knew Tim would easily bite. He would be mentally off balance from the start.

"Well, you are not in the proper position to deal with his advance," said Mr. Stewart.

Without looking at either of them, I said, "I'm pretty sure I am."

Mr. Stewart said, "I thought you had learned your lesson, Kirin."

"Like I said, I have learned my lesson."

Mr. Stewart shook his head and then glanced toward Tim's direction and gave him a signal.

Tim looked at me and said, "Are you ready?" He chuckled with confidence.

I stared directly into his eyes and asked him, "Do you actually know how to spell 'ready'?"

That was the comment I needed to put him over the top. I smiled at him as the memory from yesterday still burned in me.

Mr. Smith shouted, "Go!"

Tim shot for my legs and committed everything into that move. All I saw was his center, and I waited just long enough for him to be unable to counter out of his motion.

I moved in, like I'd always been taught, and I could see him salivating that I was an easy target. His exposed center, especially his head, was ready for the picking.

Once he flew into my range, I jammed his face heavily into the ground with a gum sau. The timing was so perfect that, even with a padded floor, Tim was knocked out cold.

Thud.

The class gasped as Mr. Stewart yelled, "What are you doing?"

I looked at him directly. "Teaching a lesson."

Mr. Stewart looked confused and asked, "What's the lesson?"

"A lesson in karma."

Gun Bill—267 Days

For the last three months since the introduction of the gun bill, United States citizens had existed under martial law for the first time in history. Everyone watched the news daily, but you could look outside your own home and see that things were different. Looking back, the tipping point of the mass killings at the school proved to be more than anyone could stomach. That was the single event that chained the impossible to finally happening. A single headline was ingrained in every mind: "The Day That Could Never Happen."

The early part of the month saw heavy protesting and rioting, but those higher up wanted to boast of the strength of this new enforcement. Soon, protests were no longer allowed, making it clear without a shadow of a doubt that this law was here to stay. The UFMF had a huge hand in this, but their tie-ins and use of their sport distracted people from laying blame. The timing of this new gun law along with the opening of the UFMF season seemed more than coincidental. Everyone knew that when a big UFMF announcement came about, it must be covering up something bad.

The government formed a new Strategic Tactical Defense squad. They were a unique breed, given rights unlike any authoritative figure; in many cases, they functioned as judge, jury, and enforcer. With the implementation of the no-guns rule, cops were reduced in rank as well as weaponry, while the highest maintenance of civil authority lay with the STDs. Outside of the military, the STDs were the only ones now armed with guns.

Several months ago, the STDs were formally introduced to the public. From head to toe, they were clad in riot gear. They were equipped with the highest tech guns, and each had a backpack that could launch multiple mini-drones and help track whomever they wished to. The future we had never once imagined was now forced upon us, and there was nothing anyone could do about it.

I was chatting with Gwen and Sage online as we watched everything unfold before our eyes.

"Can you believe what we are seeing?" I said.

Gwen said, "I can't believe the major networks are just covering useless news along with more promotional ads for the upcoming UFMF fights."

Sage said, "I never thought that this day would happen, where 'America, the land of the free,' was just a billboard saying."

Gwen said, "It's just political rhetoric now. It's been that way for some time."

As the regular TV was streaming, they continued to pump out their propaganda ads stating that it was all "for the protection of our people." The country was so apathetic that if you could come up with a cool catch phrase and ingrain it into the masses, eventually people would swallow it up as the norm. The government was Pavlov, and the masses were a collection of dogs, needing only repetition to be trained.

The news that was being streamed on air was just garbage information. They were painting a pretty picture of the last three months, when all you had to do was look outside of your own window to see the truth.

The mainstream media's information was as valuable as a grain of salt, and the internet was purposely flooded with disinformation to confuse the masses.

Fortunately for us, Gwen knew all the reliable online network sources. It had come to the point where the truth was buried within a ton of lies.

I said, "Guys, turn to channel 8, the regular station." Channel 8 was showing a very peaceful rally being held in front of City Hall.

"Are you seeing this?" I asked.

"It's such BS," said Gwen.

Sage chimed in, "I was there that afternoon, and there was no such protest. Seriously, what a load of crap! It's all staged."

Gwen said, "Give me a second; let me find out."

A few seconds passed as I watched Gwen madly typing to get us some info. Sage was also surfing and looking through other sources.

Gwen said, "Got it. Sage, you were right; my source actually has a recording that this was all paid for. He somehow got a clip of them setting up the fake protest."

I replied, "Dang, how does he get that?"

Gwen said, "He's crazy, but he's always one of the first to post info on what's happening around here."

Sage said, "I'm surprised he hasn't been arrested."

Gwen replied, "Oh, he has … many times, but it kind of just drives him to show what's really happening."

I turned the volume up on the TV as a reporter said, "This peaceful rally is still being held, as government officials want the people to have a voice." I looked at the corner, and they had it time-stamped "live."

Everyone knew that you couldn't rally or protest anymore, but putting a fake video up made it appear that it was all right.

Gwen said, "Guys, look at your other screen."

There on the bottom corner of my computer screen was Gwen's source streaming live as well at the same spot, yet it was empty.

The source said, "As you can see, there is no protest. The area is completely lifeless at the moment." Suddenly, he said, "Oh shit. I'm gonna leave my camera on, so you can see…. Time to split!"

We all turned our attention to Gwen's source as the video feed was shaking from all the action. I could hear him speaking as he began to run.

"…If you're just tuning in, I just got spotted by the STDs, and I'm trying to get the hell out of here because that was a restricted area for filming."

I was glued to the edge of my seat as this was developing right in front of us. I took a quick glance at the other channel, which was now talking about the royals' upcoming new baby to be born.

Sage said, "Wow, this guy can really book."

Gwen responded, "He's just so wild and reckless sometimes, but he's got such a huge following."

I continued to watch the reporter, and the next thing I saw was amazing. He was a parkour guy, and he was leaping from one area to another.

"Damn … I got two of them on me!" he said as he was huffing on the video and struggling to catch his breath.

Sage said, "Damn, I wish I could parkour."

Gwen didn't say a word, as she was watching intently. I could view all of them on their screens, as we had multiple feeds open.

A minute later, the chase suddenly stopped.

"Okay, I'm at one of my hiding spots. I should cut the feed, or else they can trace me, but I just wanted everyone out there to see what's really going on…." He caught his breath and whispered, "I'm pretty sure I lost them, but with those mini-drones serving as multiple eyes, you never know. They're so small now and fly silently."

I looked at the other channels, but everything else was filled with useless information—the royals, the Crackdashigans, and just how everything was hunky dory in the world today.

"Seems like I lost them," he said.

It was so cool to get this perspective of his shot, as he had a 360° camera to capture every angle.

The camera shook. "Get on the ground!" said a strange voice.

"Fuck! How the hell did you find me?"

The strange voice laughed. "The mini-drones, of course."

"What do you mean?"

"You dumb ass, the new versions have thermal vision on them. We saw you hiding and took our time in getting here."

"Okay … okay, you got me. Call the cops, and read me my rights."

"T7-49, did you hear that he wants his rights read to him? Boy, you do know that we're the STDs?"

"Government stupidity, creating a branch above the police and naming it after a disease," he chuckled.

The feed continued to show what was happening. His camera was still rolling.

"Why don't you read him his rights?"

"Ahh!" the informant screamed.

I used my hands to cover my face in shock as they began to beat him.

"Holy crap," said Sage.

We watched the brutal beating for a minute. With the 360° cam perspective, it felt like we were the ones taking the hits.

"You still think you're funny?" the first soldier said as he delivered a final kick to the gut.

"Fuck, T7-49," said the other soldier.

His hand grabbed the camera. "Fucking A, you didn't check to see if he had a feed."

Suddenly the screen went blank, and we all sat there silently. I was in shock.

One of the channels flashed, and the sound went up. "So, what do you think, America? Will the royals be blessed with a girl or a boy?"

I shook my head in disbelief and wondered how this could be. Why did people waste their time with such useless garbage?

It made me think. At what point did people become apathetic and let evil rule? Gwen, Sage, and I continued to watch the news. Suddenly a new ad popped up.

"The United States government along with the UFMF have one simple goal: to keep the world out of harm's way and to protect every man, woman, and child.

"Hi, I'm Jacob Thorne, the president of the UFMF. I'd like to take a moment to thank all the citizens of this great country for upholding and respecting our newest law.

"The Strategic Tactical Defense teams are here to serve you.

"Keep in mind the UFMF is here to help make this great country of ours even better. Join the UFMF, and you too could be the next Dome Champion of the world."

"Look at both sides before passing judgment; otherwise, you'll end up being blind to the truth."—Sifu

SECTION 2

Sifu's Journey Entry #4—Universal Harmony/ The Day After, Part 3

Dream Continued (The Next Day)

Sifu slowly opened his eyes, rubbing them several times to regain focus. Once he had, there wasn't much to see, as the only thing before him was a blank white ceiling. It had been a long night—a fun night all beginning with a single dance that led him to where he was this very morning. This was something he could declare outside the box, as he found himself stretching in an unfamiliar bed.

As he pieced things together, he realized he wasn't alone, and this definitely wasn't his apartment. He turned gently to his right. There, like an angel asleep in the bed, was Megumi. The sun's rays from the side window highlighted her features as he stared at her, studying and memorizing the shape of her face and the flow of her hair. He smiled and felt inclined to give her a kiss on her forehead.

Before he could lean over and deliver it, her eyes blinked open, and she smiled back at him.

"I'm sorry. I didn't mean to wake you up," said Sifu as he continued to be lost staring at Megumi.

"It's okay. I usually wake up early. It must've been a long night." Megumi giggled.

Sifu smiled and said, "Hopefully, it was long enough."

The two chuckled as they lay in bed together.

Sifu said, "You know … I was thinking, if you're not busy this morning, I was wondering if you'd like to grab some breakfast."

"Hmm," said Megumi, as the idea of spending more time with Sifu intrigued her. "That's not a bad idea."

Sifu was curious what Megumi had in mind. "Is there something else you'd rather do?"

"I think I had some good ideas last night," she said jovially.

Sifu laughed, slightly embarrassed as a quick flashback of last night's events popped into his head. He quickly snapped out of it and said, "You don't have to sell me.... I'm listening."

Megumi leaned forward and whispered, "Why don't you and I find the best ramen in Chicago?"

Sifu's eyes lit up as he said, "Oh, yeah. Definitely. I'm all game for that, but it's too early. It'll be a while before the ramen shops open up around here."

"You're right. It'll be a while," said Megumi.

"What are we gonna do in the meantime?"

Megumi smiled and gently caressed Sifu's face, answering his question with a kiss. It was an obvious invitation that he couldn't refuse.

An Hour Later

Sifu's head sank deep in between the pillows. It was like déjà vu, as he found himself staring up at the ceiling yet again. Sifu turned toward Megumi and said, "Hmm ... I don't think this day could possible get any better."

Megumi smiled, leaned forward, and delivered a kiss on Sifu's forehead. "I think you're losing your touch ... because you're wrong about that." She pulled away and began to get up as she put on a long, oversized T-shirt and tied her hair in a ponytail. She turned to look at Sifu, who was still in bed. "It's about to get better."

Sifu sat up with a curious look on his face. "So, should I try finding another ramen place through the internet? Or do you feel more adventurous and we should just travel wherever the force takes us today?"

"I don't think we have to do either ... because I can tell you, Mr. All-Knowing," she said cynically, "that what you're looking for is right here."

Sifu was confused as he stared at Megumi, who was looking as cute as ever. She turned quickly as her hair flowed through the air, once again mesmerizing him. At this point, Sifu didn't care what they did, as long as he was with Megumi.

"You got me. I am confused."

With a devilish smile, Megumi headed toward her kitchen. "Maybe you should put something on while I explain."

Sifu nodded and began following Megumi to the kitchen. As he put on his clothes, he said, "I thought you told me you helped make the ramen in the back ... and that you thought it was quite bad."

"I did, but how they want me to do it is not how I was taught to make it," she said smugly.

"Wait a second. You know how to make ramen? I didn't know that."

"By the end of the day, you're gonna find there's a lot you didn't know. And, yes, you could say I know how to make ramen."

She turned and grinned, adding, "Do you want to help me, or are you gonna be hopping around with one leg in your pants all day?"

Sifu nodded as Megumi sprang into action. She dashed back and forth from pantry to refrigerator, gathering ingredients to prepare the soup. Megumi started moving about, cutting, sipping, and preparing the ramen right in front of Sifu's eyes.

Sifu was amazed by her movement. This was not the first time she'd ever done this, as there was no hint of hesitation in anything that she was doing. He could tell right away that she was trained, possibly at a very young age, since her motion was so precise and natural.

As Sifu sat and stared, Megumi was stirring the pot. "So," she said, "I've finally decided what I want to call you."

"And that is?"

"I like Bing. At first, I wasn't sure exactly what it meant, but after hearing it a couple more times … I think it is pretty unique," said Megumi as she continued stirring the pot.

Sifu said, "No one ever calls me that … even my parents stopped calling me Bing after a while."

Megumi adjusted her hair and gave a quick glance toward Sifu. "Then it's decided. I'm calling you Bing from now on."

"That's a good thing," said Sifu as he slipped behind Megumi, placing his hands on her waist and giving her a kiss on the cheek. She leaned over, appreciating the affection.

Finally, Sifu sat back down and started watching her cook. Several minutes passed, and Sifu remained quiet while Megumi worked on her broth, making sure everything was just right.

Megumi broke the silence and said, "You're reading me again, aren't you?"

"Sorry about that…. It just kinda comes about naturally."

"Okay, amuse me. Go ahead and ask," said Megumi.

Sifu paused for moment and chose his words carefully. "So … someone had to teach you this and without having to be a great detective, I'm assuming it's your dad."

Megumi stopped what she was doing and then turned around. "You are correct. You were right last night, and your deduction is also correct. I was the only child, and my dad is a pretty famous ramen chef in Japan. He wanted to pass down his skills to me to continue his work … eventually."

"And so that's why you're here right now?" said Sifu.

Megumi walked toward the table and leaned forward. Her eyes pierced Sifu's as she said, "I bet you think my father is right, don't you? That I should be a good little girl and follow in his footsteps."

Sifu looked Megumi straight in the eye and said, "No. Not at all. There's no doubt you're very skillful and talented, but there is also no doubt that your passion lies elsewhere."

Megumi was surprised by his words and pulled back. "Again, you continue to surprise me."

"It's part of the skill to keep your opponent constantly off balance."

Megumi murmured, "I'm surprised you'd say that…. You seem like the traditional type of guy."

Sifu continued, "I believe you have one thing to be great at during this lifetime—something you should devote all your time and effort to so you can master it. The point of life is to live your dream, not your father's or anyone else's. Failure to do so will lead to an imbalance. Like I've always told my students, 'Find yourself, love yourself, and always be you.'"

Megumi was touched by his words and came around the table to kiss Sifu on the head. She leaned toward his ear and whispered, "Thanks … I needed to hear that."

45 Minutes Later

Sifu had cleaned and prepared the table. He sat patiently, as he enjoyed watching Megumi move about.

"You're lucky I had much of this prepped. Normally it'd be an all-day process," said Megumi.

"I think I've been lucky since last night."

Megumi giggled and said, "Okay, Mr. Funny Man," as she stared at Sifu, "it's ready. I hope you're hungry."

Megumi was carrying a steaming bowl. Sifu watched the steam rise, enjoying every second of it. Megumi sat down opposite of Sifu and just stared.

"Tabete kudasai … that means, 'please eat.'"

Before trying the ramen, Sifu mumbled in Japanese, "Itadekimasu."

Megumi stopped for a moment and asked, "Do you know the meaning of that?"

"I think I do," said Sifu.

"Hmm, if you think you do, then you probably don't. Remind me to tell you its meaning later on," said Megumi. "It's important."

He thought briefly and muttered to himself, *It's not thanks for the food?*

Sifu shook it off and stared at the soup. It looked different from anything he had ever laid eyes on before. The color was rich, the smell unknown, and he felt guilty disturbing this work of art. Eventually, his guilt was overshadowed by his curiosity about the taste. He grabbed his spoon and slowly scooped up the broth, blowing on it. He took a moment to look at Megumi, who was resting her head on both hands watching him. His lips finally touched the broth as he sipped it down.

A big grin started forming on his face. He took a full sip of just the broth and began shaking his head. "Oh my God. I had no idea.... I didn't know!"

Megumi knew from his reaction that Sifu was genuine in his response. She said, "To know good ramen, you have to taste it and experience it."

"This is just incredible!" He shook his head. "I can never go back."

Megumi smiled and said, "Are you talking about just the soup?"

Sifu shook his head and said, "What do you think?"

Megumi blushed and looked away, showing a hint of a smile at Sifu's words.

Sifu said, "Wait a second ... this might not a be a fair comparison. I've always said, the best meal you can ever have is right after...."

"Hmm, have you had that many great meals?" She leaned forward, curious of his answer.

"I've had two ... but nothing compares to this meal."

Megumi smiled. "You weren't afraid to tell me, and you didn't hesitate."

"Like I told you last night, I would never lie to you."

"So, do you believe that's why the soup tastes so good?"

"Well, I'm just saying we did build up an appetite. I'm just trying to be fair and impartial." He picked up the bowl and finished the last drop of soup. He grabbed a napkin and wiped his mouth. "That was simply incredible." He shook his head in disbelief.

"Are you done?" Megumi asked.

"Yes ... why?"

"Well, this meal isn't for free."

"What's the cost?"

Megumi got up from behind the table and sat on Sifu's lap. She gave him a deep kiss on the lips. She leaned toward his ear and whispered, "Guess...."

▲ ▲ ▲

Speaker Interrupts Sifu's Dream

"This is your captain speaking. Flight 48 is landing at Narita Airport in about thirty minutes. Arigatou gozaimasu."

Sifu took a deep breath and looked outside. He could see the city lights as the plane began its descent. His heart felt heavy, as he realized it was just a dream. He shed a tear, knowing that all he had now were dreams and memories of Megumi.

CHAPTER 5

Forced to Fight

First Week of May

I t was early evening, and Kirin, Sifu, and Angelo were hanging in her loft. Kirin was by her wooden dummy, practicing the form as the sounds of flesh pounding against the wood made Angelo flinch. The dummy was made of solid wood, about the same size as a human opponent. It was a training tool used by Wing Chun practitioners to develop their skill. Sifu was resting on the couch nearby, watching TV.

Angelo leaned cautiously over her windowsill, expecting to see a huge crowd waiting outside her loft area, but he was surprised to see it fairly thin.

"Hmm, what gives? It's surprisingly empty outside your place tonight. Where are all the fans?"

Kirin stopped for a second, grabbed a towel by the side of her dummy, and said, "Wow, can't believe that's working."

"What's working?" asked Angelo, as he worried that her popularity was dwindling.

"So, genius Gwen thought of a way to post pictures on my social media account at various locations. Last week, I went with Sage to various locations and took snapshots of me as well as video. Anyway, she's found a way to cheat the system. I post the pic, tag the location, and the next thing you know...."

"Ah, Gwen ... she's brilliant and also has excellent taste in clothes. Oh, uh .... anyway, the pics you take have everyone chasing a location somewhere in Chicago, and when you post it, they go chasing for you," chuckled Angelo.

"Yup, you got it. I feel kinda bad doing it to the fans ... but seriously, people should be focused more on their own lives instead of mine."

Angelo pulled out his phone and went to Kirin's account. He saw her most recent pic had a location pinned in the northwest suburbs of Niles. "Niles?" said Angelo. "I don't know about you, but why would anyone believe you went to Niles just thirty minutes ago?"

Kirin pulled out her phone to verify and began scrolling through the comments. "See for yourself. Check out the rants."

Angelo did as she said and began laughing. "It's so crazy! There's so much misinformation trying to hunt you down. It's unbelievable."

"Yeah, so usually an hour later after they can't find me, I post another pic at a relatively close location."

Angelo laughed even more. "Brilliant. Just brilliant." He looked down to see Bacon resting by the side of his foot.

Sifu faked a cough and said, "How come I hear only yapping?"

Kirin glanced at Sifu and then hustled back to work on the dummy form. She paused for a moment, shaking her head at the sense of déjà vu. For the next twenty minutes, the banging of her hands against the dummy continued. During that time, Sifu was fixated on the TV, and Angelo was busy planning Kirin's schedule for the week.

Kirin let out a breath and then finally stopped. She turned around to see that Sifu was still engrossed by the screen.

"Cough." She made a fake sound to get someone's attention as she waited for a response.

Sifu ignored her, watching TV.

"Mmmh." Kirin made a fist and covered her mouth once more.

Sifu finally said, "Yes?"

"I know you're busy … but I could use some instruction here."

"What do you mean?"

"Well, I'm busy working on improving my form, and you're busy watching TV," said Kirin.

"I have been giving you instructions. It's called letting you figure out what you are doing wrong."

A confused look came over her face, as she was positive Sifu hadn't checked her once. "Uh, are these instructions coming later? And besides, I thought I was doing pretty well on the dummy."

"Are you talking about the last twenty minutes?"

"Yeah," said Kirin confidently.

"Oh, yeah, those last twenty minutes were completely off."

"What? But you didn't even watch me do the form!"

"I didn't need to."

"And, why is that?"

"I could hear everything." Sifu grabbed a snack by his side and continued to munch and watch.

Kirin scratched her head and looked back and forth between the wooden dummy and Sifu. "Okay, I know you can do all these cool things, but now you have some kind of super hearing?"

"Nothing super about it," said Sifu nonchalantly.

"Explain?"

"When you hit the dummy, it makes a particular sound," said Sifu.

Kirin raised an eyebrow and asked, "What sound is that?"

"Judging from the last twenty minutes of you practicing, that would be someone who's chasing the hands."

Kirin frowned. "Why didn't you say I was chasing hands?"

Sifu looked toward Kirin and said, "In order to know right, you must experience wrong.... Besides, I was hoping you'd figure it out on your own."

"How is that a good thing?"

"Isn't self-awareness more fulfilling than someone else telling you?"

Kirin thought for a moment and said, "I guess...."

"Anyway, I thought I already told you that we always target the center."

"I know that," said Kirin.

"You may know that, but it sure didn't sound like that," said Sifu.

"Seriously. Do you do this to torture me?"

Sifu leaned back and said, "Unless you can find something more entertaining on TV for me, then the answer is yes." He smiled and chuckled.

Kirin hit the dummy several times before turning around again. "What sound was that?"

Sifu said, "Someone who hasn't learned her lesson yet."

"Ugh, I could use some instruction, Sifu ... please?"

Sifu said, "What's the target?"

"Center!" shouted Kirin.

Sifu said, "Do the first move of the dummy form."

Kirin turned around and did as Sifu had asked. She hit the dummy and turned around.

"Chasing."

"Ugh," she groaned in frustration. "You didn't even look."

"I don't have to. I can hear it. Remember?" Sifu said, "Pay attention to where your hands are going. Is it to the arms or straight to the center?"

Kirin focused for a moment and then hit the dummy again.

Sifu asked, "Center or arms?"

Kirin hung her head and said, "Arms."

Sifu said, "Yup, that last one definitely screamed, 'Wrong!' To the target, Kirin. To the target. Remember, center, target, own it."

Kirin asked, "What did you just say?"

Sifu replied, "Just focus toward the center."

Kirin took a moment to compose herself and let out a deep breath. She finally performed the first motion as the sound of her arms colliding with the dummy rang through her loft.

"Good, that's it."

Kirin turned around quickly and noticed Sifu was still watching TV.

"Again? Focus on the target ... the center," Sifu called.

Kirin hit the dummy again. She muttered, "Target, center ... own it."

"That's it. Do you hear that?"

Kirin wasn't quite sure, as she played around with the dummy some more. For the next minute, every time she would hit the dummy, Sifu would respond.

"Right, right, wrong, right, wrong ... right, right, right."

She paused and thought for a moment as she made a funny face with her mouth. "Hmm, there is a difference.... How come you never told me about this?"

Sifu grabbed another bite and said, "Because you never asked."

"You know, I knew you'd say that," said Kirin.

"Then why'd you ask?" said Sifu.

Kirin replied, "Oh, I don't know. Maybe I just wanted to hear you say it." She leaned against the dummy and touched the smooth surface of the wood. "Anyway, how could I be mad? This is your dummy you gave me."

"Take good care of it."

"You've given me too much, Sifu. Besides, this is your baby. You said yourself you've had this forever."

Sifu still didn't turn around. "There's no such thing as forever. Anyway, it's your turn to take care of her."

Kirin was saddened by his comment. She walked over to Sifu and said, "Why are you watching TV? It's always a bad thing when you do that."

"I'm watching TV to catch this." Sifu turned up the volume louder.

Kirin, Sifu, and Angelo stared at her screen as Thorne was being interviewed on TV.

"With us today is the president of the United Federation of Mixed Fighting, Jacob Thorne. Thanks for spending some time with us to talk about the upcoming season."

Thorne smiled, and he seemed more comfortable than the reporter interviewing him. "Thanks for having me here today, Greg."

Greg responded, "It's hard to believe that anything could be bigger than it was for the UFMF last year, but here we are just a mere two months away, and the anticipation is mindboggling. What do you attribute this to?

Thorne said, "I think this is a perfect example of a company prioritizing the customer first. When you keep that as the foundation everything else is built upon, then success immediately follows."

Kirin looked at Angelo, shaking her head as she rolled her eyes. He did the same, and they laughed together.

Greg added, "The numbers are staggering, with every match from all four locations already sold out—and that's only taking into account domestic numbers. As for products and advertising being sold, you've nearly tripled the demand. But, with all the good, one has to wonder about the bad, and I'm gonna play devil's advocate."

Thorne smiled and looked directly at Greg. "Come on, Greg. You make it sound like the devil's a bad thing."

Greg said, "The anticipation for the new season is huge, but the status of Kirin Rise for 2033 is unknown. Reports have stated that there's a strained relationship between the UFMF and Ms. Rise; is this true? Also, if by chance she decides not to enter the 2033 season, how will that affect the numbers?"

Thorne answered immediately, "I can tell you those rumors of a strained relationship are false. The UFMF places value in the fans as well as its own employees. We treat employees just like family. In fact, I wholeheartedly believe this is something that we internally promote as well as achieve."

"So, you've never had any run-ins at all with Kirin Rise?" asked Greg.

"None whatsoever. At most, you could say we've had some spirited debates." Thorne chuckled at his own words.

"Have you spoken with Kirin about the upcoming season?"

"All fighters have two more weeks to file. As of now, she is the last one to declare her eligibility for the league. Now, this is not unusual that last year's Dome Champion will take some time to decide."

"Will sales be hurt if she decides not to enter?"

"I don't believe so." Thorne adjusted himself in the seat.

Greg leaned forward and pulled out his tablet. He said, "Numbers show that Kirin Rise attributed for almost 40% of product sales last year. You don't believe her not entering the league this year would have any impact at all?"

Thorne stayed cool and leaned forward, which caused Greg to lean back. "Greg, you have to understand that, while Kirin Rise was extremely popular for us last year, much of the anticipation we believe is on the latest changes and the global expansion that the UFMF has implemented for this year."

"Fair enough. Can you speak of some of the changes that the league has set?"

Thorne said, "Well as you know this years' championship will be held in Los Angeles, but I'm gonna start with the biggest news for the UFMF. The league is in phase one of gaining global exposure for the UFMF. Three countries will be running their own leagues simultaneously along with the UFMF. Japan, South America, and the United Kingdom all have a league setup similar to ours. The only difference is they'll decide on their independent champion a month before we set up our round robin event in the States for the Dome."

"Incredible, you said this is only phase one. Can you explain?"

"It's a five-year process, where we will include several more countries into the league each year. Thus, for phase two, we currently have China, Korea, and Germany all lined up to join. It's a complicated process to work the schematics of this so that it's integrated smoothly into the original event, which is the Dome."

Greg asked, "So, if I understand you correctly, a month before the round robin selection occurs for the Dome, there will be three champions already determined from the outside countries?"

Thorne said, "That's correct. We felt integrating foreign and domestic matches throughout the season would just be too taxing on the fighters. Thus, we didn't want to give an unfair advantage based on traveling from one country to another, just because of a fight."

Greg asked, "So, are you expanding the brackets for the round robin with the addition of three new fighters?"

Thorne said, "Yes, we are."

Greg held out his hand and begin doing computations in front of Thorne. "Hmm, now, I'm not a math genius, but won't you be short one entry to make it even?"

Thorne looked at the camera as his voice emphasized his excitement. "Well, Greg, that's just another new exciting element that I wanted to mention about the UFMF this year. Because of Kirin Rise and her unknown status in the league last year, we've decided to create an open reality-based event for that final slot."

"How so?" asked Greg.

"You can call it a battle royal. Twenty slots open to any unregistered fighter in the league. Twenty go in at the same time, and the last man standing is rewarded with 100,000 credits and a slot in the Dome round robin."

"Wow, this is really unexpected news! When was this planned, and who came up with it?" asked Greg.

"I came up with the idea at the end of the 2032 season, and we decided to implement it this year. I honestly believe the closeness that people felt with Kirin, an underdog from out of the blue, rising to the top, could be captured again with this open-invitation battle royal."

"And you mentioned to me earlier you had one more surprise?"

"Well, this I wouldn't call a surprise ... but, as you know, the three-time champion Dryden Rodriguez is set to return for 2033. We've been previewing him training, and he looks ... in a word, unstoppable."

Kirin shouted, "TV off."

The screen went dark, and silence filled the loft until Angelo said, "You have about thirty minutes to get ready before Bryce gets here."

Kirin grabbed her towel and wiped up. "Cool, five minutes to shower and get ready."

Angelo mumbled, "Five minutes ... what girl preps in five minutes? You are using soap, right?"

Kirin rushed to her room and, just like clockwork, was ready in five minutes.

Angelo stared at the result of her effort and said, "Yeah, that looks like five minutes."

Kirin gave Angelo that look. "Angelo, do you mind? I need a couple of minutes with Sifu alone. Do you think you can make some coffee or...?"

"I get the hint. You don't have to tell me twice, but you've got twenty minutes, just so you know."

Sifu sat silently and looked at Kirin.

"You know I hate when you do that."

"Do what?"

"You know exactly what I'm talking about," Kirin said flatly.

"Honestly, I don't."

Kirin pointed at Sifu. "Ha … this time I got you. You never lie, but now you are."

"Well, I guess you do have me this time."

"Finally. I must be getting better at this."

"How'd you guess I'm hungry?"

"Ugh. It's not that." Kirin pouted and realized that Sifu was playing more games. She sat silently and stared at him, waiting.

"Oh, come on. You really want me to begin this conversation?" Kirin stared at Sifu, who smiled and waited.

"Fine. Fine … I'll begin it … like always."

"You see," said Sifu. "Why break the pattern?"

Kirin made a funny face as she realized that he was right; they always followed the same pattern.

Then, just as she opened her mouth, Sifu said, "So, is this about Tobias and Hunter?"

Kirin snapped back, taken by surprise. Her eyes widened as she mimicked an overacted Korean drama. "What…? That's not what I wanted to discuss at all!"

Sifu began walking toward her living room couch. "Why not? To have balance, everyone needs to love and be loved."

"Sifu, I just don't have time for that right now." Kirin followed him to that section of her loft, fumbling for the right words. "Why bring that up all of a sudden?"

Sifu ignored her question and said, "You don't have time, or you're afraid to deal with the situation. One is the truth, and the other is a lie."

Kirin insisted it was not the latter as she sat across from Sifu and did not say another word.

"Okay, okay … I can see you don't want to talk about this at all, but can I just say one last thing?" asked Sifu.

Kirin looked away but mumbled, "Go ahead, Sifu. I'm all ears."

"Kirin, while I know you are busy trying to save the world, don't forget that one should make time … in fact, one's priority should always be to invest in love."

"Sifu, honestly, there's just too much going on."

Sifu put his hands up and said, "That's my two cents. I'm leaving it at that."

Kirin thought for a moment as the room stayed silent. She looked gently at Sifu and said, "You've always told us to make love a priority."

Sifu nodded. "Aye, you don't want to turn your back on it, when the opportunity presents itself."

Kirin daydreamed for a second as she saw an image of her parents. She shook herself out of her trance and said, "I can't right now, Sifu. I have more pressing matters. And that's the real reason I wanted you to come by tonight. I want your thoughts on Bryce Adams."

Kirin stood up and began to pace. "You know I thought, after the fight, things would be a lot clearer. In fact, I thought there would be a domino effect of things falling perfectly in place. But, now I find myself more lost and more confused than ever. Why is that?"

Sifu was about to open his mouth when Kirin continued to rant.

"Seriously, I don't know what to do, what people want me to do. I haven't a clue. I don't know if I'm gonna join up for the next season or not. I don't know if I should help this Bryce Adams guy in making a movement for change. I'm completely clueless, Sifu."

Sifu looked up and asked, "And, that's different how?"

Kirin was about to give Sifu the look, but she caught herself and realized he had a valid point.

"A little help, please?"

Sifu let out a sigh and stood. "Kirin, I'm here like always to help you, but I'm not here to pick your path. That's always for you to decide."

Kirin asked, "Well, I'm a voice and, from what people tell me, a big voice. But, what does that mean? Am I gonna start some kind of revolution or something?"

Sifu said, "Hmm, a movement, a change for the better. Something everyone wants, but does everyone really need it?"

"What do you mean, Sifu?"

"I had to learn the hard way that you can't make the change through an act of violence. History has shown it, and karma makes sure we don't forget it." Sifu stepped toward the TV and turned it back on. Immediately, the news was flashing on the screen, as more violence erupted from some part of the world. Sifu gestured to the TV and said, "Kirin, you can't have change by forcing it."

Angelo tiptoed back into the conversation. He coughed to have his presence known and then said in a high-pitched voice, "I hate to interrupt this powwow, but you've got five minutes before Bryce is about to ring that doorbell."

Both Kirin and Sifu looked at Angelo. He avoided the direct eye contact, held his hand to signal five more minutes, and slowly retreated back to his seat in the kitchen.

Ten Minutes Later

Ding Dong. Ding Dong.

Angelo stood up in excitement. Like a little dog wagging his tail, he shouted, "It's him. Bryce is here. It's him!" He rushed to the door and straightened his outfit.

Kirin rolled her eyes as Bacon rushed to the door and began barking.

"Quiet, boy!" Kirin stamped toward Bacon, but as usual he ignored her. She pressed on the intercom and said, "Just come up to the fifth floor, 5B."

"Sure thing," said Bryce through the mic.

Kirin stood by the door along with Angelo, waiting for the sound of inevitability.

Knock. Knock.

They were both caught off guard as they jumped from the sound and looked at one another. Angelo rushed to open the door, as Kirin snapped at him, "I should do that."

"You sure? I don't mind." His hands were inches from turning the knob.

They looked at each other, wondering what was the proper etiquette. All along Sifu remained on the couch, unconcerned with the current guest. He leaned back and reached for the remote, turning on the TV.

Kirin said in a panic, "Fine. I'll do it. You hold Bacon so he doesn't jump."

Angelo nodded and did as he was told.

Kirin opened the door, catching a glimpse of Bryce in his suit. A typical exchange of greetings occurred as Kirin suggested that they have their meeting in her kitchen.

"You came by yourself?" asked Kirin as she led the way through her loft.

"I usually do. I don't like being seen with a huge entourage of yes-men, if you know what I mean, even though my PR guy constantly insists."

Kirin looked at Angelo, who smiled gaily at her.

"By the way, I don't think I've ever introduced you to my teacher. This is Sifu."

"Ah, the pleasure is all mine." He moved toward Sifu and extended his hand for Sifu to shake.

Sifu waved his hand from a distance but remained on the couch. Kirin looked at him, wondering why he was being so aloof.

"Uh, Sifu, can you join us in the kitchen?"

Sifu got up and joined the group at their little meeting.

"So, can I get you anything?" asked Kirin.

"I'm good, Kirin. Thank you.... Besides, I know you don't like to waste time, so I'll get right to the point." Bryce smiled and looked at everyone gathered at Kirin's counter.

"As you may or may not know, next week, we're holding a rally at the Southport location in Chicago."

"Why there?" asked Kirin as she thought that was a strange choice for the rally.

"I figured it would be a reminder of where we currently are. Anyway, while I have a pretty huge following who plans on going there in about a week, my advisors recommended that if a figure such as yourself were, by chance, to be there, we could pack the rally protest to an unbelievable number."

Kirin looked away and pondered the possibilities. "You know, the last time I took a political stand, it didn't go that well—if you remember."

"I remember, but I also told you it takes a while for people to accept the truth. And, let's face it: even if you did end up annoying a good chunk of America, they still love you."

Kirin looked at Sifu, who didn't say a word. Then she snapped her fingers and pointed at Bryce. "Wait! How can you do this? I thought it was illegal to protest."

"You are correct and aware as always, Kirin. However, the protest initially for the gun bill ranged in the thousands. With numbers comes power, and right now we're looking to have about 30,000 people come to this rally."

"You could get arrested."

"Kirin, there's always a price to pay when you want to do something you believe in."

Those words hit Kirin immediately. "But, what would I say?"

Bryce said, "My advisors said to give you a speech ... but I believe you work better just going with the flow. Am I right about you?"

Kirin thought about it, but didn't speak.

Bryce added, "Just say what you feel. Speak from your heart."

"You're gonna trust me to shoot out a political rant on the fly?"

"I believe you can do it. I believe you know what's on your mind and in your heart. Anyway, I hate to put you on the spot, but if you can tell me in the next two days, that would be much appreciated."

Kirin didn't say a word as Angelo jumped up and extended his hand. Angelo said, "We will definitely think about it." He shoved Kirin by the shoulder to snap her out of her daze.

"Uh, yeah. Sure. I'll think about it."

Suddenly a foul odor engulfed their meeting area. Everyone covered their noses and began waving the air around them. All eyes focused on Bacon, who was still asleep through the ordeal.

"Sorry about that … Bacon can get excited sometimes." Kirin waved her hand, trying to clear the air.

Angelo pinched his nose. "But, he's asleep."

Kirin said, "Maybe he's excited in his dream."

Bryce leaned toward to Bacon and rubbed him vigorously. Bacon moaned and enjoyed the petting, but still did not bother to open his eyes. "Well, I can take a hint. By the way, regardless of what you decide to do, I appreciate the time you've given to me," said Bryce.

Kirin nodded.

Bryce extended his hand to Kirin. "Whatever you do, promise me that you'll at least think about it, won't you?"

Kirin shook his hand and smiled as Bryce winked at her and went on his way.

Kirin closed the door and turned around to see both Sifu and Angelo staring at her.

"Well, I think that went well, don't you?" said Kirin.

"Most definitely." Angelo clapped his hands in excitement.

Kirin asked, "So, what do you think of him, Sifu?"

Sifu was in no rush to judge and gave a very bland answer. "He's an interesting guy."

Again, reading Sifu was impossible for Kirin. She attempted to dig further with some questions. "Do you mean interesting good or interesting bad?"

"No, I just mean interesting."

Kirin thought, *Of course, he's staying neutral.*

Angelo interrupted and said, "Kirin, he left his phone here."

"Crap," said Kirin. "Here, let me have it…. He's probably still close by. I can chase him down."

Angelo said, "Maybe I should do that."

"No, it's okay. What you can do is update my location, so I can sneak out of here."

Angelo nodded and said, "That I can easily do."

▲ ▲ ▲

A few minutes later, Bryce was enjoying the spring weather as he walked down the streets of Chicago. Portions of the town still reminded Bryce of what Chicago used to be, as he found himself dreaming of future possibilities. It motivated him to push further that hope still existed.

But, reality quickly set in. Only a block away, he could see what state it was in now. It burned in Bryce as he wondered why it had to be this way.

As he continued his walk, a large SUV pulled up by his side and screeched to halt. He turned to wonder why the urgency, but then immediately continued on his way.

Several gentlemen all dressed in dark suits jumped out of the vehicle and approached him. He kept his cool and calculated the situation.

"Can I help you?" asked Bryce cautiously.

"Mr. Bryce, our boss would like to have a word with you." The gentleman who spoke gestured for him to get into the vehicle.

Bryce said, "Who might your employer be, if you don't mind my asking?"

"Actually, I do mind, and I suggest we don't dillydally any longer if you know what's good for you."

"Well, gentlemen—and I do use that term loosely—I'm kinda busy tonight. Perhaps another time." Bryce smiled and began to sidestep his obstacle. The two men in front of him stood their ground while the other associate shadowed him.

The gentleman took it in stride as Bryce began to go around him. He nodded as everything seemingly was okay.

The man behind Bryce said, "Mr. Adams?"

Bryce turned toward the voice and said, "Yes?"

As he turned, the man swung toward his gut with an upper cut and Bryce fell to his knees in pain.

"Okay, fellas, drag Mr. Smart Mouth into the car," he barked. Two of the henchmen grabbed Bryce, who lay limp, toward the car.

"Hurry up, will ya?" shouted the lead guy as he scanned around to make sure no one was watching.

The two henchmen had him halfway into the car as they complained. "Geez, for a thin white guy, he sure weighs a lot."

"Dumb ass, it has nothing to do with his weight. It's coz he's all limp."

"What do you mean?"

"Yah never had to deal with a drunk guy before?"

"Of course I have!"

"Well, it's the same thing."

"So he's drunk?"

"No he's not drunk...."

The lead henchman shouted, "Will you idiots shut the hell—?" Suddenly, as he was in mid-speech, he was thrown from behind and flew against the wall. A figure in a red hoodie stood there, back against the car, watching the henchman crash down to the ground.

This stunned the other two henchmen, who were holding Bryce. The stranger turned around and removed the hoodie from her head.

Kirin had a devilish look on her face as she said, "If you don't want to end up like your friend over there ... I suggest you let him go and be on your way."

The two henchmen looked at each other, surprised to see who was in their presence. The driver came out as well as another henchman from the passenger side. Kirin analyzed the situation. She was confronted by at least four guys.

"Well, well, well, it seems to be a celebrity night."

The other henchmen snickered at his comment.

"You know, Ms. Rise, I always wondered if you were really as tough as you seemed in the Dome."

Kirin cracked her neck and looked at them. "So, we're all in agreement?" Kirin waited to see their reaction, and it was confirmed. "Time to whip out those medical cards, boys."

"You cocky bitch!" said the one thug just within kicking range.

As the last sound of his insult finished, Kirin rushed into her closest opponent and began unleashing hell. The guy with the smart mouth tasted her fist. Kirin swung a straight punch through him as the force knocked him into the car and his head cracked the window.

The guy furthest from her was rounding the car, as the other two thugs dropped Bryce on the ground.

She thought, *Two down, three to go.*

The two guys rushed into Kirin, who angled herself so only one guy had her in harm's way. He led heavily into the charge, and his exposed knee was just too tempting not to kick. She did just that, and he dropped to the ground, screaming in pain. Kirin followed up with another kick to his face, silencing him.

His partner froze from shock, but that hesitation invited Kirin in. She punched him, dazing him immediately. He took another swing that Kirin ignored. All that mattered was dominating the center line and hitting him to the root. Flashes of her hand were all he could see. In a blink, he was out cold.

The driver finally got to the other side to see the destruction that Kirin had laid out. He panicked and held his hands up.

"You can have him," he quivered. "Take him!"

Kirin kept her eye on him the entire time as she pulled Bryce to the edge of the sidewalk.

The driver did the same, shoving the henchmen back into the car. As soon as everyone was inside, the doors slammed and the car peeled away as Kirin watched.

Kirin lifted Bryce's head and asked, "You okay?"

He smiled and gritted his teeth. "I have had better days."

"Do you know who they were?"

Bryce said, "I have no idea, but I guess that's what happens when you start to rock the boat."

Kirin looked up, knowing the universe had given her a sign. "Come on. Let's get you home where it's safe."

"Respect and trust shouldn't be freely given, but earned. To do so without caution is quite foolish."—Sifu

SECTION 1

Short Stories #5—Kirin's P.O.V.

The Fan—283 Days

I t was the middle of spring, and football season was almost over. I went to the family room to see all my brothers and my father in couch potato positions watching the game. Mom was at work this Sunday on call, and the men of the house were wasting a perfectly good afternoon. Our team had an impressive record of 2–10, with absolutely no chance of accomplishing anything this year, other than getting a high draft pick. My dad had told me that, at one time, football was played in the fall. However, losing ratings to the UFMF had forced them to switch their schedule just to stay afloat.

I shouted, "Hey, lunch is ready!"

My dad said, "In a bit, princess. This is gonna be a good game."

I gave my dad a funny look as I checked the score. Our team was already down by two touchdowns.

"Guys?" I asked my brothers.

"Just give us a couple of minutes, Kirin," said Jim.

Steven, Mark, and Kyle didn't even respond.

I plunked myself at the kitchen table and began to eat by myself. Butterscotch got into position, keeping me company. I thought, *This is so dumb. I can understand being a fan, but when your team is this terrible, why invest the time?*

After finishing lunch, I thought I had a perfectly good idea to kick my family back into gear. I went to our garage and found our football lying in the corner. When I was much younger, we would often play touch football with friends and neighbors. I ran back to the family room to see that nothing had changed.

I said, "Hey, the game's pretty much over. Let's go play some real football."

Dad said, "In a minute, Kirin … I think our team is about to come back."

I looked again at the score. Now they were down by three touchdowns. I shook my head and brainstormed some more. With a quick snap of my fingers, I pulled out my phone and began texting our friends. Soon afterward, I got several responses and confirmations that people were coming over. A quick run-down of the math told me we could do just like the old days and have a six on six football match.

Fifteen minutes later, I heard the doorbell. I got to the front door and smiled as old friends came by, ready for a game.

"Give me a second," I said.

Back in our living room, it was frozen in time. I'd had enough. I did a final check, seeing that it was the third quarter and we were four touchdowns down. They were still zombified in front of the screen. I decided to take matters into my own hands and walked to the screen and turned it off.

They all shouted at me.

"Kirin, what are you doing!" shouted Jim.

"That's enough. It's one thing to be a die-hard fan, but to waste a perfectly great day glued to the screen with the most valuable asset that you have going to waste…? I won't stand for it."

My dad said, "Kirin, you just don't understand."

"You're right; I don't. I don't understand when we could spend more quality time playing the game instead of just watching a losing team. Besides, I've invited your old friends over to play a game … so let's go out and stop wasting time. Let's do something worthwhile."

My dad listened to my argument, finding it impossible to refute my logic. He finally moved from his couch and looked at the backyard. He saw that the guys in the back were already practicing with the ball.

I stayed quiet, not sure how everyone would react.

Dad said, "Get up, guys…. Kirin's right. Let's go play some ball."

10 Minutes Later

My dad shouted, "How many people do we have?"

Steve did a quick head count. "Dad, we have ten total."

I looked around to confirm, "Hey, it's eleven people, not ten, Steve."

Steve looked confused. "You sure?"

I put my hands on my waist and said, "Did you count me?"

"Oh, my bad," said Steve.

My dad replied, "Okay, we're short one person."

The doorbell rang, so I went to answer it. Good fortune shined, as it was Hunter.

"Hey, perfect timing!"

"Hey, Kirin. Perfect timing for what?"

"We need one more person to join us for our flag football."

I grabbed him by his arm and pulled him to the backyard. "Dad, I found our twelfth guy!" I shouted.

My dad came over and said, "Hey, Hunter. Perfect timing."

Still in a daze, Hunter said, "That's what Kirin said."

Dad shouted, "Okay, we have an even number for our teams. Let's start."

Hunter said, "Kirin, I didn't know you played flag football."

"I don't know the ins and outs, but I'd rather hang out with the family doing something, instead of watching a losing team's season for the next hour."

"You have a point."

"Besides ... isn't the goal to put the ball on the other team's side?"

"Yup."

"Well, see? I know football now."

My dad started shouting out orders. "Okay, let's break up in teams."

"Ugh, not picking teams." I thought, *Guaranteed I'll be picked last again.*

As predicted, I was picked last, even though both sides tried to make it seem unimportant. Roughly twenty minutes into the game, things weren't looking good for my team.

Dad said, "Okay, team, we are getting clobbered. We're down twenty-one to zero, and they're blitzing us every single time. We need to get the ball moving at least."

I said quietly, "We can run the ball into the end of the zone, right?"

"Yes, pumpkin." He brushed me off and said, "Let's try to do some quick slants so I can get rid of the ball right away."

I tugged at his sleeve.

"Kirin, what?"

I said, "On the next play, pitch me the ball."

Dad replied, "Sweetie, these guys are in their prime and play football. It's gonna be really tough to run past them."

I replied, "Dad, just this one time ... give me the ball and let me try."

Dad looked around at his team, who was less than enthusiastic about the call. He began to bark out orders, "On three, we pitch right and make sure everyone picks someone to block. Everyone got that? One, two, three, break!"

"Dad, that means I run to the right?"

"Yeah, sweetie."

We all lined up in position. Kyle was in the center ready to snap the ball, and my dad played quarterback. Mark and Steven were to my left, and Mark's friend Peter was wide right. I stood slightly behind to the left of my dad and waited.

He shouted, "Whiskey, Bravo... tango one, tango one ... hut, hut, hike."

Kyle snapped the ball to my dad, who handed me the ball right away. I could see that two defenders were already set to steal the flag from me.

I dashed hard to the right as they accelerated toward me even faster, and once I knew they'd committed their motion, I cut hard left as they both bounced into one another. I thought, *That's two down. Run, Kirin ... run!*

After that cut, I ran harder to the side, and then I was going to be contested by another two guys. These guys were regulars playing football, so I couldn't match their speed, but I made sure that I had full control of my center of gravity. The first defender stretched out, diving for my flag. I immediately spun in a circle as he landed face first into the grass. Then another defender was square upon me. I ran to engage him and shifted my center left to right. He bit on the second shift, and I got him to commit.

"Thank you!" I sang as he was grabbing air.

I was almost to the end zone when I saw Hunter from the corner of my eye running at full speed. He was fast, and I made a mad dash from the sideline. I knew he was timing it perfectly with a good twenty yards to go. As he came by and I continued my run, I stopped dead. He flew right past me. I took a quick peek backward and saw no one was left to defend. My team, including my dad, was cheering. At that point, I ended up walking the last ten yards into the end zone.

Kyle screamed from behind, "Like a boss, Kirin. Like a boss!"

My entire team swarmed me as we celebrated our first score. I started jumping up and down in excitement as I saw Hunter still on the ground, covered in mud. I tossed the ball and jogged to see him.

"So, how's the weather down there?"

"Funny," said Hunter. He extended his hand and said, "A little help?"

"Well, I guess that's the least I can do." I reached for his hand and tried to help him up. Suddenly his weight and the mud caused me to slip as I fell right on top of him.

We both sat face to face, inches from one another, and I saw him blush.

"Uh." He gave an awkward laugh. "Sorry. Here, let's move up slowly so we don't fall in the mud again."

The Second Origin—290 Days

There we were, our main group eating out at our favorite chicken spot. Sifu had decided to treat us out for lunch, so this was different from our once-a-month hangout after class. I wasn't sure if that was because we'd trained hard or if it was just to cheer us up for our pitiful performance. Either way, this lunch turned out to be much different from our typical chitchat and camaraderie.

Robert and Big T were barking at each other, having a heated discussion while everyone watched the two go at it.

Robert said, "What's your standard for the best chicken, Big T? Coz, frankly, Korean chicken has more flavor than your Southern chicken."

Big T replied, "What it boils down to is the taste. Southern fried chicken is crunchier and more flavorful."

"How can that be? You guys don't add extra flavor to the chicken after you deep fry it."

"Exactly," replied Big T. "It's so good that the secret is not to drown it in sauce, but let the recipe of the breading take over."

Robert shook his head. "I'm sorry, but to me what makes a meal worth going out for is that you can't duplicate it yourself or it takes more work than necessary to try to make it at home."

Ken jumped in and said, "Exactly! That's why I love hamburgers."

The guys laughed out loud, and some of us shook our head as Ken stood up. "Come on! That last burger place I—"

Robert interrupted Ken. "Please, just stop. Even Danny can make a burger."

Danny shouted, "Yeah, I can make a ... hey! What the...?"

I said, "Ken, 80/20 ... 80/20, it's not that difficult at all."

"Says you." He folded his arms over his chest and sat back in his seat, pouting.

All this time, Sifu chuckled as he watched how his students would argue about nothing.

"Okay, guys, enough. Both kinds of chicken are good, and it's just a simple case of preference," I argued. "Bottom line, we aren't talking about burgers."

"Hey, what the...?" Ken frowned.

Ryan snapped his fingers and said, "Hey, I know what we can talk about...."

Doc, who was always a step ahead of everyone, cut in and said, "Sifu, let's talk about how you met Sigung. You promised us last time." *Sigung* was the term used for our teacher's teacher.

Ryan pouted. "Hey, I was going to say that!"

Sifu replied, "Did I ever say that?"

The entire group shouted in unison, "Yes, Sifu, you promised."

Sifu leaned backward, surprised by our demands. "Okay, okay … but you know what? Before I do that, don't you think it'd be more entertaining if I told you how Tobias and I met?"

Still busy chomping on his food, Tobias coughed out in surprise. Rattled by Sifu's comment, Tobias complained, "Hey, wait a minute! You promised me that you'd never mention that story. Sifu, you promised you wouldn't tell anyone."

Sifu scoffed at Tobias. "I'm not telling anyone. I'm going to tell everybody."

Tobias had a confused look on his face, making it clear he'd missed the verbal loophole. He muttered to himself, but no one could make out what he was saying.

Sifu had switched baits, and the entire gang bit on it. Just like that, one by one, the gang started to cheer for Tobias's story.

Ken led the charge and began banging on the table with his fist. "Tell us. Tell us." It didn't take long before a domino effect occurred. The gang filled the entire restaurant with the chant.

Tobias tried to stare us down, but he wasn't going to intimidate anyone with Sifu around.

"Please, Sifu. Please," I begged, hoping he couldn't say no to my puppy dog look.

Sifu raised his hands to quiet the group down. There was a long pause as he drew us to the edge of our chairs, waiting for his decision. "Tobias," he began, and we all cheered.

He raised his hands again to settle us all down. As we regained control, he said, "Let's go back…. I can't even recall how far back it was. Do you remember, Tobias?"

Tobias shook his head, but failed to contain his smile. "Honestly, I don't remember."

We could all tell that this was still fresh in Tobias's memory, and a few napkins were thrown in his direction after his lie.

"Ah, yes. I believe it began something like this…. It was a beautiful summer day. I was at the local park practicing my Siu Lim Tao form. I was much younger, either my late thirties or early forties. Anyway, it doesn't matter. There I was, practicing my form, minding my own business when suddenly this young kid...."

Sifu looked at Tobias and asked, "Tobias, how old were you at the time?"

Tobias thought for a minute and replied, "Probably early teens or so ... I've tried to suppress this memory, you know."

Sifu shrugged his shoulders and said, "No matter. Anyway, I noticed him before he approached me. In fact, if I'm not mistaken ... he was busy hustling other kids in basketball one on one."

Tobias looked at everyone and said, "A guy has to eat."

Robert snickered and said, "Well, twenty is twenty."

Tobias threw his napkin across the table as the gang laughed.

I wondered, *What does that mean?*

Sifu said, "Well, that same young man came up to me. He smelled of cockiness and an over-inflated ego."

Tobias said, "Hey!"

Robert said, "You hear that? You have the smell of cock."

Ken leaned over and took a sniff of Robert.

Robert looked at him. "What are you doing?"

"I need a reference for that smell Sifu described," said Ken.

Robert sneered and punched him on the arm as we all laughed out loud.

I shouted, "Guys, stop interrupting Sifu and let him finish the story!"

Sifu replied, "Oh yeah. Where was I...?"

I said, "You were talking about Tobias being a dick."

"Ah, thanks, Kirin."

"Come on," said Tobias. He shrank from the spotlight, covering his face with his hands.

Sifu said, "Well, Tobias, it's not like I'm lying. It's all true. Anyway, I was halfway done with my first section and had my eyes closed when he asked me a question.

"Tobias said, 'Yo, old man, what are you doing?'

"I didn't reply because I wasn't that old.

"Tobias was confused by what I was doing, and he asked, 'Is that some kind of martial art?'

"With my eyes still closed, I finally answered, hoping he'd go away. 'Yes, it is,' I said.

"'I thought so,' said Tobias. 'It's weird looking … and you know people don't fight that way. In a real fight, you gotta move your feet around.'

"I ignored him, hoping the silence would bore him.

"I wasn't so lucky, of course. He said, 'Yeah, old man. It's all about moving in and out.' Tobias started to jiggle around, showing some of his quickness while he spoke."

Tobias interrupted the story. "Oh come on, Sifu. Your impersonation of me is horrible."

Robert said, "Regardless, I am entertained," and the rest of the group began to laugh.

Sifu said, "Anyway, where was I? Oh, yes … I was working on the form."

"So I said to Tobias, 'Is that so?' as I continued focusing on my form.

"'Yeah, you need to be lightning quick, like me,' he bragged. 'Otherwise, you ain't gonna hit nothing.'

"I replied, 'That's true. Hopefully, in a real fight situation, I don't move as slow as you do in basketball.'

"He was so angry, asking me, 'What did you just say?'

"'I'm pretty sure you heard me,' I said as I continued working the one side of the form, still with my eyes closed.

"Tobias was indignant. He muttered, 'I'm the best damn basketball player in this area, old man, and I'd run circles around you.'

"I scoffed and said, 'That's like saying you're the tallest of the midgets.'

"Then he decided to challenge me. 'Maybe you want to put some money where your mouth is.'

"He got more annoyed, while I stayed calm and said, 'I wouldn't mind. I just hate taking money from a fool.'

"He puffed up his chest and growled, 'Who you calling a fool?'

"I said, 'Well, seeing that you and I are the only ones standing here....'

"'Shut up!' Tobias yelled at me then. 'How much money you got? Put up or shut up.'

"I told him I had about five hundred credits that said he was a lousy basketball player.

"He took a step closer and said, 'How do you know I won't just rob you right here and now?'

I looked at Tobias as he sunk into his seat, and he seemed as if he was blushing.

"I finally opened my eyes and stared right into his soul. Then I said, 'I can tell you are cocky, but I don't believe you'd be that stupid,' as I closed my eyes and focused on my form.

"Tobias frowned, insulted but intrigued by my challenge. 'Hey,' he said, 'I don't have that kind of money for this bet.'

"I sighed, realizing that I wasn't going to finish my form. I had to deal with the pesky mosquito. 'That's fine,' I told him. 'Tell you what. Here's the deal, when you lose this challenge, I keep my five hundred credits, but you have to be my student for an entire year.'

"Tobias sneered at me and said, 'You're kidding, right?' Then he shook his head, putting both his hands on his hips as he gave me a look. 'And you think I'm the cocky, arrogant fool.'

"I decided to have a bit more fun and fueled the fire. I taunted him by saying, 'Either I'm kidding, or all your life you've believed you're an ace in basketball when, in fact, you haven't fought anyone that's actually good.'

"That was the comment that got Tobias to bite. I knew emotionally he was off his center. I added, 'You're probably that generation of kids who grew up winning trophies and awards for just participating.'

"Tobias said, 'Fine, old man ... let's play up to twenty-one.'

"I thought for a second and said, 'Let's make this more interesting. I'll give you twenty-one attempts one on one. You can shoot or drive to the hoop or whatever. If you score once on me, then the five hundred credits are all yours.'

"Tobias's face lit up. I could tell he knew the deal was too good to pass up. 'You're kidding, right?' he said. 'You don't think I'll be able to score one point against you?' He snickered and then added, 'So, let me get this straight. I get the ball twenty-one times, and I can do whatever I want. I just need to score once.'

"When I said that was right, he replied, 'Fine. Let's do this.'

"He tried and tried but still hadn't gotten anywhere ten minutes later. I said, 'What's wrong, kid? You've got two more chances to score. All this time, you still can't shoot or drive to the basket.'

"Tobias was fuming. 'Old man,' he said, 'time to eat humble pie.'

"Tobias showed off his fancy dribbling, but I was not fooled. I continued to watch his center and attack it. As fast as Tobias was, his speed was no match for a superior center of gravity. No matter what he did, he could not create any kind of gap between the two of us. Frustration was all over his face. He went for a short mid-jump range about twenty feet away. As he was about to release the ball, I caught the timing of the release and blocked his shot.

"I asked, 'How's the pie taste?' as I smiled and handed him the ball at the top of the perimeter. I could tell his confidence was already broken.

"When he didn't respond, I said, 'You know that counts as a shot.'

"He muttered, 'I know the rules of the game.'

"'Well,' I told him, 'you got one last shot. In my book, the odds don't look good for you, kid.'

"Tobias shook his head, frustrated.

"I decided to back down as he stood at the top of the three-point line. 'Go ahead,' I said. 'Take the shot. This will be your first uncontested attempt. Be the hero, and the five hundred credits are all yours.'

"He looked at me and said, 'You're gonna let me take a free shot?'

"I nodded, and he bounced the ball several times as I took a further step back and stared directly at him.

"He released the ball and said, 'Money.'

"I turned around and watched the ball bounce and hit the rim and bank off to the side. I started walking away and said, 'I'm looking forward to seeing you in my next class.'"

Robert finally broke into Sifu's story and said, "Wow, that is bad ass!"

Tobias shook his head with a slight smirk and a look of embarrassment. He said, "God, that's as painful to hear it now as it was back then."

Ryan said, "Well, have you played since then?"

Tobias said, "Hell no."

"See, that's a good thing," Ken said. "You only got schooled that one time."

Tobias yelled back, "What the hell are you talking about? Ever since I joined, he continues to school me in Wing Chun."

I couldn't help laughing along with the rest of the guys.

Robert said, "Well, it sucks to be you."

Tobias looked at Robert and slowly raised his middle finger.

Sleepover—297 Days

It had been a while since we'd done this as little kids, but one Saturday Gwen suggested that we have a sleepover at her place. It was early evening as we both had finished the meal that Gwen's mom had prepared.

"Oh my God, I'm so full, Gwen," I said.

"Kirin, maybe you should see a doctor?" said Gwen.

"Why's that?"

"It's not normal for a girl your size to eat that much."

I grabbed a pillow and threw it at Gwen. "Oh, stop being silly. I'm gonna get changed in your bathroom."

Several minutes passed as I got dressed for bed. While in the bathroom, I could hear Gwen talking to someone.

"I'm all ready for bed," I said as I came out of Gwen's bathroom. Gwen was by her computer work station as she turned around and said, "Bed? It's 8:30 on a Saturday night. What are you, some kind of old fart?"

"Yeah, you old fart," said the voice on the computer screen.

"Who are you talking to, Gwen?"

"Who else? Sage," laughed Gwen.

"Hey, Kirin. Nice PJs," said Sage.

"Are you being sarcastic, Sage? Because I can't tell."

"No, seriously, they're cute. Love the penguin PJs," said Sage.

Gwen said, "Okay, we gotta go, Sage. Go play your *King of the Kage* game."

Sage whined, "Seriously, I can't hang out with you guys tonight?"

Gwen made a face and said, "It's girls' night. Notice the emphasis on the word *girls*."

"Fine," huffed Sage, logging off his chat.

"Okay, so what do you want to do tonight, Kirin?"

"I honestly don't know. I finished all my homework. Does that help?"

"Again, like I said, go see a doctor." Gwen began checking me out from head to toe. "I know you're not used to doing girly things, but let's do some makeup and hair stuff tonight."

I shrugged my shoulders and said, "But, we're going to bed and not going out."

"Come over here, Kirin. Now!"

I walked over to Gwen and stood in front of her.

"Raise your right hand," she said.

"Why?" I asked.

"Just do it. Repeat after me … I swear to do whatever my best friend tells me to do tonight."

I raised my hand and repeated it to Gwen. "I swear to do whatever my best friend tells me to do tonight."

"Perfect," said Gwen. She finally left her computer and headed to her closet. "Now follow me."

I followed her into the walk-in closet as she turned around in her wheelchair. She smiled and said, "You can keep the PJs on … but do you trust me?"

"Is there a right or wrong answer to this question? Then again, I just swore an oath to you."

She giggled and said, "Oh yeah, I forgot."

I rolled my eyes and shook my head as I took in her walk-in closet. It was unlike any I could ever imagine.

"No, seriously, come over here, and let's get started," said Gwen.

For the next several minutes, Gwen was busy explaining the finer details on selecting the proper outfits and color-coordinating on a daily basis. She then switched gears and educated me on skin care and makeup application. I personally never bothered to put makeup on. It always felt more like work than was necessary, especially for school.

Gwen was busy applying eyeliner to my face. "You have such beautiful features, Kirin. I know you are too lazy to do this, but just a few minutes a day and a little makeup just enhances your features."

"Can I see?"

"Not yet, I'm almost done," said Gwen.

Gwen whipped out another box as she said, "Now, I want you to select a lipstick color you prefer.'

I opened the box and shook my head in surprise. "Gwen, there's like over a hundred different kinds of lipstick in this box. I have no idea what's good."

"Fine. I'll pick it." Gwen reached in and started holding different colors of lipstick up to my mouth.

"Ah, this one is perfect," said Gwen as she stared at me like I was her art project. "Yup, this is the one. Now pucker your lips, and we are all done."

After a few more dabs here and there, Gwen finally finished my makeup and hair.

"Let me see now." She stepped back and was examining me from every angle. She grabbed my hand and started dragging me away. "Now close your eyes just for a second."

I was being tugged around, not knowing where I was going, and then suddenly Gwen stopped. "No peeking."

I said, "Can I look now?"

Gwen said, "Let me fix you just a pinch here."

I waited. Strangely enough, I was kind of excited to see what she had done.

Gwen shouted, "I give you the new Kirin Rise!"

I slowly opened my eyes, and I saw a different person staring back through the mirror. I said, "That's me?"

"That's you all right." Gwen wheeled up behind me, holding my waist.

I smiled and said to Gwen, "I like it. I really never knew I looked like that."

We both stared at the mirror, admiring Gwen's work, until our moment was interrupted by her phone.

Gwen shouted, "Oh my God, I almost forgot."

"Forgot what?"

She spun around in her wheelchair and headed back to her room.

She shouted, "Hurry, Kirin. Hurry!"

I ran when she called me. I was thinking something was wrong. I got to her bedroom and saw what the excitement was all about.

"Ugh, you can't be serious." I hung my head in disbelief.

"Just one hour. I've been waiting all week for this episode to come up," said Gwen.

"How is it that you got hooked on Korean dramas?"

"Since my BFF is always sneaking out practicing her Wing Chun, I'm assuming Koreans probably live pretty fascinating lives. So, it's all about the stories, Kirin. If you give it a shot, you'll probably be hooked on it as well."

We both got into Gwen's king-sized bed and started watching her K-drama on the screen. Forty-five minutes into the show—and a lot of explanation from Gwen—and we were both holding tissues in our hands, crying from the story.

"I can't believe I'm crying from this stupid movie," I said.

"It's always the same. Cute rich Korean guy and poor homeless Korean girl fall in love. Next thing you know, someone's either sick or dying," said Gwen.

"Oh my God, I have no idea why I'm crying. Korean dramas are filled with over-exaggerated B acting." Even so, I sniffled through the scene. "Change the channel."

A few flips on the screen, and Gwen stopped at a K-pop music video. Her eyes lit up as she smiled. Gwen turned to me and said, "Kirin, tell me a secret?"

"I don't have any?"

I saw her grab her cell phone as she said, "I'm calling your mom right now if you don't come up with one."

"That's blackmail!" I shouted.

She grinned evilly as I scrambled to think of something. "Fine … fine … uh, Sage is a really good dancer."

Gwen looked at me and said, "What? For real? How do you know that?"

"I went to his house one day, and his mom let me in without his hearing me. Anyway, I saw him busting some moves like you wouldn't imagine."

"No kidding? Hmm."

"Yup."

"I never knew that." Gwen was really caught off guard.

"You know, Sage is pretty cool, but I never tell him that. As smart and brilliant as he is, he's still the typical guy who'll get a bloated head."

"I talk to Sage all the time. I never thought he could carry a beat. He's always his goofy and nerdy self."

I said, "Hmm, maybe he likes you and just acts awkwardly. Sounds like you two could be an item."

Gwen grabbed a pillow and threw it at me.

"What?"

"Are you crazy?" said Gwen.

"What's wrong with Sage? Like I said, he's cute, the smartest guy in the school, and he can dance. That's three positives most guys don't have."

I caught Gwen in mid-thought and wondered if I had just planted a seed in her head for the future.

Gwen turned up the volume on the TV and said, "Come on, Kirin! Now show me some of the moves. It must be in your blood."

"Now, that's racist."

She giggled and pointed to the TV. "Pretend you're number eighteen in this K-pop girl group. So, don't worry; you'll be in the back."

"I'm so embarrassed, I can't."

"It's just me. Come on," she insisted.

I listened to the music and watched the video as I began to feel for the beat. Next thing I knew, I found myself strangely lost in the song and just busted out some dance steps. As the music video ended, I turned around and looked at Gwen. She had a befuddled look on her face as she stared at me.

"Gwen, what's wrong?"

"Uh, were we listening to the same song? Because it looked like you were dancing to a different beat."

I folded my arms and looked away.

She said, "I'm sorry, I just didn't expect those very interpretive dance moves."

I began ranting to Gwen that, for whatever reason, I just couldn't relax and feel the beat of the song. It was nothing like Wing Chun, which allowed me the most freedom of expressing what I felt. I snapped back and turned around. "Okay, okay … I can't dance. I have two left feet." I paused for a moment to gather my breath, as I noticed some sadness on Gwen's face.

"What's wrong?" I jumped back onto her bed.

"It's nothing," said Gwen.

"Come on, Gwen. We always tell each other everything. Something's definitely bothering you."

Gwen looked teary eyed for a moment and said, "I miss it."

"What?"

"No matter how goofy your dancing may look, I just miss dancing and doing the things I once was able to do."

I felt so bad for Gwen. Had she been born not being able to walk, it would've probably been easier to swallow. But, since her accident when she was little, she has always clung onto the hope that, one day, she would walk again.

I leaned forward and whispered in her ear, "I truly believe that you'll be able to walk again someday. I'm not just saying that. I promise you it'll happen."

She started to tear up and gave me a big hug.

"When two people can be themselves, it brings a natural balance to the universe."
—Sifu

SECTION 2

Sifu's Journey Entry #5—Odd Encounter

Late Spring 2030

Weeks passed by like a blur as Sifu found himself wandering through the streets of Tokyo. He had walked for hours each day, stopping only to eat when needed, but his feet felt the ache of all the monotonous activity. All this walking was the most exercise he'd ever had. His pants felt loose around the waist, and his shirts no longer hugged him. He had gone down the same streets before, but he continued to delay the inevitable. Sifu sighed, angered by and dejected over himself for being so weak. He thought, *I am doing the exact opposite of what I've always taught.*

The wound in his heart felt amplified since he'd landed in Japan. He felt in a daze most of the time, as memories of the past continued to haunt him. The places he had gone with Megumi when they first came here many years ago, he no longer could bear to walk. Hints of memories seemed to linger around every corner. Sifu avoided them and fought to hold back the tears.

His lack of attention walking the crowded streets of Tokyo caused him to accidentally run into a person. His center held, as it always did, but the unfortunate soul who was busy texting on his phone ended up on the ground. Sifu snapped quickly to help the stranger up. A quick exchange of bows and apologies, followed by a smile, had Sifu parked in the middle of the road.

He stood still as he turned slightly toward a street which he had not noticed before. There, in the distance, lay a narrow passage, unknown to him. He decided to go with his feelings and alter his path.

Several minutes later, as he walked down this empty road, he saw a very odd thing. A person dressed in a robot suit was sweeping in front of a store. This was Japan. While odd things were the norm, he found this act intriguing enough that it captured his attention. He continued walking at a normal pace and forced his head to stare straight as he used his peripherals to sneak a peek. But he noticed the robot had stopped sweeping and whoever or whatever was underneath that suit was staring at him, making him feel uneasy. He thought,

Hmm, what's up with that? He wondered why the stare, since he thought he blended in well with the rest of the Asian community strolling down the street.

Sifu stood still as he slowly turned around to confirm that he was correct. After finally getting a full glimpse of it, he found it even more odd. Sifu felt things in energy, and whoever was under that costume seemed to be surrounded by an aura of rainbows, unicorns, and other magical creatures. It was unlike anything he had ever encountered before.

The robot tilted its head, mechanically gestured several steps forward, and spoke. "You seem lost. *Beep. Beep. Bop.*"

The voice immediately answered a few questions. First, the it was a girl, and, second, she spoke perfect English.

Sifu replied, "I'm not lost," drawing closer to this person. As he bridged the gap between them, he could feel a warmness about her. He rocked back and forth in his stance several times, checking to see if he could feel the difference. When he pulled away from her, the feeling would lessen, but a quick rock forward led to the warmth. A single eyebrow raised when he realized this was not the norm. There was something about this girl which now had his full attention.

The robot spoke, "I didn't mean literally ... but you seem, you know, lost." She used her hands to mimic quotation marks.

Sifu narrowed his eyes, taking a single step forward. "I'm sorry. Have we met before?"

The robot lifted her hand and scratched her head but remained in character as the motion was, well, robotic. She said, "You know, I was about to ask you the same thing." She fidgeted with her costume, and Sifu waited to see who would pop out from underneath the helmet. Upon plucking off her helmet, a huge puffy fuzz ball of hair exploded in front of his face.

"Howdy, the name is April ... April Welch, that is." She extended her hand for a shake. She smiled from ear to ear as a little gap showed between her top teeth.

"Nice to meet you, April. My name is Kwan ... uh, Gordon Kwan." Sifu shook her hand as her vise-like grip felt like a juggernaut. Sifu was surprised, not knowing how someone her size could be generating so much power. She was short and a pinch stout, and her dark skin made her look different from everyone in the area.

"I bet you didn't expect to find me underneath the outfit," she said confidently as she continued to beam with energy.

Sifu let out a little chuckle as he looked above her and read the sign on the store.

April looked at Sifu and said, "Hmm, so can you read Japanese?"

Sifu quickly apologized and greeted her in the traditional Japanese way. April reciprocated, speaking fluently in Japanese.

Afterward, she said, "Great. But, if you don't mind, it's been a while since someone's come around here who speaks English. Mind if we stick to that?"

"Uh, no. By all means."

"Tell yah what, why don't you come inside and I'll show you around?" said April. She was quite forward and grabbed Sifu by the arm, clenching it tightly.

"Thanks for the offer, but I really need to go somewhere." Sifu began to pull away.

April scrunched her face and began to laugh. Her boisterous laughter shook the glass in front of the store as she continued to drag Sifu toward the entrance. "No, I insist. Come hither…. Besides, if you really wanted to go where you need to, you'd be there already."

Sifu took a deep breath and thought about it. *She's right … but, who the heck uses the word 'hither'?*

Seconds later, Sifu found himself in this small, quaint, yet odd store. As soon as he entered, the smell intoxicated him, causing his stomach to grumble. His eyes scanned the entire area, noting the walls were covered with shelves from top to bottom. On each shelf were toys lined next to each other. He couldn't quite put his finger on it, but so far he had a black robot girl, a toy shop, and the smell of some kind of delicious food. Had he entered these criteria in a search engine, it would've come back blank.

"I bet you're wondering what you just walked into?"

Sifu ignored her question and continued to gaze at the wonders before him. He walked toward one of the shelves and was about to touch one of the sealed containers, when he stopped just inches away. He looked toward April and made eye contact, asking permission without speaking.

"Yeah, you can touch it. It's sealed tight, though. Over there are the toys that aren't, which people can play with."

Sifu shook his head in surprise, which led to awe, and eventually admiration for what lay before him. He reached forward and grabbed one of the toys as memories of his childhood immediately rushed back. *Fascinating,* he thought, as he ogled one of his favorite toys from years past. It seemed to be in mint condition.

His concentration was suddenly broken as a thin Japanese fellow came from behind a curtain. He yawned and scratched his head and weakly said, "Ohayou gozaimasu" and let out another yawn.

April yelled at him, "You're late again, Takashi! I've already started preparing stuff. Why don't you get the usual for my friend here?"

Takashi, who looked half-asleep, responded, "Hai," as he turned around and mumbled something.

"I heard that, Takashi. Don't make me go Godzilla on your ass." April took her fist and slammed it on her other hand.

Sifu chuckled at the comment and then forced a serious look on his face.

April turned around and asked, "Care to take a guess what we're known for?"

Sifu shrugged his shoulders and pretended not to know. Sifu took another sniff, stared at April briefly, and silently thought, *What are the odds it would be chicken?*

April laughed, "You know I'd say you're racist if your first thought was chicken?"

Sifu coughed and cleared his throat. He said with a surprised expression, "Chicken? Honestly, I had no idea.... That's the last thing I would've ever guessed. Besides, I'm not hungry."

"Trust me. I insist. Besides, turning down chicken and waffles is like saying no to cake ... and we all know that didn't work for Tina."

Sifu had a confused look on his face. "Huh?"

April replied, "Never mind. Anyway, chicken and waffles isn't the answer to everyone's question, but once you eat this, you'll feel a whole lot better."

Sifu threw his hands up in surrender and said, "You win."

April took it as an opportunity to high five Sifu, which caught him slightly off guard. As she landed back on the ground, she blurted out, "My two favorite words: 'you win'!" She began laughing to herself as Sifu looked at his hand, which turned beet red, and then all around to see if there was some kind of camera that was capturing all this.

20 Minutes Later

In a bizarre twist of fate, the universe had thrust two perfect strangers to finally meet. Just twenty minutes ago, not a single word had ever been spoken between them, but now they were chatting up a storm as if they were old friends who had finally reunited. Each sensed that, maybe in a past lifetime, they had known each other. Somehow the stars were aligned again for them to encounter each other and begin a new journey.

Sifu paused before speaking again, closing his eyes and taking a deep whiff. The doors swung open as Takashi came by with a plate in each hand. He stood in front of them and gently placed the food on the table. Speaking in Japanese, he muttered, "Please eat and enjoy."

Sifu looked somewhat surprised that Takashi had brought two plates. He said, "You're also eating?"

April was already positioning her napkin around her neck as she said, "But, of course."

"Don't you eat this all the time?"

"I do, but if it's a good thing … why wouldn't I want to have it again?"

Sifu shrugged and blurted, "Oh, I don't know. Maybe some balance."

April picked up a knife and fork and was about to dig in. She looked up at Sifu and said, "I hate eating alone. Don't you think it's best to have meals with someone?"

Those words hit Sifu like a brick, and he tried his best not to show the pain. However, April felt it. She tried her best to soften the moment, but for the first time an awkward silence fell between them.

Sifu smiled and asked, "What?"

"Nothing." She shook her head and uttered again, "I didn't say anything."

"You didn't have to."

They both stared at the food they were about to eat and simultaneously said, "Have we met before?" Both Sifu and April chuckled, as their timing seemed surprisingly less coincidental by the minute.

They both laughed. Quietly and simultaneously, they said, "Itadekimasu."

Sifu asked, "Do you know the meaning of *itadekimasu*?"

"Of course I do. It means, 'I humbly receive you' or simply 'let's eat.'"

"Well, that's the literal definition, and you are 100% correct in that sense."

"Okay, now I'm curious. You seem to have knowledge of a deeper meaning."

Sifu paused as he recalled Megumi explaining the meaning when they first met. He took a deep breath and recited the same thing. "Itadekimasu, in a deeper sense, means 'thank you for sacrificing your life.'"

"Hmm." April put down her knife and fork and thought about what that meant.

Sifu said, "I was taught that a long time ago … that which we eat gave up its life so that we live."

April smiled and said, "I really like that, and I never knew about its deeper meaning."

They both looked at each other briefly before staring at the scrumptious meal. In front of each was a plate filled with two waffles drizzled with fine sugar and coated with a special butter that made it look like the sun. Next to them were two pieces of extra crispy dark meat fried chicken. The oil glistened from the light; nothing from this meal could be deemed healthy.

Sifu said, "This food may have given its life up for us, but I'm pretty sure if I eat this … it's going to kill me."

April barked a laugh. "Oh well, I had a good run. What can I say? Karma."

Sifu smiled. "Agreed … karma."

"Okay then, let's eat." April broke formalities. She dove in, seemingly eating this meal as if it were her last.

The taste immediately put a smile on Sifu's face. He shouted, "This is incredible!" He shook his head in disbelief and dug in for another bite. "No, seriously … I've never had chicken and waffles like this before."

April gave a thumbs-up but continued to eat. "Thanks … can't talk, too busy eating."

Sifu chuckled and watched April devour her food. He was amazed at the ferocity with which she was eating the meal. Eventually, he snapped out of the hypnotic stare and continued to eat. Several minutes passed, filled with mmms, grunts, and lip smacking. They ended up in the typical leaned backed position, each with a single hand on their belly. Takashi came from the kitchen and asked if they were done. They both said they were as he begrudgingly took their plates.

Sifu stared at him as he headed back into the kitchen and said, "I hope I'm not to forward on this…."

April interrupted, "I doubt you've ever been too concerned with being too forward."

Sifu laughed and said, "Yes, yes … but Takashi, he doesn't seem to have the same … oh, I don't know … uh, the same vibe that you carry."

April snickered. "I'm working on it. You could say he's a work in progress. Besides, I owe his father a favor."

Sifu looked at April, somewhat confused. "You don't say."

April pointed toward the back counter. There, encased in a glass structure, was a beautifully designed samurai sword.

"Do you see that sword over there?" said April. "That is a one-of-a-kind Shinzuki samurai sword. He's known as the greatest living sword maker left in Japan. He is descended from great sword makers, and his great-great-great-grandfather forged one of the oldest and most valuable swords that's still around today."

"Wow, that's incredible."

April leaned forward and whispered, "Care to guess what he and Takashi have in common?"

Sifu's eye lit up as the answer was too obvious. "No way. Let me guess: Takashi's dad is … Shinzuki."

April nodded to confirm. "We met several years ago and immediately became friends."

Sifu said, "Is there anyone you meet that doesn't become friends with you?"

April laughed hard, so hard she apologized for several uncontrollable snorts.

"Oh, where was I? Oh yeah … basically, Takashi's working for me. You could say his job is a ruse, as the main goal is to straighten himself out. His dad felt, if he hung out with me more, it would shake him out of his funk. So, I got the sword as payment to fix Takashi."

"So, how's it going?"

April laughed. "You should've seen him several months ago. I was this close to using the sword on him." April face-palmed as she recalled a painful time, but she sprung from one emotion to another in a blink. Smiling once again from ear to ear, she said, "His dad visited recently and was actually happy with his progress."

Sifu thought for a moment and dreamed of the possibility. "Hmm … uh?"

April encouraged him, "Spit it out. What's on your mind?"

"I was wondering…." Sifu hesitated, thinking he was being too forward with his newly formed friendship. He waved his hands and said, "It's nothing."

April didn't particularly like that response as she began to slither side to side on her seat, staring at Sifu directly.

"Are you trying to read me?" said Sifu.

She switched voices to a scratchy old pitch. "Try, you say? Maybe what you see, I've already done." She bobbled several times in laughter.

Sifu kept his poker facing, waiting to see what April would say.

Her eyes squinted as she snapped her fingers. "I got it." She sat erect, confident that she was right, waving her index finger at Sifu to let him know that he couldn't fool her. "You teach something." She phrased it as statement and not as a question. "In fact, now that I think about it, from your walk, your energy, your confidence … it's not by method of books, but a ….." she shook her head, assured that this was correct, "a martial art!"

"Your insights serve you well." Sifu nodded in confirmation.

April clapped her hands once and spread them open to welcome a question. "Say your peace and tell me what's on your mind."

Sifu said, "I don't' even know if it's possible."

"Oh, just say it … you won't know till you ask."

Sifu was about to repeat the words of defeat, but caught himself. Instead, he said, "You know, I have a sword design that I've wanted to make for years. Problem is I need someone skilled enough to make it and with quality steel. I know this is kinda forward, but … any chance…? Well, you know."

April smiled and said, "Consider it done. Give me the specs, and I'll have Shinzuki work on it. But, you know, it's gonna cost you."

"What's the cost?"

"Isn't it pretty obvious? A teacher of your caliber, I'm sure has the skill to transform and mold future minds. I figure with you and me combined, we can turn Takashi's personality over."

Sifu said, "For all you know, I'm a lousy teacher."

April snarled and said, "I know for a fact that you don't believe that."

Sifu rolled his eyes and snickered.

April slammed her fist on the counter and said, "Then it's agreed upon. Henceforth, from this day forward, we work together toward a common goal." April extended her hand, looking to seal the deal. "What say you?"

Sifu thought, *Thank God she didn't seal the deal with a spit handshake.* Then it occurred to him as he laughed inside, *Henceforth.* He reached over and shook her hand, and she waved it vigorously like a wet noodle.

In just a short time, it seemed to Sifu that he had accomplished more in less than an hour than he had done this entire trip. He blurted out, "I know I said it before, but that was one of the best meals I've ever had."

"Arigatou." April smiled and then suddenly let out a little burp. "Excuse me."

"Did you come up with this recipe?"

This time, Sifu's words hit April. Her face slightly saddened as she forced a smile and said, "No, it's not. This is actually my, uh … my father's recipe."

Sifu recognized that look as he came to understand their common bond. He quickly snapped, "You know … your father would be proud that you created something that brings a smile to so many people."

They both sat silently for a moment, as each one knew without another word spoken what the other one was feeling.

April broke the silence. "It doesn't bring him back."

Sifu stayed silent and bit his lip to stop it from quivering. "Hmm?"

"You know earlier, I said you were lost." April stared at Sifu with a serious look.

"I'll be honest. I feel better, but I still feel lost." Sifu couldn't make eye contact.

"Well, you don't seem like a guy who gets lost often. Do you mind if I give you some advice?" asked April.

"I'm always open. Besides, I'm pretty sure you'd force it on me regardless."

"True that," said April. Suddenly she showed a serious side for the first time. She spoke with a kind voice, as if someone else were speaking through her. She said, "Whatever it is or wherever you have to go, just remember this: you go when you're ready to go and be when you're ready to be. In other words, trust in the timing of the universe."

Sifu listened intently and let the words sink in. "That's really brilliant."

"I can't take credit for it.… It's something my father taught me a long time ago."

Sifu began to chuckle and reached into his fanny pack to pull out a piece of paper. "I've carried this with me for over twenty years. I saw it back in my college days and wrote it down. I never knew why I did that, but I think this is the moment I'm supposed to read it."

"What is it?" asked April as she leaned forward, intrigued.

Sifu said, "It reads, 'Amicitiae nostrae memoriam spero sempiternam fore.'"

"What's it mean?"

"I think it has greater meaning if you find out for yourself," said Sifu.

April jerked back and rested comfortably on her chair. "Do you believe we met by accident?"

Sifu said, "No such thing," as he smiled and enjoyed the moment.

CHAPTER 6

The Day of Silence

Mid May

I t was a bright and sunny day, but one couldn't tell from the tinted glass inside the limo. Watanabe and Kristen were side by side as they were getting ready for a busy day. It was an unusual moment, for it was rare for Watanabe to ever leave the comforts of his office.

Kristen wore tension on her face as she was busy going over final details. She peeked at Watanabe, who appeared to not have a care in the world. He sat quietly looking outside with an occasional glance toward her to see if there was anything needed.

Kristen asked the driver, "How much longer?"

"There's tons of traffic today, ma'am. I'd figure another twenty minutes before we arrive."

Staring outside, she saw traffic was heavier than normal. Kristen shook her head in disapproval and sat quietly. She resorted to the only option that was available while being stuck in the car, and that was work. For the next several minutes, she continued to work on her tablet as the car remained quiet and lulled through the morning rush hour.

Watanabe finally broke the silence. "What is it, Kristen?"

"Nothing, sir …." She started to say something before abruptly closing her mouth.

Watanabe looked at her directly, but did not utter a word.

She shook her head as his silence and stare forced her to speak. "How do you stay so calm, sir?"

He chuckled and stretched to find a more comfortable position.

"I know you hate it when I compare you and Thorne," said Watanabe.

Kristen kept a straight face, refraining from showing any emotional reaction to that statement. She said, "How so, sir?"

"Well, I guess it's good that my two best companions do the worrying for me."

She smiled but pressed for an answer. "Seriously, sir. How do you stay so calm in light of what's happening tomorrow?"

Watanabe looked away as something caught his eye. It surprised Kristen that there could be anything more important than tomorrow's rally.

"Kristen, we've done the work. We've laid out our plan, and now we will see where the cards fall."

"I don't like to leave so much to chance," said Kristen. She caught herself reflecting on her words, which is exactly what Watanabe was referencing. Kristen had a smirk on her face, as Watanabe's observation skills were always on.

Watanabe broke her trance and said, "Don't you think life would be too boring if everything went exactly as planned?"

"I like boring."

Watanabe enjoyed Kristen's comment and honesty. "We can't control everything, Kristen." He snickered, as the words oozed with irony.

Kristen smiled and continued to do her work. Several minutes passed as they continued on their route when a screen popped up in front of them.

Kristen said, "It's an incoming call from Thorne, sir."

"Please." Watanabe nodded.

Kristen gestured toward the screen, which brightened and showed Thorne from his Chicago office.

"Good morning, sir. Good morning, Kristen."

Kristen adjusted her glasses and looked at Thorne.

Watanabe said, "I'm assuming you're calling to tell me everything is in place."

"It is, sir."

"Good." Watanabe glanced at Kristen.

Kristen said to Thorne, "We're all set for tomorrow."

"I'm curious, sir. How long do we allow it to go?"

Watanabe took some time to answer. "Let them have their moment."

Both Thorne and Kristen said, "Sir!" They immediately looked at one another through the screen.

"Yes, allow them to win this round."

Thorne didn't hesitate to voice his opinion. "Sir, I want to point out that we have no idea what Kirin could say at the speech tomorrow. Also, we already know she has huge influence with the masses."

"I'm well aware of that," said Watanabe, even though he knew otherwise.

Kristen said, "I agree with Thorne. The impact of tomorrow's rally is too big a factor to leave to chance. You could be leaving the company open to exposure."

Watanabe raised his hands as he tried to calm both his associates. "Neither of you likes the unknown, correct?"

He waited as both acknowledged that to be true.

"Well, I'm guilty of that as well."

Both Thorne and Kristen wore confused expressions.

"You see, this movement … this rally has quite a bit of steam behind it, and Kirin's pull is powerful. But, you see, I don't know how strong it is, or could possibly be. So, tomorrow's rally is to allow them the ability to flex their muscle. In fact, I'd very much like to see how just how much, personally. We will allow Bryce to do his work, and Kirin, I'm sure, will follow afterward. Besides, I'm not the only one who needs to see their muscle."

Thorne said, "Won't people wonder how it's possible they were able to hold such a protest?"

"They will," said Watanabe, "and at the very end, we'll arrest both of them."

Kristen said, "You'll add more fuel to the fire, sir."

"Exactly, like I said … I want to know just how strong and deep this movement is.…"

"Very well, sir," said Thorne. "Oh, and by the way, sir, my hunch was correct. It took some more digging than normal, but we found what we needed."

Watanabe asked, "Will it be difficult?"

"Not at all, sir. Everyone has a price." Thorne had a devilish smile on his face.

"Very well, Thorne. Good work. Keep me up to date, please."

"As always, sir … Kristen." Thorne gestured as the screen finally went blank.

Kristen gazed outside for a second and saw they were almost at the office.

"We're almost here, sir." She looked relieved to finally get to work.

Watanabe cautiously opened the window, and the warm breeze hit his face. Kristen began packing up her belongings, ready to head out of the car and into the office. The work preoccupied her, so she didn't see Watanabe made no preparation to leave the car.

"Driver!" shouted Watanabe.

"Yes, Mr. Watanabe?"

"Would you be kind enough to spin us around for another fifteen minutes?"

"Yes, sir."

Kristen looked at Watanabe in surprise. They were packed with a busy schedule, and now she would have to make some changes. She kept herself in check and held her tongue.

Watanabe knew she was staring at him as he continued to gaze outside. He did not look at Kristen as he said, "The weather is too nice not to enjoy. Sit back for a bit, Kristen, and relax."

She tried to keep a calm face and did as Watanabe said, but Watanabe was going to be the only one enjoying the ride.

▲ ▲ ▲

The Night Before the Rally

It was almost 11:00 pm, and the TV was keeping Kirin company. She was killing time practicing her punches a few feet away from it. The channels were flashing the same news from around the country. She watched as every story seemed to paint a bleak outlook: police brutality, unemployment at an all-time high, and more Americans struggling to hold on to what they had. All the sadness finally broke her concentration as she stopped in mid-punch and crumpled to the ground. She spent the next several minutes scanning through all the channels and eventually lay down on the ground.

She thought, *One year later, and nothing's gotten better. In fact, things have gotten worse, but we've done a great job covering up the truth of it.* Kirin tilted her head to the side and stared at the phone lying on the ground. She grabbed it and looked at the time. She thought, *I wonder....* Kirin was doing a great job of evading her worries and did one more thing to prolong the inevitable.

She hesitated and then forced herself to dial the number. She cowered with the first ring and was about to hang up when that voice of comfort spoke.

"I thought you'd be up," said Hunter.

Kirin stared outside as she held her phone just to the side. "Are you sure it's okay that I bothered you so late at night?"

Hunter replied, "What have I always told you?"

Kirin knew the answer to that question, but felt bad that her own insecurities and indecision placed her relationship with Hunter on hold.

"I know," she said with a soft and tender voice. "Hunter...."

"What is it?"

"I'm sorry." Her voice choked as her eyes began to get watery.

"For what?"

"For leaving you hanging, for making you wait, for being so unsure about my...."

Hunter put up a strong front on the other end, but his heart ached knowing the truth. "I know you've got other pressing matters."

Kirin was silent as she thought, *He's always been there for me. Never doubting, never asking, but a friend one could only dream of ... what's wrong with me?*

"Kirin?" said Hunter.

"Pressing matters," she uttered back. "I'm going to speak tomorrow, and I don't even know what I'm going to say."

Hunter said, "You've always had the fight in you. You've never beaten around the bush when it comes to this. Be yourself; be direct."

Kirin snickered, unable to stop herself.

Hunter wondered, "What's so funny?"

"Everyone always thinks I have this incredible master plan, that I know every step of what I'm doing. The fact is: I don't. I'm gonna be speaking in front of thousands of people live and possibly millions of people at home. And, right now ... all I've got written is ... 'Uh, hi, I'm Kirin Rise. Listen to me, or I'll punch you hard.'"

Hunter chuckled at the joke.

"Don't laugh. I'm serious."

"Well, you said you can apply Wing Chun to anything. Why not do that to this situation?"

"I've talked to Sifu about that ... and he mentioned you can't solve anything with more violence. Otherwise, the circle keeps continuing."

"Okay, I've got an idea. What's the main point you want to get across to everyone?" asked Hunter.

Kirin thought about it for a minute and finally replied. "Hmm, I wanted to tell them that the people still have the power—not the corporations, or the government, or the filthy rich who basically do whatever they want."

Hunter said, "That's great and all, but those are just words, Kirin. You need to hit a homerun.... You need to prove to the people that they do have the power."

"How do I do that?"

Silence stretched until Hunter's excited voice said, "Can you give me five minutes? I just remembered something that just might help."

Kirin waited and watched as Bacon was sleeping on her bed. Finally, she heard Hunter shout on the other end of the phone.

"I got it!"

"Got what?"

"Well, I got your idea.... The rest is up to you." Kirin could feel his excitement over the phone.

"Give me a second, I'm texting you the link.... Take a look at it."

Kirin heard her phone ding and clicked the link to see what Hunter had come up with.

"I got it."

"Good. Now read it."

Several minutes passed as the phone call between the two remained silent. Kirin was doubtful at first, but with each sentence, her tension and renewed hope sunk in.

Hunter asked, "You still awake?"

"Of course I'm awake." Kirin smiled and shook her head. "I can't believe it. This is absolutely brilliant.'

Hunter smiled and said, "Well, did I come through for you or what?"

"You did ... like always. Now I know the direction I want to go with my speech tomorrow. Hopefully, this will work." Kirin's smile was devilish. "Thank you. Thank you. Thank you."

Hunter thought for a second and said, "Just don't go overboard Kirin, okay?"

"You know me."

"I know you, and that's why I'm worried."

Kirin smiled at the thought that Hunter's words were true—that he did, in fact, know her so well.

"Uh, Kirin?"

"What is it?"

"I won't be coming home this summer. There's an opportunity for me at school, so I'll be gone for those three months."

"Oh ... I won't get to see you?"

"You won't miss me."

"I'll miss you," Kirin protested. "Don't say that."

Even if it was just a quick reaction, those words coming from Kirin felt good to hear. "Besides, you'll be busy as ever."

Kirin thought about it, knowing that Hunter's remarks hinted at another issue that remained unresolved.

"Promise me you'll call me as often as you can?"

"I promise. Okay, I better let you go. You have a speech to write."

Kirin was saddened, but Hunter was right. There was work to be done, and she found herself back in high school doing a last-minute assignment.

"Good night, Kirin."

"Thanks again, Hunter. Good night." As she hung, she day-dreamed for a moment and thought, *I really care about him … Is it possible I….*

▲ ▲ ▲

Two Days Later

"After you," said Sifu, as he extended his hand.

Kirin opened the door to her loft and was immediately greeted by a boisterous cheer.

"Surprise!"

Kirin was caught off guard, and then immediately covered her reaction, embarrassed. The entire gang was in her loft along with Sage and Gwen leading the cheer.

"What are you guys doing here?" She began removing her jacket. Bacon came running toward her, his little butt wiggling from side to side in excitement.

"Good boy, good boy! Did you miss me?"

Bacon smothered Kirin with wet kisses and licks. She spent a few seconds enjoying the attention and then looked around. She could see food laid out, as if a party was about to begin. And then the banner caught her eye, making her shake her head. Someone had spent the time to blow up a poster of her mugshot, with "Jailbird" written in huge letters.

"You guys are terrible!" Kirin blushed with embarrassment.

Sifu finally entered from behind and began to close her door. He said, "I hope this doesn't become a regular occurrence."

Looking at her teacher, Kirin said, "At least you took it in better stride than my parents."

Sifu said, "Maybe that's because they had to pay for your bail."

Robert began clapping and said, "I've never known anyone who's gone to the slammer before. Kirin, you are officially the first."

Kirin said, "I'm kinda surprised by that, Robert."

Robert replied, "I'd bet you'd be more surprised if Big T had said that."

Big T shouted back, "Hey, man, you know my people are oppressed!"

Danny said, "Was your uncle T-Bone oppressed when he tried to rob that electronics store?"

Big T laughed. "I should've never told you about that … and, yes, he was oppressed. He told me he was just gonna borrow it."

Everyone began to laugh at Big T's expense. "Y'all think that's funny, but I'm telling you, it's racist."

"Remember, it's only racist if it's not true," said Ryan.

Tobias walked up to Kirin and looked her straight in the eye. "You okay, jailbird?"

"Yeah."

They hesitated, but then Tobias moved in and gave her a hug. He whispered in her ear, "I'm glad." Kirin closed her eyes and enjoyed that moment. It was surprising to see Tobias show some emotion, especially in front of everyone else. Afterward, one by one, each of her friends greeted her and gave her a hug.

Angelo stood up and shouted, "I protest! She should be getting her rest after such an ordeal."

Kirin tapped him on the shoulder and said, "It's noted."

Angelo begged, "I only want what's best for you, Kirin."

"I know. I know."

Gwen asked, "So, how much do you know?"

"Know about what?" asked Kirin.

The room immediately went silent, as they were surprised by the fact that Kirin was totally in the dark. All eyes were staring at her as Kirin had the look of a wide-eyed puppy dog.

Sage jumped in and said, "So, you have no idea what happened after you were arrested?"

Doc cleared his throat. "You might want to sit down and watch it for yourself."

Ken shouted, "Someone lower the lights."

Danny said, "This isn't a movie?"

Ryan shoved Danny onto the sofa and sat next to him. "We all know that, but it'll make for a more dramatic effect when she watches it."

Kirin said, "What are you talking about?" Her voice feel upon deaf ears, as no one would answer her.

Kirin's heart began to race. She had no clue what everyone was talking about. The car ride home had been difficult enough, having to deal with her parents, but Sifu was surprisingly quiet. She peeked back to see if he looked any different, but he held his emotions, if any, in check.

Doc asked, "Ken, can you turn on her TV and playback her speech?"

Ken ran to turn on her TV as everyone gathered around. Kirin slowly took her spot on the center of the couch and remained silent.

Ken asked, "Just play the speech first?"

Doc said, "Yeah, I'm sure everyone wants to see the greatest speech again."

Kirin's puzzled look continued to grow as she had no clue what everyone was talking about. She thought, *The greatest speech?*

Tobias said, "Kirin, I can't tell you how many times I've watched this already."

Ken said, "If you thought your knockout last year was viral, this blows it away."

"No kidding, only two days and you've got a billion views online," said Robert.

Kirin's head twitched from one comment to the next, confused by all the excitement.

Doc said, "Guys, will you all just be quiet and let her see it for herself? You can tell she has no idea what's been happening."

For Kirin, everything was still in a blur. The last forty-eight hours sitting in the jail had left her dazed and confused.

A silence fell upon the entire loft as everyone gathered around her TV. A few seconds later, it began to play.

Ryan waved his hands to calm down the group. "Shh ... everybody."

Bryce was on the screen, saying, "I'd like to introduce someone who needs no introduction. Many of you may recognize her as the Dome Champion of the world, but before me is a person I truly admire and look up to. I am glad to call her my friend. Here is ... Kirin Rise." Thousands of people clapping and cheering could be heard and seen. On the screen, Bryce gave Kirin a hug and led her to the podium to speak. The camera zoomed out to show the immense crowd waiting for her. Finally, all eyes were focused on Kirin, and she began to speak....

"Last year, I stood in front of a crowd much smaller than this, unknown to the world, I was armed only with a single thought. But now look, before you is what a single thought put into action can create. One punch ... a single punch captured the attention of millions of people all over the world. That is the power of one. Now imagine if we take that single idea amongst each and every one of us and unite it together ... imagine a million focused punches and how one punch by all of us can change things forever. You see, that's why we're gathered here today, to capture the world's attention unlike ever before.

"I am speaking to the tens of thousands who have gathered here to listen to my message, as well as the millions who are watching at this very moment. Take a second right now, because I want you to see what I see, to look into the faces of those nearby and from afar ... to know that a common bond exists in all mankind that transcends one's sex, race, or nationality. We the people, united in a single thought, here today to make a better world for all to live in. I want you to remember this very moment."

Onscreen, Kirin paused before she began speaking again. She thrusted a punch straight into the air, but at the last second extended her index finger to the sky. That was the symbol of the power of one, as everyone around followed her gesture. After watching everyone mimic her motion, she lowered her hand and continued.

"What I see and feel in your eyes tonight is the silent pain that each one of us carry. The pain of hopelessness, the pain of accepting what will never change, the pain of knowing the next generation will come to live with the same desperation. I stand in front of you tonight telling you that we can change our world and we must! The possibilities of what can be do exist, for I feel it within, all around, in the air, and through my very bones. And it begins here, tonight, at this very moment. This moment in history is when they look back years from now and say ... this is where it all started, this is the day the masses became one."

The crowd cheered as Kirin adjusted on the couch, feeling a little uncomfortable watching herself on TV.

"Now, in order for this to happen, we must first come to accept the truth. The difficulty lies in taking responsibility, for that burden falls upon us and not those individuals governing. It begins with you!

"For too long we have feared dealing with reality, and now the inevitable is upon us. The fact is we have allowed this to go on. We have deemed this to be the standard, that poverty, hunger, lack of education and opportunities are our way of life. For too long, we have put our faith in the hands of others, believing in their lies and thinking that they're doing what is best for us. We are given false hopes and promises that through their system we can make change happen. And each and every year, through every term, promises continue to go un-kept, and we wonder why things can't get better when the solutions are right there in front of us. The balance we seek is but a dream for the masses and a reality for only the handful that control our destiny. Thus, we have lost our way.

The crowd on screen was silent, as the weight of the truth set in.

"Those in charge have kept us in dissension with one another, divided us so that we can bicker and squabble over the scraps. We have allowed our petty differences to fuel their fire. They know all too well that, together, we have the power. Together we are strong. Together we can make the impossible a reality. So, I ask you today to embrace our differences and see that we have a greater goal … that we as human beings deserve and are entitled to a better way of life.

Kirin paused as the crowd's cheers rose in volume.

"The time to act is now. Driven by greed, they have taken everything … our identity, our dignity, and our humanity. They want to destroy the light and hope in each of us, because it is the last thought we cling to and the very core of our existence. Without this single thought … without hope, we are powerless and there will be no return from the darkness that ensues.

"To win this game we cannot play by their rules. Those were designed to make you fail. The vote they pretend to give you is only the illusion of choice. Your protest goes unheard and forgotten over time. Only unified, indivisible action by all of us will bring the change we want in our lives. The power of a focused action, delivered in unison by millions will be what history remembers. Today, together, we can once and for all flex our muscle and remind those individuals who lead and govern us that we have the ultimate power—not the handful, but the masses united as one.

The crowd began chanting 'The power of one', as the thrill of the moment electrified the air.

"I believe if greed can have its day, then the time for justice and common sense has arrived. Those in charge are the ones now afraid. They have feared for many years the coming of this day when the masses realize the power from within and refuse to be their pawns for profit any longer.

"A wise man once told me that the world will go on without you, unless you give it a reason to stop. I say on this day, this very moment … let the entire world take notice…. We, the forgotten, will rise from the shadows and make the world stop. Our action will not be through violence, but we will make them feel our pain and suffering in the only form they can understand … financially. Our non-action through holding back production and consumption, will show them how much we truly matter, because we … the men and women working across this country are what keeps their machine of profit and greed running. Today we proclaim our awareness of the power that we as individuals have. And, we will unite on common ground no longer denying the world of the endless possibilities of our greatness.

Energized by Kirin's speech, the crowd onscreen cheered again and began the chant 'The power of one.' Slowly a sea of humanity began raising their hands symbolizing the power of one.

In the loft, fifteen minutes passed as the group finished watching the last word spoken by Kirin. And, just like on TV, everyone in Kirin's loft stood up and began to clap around her.

"I don't get it," said Kirin, who was no better off knowing what had happened than at the beginning.

Sage said, "Kirin, you have no idea what your speech has done. Do you?"

Tobias looked at her and said, "Kirin, seriously … you've done more with your speech than most politicians have done in their lifetime of promises."

Kirin shrugged her shoulders. "Wait. What?"

Doc glanced at Gwen and said, "Were you able to splice all of it together?"

Gwen nodded. "Yes, I got it all nicely placed together."

Turning to Kirin, Doc said, "Gwen was kind enough to put together the last forty-eight hours of what you missed, Kirin."

Gwen swiped her finger across her tablet, and her work popped up on the TV screen.

Kirin sat silently studying the collage that Gwen had arranged. Flashes of headline news and the impact seemed almost surreal to Kirin.

Sage said, "Kirin, what Tobias said was right. While your actions created a temporary disruption, it made the entire world stop for a moment and think. The market took a massive hit the day after the speech, and they've suspended it for a day and could possibly do it again tomorrow. They are thinking of putting market limits just in case it drops any further."

"Why?" asked Kirin.

Doc explained, "Your *Day of Silence* resonated through the land. How can I put this so it doesn't create a shock to the system? A country run by consumption was brought to its knees when the people didn't purchase major products for just one day. Stock prices fell; companies for the first time bowed down. There's a sense of jubilation at the demonstration of what we can do unified. Even those making minimum wage went on strike, and not a single person broke it."

Sage said, "Imagine: no one bought, no one worked, no one did anything. Your speech got the majority to listen and do nothing."

Ryan said, "You could say your nothing made the biggest something."

Gwen asked, "Kirin, it was just brilliant that you came up with this speech."

Kirin said, "I can't take credit for this. It was Hunter who gave me the idea."

Doc asked, "What do you mean?"

Kirin said, "Hunter sent me a link to a story about Women's Day Off in Iceland. It was October 24, 1975. It was a day when all the women united and went on strike, bringing the entire country to a standstill. That little idea gave me the motivation to do the speech. The only difference was, instead of just women, I made it for everyone who shared the common goal of being treated fairly."

Sage said, "Now, that is brilliant."

Kirin said modestly, "I can't take credit. He gave me the idea."

Sifu said, "Don't sell yourself short. Every little idea needs motion; otherwise, it just becomes a passing thought."

Ken said, "Kirin, guess who took the biggest hit?"

Kirin thought for a moment and said, "The UFMF."

Robert smiled. "You got what you wanted. Their stock took the biggest hit of all."

Kirin took a moment to let everything sink in. She knew, deep down, that this was just the beginning.

10:00 pm

Kirin was busy cleaning up her loft as everyone but Sifu had left. Sifu had been quite distant all night, staring at the crowd outside her window.

"You're extremely quiet tonight," Kirin said as she was finishing the last of the dishes.

Sifu stared outside and didn't respond.

"Sifu?"

He turned around and said, "Sorry, I was just thinking of something."

Kirin turned off the water to the sink and began drying her hands. "What is it?"

"I don't like it."

"Like what?"

"It's nothing."

Kirin walked toward Sifu. "There's no such thing as nothing is nothing with you, Sifu. Please, tell me what it is."

"The protest was illegal from the very start. They could've squashed it immediately. Someone wanted you to deliver the speech. They wanted you to reveal your hand. They were banking that you would fuel the fire."

Kirin paused and thought about what Sifu had said. "Sifu, that doesn't make sense. Why give me the upper hand?"

Sifu said, "Kirin, aren't you the least bit worried tying in your message with Bryce?"

Kirin said, "Sifu, this is beyond anything a twenty-year-old girl can do by herself."

"Why? Who says it's not possible?"

"I'm not a leader. I don't know the first thing about politics."

"You know something far greater than politics, Kirin. You have common sense, and you know right from wrong. Do not place such little value in what I've taught you as well as in believing in yourself."

Kirin looked away, unsure she could handle the burden that continued to grow upon her.

Sifu said, "Are you not passing the very responsibility you talked about in your speech over to Bryce?"

The room went silent as Sifu's words lingered.

▲ ▲ ▲

It was just past midnight, and Kirin found herself restless. She stared at the clock and blew the hair from her face. A quick peek at the side of her bed showed her Bacon was snoring and farting in sequence. Kirin thought, *Hmm, maybe that's what's keeping me awake.*

Kirin got up and headed to the fridge. She stared at a handful of leftovers and a half-empty bottle of juice. She picked up her phone and quickly checked to see if there was any place open that delivered. After several minutes, the feeling of hunger went away, and she went back to her bed and tucked in Bacon, who was still sound asleep.

Kirin then headed to her computer and began surfing the net. Several quick glances showed her nothing important was online, which wasn't unusual. She then clicked on her mailbox to see if anything was new. As she scrolled down, an email addressed to her stuck out. It read, "Important Read for Kirin Rise." At first, she thought it was some kind of junk mail or spam, but curiosity got the best of her as she clicked it open.

As she opened the email, the screen flickered and went black. She sat back, wondering what she had just done. A video popped up with a shaded figure, who began speaking. His voice was altered so it sounded robotic.

The voice said, "Kirin Rise? Kirin Rise?"

Kirin wasn't sure what was going on. No app or chat was open on her computer, but yet a voice was coming through it. The voice said it louder, "Kirin Rise?"

Kirin panicked and immediately hit the off button. The screen turned black as a moment of silence gave her some relief. She stared at the computer and let out a sigh. She thought, *What was that all about?*

Suddenly, right before her eyes, the computer booted itself back on. Kirin leaned back with her hands up away from the machine. She muttered, "How's this possible?"

The same image reappeared onto the screen. The voice repeated, "Kirin Rise?"

"Yes!" she said apprehensively. "This is her ... Who is this?"

The stranger spoke, "Who I am is not important. What we have is. If you do not fully follow our instructions 100%, then what you desire will be forever lost. If you tell anyone about this conversation, the deal will be off as well. Stay tuned for further instructions."

Kirin was unsure what the message was referring to, but in a flash a picture popped up on the screen that turned her world immediately upside down. Kirin's mouth dropped open, and she began to cry uncontrollably. She stared at the screen confused at what she was looking at. It was a picture of her mother and father—her biological parents. She trembled and mumbled their names in Korean. She thought, *How is this possible? I thought they were dead! Is this for real?* She shook her head, skeptical of the possibilities, but her eyes could not look away. She touched the screen as her fingers trembled; her emotions ran wild. She leaned forward and looked at her father's face, there it was, a mole on the side of his cheek. *It's him,* she thought. Both of them looked older, but it really looked as if it were them.

The voice said, "If you want to see them again, you will do everything we say. Betray us, and you put their lives in jeopardy. Do you understand?"

Kirin stared at the blank figure on the screen and quickly replied, "Yes … Yes, I understand."

The voice said, "Wait for further instructions."

As the screen went blank, Kirin panicked. The same questions began to race through her head, *Is this for real? Can they possibly be alive?"*

Kirin picked up her phone and was about to call Gwen, but before she could dial her, her phone began to ring. It was a number she didn't recognize. She picked up the call and said, "Who is this?"

"Kirin Rise, we warned you about telling anyone. I guess you don't care to see your parents ever again," said the voice.

Kirin said, "I'm sorry! I'm sorry. Yes, I won't tell anyone…. Please, give me another chance."

The voice said, "You've been warned." The line went dead.

Kirin stared at her phone and then looked around her loft. She wondered how any of this was possible. *Could they really be alive? How did they know I was going to make a call?* Kirin didn't know what to do, as the picture she'd seen was now ingrained in her mind. She had a sense of excitement and sorrow. If that the picture was true, could her parents have survived and still be alive in North Korea?

"If we can divide people and distract them, then they will allow themselves to be dominated."–Watanabe

SECTION 1

Short Stories #6—Kirin's P.O.V.

<u>April Showers—299 Days</u>

Mondays were such a drag, but I had such a great time with my sleepover at Gwen's that I guessed this was the universe balancing things out. It was the end of a long school day, and I went through the usual routine. I made sure I had all my stuff for homework, and the walk home with my two bestest friends would be the conclusion to a tiring day. As I stared at my locker and reflected, something odd came up that took a moment to sink in. I thought, *I haven't seen Hunter all day, not even once.*

That's strange. He always talks to me. I checked my phone but didn't see a text or phone call. I was about to give him a buzz, but the time was short and forced me to hurry. I concluded that he was probably home sick or just busy.

In the distance, both Sage and Gwen were already waiting for me. The outside ground was all wet as the rain matched the gloom of a Monday.

Sage waved at me and yelled. "Hurry up, Kirin! It's probably gonna rain some more."

I sprinted toward them and said, "Hey, guys, what's up?"

They gave me a weird look and then stared at one another.

Sage asked, "Gwen, can I put my backpack on your chair?"

She looked at him for a second and said, "Fine."

"Come on, we better get home. It looks like it's going to rain again.... Oh, by the way, did you guys see Hunter today?"

Suddenly, they stopped dead in their tracks. Gwen slowly turned around and said, "You're kidding me, right, Kirin?"

"What do you mean?"

"Oh my God, you didn't hear?" said Gwen as she gave me a horrified look. She glanced at Sage for confirmation. "Sage, she doesn't know?"

Sage shrugged and said, "I only found out when you told me."

"Is something wrong? Did something happen to Hunter?" I asked in a panicked voice.

"No, no, physically he's fine, but remember you slept over at my place this weekend, right…?"

"Yeah, so what's the problem?"

Gwen shook her head.

"Come on, Gwen. Spit it out."

"I guess when you were at my place, Hunter had an elaborate plan to ask you out to prom. He had it all planned with a band, dancers, and the works. He didn't realize you were at my place."

"Oh my God … I can't believe it. I gotta find him," I said.

Gwen asked, "What are you gonna do?"

"I don't know, but I have to find him." I dropped my stuff and took off.

I began calling Hunter. He didn't respond. I texted him and waited for about a minute, but still no response. "Pluck a duck! I'll find him the old-fashioned way." I ran toward his home, taking a wild guess about which direction he took to get to his house.

After five minutes of running around, I thought, *Is that him? That looks like him.* He was about to cross the street.

I yelled at the top of my lungs, "Hunter. Wait up, Hunter!"

I ran toward him, but he didn't respond.

I felt so bad about all the effort he'd put into it—and right on the odd day I picked to sleep over. I wasn't sure what to say to him, but he was my friend, and I didn't want him to feel bad.

"Hunter!" I shouted.

He finally stopped in his tracks, but didn't turn around. He stood there with his head hung low and his shoulder slumped. I could feel it. I could feel what he was feeling as I got closer.

"Please just hear me out, will you?" I said it with such confidence, but I knew it was a bluff.

He still didn't turn around, but I approached him, so he knew I was right there.

I grabbed him gently by the arm and spoke. "Uh … hey," I said as my nerves finally kicked in and I could feel a lump in my throat. "I'm not sure what to say, Hunter, but I just found out all that you did for me … and, I'm, uh … I'm really flattered."

Hunter finally turned around. When he did, I took a step back. He still avoided eye contact with me and remained silent.

I stood there helplessly, unsure what to do.

"I'm so stupid. I can't believe I planned all that, and the most important thing was to make sure you were there." He shook his head and continued to stare down toward my feet.

"I think it's really cute what you did, and any girl would appreciate all the effort you put into it."

"Sorry, Kirin, I blew it."

"You didn't blow it."

Hunter finally looked up; his eyes had a shimmer of hope in them. He blurted, "So, will you … uh, go to prom with me?"

I didn't know what to say. I was prepared to find him, but I hadn't thought about even answering the question. He caught me off guard as I stuttered to answer him. "Uh, I'm not sure, Hunter. I've never done anything like that before, and I…."

Hunter walked past me, and I could feel his sadness from my answer. He didn't say another word; he didn't need to. I was clueless about how to respond.

I hated this feeling of uncertainty. This was foreign ground to me. I searched my Wing Chun teachings and thought, *What would Sifu say in this situation?* I turned around to face him, my back to the corner of the street.

I closed my eyes and tried to quiet my mind. I failed miserably, as my head was full of confusion. The pressure of the moment was just too much for me to handle.

Suddenly, I felt Hunter grab me by my arms, spinning me around. We immediately switched sides as his back was now facing the street. All I saw was a car speeding by as it hugged the curb, creating a huge splash. Hunter shielded me from the splash, but he ended up getting drenched to the bone.

The jerks in the car speeding by shouted, "Have a wet day, blink!" and continued to chuckle away.

I looked up at Hunter. The first thing he said was, "Are you all right? Did you get wet? You okay, Kirin?"

"I'm fine. I'm fine, but you look like a mess," I said. I couldn't believe that he was more concerned about my welfare than being drenched from head to toe.

I stared into his eyes. "Yes."

Hunter asked, "Yes, you're okay?"

I shook my head. "No … I mean, yes, Hunter, I'd love to go to the prom with you."

He smiled from ear to ear.

I heard a loud crackle in the sky as we both looked up at the sound of thunder. Just like that, before we could say another word, it started to rain harder than I could imagine.

We looked back into each other's eyes and laughed at the irony of such things. I approached him, and he finally came close to me, and we both hugged each other tightly as the rain continued to fall down upon us.

Off Key—307 Days

I was waiting by the window for Sage to come. Most of the family was home, but I had more pressing matters that needed my attention. Finally, I saw Sage walking by our front door.

"Awesome, he's here!" I said as I sprang to my feet.

My mom somehow reached the door before me.

"Mom, I got it."

"It's no bother, Kirin," said my mom as she welcomed Sage in.

"Hi, Mrs. Rise," said Sage.

"Ah, Sage, come on in," said my mom. "Honey, Sage, is here."

My dad came strolling by and said, "Hey, Sage … you here to practice music with Kirin?"

Sage paused for a moment. "Not exactly … I guess we could work on that as well."

My dad looked confused. "Sage, aren't you in the same band as Kirin is?"

My eyes opened as much as eyes could open for an Asian girl, and I quickly bit my lip.

Sage said, "Yeah, we're in band, but Kirin's in the beginner group."

"You don't say. You know what? I just thought of this…. I've never heard Kirin play yet." He glanced at me and said, "Kirin, why don't you and Sage play a song?"

"Hey, Sage, shouldn't we be working on our school project instead?" As soon as my dad looked back at him, I made hand signals not to go further with this band talk.

My mom turned around and stared at me awkwardly.

"Kirin, what's wrong with you?" asked Mom.

"Uh, nothing, Mom. I just saw a fly and was trying to swat it." I stifled a giggle as that was the best excuse I could come up with.

My dad said, "Oh, come on. Now I insist. A few seconds won't kill you, Kirin."

Sage said, "Yeah, Kirin. I'd like to hear you play it as well."

My dad gestured to head to the living room. "Honey, go upstairs and get your instrument so we can all hear you play."

When both my parents had their backs turned, I snapped a punch to Sage's arm.

"Ouch!" yelled Sage.

My parents turned around to see what was wrong, and I stood their innocently.

Sage said as he rubbed his arm, "Ah, been lifting way too many weights lately. My arm is kinda of sore."

I said, "Yeah, Sage, I can really tell the difference now."

We both gave each other a dirty look.

My dad said, "Princess, hurry up and get your instrument."

I swallowed and went back to my room. I thought, *Oh my God, I've never even opened the case, let alone practiced.* As I ran into my messy room, it took me several minutes to figure out where I placed my instrument. I found a big suitcase buried under my clothes. I looked at the size of the instrument and wondered what the heck was I assigned to. As I opened up the case, for the first time my eyes laid upon a golden metallic thingamajig. I thought, *What the heck is this...? A tuba? Trumpet?* I honestly had no idea what it was or what exactly I was supposed to do with it.

"Kirin, hurry up!" shouted my dad.

I carried my instrument down the stairs in the living room, where Sage and my parents were waiting.

Mom said, "I didn't realize your instrument was so big."

I thought, *That makes two of us.*

Mom asked, "Is that a tuba?"

Sage laughed. "Hey, Kirin, you are so lucky to have such a big instrument."

I gave him a look as he kept his stupid smile on his face.

I said, "Yeah, Mom. It's a tuba."

Sage stepped in and corrected, "Mrs. Rise, it's actually called a baritone. Most beginners have trouble telling the difference between the two."

Dad asked, "So, what are you going to play?"

"Uh, I've been practicing this for a bit," I said. I had no idea what I was doing, other than just blowing into the hole and moving my fingers around.

For the next several minutes, the sound of an animal in pain spread throughout my entire house. I watched as my parents tried to keep a supportive face, but the sound was painful for all of us.

I could see Sage was doing his best to keep a straight face.

"Well, that was a good beginning, uh, Kirin." My dad tried to encourage me.

"Uh, yeah, Dad. I still need lots of practice." I blushed, wondering how painful it had been for everyone.

Both my parents got up with a dazed look on their faces. As they left the room, Sage began to howl in laughter. I punched him in the arm.

"Ow! That really hurt," said Sage.

"You jerk! Why'd you put me in that situation?"

"Hmm, I've heard you philosophize about Wing Chun teachings, and I believe the correct question is: how did you put yourself in that situation?"

"Quiet! Now are you going to help me out or not?"

Sage said, "Yes, let's head upstairs to your room."

We ran upstairs to my room.

"Close the door," I said.

"Okay, so what do you need help with, Kirin? It's not like you aren't getting all As," said Sage.

"No, no ... it has nothing to do with homework or school. But, as you may or may not know, I said yes to Hunter for prom."

"That's awesome! So, what's the problem? Do you need me to explain the birds and the bees to you?" chuckled Sage.

"Please don't talk. This is a serious issue."

"What is it?" Sage's brain was scrambling to figure out what it might be.

"I don't know how to dance!"

"Are you serious? That's why you asked me to come?"

"Yes. I know you're a really good dancer, Sage." I said.

"That's BS. Who told you I could dance?" Sage said angrily.

"Your mom showed me a video of you dancing several years ago."

Sage turned around and muttered something.

"Come on, Sage. You're my only hope," I said, hoping to appeal to his empathic side.

Sage laughed out loud. "Nice one, Kirin. Just for that line, I'm willing to help you out."

I thought, *What line?*

Sage clapped his hands and said, "Okay, let's see what you can do first. Let me pull up a simple jam for you to dance to."

The music began to play as I started going to the beat as best as I could. At first, I was nervous dancing in front of Sage, but I quickly settled in and started doing my thing. I honestly forgot that Sage was there, and as the music ended, I continued to dance, regardless.

His mouth was open, and his face seemed frozen.

"So, what do you think?" I asked.

Sage didn't answer right away. He almost looked constipated.

I waved my hand in front of his face, and he still didn't respond.

"Let me ask you something, Kirin. Were you listening to the same song that I was?" asked Sage.

I grabbed a pillow and chucked it at him.

"What? I thought you wanted me to be honest," said Sage.

"Seriously, is it that bad?" I asked as I tried to envision my own dancing.

"I can tell you this, Kirin … if it was interpretive dance, you're definitely dead on."

"Ugh, okay. Well, it isn't. So, now I'm begging you.… You have to teach me how to dance."

Sage took a deep breath and placed both hands on his hips. "A promise is a promise. This is gonna require quite a bit of work."

I looked at him, hoping he had the magic.

"Okay, turn on the music and just watch," said Sage.

I pulled up a song on my phone and began to play it. Immediately, Sage's personality changed as he began dancing to the beat. It was mesmerizing watching him do all his moves. He was mixing several types of dances together, but he looked as smooth as Sifu doing the forms. When the music finally stopped, he smiled at me and waited.

I sat on my bed and just began clapping. "Wow, that was awesome! I never realized you had it in you. How'd you learn how to dance?"

"Well, being a bookworm, I needed some kind of avenue to let go. When I was a little kid, I would watch people on TV do dance moves and just mimic their motions."

"Sage Parker, you never fail to surprise me."

"Can't say I don't hear that enough," laughed Sage.

"You jerk." I laughed along with him.

When we were quiet again, I said, "Teach me. Teach me to dance like that, Sage."

Sage said, "No guarantees that you can dance like that, but I'm willing to go off the edge for you and say … I can at least teach you to catch the beat."

He extended his hand to me, and I didn't hesitate to lock in the deal.

An Hour Later

Sage looked flustered as I tried my very best to listen to what he was saying.

"Okay, we've tried almost all the dance steps, but you aren't really catching the beat. You're trying too hard to copy my motions. Let's do this: let's keep it simple and do the white man step side-to-side dance."

"Watch me first, Kirin," said Sage. I watched him move; he looked so graceful and on beat. "Okay, it's your turn."

I tried my best to get the beat but honestly felt like I had two left feet.

Sage scratched his head in frustration. "Okay, forget all the steps I've taught you so far. Dancing isn't about memorizing motions. The main goal is to feel the beat. To go with the flow. Just to be you and be natural. Do you understand?"

I knew exactly what Sage was talking about. It was no different from doing drills in Wing Chun. I had to look deeper than just copying motions.

Another Hour

Well, you're not gonna win any dance contest, but I think those simple steps will keep you safe from looking too weird on the dance floor."

"Thanks, Sage, for all your help. I'm sure prom will turn out to be awesome."

<u>Prom Night—332 Days</u>

Staring into the mirror, I was unsure of the person who was on the other side. I thought, *Is this really me?* Makeup, hair, perfume, and a dress—this was something out of the norm from my daily routine of soap, water, and my trusty red hoodie with jeans.

"You look beautiful, Kirin," said Gwen with a beaming smile as she stared at me, her pet project.

Gwen's words shook me out of my trance as I turned slowly to look at her and returned a smile. I squirmed and fidgeted in my dress, finding it extremely difficult to relax.

"I hate to brag——" said Gwen.

I interrupted and giggled. "Are you sure? Coz you do it quite often."

Gwen frowned and looked away, crossing her arms with disapproval. "Hmh!"

I quickly rushed over and gave her a big squeeze. "You know I'm joking. You're my best friend, and I wouldn't have been able to pull this off without your help." I kissed her on the cheek, leaving a red stain from my lipstick, as we both looked in the mirror and smiled.

"Seriously Gwen, I don't know how you do this every day."

"Uh, Kirin, this is what girls do…. News flash: you … are a girl."

I didn't want to upset Gwen, so I just smiled and didn't say anything. I thought, *I always favored the more natural look.*

"I can't believe I'm going."

Gwen smiled. "You're the lucky one, going to senior prom as a sophomore."

I replied, "I guess you and I have different definitions of *luck*."

Knock. Knock. Knock.

"Can I come in?" My mom's muffled words snuck in from behind the door.

"Sure thing, Mom."

The door creaked open as I continued to stare at myself in the mirror. Still in a state of shock, I honestly couldn't recognize who I was looking at.

"Oh my god. My little girl. You look so beautiful." I turned around to see my mom cover her mouth as she struggled to stop the tears from running down her cheeks. She came rushing toward me and hugged me from behind. We both were engaged in a stare, as the mirror trapped us.

"Thanks, Mom." I held her arms, enjoying her touch more than her compliment.

"I swear I'd give you a kiss, but I don't want to ruin your makeup. Anyway, if you're ready … Hunter's been waiting downstairs." She leaned over and gave me a pretend kiss.

"Just one more minute, okay, Mom?"

She nodded and headed toward the door. I laughed as she kept turning back as she was trying to leave. I thought, *I wonder if this is how she'd react if I ever entered and won a beauty pageant.*

The door closed, and the room turned silent. I took a deep breath and slowly let it all out.

"Nervous?" asked Gwen.

I nodded, bit my lip, and made sure my little scar was covered by my hair.

"You'll be fine. You said you and Hunter have been hanging out and getting along well."

"I know. It's not that."

Gwen started giggling.

"What?" I smirked, as I knew what she was thinking.

"I can't believe you're nervous about that." Gwen was trying to keep from bursting out in laughter.

"Well, you've seen me. Who wouldn't be nervous?" I cracked a smile, and then we both started laughing.

"Seriously, Kirin, you're the only person I know who goes to prom and is worried about dancing," said Gwen.

"I can't help it. Even with Sage's help, I still feel like I've got two left feet," I said.

Gwen said, "Do you want a little advice from your BFF?"

"Of course."

"All that Wing Chun that you yap about with me, you always mention that it's based off the feel, right?"

"Wow," I said in a state of shock.

"What?" Gwen asked curiously.

"I always thought you zoned me out when I talked about that."

Gwen snickered. "I do zone you out, but you keep saying it so much, some of the stuff actually stuck. Besides, I kinda like your attack and defense philosophy and I sorta use it when I do my hacks."

I couldn't help but giggle and turned to face her.

"I know Sage has helped you learn how to dance. But, seriously, forget all that. When it's time to dance, just do what you do. Just like you always say to me, trust what you feel."

I came behind Gwen and gave her an immense hug. "Gwyneth Albright, you surprise me sometimes."

"That makes two of us." Gwen giggled.

Suddenly I heard my dad shout from below, "Kirin! Honey, are you ready?" His voice carried more anxiety than I felt about dancing.

I took one last deep breath and stared at Gwen. "Well, there's no turning back now."

I stood outside my room and blew into my hand, a quick check to make sure my breath was okay. I grabbed a piece of tissue to dry my hands. They always seemed to sweat more when I was nervous. I was ready for the long walk down the hallway for the first encounter. It seemed almost like it was from the movies. It appeared to stretch longer than it should before I got to the top of the stairs. In a way, I was just waiting for the director to shout, *Action!* Gwen followed behind me in her wheelchair but gave me enough distance to be the center of attention. I honestly didn't need to be, but she had a flair for the dramatic.

I looked down from above and saw all the faces staring at me. My hand was shaking uncontrollably, so I clenched my fist, trying to stop it, and brushed the side of my hair like I always did when I got nervous. Seconds seemed like an eternity, as my nerves were getting the better of me. I tried controlling my breathing, like Sifu taught me, but it wasn't helping. I thought, *Dang ... more practice. I hope one day I can learn that.* Flashes started popping as my dad began snapping shots. My mom stood by Mark and Kyle with Butterscotch wagging her tail and circling everyone.

Finally, I glanced over, and there he was ... Hunter. We made direct eye contact as he smiled. He looked at me with those kind eyes that I was so used to seeing. He put me at ease, and I let out a little breath and slowly started settling down. Dressed in all black, he stood proudly in his tuxedo and his traditional red bow tie. I thought, *Wow, he looks really good.*

I walked down the stairs, and it felt magical, almost like a movie short of music being played. Eventually, the slow walk led me face to face with Hunter. At the base of the stairs, I stumbled slightly. I thought, *How does one walk in these high heels?* Then I frowned, briefly realizing my center wasn't working either. Unfortunately, that brought my nerves back, and I turned away slightly.

"Uh, hi." I brushed the side of my hair again.

Hunter smiled and replied, "Hi."

Mark said, "Kirin, seriously ... you look great."

Crunching on a snack of potato chips, Kyle added, "Yeah, I didn't recognize you. You look really good, sis."

Mark added, "Yeah, I concur. You actually look like a girl."

Mark's remark snapped me from the moment, and I punched him in the arm.

Mark rubbed his arm, saying, "Ouch, that hurt! That was a compliment."

Both Kyle and Hunter began laughing. I looked back at Hunter and said, "Uh, sorry about that." I gave Mark a look afterward.

"Don't worry about it," chuckled Hunter.

Mark whined, "Okay, Mom ... do we need to be here for the rest of this?"

Mom shooed them away and said, "Go, go ... go watch your UFMF fights, or whatever that is." My brothers perked up with excitement and scurried their way to the living room. I was relieved that some of my stress left with them.

Dad said, "Okay, I want the both of you to have fun." My dad stared at Hunter with a serious look. "And ... Hunter, remember what time I said I want Kirin back home."

Hunter said, "Of course, Mr. Rise. She won't be a second late. I promise."

Several minutes passed as my parents gushed and took pictures of both of us. Then we were finally inside Hunter's car ready to go.

Hunter turned to me and stuttered, "Uh ... you ... no, um ... I've never seen you so beautiful. Wait ... that's not what I meant! I mean you've always looked good, but tonight you're, like, extra pretty." He chuckled nervously, which brought me a sense of comfort that he was feeling the pressure just like me.

I blushed and couldn't think of something clever to say. "I thought the same about you." I shook my head and turned away. *Oh my gosh ... why did I say that?*

Suddenly I heard a text. "Oops, sorry about that." I took a quick peek and saw it was Gwen.

"Um ... ready to go?" I said, trying to help the situation with motion.

"Yeah, sure thing," said Hunter.

My phone beeped with another text, but this time I ignored it.

The twenty-minute car ride went by fast. We both eventually settled down and felt comfortable after a shaky start. It felt like how we normally hung out when we were in school; the only difference was we were all dressed up.

"Well, we're here," said Hunter as he parked the car. Droves of students were headed inside the banquet hall.

"Yeah, we're here. This should be fun," I said with a smile. My phone beeped again with a text, breaking our moment. "I'm sorry. I'm sorry." I thought, *Bad timing, Gwen.* I smiled to cover up my frustration and said, "Gwen can be pretty nosy at times." I didn't bother checking if it was her and set my phone to vibrate.

"Ready?" asked Hunter.

I nodded and sat there. Each moment felt like a nervous milestone of achievement.

"Oh wait, don't move," said Hunter as he flashed his hand at me to stay put. He sprang out of the car seat and rushed to go to my side. I watched as he ran around the car to get my door. He opened it for me like a gentleman and extended his hand to help me.

"Thank you."

We began walking to the entrance as the celebration and the loud music were bustling. Inside the banquet hall, the bright lights and the nice decorations were something to be marveled at. I found it hard to believe that one day of preparation and a very limited budget from our student council were able to pull off something this decent.

Hunter said, "Wow, they really went all out!"

I nodded, bit my lip, and stood frozen in my stance. He offered his hand for me to hold, and I did just that, thinking, *Please God, don't let my hand be sweaty.*

His touch was soft and comforting as we gazed at each other. I thought, *This will be a night I'll never forget.* Our smiles grew even more; for the first time, I had the courage to look deep into Hunter's eyes. Suddenly, I hung my head again as Hunter asked me, "What?"

"I'm so, so sorry. My phone keeps vibrating nonstop. Let me tell Gwen to stop bothering us, okay?" Hunter was always understanding, and he smiled and assured me it was okay.

I grabbed my phone and then finally looked at the text.

My hands shook as I reread the message.

"Kirin, your phone!" shouted Hunter as he tried to reach for it before it hit the ground.

Crack.

I fell to my knees as the room started to spin.

"What's wrong, Kirin?" Hunter kneeled to check on me.

I started to cry. "I'm sorry, Hunter. Please forgive me," I stuttered to get the words out of my mouth, but I couldn't.

"Kirin, what's wrong? Please tell me."

I couldn't speak. I stayed on the floor in a daze as my world felt like it was crashing all over again.

Hunter grabbed my phone and looked at the text.

"Kirin. Kirin, can you hear me?"

My eyes began to refocus, and the sound of Hunter's voice became audible.

"I'm sorry, Hunter.... Please, please, take me to the hospital now! Please," I cried.

He pulled me up and led the way. "Sure thing, let's go. Right now."

Twenty Minutes Later

We ran into the emergency waiting room as I searched frantically for the guys. Hunter tapped me on the shoulder, pointed, and said, "I think that might be them, over there."

I jerked quickly to look and saw that the gang was all there. Tobias had already spotted me and was walking in my direction. I could barely stand, shaking all over. I couldn't believe what was happening. Hunter put his arms around me to support me, as I felt ill to my stomach.

Tobias came up to me and didn't say a word. He stood there, teary-eyed with his head hanging down. I pulled away from Hunter's embrace and walked toward Tobias. He couldn't look me straight in the eye, but once he was near enough, I hugged him tight. We didn't speak, but the pain was for real, and we both began to cry.

"Where is he?" I said as I continued to tremble, and my words carried the pain of the moment.

I looked up and finally saw him. There he sat, hunched over on a chair. For the first time in my life, he looked so vulnerable.

Tobias let go, and I headed slowly toward him. With each step I drew closer, my heart ached. The rest of the gang was there, hanging their heads as they cleared a path for me. I didn't bother making eye contact with anyone; all I could see was him. I didn't need to know. I could feel it. I could feel the sorrow in the room. It was silent, yet my heart was screaming in pain. When I finally got to him, I got down on my knee, but I didn't know what to do or say. I was hesitant to even touch him.

I cried and hugged him and just let instinct take over. "Si ... fu." I shook my head and held him even tighter, hoping that a single action could ease the hurt. I was searching for words, for anything I could do to help him. I thought, *What can I do? What can I say?* I continued to cry while hugging him as he sat there, silent and unresponsive.

Then he looked at me tearfully and hugged me tightly. His bloodshot eyes were drowned in tears. He leaned closer and whispered, "The kids. The kids are ... gone ... and Megumi's barely hanging on." His voice became quieter, and I had a hard time hearing him. "I'd give up all the skill in the world ... if I could—"

"Mr. Kwan!" a doctor spoke, garnering everyone's attention.

Sifu immediately sprang up and approached him. I watched as the doctor began to speak, hoping for some good news. Everyone was watching when the doctor put his hand on Sifu's shoulder. Sifu's dejected reaction spoke louder than words. I thought, *Oh no, this can't be happening! Why?*

I tried listening in and caught just a sliver of what the doctor was saying. He said, "She's not gonna make it. I'm sorry, Mr. Kwan. Take this time to say your goodbyes."

I could see Sifu shaking as the doctor walked away. A nurse came by and said, "Mr. Kwan, please come with me."

Sifu stood there, frozen; he looked so frail and helpless. The nurse spoke, "Mr. Kwan, you must hurry. Please follow me, sir."

The guys stood confused, not knowing what to do. I ran up and immediately grabbed Sifu's arm and began walking toward the nurse.

She spoke, "I'm sorry, miss, but only family is allowed back there."

Sifu choked up and said, "She's family."

We both began walking toward the ER, following the nurse. Sifu hesitated for a second before entering, and then we finally saw her. Simo was hooked up to a thousand things, and the sight of her caused Sifu to grip my arm tightly. It was a shocking sight, because it was difficult to make her out. I helped Sifu to the bed as the nurse left the room, leaving us with some time alone. I stood silently and just put my hand on his shoulder. The sounds of the machines, along with Sifu's whimper, were difficult to take in.

Sifu held her hand, which had an IV stuck into it. He bowed his head and began to cry some more. I did the same, but tried to remain silent. I could feel his tears, his pain, as every second brought further sorrow. It brought back memories of my past, which I had locked away for some time. I knew all too well that feeling of losing the ones you love. I gripped my chest as the pounding grew stronger.

A minute passed, which felt like an eternity, and then I saw it. Simo slowly opened her eyes.

I gasped for air and called, "Sifu!"

Simo struggled to turn her head, as Sifu immediately stood up and leaned forward. He came face to face with her and, for a split second, cracked a small smile.

I stepped back, with a side profile view of both, trying not to make a sound. A sea of tears streamed down my face as I held my hands tightly, watching as the two were looking at one another. That look spoke volumes; it defined what love was about.

Simo struggled to open her mouth as Sifu touched her face gently and whispered, "Don't speak."

She stared deeply at Sifu; even in pain, her eyes tried to comfort him. A tear crawled down her face, and Sifu wiped it with his hand. She whispered in pain, "The kids ... the kids, are they okay?" The words were a struggle for Simo, but she desperately wanted to know.

Sifu stayed steady as I heard him say, "Don't worry about the kids. The kids are all fine. I promise you, I'll take care of them." He smiled and assured her. I bit my lip, realizing how painful that must've been for Sifu to say. I thought, *This is the first time I've ever seen Sifu lie.*

Simo made a hint of smile as she said, "I'm so sorry. I didn't see the other car—"

Sifu shook his head and, for a moment, laid it low upon Simo. The sight of Sifu crumpling made Simo tear up. She wanted to help him, so she gently touched his head. He quickly jerked up. In a tearful voice filled with sadness, he spoke with determined conviction. "I swear ... I swear to you, in the next lifetime or however many are needed, I will find you, and we will be ... together again."

Simo looked kindly at Sifu as more tears formed. The two stared at one another. She clasped Sifu gently by the face and said, "Not bad, not—"

Suddenly her monitor went flat, and Sifu stood still, just holding her hand. His glimmer of emotion disappeared, and he himself looked lifeless. The alarm sounded, prompting people to rush in. Roughly fifteen seconds passed before a doctor and several nurses came rushing in, surrounding her.

A nurse shouted, "Mr. Kwan, please step aside."

While all this activity was taking place, I stood by Sifu and grabbed his arm. It was so surreal, as everything felt like it was moving in slow motion. I pulled him out of the way and stood in the corner. I held him tightly, and he didn't make another sound. He stood there, hunched over in darkness as he froze and stared at Simo.

"Accidents don't happen, karma does."—Watanabe.

SECTION 2

Sifu's Journey Entry #6—Let It Rain

First Day of Summer 2030

L ance asked, "How are things going in the land of the rising sun?"

Sifu spoke into the phone as he stared outside the window of his room. He leaned his head against it and did his best to hide his frustrations. "Same old, same old," he muttered.

"You know, Sifu, you'd be terrible as a tour guide," chuckled Lance.

"I'm just being honest. Unless I see Godzilla or Gamera, being in Japan is no different from being in the States."

Lance said, "Wait a second, is Gamera the giant turtle or the robot dude who could fly?"

"It's the turtle. You're thinking of Ultraman."

"Oh yeah, that's right." Lance paused and invested more time into useless info than what was necessary.

"Dang, Sifu. You've side-tracked me. What were we talking about? Oh yeah, I doubt you'd give me the same answer if I asked you that about the food."

Sifu laughed, but he was not in the mood to talk. "Uh, yeah ... I think my reception is going bad, Lance. I'll have to call you back. Shhheeesshh."

Lance said, "Wait, I had a question about the punch."

Sifu said, "Yeah, it's coming in real staticky now ... creeekkksshh." Sifu continued to make a sound as a he grabbed a paper lying nearby and began to crumple it.

"Come on, Sifu, I really have a question about it."

"Have you done 10,000 punches yet, like I told you to do?"

Unfortunately, his hesitation was the answer to Sifu's question.

"I thought so."

"Dammit, Sifu! Okay, before you go, how much longer are you gonna be there?"

"I'll answer that as soon as you finish all your punches," said Sifu.

Sifu hung up and stared outside of his apartment. He looked at the lights glimmering from the building as he pulled away from the window. Since he'd arrived in Japan, he'd been spending his days wandering the streets, wondering when the right moment would be for him to finally take some action. The days seemed to be all the same. Only his occasional visit with April broke the monotony and brought him temporary solace. While he enjoyed seeing her, deep down he knew it was only a distraction from what lingered and pressed in the back of his mind.

Time continued to drift by as dusk suddenly turned to darkness. He found himself staring outside again into the heart of the city. It kept calling him, as unfinished business remained. The blank expression on his face hid the truth as the rain suddenly began to fall. The light drizzle came to life, as if the universe above had lost its patience and was now sending a message to him. Drop by drop, every sound it made caused a shiver throughout Sifu's entire body.

Sifu had enough. It had all boiled down to facing his fears and finally taking steps toward making it better. His eyes began to water until he shed a tear. As that single drop hit the floor, in that very instant, he grabbed his things and finally made a dash for the door. Something at that very moment drew Sifu to action. The universe had spoken that it was now time.

Sifu ran through the streets of Japan, oblivious to all the elements and his current surroundings. After sprinting through the streets, creating seemingly endless patterns from the water, he finally froze dead in his tracks. He could see a familiar building in the distance. He checked his phone and made a futile gesture of wiping the rain from his glasses. It had been a while since he'd felt this way, that he was exactly where he needed to be at that very moment in time.

It was late at night, almost 10:00 pm, but he could see the goal beforehand. It was the first time he'd seen the place in quite a while, and avoiding it was no longer an option. He waited at the corner and watched as the elements continued to show no mercy and poured heavily. He remained distant, observing from afar the little shop as the lights stayed on and some staggered activity inside continued.

More time passed before the lights began to fade and the silhouette figures that were once animated disappeared from his view. Sifu took a deep breath, made a decision, and began taking steps closer toward the entrance. As he got within inches of the door, he hesitated as his heart began to thump, wanting to escape from his chest. He told himself to just do it, to face the music and do what must be done. However, memories quickly flooded him, bringing back the pain, as each drop of rain seemed to blend in with it. He leaned back slightly and then took several steps back away from the door. The rain continued to hammer him as a few onlookers passed by, staring at this odd, soaked individual.

He stared straight ahead as the tears were covered by the rainfall, and Sifu stood there alone and ashamed, torn by an array of emotions. Eventually, he froze in his stance and hung his head. The single light from the shop finally dimmed to a flicker as he took a deep breath and just stood.

Several Hours Later

Just above the ramen shop was the bedroom of Megumi's parents, both of whom were lying down on their tatami, the traditional Japanese bed. Megumi's father, Hiroshi, found himself restless that night, and he continued to toss and turn. He looked toward the window and was drawn by the sound of the rain outside. His aged body struggled to get up, so he took his time. The wind and the rain continued to batter his window, screaming to look outside.

As he reached the window, the condensation formed a haze, making the outside a blur. While it was raining unusually hard, he saw nothing from his quick glance to indicate anything out of the norm. The usual single light that cast its glow struggled to shine against the elements. Exhausted, he decided to give sleep another try. He turned around slowly to head back to his bed, but caught a hint of a shadow below. He rubbed his eyes to clear his sight and then used his hands to remove the moisture from the window. As he leaned closer to see what it was, he mumbled to himself, "Nani?"

Hiroshi began wiping the window feverishly, pressing harder just to make sure he could see things clearly. As his forehead pressed against the window, his eyes squinted to focus on the subject. He finally realized what he was staring at. There in the distance, highlighted sparsely by the single streetlight, stood a man drenched from the pouring rain … Sifu. Surprise quickly changed to anger as he muttered some words in Japanese. He snapped away from the window, crossing his arms in disgust, as he could not bear to look outside anymore.

Two Hours Later

Megumi's mom, Yuki, rolled over to her side. Even in her deep sleep, she realized something was missing. Forty plus years of marriage ingrained a pattern between the two, as the usual brush of her husband's touch was missing. She reached over, blindly feeling for him, but her hand felt an empty space along with the bristle feel of the tatami. She slowly opened her eyes, confirming what she felt, and wondered where he might be. She sat up and looked around the room before finally seeing him nestled in the corner standing by the window. She asked him politely what he was doing, but he did not respond to her question. She was used to his stubbornness, but this time she pressed him further. "Hiro ... nani?"

Again, Hiroshi didn't respond, as he was to focused on the event outside and continued to stare. Yuki called out his name once more. The sound of her voice cracked like a whip, demanding a final answer. He edged slightly in her direction and mumbled in a crackly voice, "He's here."

Still in a daze, Yuki found herself sitting up and wondering what her husband meant. She questioned him again. "Who's here?"

Hiroshi mustered up the nerve to look at his wife straight in the eye. Without a single word spoken, she covered her mouth in surprise. Her eyes began to water as suppressed memories found a reason to escape. Somehow, she found the strength to get up and cautiously headed toward him. Several seconds passed, and Hiroshi pointed out the window. She followed the direction of his finger. There, standing motionless and being bombarded by the rain, stood Sifu.

Yuki leaned forward and rubbed her eyes, as it took a moment for her sight to adjust to light. She mumbled to her husband, "What's he doing? Why's he here?"

Hiroshi shook his head, unsure of the answer to his wife's questions. They both looked at each other, befuddled, and then slowly turned their attention back toward Sifu.

Hiroshi said, "Hmm, he's been in that same position for two hours. He hasn't moved a muscle. No telling how long he's waited outside."

Yuki lowered her head and said to her husband, "We should do something, Hiroshi. His loss and his pain were as great as ours." She reached to touch her husband, but his stubbornness made him pull away.

Hiroshi was steadfast and remained fixed. He grunted something incoherent and pretended to concentrate on Sifu instead. A sliver of a tear formed at the corner of his eye, as the pain of the moment could be felt by both.

Yuki stopped short of touching her husband and gently whispered in his direction. "He is not to blame for her path. Megumi chose to go to the States.

As much as we would all loved our children to continue our work, sometimes our work ends with us, and their choice becomes just that … their life."

Hiroshi turned toward his wife and planted a kiss on her forehead. "Hmm, that may be true, but I need him to suffer some more outside. Besides, he can't possibly keep this up much longer." With that, he finally walked away from the window and headed back to his bed.

"What are you doing?" asked Yuki.

"I'm going to sleep. If I happen to wake up and he's still there, then maybe…." Hiroshi turned around and pouted, "Well, then, maybe I'll talk to him."

Yuki shook her head, but realized her husband would not budge. She looked outside again to see Sifu get pounded by the rain, as he stood still and waited. She was saddened and knew all too well what he was going through.

Still with his back to his wife, Hiroshi mumbled, "Yuki, come back to bed."

This time, it was Yuki who was ignoring the words. She decided to stay put and keep an eye on Sifu.

Several Hours Pass, 4:00 am

Hiroshi continued to toss and turn for the next hour. As much as he tried, he could not sleep. Sifu's presence would not allow him to rest. He finally opened his eyes to see that his wife was not in bed. He quickly turned around to find that she was standing by the window.

"Have you been awake this entire time?"

"Yes."

The news jolted him further as he finally sat up. "Is he still there?"

"Yes," said Yuki. She looked at her husband and added, "He has not moved an inch."

"Impossible!" Hiroshi was surprised at the persistence of Sifu, but he was determined not to bend to his will. He said in a stern voice, "Yuki, come to bed already, please."

"No! I refuse to go back to bed. In fact, I will not go back to bed until you let him come inside and speak with him." She continued to stand but cringed slightly from being on her feet for so long.

Disgusted, Hiroshi looked away, but he saw that his wife's will was stronger than his. He also knew that, even with her arthritis, she persisted through the pain. He realized that his wife need not suffer for his own stubbornness, and his love for her overcame his own ego.

Hiroshi sighed and asked, "Is that what you want, Yuki?"

"You know what would make me happy is for things to be the way they used to be. I know that can never be, but there is no question how much this man loved our daughter and our grandchildren."

Hiroshi breathed in deeply and finally found himself at the edge of the bed. His mind was racing, but he knew what he had to do. Yuki continued to watch Sifu, and took her stand against her husband.

"All right. I'm going downstairs to talk to him." He watched his wife, who still did not budge; in fact, she had no reaction. Hiroshi knew when he had been beaten. He swallowed his pride, gathered his slippers, and headed down the stairs.

▲ ▲ ▲

Like a statue, Sifu was frozen in his stance, drenched in water. He had not moved for close to six hours. His eyes remained closed as the rain and tears continued to blend. The cold, brisk morning air would have made anyone shiver, but the energy flowing through Sifu made glimpses of steam rise from his body. He continued to hang his head as his breath formed a slight mist with each exhale. Suddenly, without even looking, he felt a change, an energy that he had waited to confront. Sifu did not make eye contact and refused to look.

From several feet away, some activity began to happen inside the ramen shop. The pitch dark store flickered with a gleam of light inside. Footsteps dragged from across the room and drew closer to the entrance. Sifu remained unfazed, and his stance continued to remain perfectly in place. A few minutes passed before the door finally slid open.

Sifu used his other senses and reacted to the sound. The storm continued to show no mercy as the silhouette figure stood several feet from Sifu. No sound was made from either individual, as the rain's constant pouring dominated the night.

With all his might, he summoned the strength to look up and tried to stare straight ahead. Immediately, he knew it was Megumi's father, as his mouth quivered and his heart ached with pain. Sifu's guilt pushed him to try to make eye contact. For that brief second, he achieved it, but the pain of seeing the truth caused Sifu to crumple to the ground. He questioned whether he should've even come by, but he was out of answers, seeking some form of redemption. Sifu fell to his knees and hung his head in shame. He whimpered endlessly, alone, and wished the pain would go away.

Only a minute had passed, but that time felt like an eternity. Megumi's father took several steps toward Sifu. He was also drenched to the bone, but try as the elements did to distract, neither man cared about the weather. Sifu opened his eyes only to see a pair of slippers just before him. Hiroshi broke all code of tradition and fell down on one knee. There, he placed his hand on Sifu's shoulder.

The instant he touched him, the pain was immediate. Sifu felt helpless.

Hiroshi was staggered in his speech. He found the strength to say what he'd wanted to say to Sifu since the funeral. He said, "Punishing ourselves does nothing. Megumi and the kids are gone, and nothing we can do will ever bring them back."

While the words spoke the truth and both of them had to face reality, it stabbed deep into Sifu's heart. Sifu cringed and focused hard to keep from breaking down. "If I could give my life for all of them, I would do so in an instant.... I would not hesitate at all."

Hiroshi closed his eyes and leaned closer to Sifu. He whispered, "I know you would." He stood up, drenched from the rain, and finally extended his other hand for Sifu.

Sifu looked up, saw Hiroshi's hand, and reached out for it. Hiroshi helped him back to his feet and spun around. He began walking back to the entrance and stopped just short of the door. He said, "Come … come inside and get out of the rain."

"It's possible that our worst expectations are as bad as we imagine, but one cannot escape the inevitable. At some point, you'll have to deal with it in this lifetime or the next."—Sifu

CHAPTER 7

Into Action

Mid-June

S ifu and Lance were busy in the back of the kitchen preparing for the large crowd outside. Several bowls lay empty in a row as three huge pots behind them were still brewing with the ramen broth. Each of them was scrambling to make sure every bowl was done to perfection.

Lance looked at Sifu as beads of sweats were forming around his head. "This is starting to feel like work," he grumbled.

Sifu paused for a moment and said, "You're right. I think we just got caught up in the moment." Sifu stood straight up and stretched. He laughed and made an odd face. He said, "I sometimes forget that the soup is free."

Lance grabbed a towel and wiped the sweat from his brow. He also took a moment to catch his breath and reflected on Sifu's statement. "So, what should we do about it?"

"Take ten," Sifu said nonchalantly. "I'm gonna go back out front and mingle a bit." Sifu removed his apron and his hat.

"Sounds like a plan," Lance said as he did the same.

Sifu looked at him and asked, "What are you going to do?"

"Have you seen my twenty-single man technique in a while?"

Sifu paused to think about it. They both stared at one another for a brief moment and then said in unison, "Practice."

Sifu confirmed. "Good idea!"

In front of the restaurant, the crowd had a playful atmosphere that night. As soon as Sifu walked into the dining area, they cheered. Sifu waved and began chitchatting with everyone. In the middle of the room, he saw one of his most consistent regulars, Newton. He was in the middle of a conversation with an attractive young lady.

Sifu stared for a moment and thought something was weird. He walked toward Newton and patted him on the back. "You know, you don't get a prize for coming here the most."

Newton chuckled and said, "I can't help it. I need to eat every day."

"Well, I'm not taking count, but since I've opened, I think you have."

Both Sifu and Newton laughed; they had formed a close friendship over the last year. The girl who had been talking to Newton leaned over and said, "If you don't mind, will you excuse me? I have to go to the ladies' room."

Newton stood up and said, "Sure."

The young lady smiled and excused herself as Sifu nodded to his customer. Newton took a quick peek to enjoy the view and then nudged Sifu in the belly.

"I've been coming her quite often, but this gorgeous chick just came out of the blue and began to talk to me."

"You don't say," said Sifu.

"Yeah. Been talking to her for the last hour, and we've got so much in common."

As she walked away, Sifu looked at her a second time. He stared and said, "So you two just met?"

"Yeah, do you know who she is?"

"Yes and no."

Newton was so excited that he didn't catch Sifu's odd comment. He rubbed his hands and dove in for more of Sifu's ramen. "Man, today must be my lucky day."

Sifu leaned forward and whispered into Newton's ear, "I hate to burst your bubble, but … uh, I'm pretty sure that's a guy."

Newton coughed out loud, choking on his ramen. "What?"

Sifu pulled away and said, "You can tell me later if I'm wrong."

Newton sat frozen in his chair with a glazed look on his face and a single noodle hanging from his lip. Sifu patted him on the back and walked away. Suddenly, the TV caught everyone's attention as something out of the norm popped up on it.

Sifu stared at the screen, wondering what it could be. The restaurant stood silent as everyone was kept on the edge of their seats.

"This has officially been confirmed by the UFMF. The biggest star from last year will be returning for the 2033 season. Kirin Rise has officially said she will be returning to the ring to defend her championship."

Everyone at Sifu's establishment began to clap and cheer.

"Go Kirin!"

"Man, I can't wait for the season to begin."

"I knew she'd be coming back."

Sifu stood silently, caught off guard by the announcement. It had been only the other day when he and Kirin had worked out together, and she'd made no mention of a decision. Sifu found it odd and watched as everyone was celebrating. He continued to listen to the details when a large crash from the back kitchen interrupted his train of thought. Sifu excused himself and hurried to the back room.

Lance had dropped several bowls, and he stared Sifu in the face. "Did I just hear what I thought I heard?"

"Yes."

"Didn't you just work out with her the other day?"

Sifu nodded and turned away. He thought, *Something's just not right.*

Lance was already on the ground cleaning up his mess. "Sorry about this, Sifu."

Sifu continued to listen to the announcement and ignored Lance's apology. He turned toward Lance and said, "Can you cover solo for a while?"

"Yeah, of course. Why?"

"I've got some digging to do."

As Lance looked at Sifu, his expression became concerned. "I don't like that look."

"It's nothing. Really."

Lance had grown to know Sifu well enough to not press any further. "You should go, Sifu. I got this." Before Lance could finish his words, Sifu had already exited the back door, and it slammed shut.

Fifteen minutes had passed when Sifu found himself in a really bad area of town. Underneath a darkly lit part of a bridge stood droves of little shacks, each one unique in its looks. The community was of homeless individuals who were forced into this existence with the state of the economic situation.

While he had many sources throughout the years, little Billy was the most dependable and most reliable source for information. As he walked, he recognized one of his homeless friends and began to speak with him.

Sifu said, "Hey, have you seen Billy?"

Jordan replied, "Yeah, I have. Is everything okay, Sifu?"

"Yeah, everything's okay." Sifu maintained a straight face.

"You sure?"

"I'm sure. Thanks for asking, Jordan. Where's Billy again?"

"He's just under the bridge over there, probably asleep." Jordan stretched out his arm and pointed Sifu in the direction. Sifu trudged through the trashy area and stood in front of a little fortified shack. He bent over slightly and knocked on the box. "Billy, you there?"

"Who is it?"

"A guy holding some really delicious ramen."

"Holy shit! Sifu," said Billy. The muffled voice vibrated through the walls, coming to life as Billy's makeshift door swung wide open.

"You shouldn't have," said Billy.

"So, you don't want this?" asked Sifu.

Billy quickly swiped it from Sifu and said, "You're kidding, right?" Billy hugged his ramen and invited Sifu into his little abode. At first, Sifu was taken aback by the sight of Billy's living quarters. From corner to corner, garbage was littered everywhere.

"You know, Billy … the offer's always open for you to move into my restaurant."

Billy smiled and said, "It's a dump, isn't it?"

"Um, it's got character," said Sifu.

Billy chuckled and said, "Sifu, close the door."

Sifu did as he was told, and Billy made sure everything was sealed for no one to peer inside. Once he was satisfied it was safe, Bill shoved an old decrepit microwave sitting in the corner of the room.

"Sorry about this, Sifu. You're gonna have to crouch down to get through this," said Billy.

Billy opened a small door, and he turned on the light to the other side.

"Come on in," said Billy.

As soon as Sifu walked through, his eyes bugged. Inside was a large room, built of four solid red brick walls. It was the total opposite of the place he had just stepped out from. It was spotless and didn't carry the same odor. In the corner, he noticed a little shrine that seemed to be the center of attention. It looked to have some Native American artifacts with a picture hanging on the top.

Sifu asked, "Who's that, Billy?"

"That's my great-great-grandfather. He was head of the tribe."

"Hmm," said Sifu. "I guess this explains why you haven't taken me up on my offer."

Billy was busy scarfing down his soup. He paused, not to be rude, and said, "You know I appreciate the offer, Sifu. But, as you can see, I do like my little home that I have." Billy took one big slurp and spoke again. "The building this is connected to is abandoned and sealed off. So, this is a perfect little spot for me."

"It is, Billy. It's quite nice."

Within minutes, Billy had downed the last of the ramen noodles and said, "Besides, I'm more good to you out here than I am working for you in the restaurant."

"Oh, I wouldn't say that," said Sifu.

Billy chuckled and said, "This time I got you on that, Sifu. You wouldn't be here in the wee hours of the evening if you weren't looking for some answers.... Am I right?"

Sifu patted Billy on the back. "Your skills in reading people are as good as ever."

Billy smiled and said, "Thanks, Sifu, but it wasn't that difficult to piece this one together."

For the next several minutes, Sifu discussed with Billy certain things he was looking for. He was surprised that Billy had already heard some information pertaining to his situation, but he wanted even more.

"Okay, Sifu, I can definitely dig deeper into the stuff you're asking, but once I get to the stuff that's really hot, even I'll have to be pretty careful about that."

"Of course, be careful about it, Billy.... About how long do you think it'll take before you can get me more info?"

"I'd say about forty-eight hours. I'm gonna have to network this pretty deep."

"Sounds good. You know how to get a hold of me?"

"Of course, I'll just follow my nose to your restaurant."

"You know, technically, ramen really doesn't have a distinct smell to it," said Sifu.

Billy laughed and finished the remaining broth in his bowl.

At Kirin's Parents' Home

Kirin was in the living room, and the discussion grew heated once she told her parents that she was going to do another season of UFMF. The bombshell ended up disrupting the peaceful evening they'd planned. Both her father and mother were standing and yelling back and forth with one another, while Kyle was sitting on the couch watching the exchange.

Kirin paused for a moment and thought, *Déjà vu.*

Kirin's mom, Diane, was noticeably upset, shaking her head in frustration and anger. "I don't understand why you feel you need to go back and fight again. Please explain it to me."

Kirin looked away, knowing what she was about to say wasn't the truth. "Mom, you saw my rally...."

"Yes, I did. I saw that fine display of my daughter being dragged off by the police," Diane muttered as another bad memory entered her head.

"Let me finish. The people need a voice. They need that someone to show them the possibility of a better way, and my voice carries more push if I enter the ring for a second season."

Diane knew exactly where Kirin was going with this, but the plight of the people was not a mother's main concern. Diane said, "I understand your cause, Kirin. At the same time, you have to realize how much it kills your father and me having to watch you in the ring."

"Mom, I know how to fight!"

"Princess, it has nothing to do with that. We know you're an incredible fighter. You just have to understand your last fight ... you taking those hits from Diesel...." Kirin's dad choked up as he struggled to keep his eyes from tearing.

It was difficult for Kirin to argue after watching her father show his pain. She bit her lip and decided to let it play out.

Diane went to comfort her husband and said, "You don't need to fight anymore.... Your voice is more than powerful enough to carry this nation."

Kirin shook her head as images of her last message from her anonymous stranger flashed back.

"Mom, you and Dad don't have to worry about me. And, I've hired extra security to make sure the family is safe during this time."

Her dad said, "Kirin, it's not that.... One day, when you have kids, you'll understand."

Suddenly Kyle's stomach grumbled. Everyone stared at him, and Kyle said, "Hey, I can't control bodily sounds. I'm just sitting her, being quiet."

Diane looked at Kyle suspiciously, but his neutral choice of words saved him from his mom's wrath.

"Why are you always so stubborn, Kirin?"

"It's not my fault. Besides, Dad told me that I'd be doing this one day," said Kirin.

Diane gave a sharp look to her husband, who shrugged his shoulders, wondering what Kirin meant. "I, uh ... I said what now?"

"Dad, don't you remember several years ago when we were going through your comics? You said the day may come when I could be a hero."

Her dad struggled for a second with that memory and then suddenly recalled what she was referring to. "Jesus, Kirin. When I said that, I didn't think you'd be going into a ring and risking your life."

Kirin looked at her dad and said, "That's what makes you a hero, isn't it? Doing what is necessary, when no one else will rise to the moment."

Dad looked at Kirin and said, "The problem is that being a hero is about pain and sacrifice. And, it's not just you, Kirin. You have to remember; it affects everyone you love."

▲ ▲ ▲

Opening Night, Before the Fight

Tobias shouted at Kirin, who was in her locker room. "Come on, Kirin. What gives?"

Kirin looked at her cell phone and clenched her fist. She tossed it back in her locker and ran toward Tobias. The weight of the message was something that she could not run away from. Whoever it was pulling her strings was watching every single one of her moves.

"Geez, Kirin. Get your head in the game," said Tobias. "You still have to fight, you know."

Kirin put on a fake smile and said, "Relax." She punched Tobias on the arm.

Tobias rubbed his arm and said, "Ouch. Well, that's more like it."

As they exited the locker room, Kirin stared at the long, stretched out hallway. She noticed someone at the end she'd never met before. She continued to walk as the stranger approached her. It was Dryden Rodriguez, who took a moment of his time to greet Kirin. Kirin told Tobias to wait for a minute so she could speak to him all alone.

"Sorry, for my bad timing, Ms. Rise, but I don't think we've formally met before." He extended his hand.

Kirin reached out and shook his hand; his grip was firm and strong. "Sure, Mr. Rodriguez."

He smiled and chuckled. "If you don't mind, please call me Dryden."

Kirin smiled and said, "Oh, sure thing ... and uh, you can do the same. I mean, you know ... uh, call me Kirin."

Dryden nodded. "Anyway, I know you have a match, but I just wanted to take the time to tell you that I admire your fighting style."

Kirin leaned back, surprised by his admission. "Oh, I'm kinda surprised to hear that."

Dryden replied, "Not all of us UFMF fighters are meatheads, Kirin."

Kirin looked down, feeling guilty for feeling that way. "I didn't...."

"No need to apologize. Anyway, I'm hoping the only time we do get to fight one another is in the championship."

She nodded and looked him in the eye. Upon gazing at him, she saw he was sincere.

"Good luck," said Dryden as he walked away.

Kirin waved Tobias back in; they would now make their way to the entrance of the arena.

Tobias said, "What was that all about?"

"I'd say ... surprisingly, it was about respect."

Tobias replied, "You don't see that in martial arts anymore."

Kirin paused and said, "No ... you don't."

The hysteria and the pandemonium never got old. It was something not to be forgotten as they stood at the entrance once again. The crowd grew energized, as Kirin was the main event for opening night of the new season.

Tobias looked at her as they waited. "You know, I'm afraid to ask what the opening entrance song is going to be."

Kirin said, "Don't ask; just listen."

"I swear I'm more worried about this than your fight," joked Tobias.

The crowd tried to silence themselves for the opening as the ring announcer began introducing Kirin. The arena darkened as the music popped through the air and the lights flashed brightly on both of them.

Tobias immediately recognized the music, and he pinched his brow and shook his head. He looked at Kirin and said, "Come on. Let's get this over with."

"You're not gonna ask me what song this is?"

"I remember it from back in the day, when Sifu would play his '80s music," said Tobias.

"Would you prefer I sang along with it?"

"No, I've heard you sing."

Kirin punched Tobias in the arm again.

The crowd roared with excitement, the loudest that could be heard for any fight, as Kirin was not only highly favored, but anticipated to do extremely well for her first match back.

After the Match

Connor was shaking his head as he spoke on camera. "For all those watching this match, I'm probably as stunned as you."

Linkwater added, "The 2033 season was hyped to be bigger than ever, and our opening night main event did not disappoint."

Connor said, "Wow. Just looking at the audience members, they're as stunned as we are."

Linkwater said, "Kirin Rise starts the season 1–0, but no one expected the first match to be that close, and for her to struggle to get that victory."

Connor replied, "Oddsmakers and analysts are going to figure out if tonight was just a fluke or…."

Linkwater said, "Or, it's possible Kirin's entered her sophomore slump, and the fighters at the UFMF have finally figured out her game."

Connor shook his head and smiled at the camera. "Anyway, stay tuned for in-depth post analysis of tonight's fight. Kirin Rise, once again, surrounding herself with attention."

Inside the Locker Room

The reporters outside were in a frenzy as they began shouting more questions and taking pictures. They began shoving one another, trying to get a response from Kirin, who remained quiet the entire time. Tobias did his best to shield Kirin from all the craziness as they finally entered her dressing room. As soon as she was safe in the confinement of the room, he slammed the door behind him, and Kirin plunked down in a chair.

Tobias raised his hands in anger and shouted, "What the hell was that?"

Kirin refused to look up. She was not in the mood to talk about it. "What are you talking about?"

"What am I talking about? That pitiful performance you had out there."

"What are you complaining about? I won. What does it matter how I won?" Kirin rubbed her face.

Tobias grabbed a bag of ice and began to approach Kirin. "Here, put this on your face."

Kirin took the bag and threw it across the room. The ice hit the wall and scattered to the ground.

Tobias stared at Kirin, still in shock at what had just transpired in the ring. "You know, Kirin, it's not all about you."

Kirin stood up, raising her voice in frustration. "You honestly think I'm doing this for me? That somehow this is fuel to feed my ego?"

Tobias turned around and grabbed Kirin by the arms. "Look, you just don't get it. Last time I saw you in the ring and you took that beating from Diesel, it tore me apart inside. I couldn't stand watching you in pain."

Kirin looked down, surprised by Tobias's comments. Ever since Kirin had known him, he had always kept his feelings in check with her.

"I'm not going to watch you go through this again. I can't handle it, and you have no idea ... how much it tears me up inside."

Kirin mumbled under her breath, "I'm sorry." The burden weighed on her heavily, as she felt bad for Tobias.

Tobias said, "Look, I didn't mean to shout, but ... when you got knocked down in your first match of the year ... it really caught me off guard." Tobias lifted Kirin's head up by the chin and gazed deep into her eyes.

Kirin stared into Tobias's eyes, searching for comfort.

Tobias gently touched her bruise, and she flinched immediately. "Oh, I'm sorry." He pulled his hand away.

"No ... no, it's okay," said Kirin.

Tobias winced, concerned for Kirin's well-being. He touched Kirin gently by the side of her face and said, "Does this hurt?"

She shook her head and replied, "No." She leaned in closer, as his breath was caressing her skin.

He matched her distance, and their heads touched. "How about this?"

She touched his hand that was against her face and spoke softly, "No, that doesn't hurt either."

He tilted his head, angling his lips so that he could finally taste her softness. He planted a gentle kiss on the side of her bruise. "Does this hurt?"

Kirin shook her head and looked up to him. Her heart began to race, and it felt like it wanted to escape, but was trapped in her. The anticipation between the two had built up throughout the years.

Tobias grabbed Kirin firmly by the arms, his eyes flickering to her lips. Kirin didn't struggle from his grasp. She felt safe. She was unsure where this was going to lead, but wanted to connect with Tobias for the first time. As his lips approached hers, she closed her eyes, waiting to experience his taste.

Suddenly, the door swung open, and a familiar voice caught their attention.

"Man, these people are crazy!" Sifu entered through the door and spun around, securing it.

Both Tobias and Kirin pulled away from one another, and they stood awkwardly in front of Sifu. Kirin broke out of her daze and headed in Sifu's direction.

Tobias let out a sigh and leaned into the lockers for support. He muttered to himself, "Dammit, maybe the third time will be a charm. Still can't land that first kiss." He scratched his head and thought, *I guess this is how Ryan must feel.*

"Many join the fight; few know how to win it. Their failure is not understanding that who they have to become is different from who they were from the start."—Sifu

SECTION 1

Short Stories #7—Kirin's P.O.V.

It's Just Glasses—342 Days

Staring into the mirror, I felt lost. I didn't even know why I even cared. Black, oddly shaped, and oversized, I wasn't sure what I was thinking when I picked them out. The glasses were not important, but they distracted me from the real big issue that was pressing.

It had been a week since the funeral. While on the outside, everything seemed normal, it was far from that. The world continued to move forward, but inside I had felt this hollow feeling before and was condemned to relive it again. It was almost a reminder that I could never escape it, and what joy I had was quickly taken away. The guys had been helping to teach the classes while Sifu took his time to recover. Then out of the blue, Sifu gave me a call, asking for some help at his house.

I had grown close to Sifu and his family and just like that, everything was so different. It was just him, all by himself. For the first time, he seemed so lost … so human, just like me.

Several minutes later, I went through the routine of saying goodbye to my mom and Kyle. They were preoccupied with their own things, and I hit the garage to pick up my transportation.

Twenty Minutes Later

I got to Sifu's house and parked my bike at the side of his garage. The last time I visited Sifu was when I babysat their kids. I could feel my heart racing, and my nerves clinched as soon as I pressed the doorbell.

Ding dong. Ding dong. Ding dong.

There was not the typical response from Sifu shouting that he was coming or the pitter-patter of feet bouncing and kids shouting by the door. Instead, a somber feeling followed me, ready to make itself at home. From afar, I could hear the foot work shuffling my way.

Sifu opened the door and said, "Sorry to bother you, Kirin. I'm glad you came. I was wondering if you could help me?"

I looked at Sifu, who appeared as normal as one could be, and I said, "Anything I can do, I'll do it for you." Even though I was wearing glasses for the first time, he seemed either unaware of or unfazed by my appearance.

Sifu waved me in and said, "Please come in. Please."

I stepped into the house and immediately saw what was happening. The living room was filled with boxes, and some of the stuff looked like it was being prepared to be shipped out or put into storage.

"Uh, Sifu. What do you need me to do?"

Sifu paused for a second before answering. He seemed somewhat choked up from my simple question, as I saw him struggle to answer.

"Kirin, I need your help … packing all of Simo's stuff as well as the kids."

I nodded and asked, "Where should I begin?"

Sifu sounded sad. "Can you start off with the kids' room so we can work our way down?"

"Sure thing, Sifu, anything."

I headed upstairs and got to the twins' room. As I opened the door and took a quick peek inside, I was shocked to find that everything looked exactly like it was before. I could hear Sifu walk down the hall and realized he must've been working in another room as well.

Both Hideo's and Akira's pictures were plastered all over the room, from their very first day at the hospital and a row for each year since then. As rambunctious as the twins were, I always found it surprising that they kept quite a clean room. I walked into the center and realized that I didn't know where to start. I grabbed one of the boxes and began taping it up. All the supplies that were needed were right there in front of me. When I finally had the box ready, I placed it in the corner of the room.

Looking through the twin's bedroom, I began tearing up. I grabbed several of their toys and was wrapping them up properly so they wouldn't break when Sifu moved. I wasn't sure what Sifu was going to do with it. Was he just gonna store it away or donate it?

I finally dried my tears and forced myself to work. I thought, *I have to be strong for Sifu.* Each minute of packing was painful for me. I understood now why Sifu needed my help. Doing this would've been torture for him.

I checked my phone to find thirty minutes had passed. It was quiet in his house, and I no longer heard Sifu. I decided to find him, and I left the twins' room and quietly moved around in the upper area.

I peeked into Hana's room as well as his and Simo's, but no one was there. At first, it didn't seem like a big deal, but I felt a chill down my spine that something was wrong. It was eerily quiet all around. I started to panic and called out his name. "Sifu?"

I yelled several more times, but still no answer, and I was now dashing through each room to see where he might be. Suddenly, something told me to check the garage. I ran through the kitchen and opened the door to the garage. He was sitting inside the car with the garage door closed, and I wondered what he was doing.

I move toward his closed door. As I peeked inside, I saw he was holding a picture of Simo and the kids as tears rolled down his face. I opened the door and said, "Sifu...."

I noticed that the car keys were inside with the car halfway turned on. I turned toward him in disbelief, as it finally registered to me what he was planning to do.

"No! No, Sifu." I swung the door open, reached into the car, and pulled out the keys. I couldn't believe what I was seeing. I threw the keys away and crumpled to the ground, crying uncontrollably. The possibility of what he had been considering finally sunk in. We both could feel each other's pain, as this was so difficult to bear.

As I continued to cry, I finally felt a gentle touch come over me.

"I'm sorry, Kirin. I'm so sorry," Sifu said in a crackly voice. "I'm sorry for asking you to come over, but you are the closest thing I have left to—"

I turned around and hugged him back hard. "Don't ... don't you ever.... Promise me, you'll never leave me."

Sifu shook his head and looked embarrassed. "I wasn't ... sounds so stupid, but I thought nearing it ... it might bring me closer to them again."

I hugged him even tighter, hoping I could neutralize the pain and suffering with my touch. I kneeled next to Sifu for several minutes, holding him tight, hoping that the pain would go away.

Sifu whispered. "Thanks for coming. Go home, Kirin. I'll be okay."

I didn't want to leave him. I knew he wasn't okay, and I wanted to make sure he didn't do anything stupid. I tried desperately to think of something to get our minds off the pain and to find an excuse to stay with him.

"Sifu...?" I said.

"What is it, Kirin?" he asked.

I thought of the one thing that might bring both of us solace. "Help me with my Wing Chun, Sifu. Let's train."

Sifu's swollen eyes stared at me, as he paused to gathered himself. He uttered, "Okay.... Give me a couple of minutes, Kirin. Let's go back inside, and we'll do just that ... train."

I headed to the living room and found an empty area. I opened my stance and began punching, trying my best to focus on a single thought. I kept it as simple as possible, as each punch cracked through the air with ease. Suddenly, I felt lost in my own focus and continued to punch. It did not matter that the tears were still falling down. I focused on my target and just punched.

While I kept my focus, I suddenly felt Sifu nearby. I had never felt that before, but I knew he was right there.

Suddenly from behind, I heard his voice. "Not bad, Kirin. Not bad."

His words seemed fresh again, like before. Sifu then came near and opened his palm in front of me.

"Now, punch," said Sifu.

I began punching his hand, using it as a target. With each hit, he would adjust his hand for me to feel the solid impact of my motion. Sifu said, "Watch the timing of your punch, Kirin. The speed of the punch and pull should be the same. The tension from going forward as well as pulling back should be equal. The distance of the punch and the pull should be equal distance as well."

"Got it, Sifu."

For the next several hours, all we did was train. We worked on everything imaginable that day. While neither one of us was able to pack Sifu's stuff, in some way, what we did was just as important to keep the healing progress moving forward.

Environment Cares—1 Year, 25 Days

Right after school, for the last couple of months, I would head over to Sifu's house to see how he was doing. The goal of packing up his family's stuff was never accomplished, as both of us found it easier to just train and not talk about the matter. The way I figured it, it was our way of dealing with the pain and the loss.

Today was a high pollution alert in our area, so everyone had a mask on to deal with it. Riding my bike and seeing everyone like this made for an eerie sensation. Those who suffered from asthma were told not to venture out on days like this.

I knocked on the door and heard Sifu shout, "Just come in, Kirin." It was a ritual to go through the same process, but I liked the consistency. It felt like how it used to be, even though, deep down, I knew it would never be the same.

The house was exactly as it had been two months ago. Sifu was in the living room practicing his form. From the outside, he seemed to be doing better, but I could still feel his pain. It felt no different. I was sure it was difficult for him to stay at home, with everything around him as a constant reminder. Yet, the most important things in his life were clearly missing.

Sifu broke from his form and asked, "How about we do some chi sao today, Kirin?"

I nodded and said, "That's fine ... Sifu, is it all right if I grab a drink first?"

"Yeah, just go into the fridge and help yourself. I've got some cold bottled waters inside." It was my favorite drink, second only to coffee. The simple and natural way always seemed to appeal to me.

I headed over to the kitchen and opened the fridge. Inside, a quick peek revealed a case of bottled water, some fruit, and a box of baking soda which I was sure was expired. I reached in and grabbed a bottled water and downed it right away. The ice-cold water was refreshing, and I got every last drop.

I looked around his kitchen and searched for his recycling bin.

"Sifu?"

He didn't respond at first, so I continued to search for it, thinking I probably missed the obvious.

"Sifu?"

"Yes?"

"Where's your recycling bin?"

A few seconds later, he strolled into the kitchen and poked his head inside. "I don't have one."

I was caught off guard by his statement. In fact, I stood frozen, holding the empty bottle in my hand with a confused look. "How can you not recycle?"

"Kirin, it's good to recycle, don't get me wrong ... but there's a flaw with the entire system."

"Uh … how so, Sifu?"

Sifu stepped into the kitchen and began preparing some tea for himself. He said, "I know that everyone wants to do their part to save the planet."

"Yeah, if we don't take care of the planet, we'll destroy it," I said.

"You know, I was born in the period when they began to recycle, and the thing is, it's gotten worse. Now mind you, in theory, there should be a greater sense of awareness of the situation, yet … many years later, look at where we are now."

Sifu's statement got me thinking. *He's right. Everyone's aware of being green, but things haven't gotten better. Why is that?*

I asked aloud, "Why is that, Sifu?"

"That's a good question. How is it possible things are getting worse, when everyone's recycling and each and every company has gone green?"

I stood there waiting for the answer.

Sifu paused and sipped his tea. He took his time to keep me further in suspense. "Just like with everything else, the sell of recycling was to make money for the guys in suits, to give people a purpose to believe in—that we, as the average Joe, somehow truly are making a difference. But, the truth is, the guys running the show couldn't care less what their effect on the environment really is."

I continued to look puzzled and asked, "I still don't get it, Sifu?"

"First, the statement that we can destroy the planet is delusional. Mankind can do everything it wants, but this planet will never be destroyed. The arrogance of man … I sometimes think that's why we have typhoons, hurricanes, and earthquakes … just a reminder of how little we are compared to Mother Nature."

"But, Sifu, much has changed with the environment due to us."

"You're correct. The environment has changed, due to us. But the choices we make will destroy us. The planet will still survive, while technically we're killing ourselves off. And by the way … all our hard efforts in being green are really not even coming close to the source of the problem."

"So, what do you suggest is the best approach to it?"

"Wing Chun theory is applicable to everything, Kirin. Right now, the majority of the pollution created on this planet isn't by individuals, but by the companies and corporations that are cutting corners to make a profit at the expense of the planet. Think about the phones people love so much. That material comes from somewhere. It's not just artificially created."

"But you said most companies have pushed hard to be green."

"Don't sell me on what you say, but what you do, Kirin. Always remember that. There are two sides to everything. You always have to look to see the bigger picture."

"Maybe this is beyond me, Sifu. I don't get why that is."

"Ultimately, if you want to change anything, you have to attack the source. Remember that."

"The source?"

"Of course. Most people like to deal with the problem only and not the source of it. That's why it continues to happen, and that's why you never see the change. It's no different from Wing Chun, Kirin. I don't care about your attack. All I care about is your center. If I destroy the center, automatically I stop your attack."

"I see, Sifu … but you make it sound so depressing, like there's nothing we can do. Why can't things get better?"

"The problem is most people won't act upon it."

"That being …?"

"The state the world is in financially; it's difficult to have people care when they're too busy trying to survive. I've met many great people who want to change the world, but when you have several kids who need basic necessities…. It's quite difficult attacking the source when they need their next meal first. It's just the right amount of distraction to put us in place, keep people separated from one another. Basically, keep us distracted by any means necessary."

"So, the system stays in power that way?"

"You could say those in charge just know how to keep everything at the level of acceptable humanity. Their job is to balance it to the point where people don't revolt. But, if you pay attention, every day they are scheming about how to take more and more away from us. It's all part of the game."

I sat down on a chair as Sifu's words made me think. "I'm afraid to ask…. What else don't you do?"

Sifu grabbed his tea and said, "Let's see … you already know the reasons I don't go to church … but I don't vote either."

"You don't vote? Oh, and by the way, I spoke about the church view with my mom, and that didn't go well."

"Most people have a difficult time seeing both sides. They get emotional," said Sifu.

I had a momentary flashback of that day and quickly shivered. "Anyway, you were saying ... you don't vote?"

"Yup, never voted, and I'm sure you'll hear people spout that if you don't vote, you don't have the right to complain. You know they spend millions of dollars brainwashing people into believing that or even believing their actions make a difference. They repeat and sell a line. It doesn't have to be true, but if you repeat it enough, it starts with doubt and they build upon it."

"Explain, Sifu."

"People want change, but how can they get that if the system was designed for them to fail?"

"So, what do you do?"

"Like I said, you either play along with the game, or destroy the system entirely."

"It sounds like a revolution."

"Wearing suits and being rich doesn't make things legal, but the world is so dependent on perception. People would rather look good than face the truth. Both these ideals for years have been used as a form of control. Remember: at one time the founders of these countries were labeled traitors."

"But I thought you told me solving it with violence is flawed."

"It is, Kirin, because if you use force, the cycle continues. That's why we are where we are."

"So, do we do nothing?"

"I didn't say that."

"What can one person do?"

"One person isn't enough; you'd need a mass far greater than those in control ... but it begins with one. People will not move unless it's in extreme; thus, you need the two overwhelming forces to combine to make action."

"And that is?"

"Passion and fear. They need to believe in a cause, and they have to feel the fear; otherwise, they'll never act. The two sides work together to create action. Only then when it's real, will you see the change that everyone is seeking."

For the next several hours, we did a different kind of training. Everything Sifu did was always based on Wing Chun. It fascinated me how he saw the world and how an art so true in fighting could be applied to the everyday world.

"When you look around and see the chaos surrounding the world, it's difficult to comprehend that the world is as it should be."—Sifu

The Dog Days of Summer—1 Year, 56 Days

It had been over three months since I had been coming over daily to Sifu's place. I was the beneficiary of such tragic times, but I felt guilty in the process. Training with Sifu privately was intense, unlike his regular classes. I could feel my skills improving exponentially working with Sifu alone. It almost felt as if his skills transferred over every time we touched hands.

It was nearing the tail end of the dog days of summer. The sun's heat was pounding as beads of sweat formed around my head. I could see Sifu's house in the distance and decided to pedal faster on my bike to squeeze in every second with him. I dropped my bike on the front of the lawn and ran to Sifu's door step. I rang the doorbell, once, like always, and waited to hear his voice. A minute passed, and I thought nothing of it, but there was no answer. It was strange, since I would normally hear his warm voice and feel his presence right away. I thought, *Hmm, that's odd*, as I pulled my phone out and checked the time.

I began to knock on his door and then oddly heard scratches on the other side. *Hmm, what could that be?* I put my face against the glass, trying to see through the door. I decided to take the initiative and turned the knob; strangely enough, it wasn't locked.

"That's ... weird," I muttered.

As I opened the door, a tiny nose poked through, which made me lunge back. "What the heck is that?" I reached for the door again and edged closer. This time, there was nothing but the sounds of whimpering from behind.

What the heck is going on? I thought. I finally stepped through, but before I could ask for Sifu, I saw the cutest little puppy wagging its butt back and forth, unsure of whether to jump toward me or stay in place.

"Sifu? Sifu!" I shouted several times. I waited for an answer and still got no response.

"Come here, boy," I wasn't sure whether it actually was a boy, but it was my natural instinct to call him that. A quick peek below confirmed my guess was right. I grabbed the tiny bulldog and picked him up. I was wondering where Sifu was, why his door was left open, and who this little guy was.

I spent the next several minutes calling throughout the house and searching the rooms. Everything looked exactly the same as yesterday, but my unanswered questions remained. I looked around to find any kind of clue and eventually found a note. It read the following:

> *Mr. Kwan, here's the puppy we spoke about a couple of months ago. Hope you and your family—especially your kids—will enjoy him.*
>
> *Alice of Pet Land Kennels*

The little puppy was sitting by my leg as I read the short note several times. I put two and two together. From what I gathered, Sifu must've planned months ago on getting the dog for the kids from the breeder. It was probably just old enough to be weaned away from its mother, and the puppy had been delivered today.

I dropped the note, realizing what might have happened. At first, I panicked, thinking the worst as I ran to the garage to see no one was there. I began calling Sifu on my cell phone, but it was now saying the number I had contacted was no longer available. I checked the entire house for anything further, but everything seemed to be intact. I thought, *Would he just leave? This must've torn him apart seeing the puppy. Sifu wouldn't just leave, would he? Where would he go?*

The moment finally sunk in, as a pit formed in my stomach, making me feel ill. I thought, *This can't be happening. What should I do? Think, Kirin. Think.* After a few minutes of panic, I figured I'd go to the class and see what the gang thought. I grabbed the puppy and found a set of Sifu's keys and left a note just in case.

At the School

I rushed to the school, slamming the door wide open. The little puppy was squirming the entire time. Inside, I could see that Robert was busy teaching class. None of the other seniors were there today as they had been taking over for Sifu the last several months. Robert had a cast on his left arm and was working single stick with his students. It was a small class with a few of the newer students.

Robert said, "Wow, what a cute puppy!"

I shook my head. "Robert, we need to talk ASAP!"

"What's wrong, Kirin?"

"One second." I called out for Carlos. He was a recent student who had only six months of training. He came up to me and asked, "What's up, Kirin?"

"Do me a favor and watch him for sec."

"Sure, thing." He grabbed the dog from my hands. "Hey, what's his name?"

"Uh ... just call him 'Puppy' for now."

Robert yelled out to the rest of the class. "Guys, continue practicing the shift and punch technique until I get back. If any of you stop, I'll make you guys do this for another thirty minutes."

I grabbed Robert by the arm, and I brought him to Sifu's office.

"Hey, what's going on? What's wrong with you?" asked Robert.

I had a look of panic as I said, "He's gone. Uh, I could be wrong, but deep down, I ... I think Sifu's gone."

"What do you mean he's gone?"

I gave Robert the note and began to explain. "I saw this note. I've tried calling him. He's gone. I don't know what happened. I thought he was getting better, but this puppy arrived today, and this may have caused Sifu to snap. That's what I'm guessing."

"Slow down Kirin. You're not making any sense at all. What about the puppy?"

For the next several minutes, I tried clearing things up for Robert, and then it clicked. It finally hit him, and he began texting and calling the others.

"What are we going to do?" I asked.

"I honestly don't know. Maybe he just needed to get away. Sifu wouldn't leave just like that, would he?"

I began to tear up. "The man lost his entire family. For the last three months, he seemed as normal and unaffected by the everything. But, something like this ... I mean, who knows? Anyone can snap. He had probably even forgotten about ordering the puppy for the kids."

Suddenly, while Robert and I were discussing things, the door swung open.

I hung my head and prayed I was wrong. I thought, *Not now. This has to be the worst timing possible.*

"Oh, crap," said Robert.

"Let me guess, a challenge match?" I said. I forced myself to look, and my feelings were instantly confirmed.

"I got this, Kirin." Robert walked away from me and headed to both guys. He tried staying cool and said, "How can I help you guys?"

"Challenge match," the guy said cockily.

Robert sighed and said, "Well, you're gonna have to come at another time."

"You afraid?" said the challenger.

"Afraid of you?" snickered Robert.

The guy began to quote the rules as he opened the paperwork. "In the event of a challenge match, all schools must have a representative to defend the school at all times, otherwise forfeiting their right. No exceptions to this rule. If you do not accept the match, you hereby forfeit the school and must immediately shut down all forms of business."

Robert looked at me and the rest of the guys. He then walked by me and said, "Kirin, try texting one of the guys and see if you can get them to come to the school ASAP."

I spent several minutes relaying texts back and forth with the guys. They were all tied up, and Danny was the closest one to coming, but that was a good hour away. I told Robert the situation.

He said, "Shoot. What are we going to do? I can't fight with this cast on."

The challenger spoke. "Come on, you pussies. Either have someone to challenge me, or this school will be officially closed."

The words infuriated me. I looked up toward him and then turned to Robert. Without giving it a second thought, I said angrily, "I'll do it. I'm gonna fight."

Robert shook his head. "Kirin, are you crazy? You've never done this kind of fight before. I can't allow you to do it. You're not ready."

I stared Robert straight in his eyes and said, "I'm the only one available. I'm the most senior student, second only to you.... I'm gonna do it. You have no other option." I didn't utter another word, as I made it clear to Robert there was no changing my mind.

For the first time, I must've caught Robert off guard, because he didn't have any snappy remarks. I was about to walk away, and then he finally blurted, "You know everything is riding on this?"

I didn't answer him as I turned away. I started walking toward the opponents and shouted, "Robert, sign the papers."

He approached the challenger, waited for a second, and signed the paperwork.

The guy looked at me as he said, "This should be a lot of fun." He was looking me over from top to bottom as he said, "First fight, little girl?"

I ignored him and didn't make eye contact. I was nervous, but I also knew I wasn't going to lose. I wasn't going to be the reason for the school to shut down. I let my sadness drive my rage and become my source of power.

"You got nothing to say?"

I answered him with my eyes, as I stared dead straight into his soul.

Several Minutes Later

Robert was trying to give me some last-minute tips before the match started. He said, "Remember, just keep it simple, Kirin. Dominate the center, and finish it as quick as possible."

"I know," I replied as I pretended I was listening. Everything he was saying was passing right through me. I took a quick glance at my opponent, who was standing in the center of the school ready to fight. I had so many thoughts running through my head. All the lessons Sifu had given me seemed to be bombarding me at the worst time possible. I couldn't think of or remember any of them.

He shouted, "So, are we gonna do this or what?"

I looked at Robert and said, "I'm ready."

He took a deep breath, and I could tell he was nervous. I turned around, and the rest of the school was watching cautiously from one side of the room. I walked slowly toward my opponent and stood several feet from him. I knew what was on the line, and so did everyone who was watching me.

I didn't even hear anyone say that the fight began, but suddenly my opponent charged in to me. I stepped back, as it caught me off guard, and we began to exchange blows.

Things were moving in a blur, and I spent most of the time blocking. I found myself thinking of what to do, as nothing felt like it was flowing.

I heard Robert shout something out loud, but I couldn't make it out.

Suddenly, my opponent swung an upper cut that got through my defenses. I found myself clenching my stomach and crumpled to the ground. I struggled to get my next breath, but I refused to cry.

He stopped and towered over me. "I'm so gonna enjoy being the one to shut down your school," he chuckled.

I was on the floor, grasping my stomach from the hit. I looked up at him and was gathering my breath. I closed my eyes for a second and heard Sifu speak to me, as his one lesson formed clarity in my head. Sifu said, "Suspend the heart."

Sifu's words were the fire, and my opponent gave me the fuel to fight. This time, there was no holding back. As he hovered over me gloating, I sprung up and punched him straight to the groin. He howled a high pitch as he grabbed his privates. He was wide open for the picking, and I kicked him so hard he flew to the ground.

His friend shouted, "Get up!"

I was mad. The decision was clear, and there was no stopping me. I dashed forward, with no fear of any attack, as his center resonated a huge, pulsing target, one that kept beating, one that needed to be shut down immediately. Before he could even throw out an attack, he was too busy with the one I had just served him. After the first hit landed, the flow of attacks would not stop until he was on the ground again. He was done, but I wasn't. I mounted him and began to pound him further and continued to rain the punches on him.

His friend yelled out, "It's over. Stop! Stop!"

I heard it echo through my head, but I was focused on finishing it.

Suddenly, I felt myself get yanked away from him.

"Holy shit, you're gonna kill him, Kirin!" Robert pulled me off him, and blood was dripping from my hands.

Robert held out his hands. "Calm down, Kirin. The fight's over."

"You're fucking crazy, bitch," said his friend as he was helping the guy up.

I couldn't turn off the switch. I broke out of Robert's grip and charged in again. Carlos stepped in front of me, and Robert grabbed me again. It took several students to hold me back. I wanted him.

Robert shouted, "Get the hell out of here … quickly."

I could see his friend tremble as he dropped him accidentally and eventually picked him up. The challenger was covered with blood, and the floor showed evidence of the damage I had done. I wanted to watch the entire thing. I wanted to see him suffer. I wanted someone other than myself to feel my pain.

"Let me go," I said.

Robert said, "I'll let you go once you tell me you can control yourself."

"I'm fine … I'm fine, now."

The adrenaline quickly wore off, and then I realized why I was there in the first place. As soon as they let me go, I fell to my knees and began to cry.

I whimpered. "He's gone. He's gone, you know, and I have no idea where he's at."

The guys surrounded me as the news shocked the entire school.

Robert said, "We don't know that for sure."

I shook my head, but I knew he was gone. The tears began to fall uncontrollably, and then suddenly the little puppy came jumping up and began smothering me with kisses. My puddle of tears was being mixed with his drool.

I looked at Robert and cracked a smile.

Robert said, "So, what are you going to name him?"

I hugged the little bulldog and thought about it for a minute. "You know … I think I'm gonna call him…."

"Be very cautious to exert your power, as the price is a heavy burden few are willing to pay."—Sifu

SECTION 2

Sifu's Journey Entry #7—Back to Square One

Four Hours Later

The sun breached the morning sky, signaling a new beginning. Most of the streets had scattered remnants of last night's torrential rains. Puddles lay still undiscovered by little children, umbrellas were left outside the houses to dry, and sewers ran continuously, preventing flooding from occurring. Surprisingly, the buzzing and chaotic noise that comes with living in metropolitan Tokyo was still sound asleep. However, inside this quaint little ramen shop it was a different story.

Hiroshi's ramen shop was exactly how one would imagine it. Simple in design, but filled with character, it stood the test of time. Hiroshi had spent his lifetime perfecting his craft, earning him the nickname 'the god of ramen' from the locals. Set in tradition with handcrafted wood throughout the restaurant, it sat a mere twenty people at any one time. Thus, customers were accustomed to lines beginning early and would only end when Hiroshi put his sign out, indicating he was done for the day.

Sifu was already busy preparing ramen as Megumi's dad awaited. Running on a few hours of sleep as well as last night's demonstration of dedicated stillness in the rain, he was back up and working.

Hiroshi stared at Sifu, watching his every move, regardless of how minute a task. He remained silent throughout, but he was impressed that a man untrained in the ways of preparing ramen looked anything but that. On the counter where his customers normally sat lay the picture of Megumi with the recipe on the back. It was, as Sifu would say, the catalyst from which everything originated.

Saddened yet proud, he smiled as the words written by Megumi reflected his teachings through the years. He realized that all those times he mentioned little details to Megumi, she was in fact paying attention. The words that he'd felt were lost found their way back to him, in a way he never expected. Hiroshi began flipping between staring at Megumi's picture and the recipe on the back.

As Hiroshi was lost in his thoughts, Sifu was working hard to make the best soup yet. For over a year, he had been working diligently on trying to perfect his wife's recipe. Armed with only a piece of paper and the memories of its taste, he was trying desperately to recreate what he had once so loved. His efforts, when time allowed, compared to him mastering his own art. He knew that, regardless of the task, the tools needed to decode the art of Wing Chun would help him figure out how to make the perfect ramen. Thus, knowledge only becomes wisdom when it can be applied to anything that you do. The formula always required the most important ingredient, that being work. Sifu always said that, when you want something, the truth is not in your words, but in your actions.

Sifu was lost in the moment. Time carried no meaning when his focus was so determined. Minutes quickly passed, turning to hours. Before Sifu knew it, he had slaved away the entire morning so that his soup was ready for tasting. He put his hands on his waist and took several deep breaths, gathering every ounce of his strength to put his finishing touches on the dish. This was truly his best, but he was still in search of the missing touch.

Sifu gently held the bowl of ramen and put it in front of Megumi's dad. The steam was the first to greet him, and Sifu bowed and stood silently in place.

Hiroshi, like a true connoisseur, took his time before proceeding to eat. He watched as the steam continued to rise and stared into the soul of the soup which seemed to be in perfect harmony. After several seconds examining just the exterior of the soup, he finally reached to his side and grabbed his spoon. There the spoon and broth were finally introduced as he began stirring it. Hiroshi stirred the ramen, blending the soup even further; he appeared to be searching for a specific part of the broth. Finally, he found what he was looking for and brought it close to his lips. He blew on it gently and teased Sifu as the soup stopped just short of his lips and remained untasted.

Sifu watched Hiroshi. His movements were exactly how Megumi used to taste her soup. It looked almost like a form that the two had performed hundreds of times with each other. It was now crystal clear where all her training had come from. He had reached the source of it all. His heart was skipping a beat in anticipation, waiting for the verdict from her dad.

Hiroshi inhaled deeply and blew gently upon the soup so that it had a slight indent from the wind. The sounds of slurping followed shortly afterward as Hiroshi closed his eyes.

Sifu watched, knowing he had done his very best. He felt his center off as he leaned in anticipation and swallowed with nervousness running throughout his entire body.

He watched intently, but there was no reaction at all from Hiroshi. He dug deeper and felt for anything, but all his senses came up empty, matching the silence of the room. Sifu showed his human side and quickly doubted himself as he thought, *Could it be that awful?*

Hiroshi finally opened his eyes, staring blankly into space. He bypassed Sifu and lowered his spoon to the side of the bowl.

Sifu thought, *That's it. He's not gonna try another sip.*

Seconds later, he finally looked Sifu straight in the eye. He said with a stern voice, "I want you to be totally honest with me. Did my daughter show you how to cook this, or did you learn this all from the back of this picture?"

Sifu was surprised with the line of questioning. He looked at Hiroshi and said, "Megumi never showed me the recipe, nor did I have any interest in it other than to eat it."

"So, you did all this from my daughter's recipe?"

Sifu nodded and answered, "Yes. What you have in your hand is everything I used to work with. The rest has been countless hours of practicing and making it for over a year now."

Hiroshi took his eyes away from Sifu and then looked at Megumi's picture. "I'm curious," asked Hiroshi. "You came all the way to Japan for a reason. What is it?"

Sifu took a deep breath, feeling the weight of the answer and finally revealing it to Megumi's father. "Your daughter's recipe, Megumi's recipe … I know right away what it tastes like, and no matter what I've done or continue to change … I just can't duplicate it." Sifu hung his head, dejected, but feeling some relief from finally revealing his intentions to Hiroshi.

"I'm sorry if I've failed to meet your daughter's standards, as well as your own, Hiroshi-san. Please accept my apologies." With that, Sifu bowed the maximum amount required. He was on the ground as he hung his head down in shame and dared not to look up.

Hiroshi sat back and felt Sifu's sincerity. He leaned over the counter and saw Sifu still on the ground, holding his bowing position.

He said, "I admit it. I am impressed, even more so that you were able to do this with only with a recipe and trial and error. But as you already know, it's missing something … and that's why you're here."

Sifu stared Hiroshi directly in the eye and said, "I remember the first time your daughter made me the soup. It immediately brought a smile to my face. It was unlike anything I had ever tasted before." Sifu shook his head and continued, "While I think what I did was the best I could do for my standards … it did not bring that same feeling back."

Hiroshi knew what Sifu was feeling, as they both shared that moment of understanding. He asked, "And you're hoping to duplicate that?"

"Yes," said Sifu.

"What are you willing to do?"

"I'm willing to do whatever it takes, no matter how long it takes. I'm willing to start from the very beginning."

"Hmm," Hiroshi murmured, caught by surprise from Sifu's words. "Most people aren't willing to go back to the beginning. In fact, ego prevents many from doing that."

"That's because most people aren't willing to do it right."

"I now know why you caught my daughter's interest." Hiroshi leaned forward and said, "You possess a rare quality … to quiet the ego and start from scratch…. Very few, very few people indeed can do that." Hiroshi snickered and shook his head.

Sifu was surprised, as he had never seen Hiroshi laugh—or smile, for that matter. He added, "I believe everyone can do it, sir…. It's a question of whether you want to or not."

The room was silent for several minutes, and Hiroshi finally stood up and walked past Sifu. From behind the counter, he grabbed a smock and threw it at Sifu.

Sifu clung to it, waiting for him to speak.

"Okay, let's get to work."

"Understand what the mind says you can't do; it can also say you can. The question is: who is in control of answering that?"—Sifu

CHAPTER 8

All in One Week

Mid-September

H alfway through the season, the new format setup by the UFMF had kept everyone on their toes. It seemed as if the UFMF was now on the air 24/7, as people tuned in to the fights that were occurring overseas. Now the entire world was connected and wondering who would emerge to qualify for the Dome tournament. On the air, a panel was busy discussing the current events.

The camera focused on Linkwater as he cleared his throat and spoke in his usual hoarse voice. "So many things to cover today, but first let's talk about the current champ, Dryden Rodriguez."

Connor spoke while a clip of Dryden's highlights played in the background. "A champion will always be a champion. You can't count out a man who's won the Dome three times. He's had one loss for this season based on a controversial decision, and many believed—including me—that he won that fight."

Stabler chimed in, "I think the loss is insignificant, gentlemen. I think what everyone's looking to see is how his body is holding up and if he's healthy. So far, he's been dominant, and there's no sign that his knee is not keeping up with the demands of this season."

Grandmaster Chang stepped into the conversation to give his two-cents' worth. "Agreed. While it's not a stretch at all to say this, I honestly believe he looks to be the favorite to take this year's Dome."

Krenzel said, "It's hard to believe that the UFMF can keep stocking such quality fighters. But, looking at this year's cast compared to last year's, and you really see that they once again raised the bar, and the skill level is at an all-time high."

Stabler said, "It's funny you should say that, because I'm wondering if that's the reason that the current champion Kirin Rise is struggling this year?"

Grandmaster Chang, always the opportunist, wanted his moment of glory. "I'll answer that, if you don't mind. You see, with a mixed fighting-based art, it's quick to adapt. That means people saw what Kirin used last year and have adapted to it, so you can see why she's struggling severely this year."

Connor, "I have to agree. She has obviously been struggling, and at her size, I honestly don't know how she can continue to take a pounding. But if the season were to end to date, she's on the borderline to actually qualify for the Dome."

He looked around, and everyone was agreeing. Connor added, "Is this the sophomore jinx that we are seeing, or is Kirin Rise yesterday's news?"

Grandmaster Chang said, "Keep in mind that I've been consulting several of the fighters in dealing with her style, and I don't mind taking credit for several of her losses."

Linkwater said dryly, "Thanks again, Grandmaster Chang, for your continued self-promotion and valuable contribution to our chat."

Grandmaster Chang, unaware of the sarcasm, accepted the compliments with a smile. "You're most welcome."

Stabler took a stab, "I'd like to say maybe it's her lack of focus on fighting. At times, she seems almost hesitant in finishing her opponent, unlike last year. Who knows? Maybe she's more focused on fixing the country than she is on training for her matches."

Krenzel said, "Maybe if she stopped giving away her money, she could fix the country."

The group laughed snidely before Grandmaster Chang's awkward cackling laugh broke the joy of the moment and led to the next topic.

Linkwater said, "Okay, gentlemen … give me one name that strikes fear when you mention it. Who's fighting overseas right now that will definitely qualify for this year's Dome round robin in L.A.?"

Connor said, "Well, from South America, Gabriel Santiago has been dominant. While he's mixed in all forms of fighting, his specialty is on the ground. I'd liken him to a python because, when he gets his grips on you, it's pretty much over."

Stabler said, "Yeah, I really like him as well, and he's quickly amassed a huge following with his technique, personality, and style."

Grandmaster Chang said, "While Gabriel is an eye-catcher, Kurasawa from Japan has been brutal. He's hardcore when it comes to training for pain, and he's exceptional at delivering it as well."

Krenzel said, "I like Kurasawa, but from England, the old-school brawler Duncan McMillan has really caught my eye. He's not technical like most other fighters, but his years outside the ring and implementing his bar room brawl style has been really effective."

Stabler said, "Like we've always said, there's no one style that has it all, and the league is quick to adapt, which brings us right back to the struggles of Kirin Rise…."

The crew continued discussing the current season, and it began to become heated. Even with Kirin's lackluster performance this year, she still ended up dominating the majority of the conversation both on air and with the masses. The panel's voices began to fade away from the TV set as Watanabe sat back in his chair and said, "TV change channel."

The TV quickly changed in front of him, and news of another protest breaking out was being reported. Since Kirin's speech, the masses had gained some momentum and were more daring with the authorities. The possibility of re-establishing martial law was being heavily discussed by all. Many wondered how the current administration would handle this situation.

He watched, listened, and remained unaffected by the information. Suddenly, his secretary's voice popped out from the air and said, "Mr. Watanabe, Senator Collins is on the line."

The ties between Senator Collins and Watanabe were strong. Neither one was particularly fond of the other, but their differences were always put aside due to the common interest they shared. Each one realized that true power wasn't in the name but more so in the position. Watanabe had no problem allowing Thorne to bask in the spotlight of the company's name. Senator Collins had relinquished interest in ever obtaining the seat of the Presidency, since its power was more in name than in actual authority. Collins remained in Congress, being the buffer between large companies and the governing body. He knew far too well that for anything to happen, it had to go through him.

Watanabe's expression quickly changed as a glimmer of a smile could be seen on his face. He reached into his pocket and grabbed a small object. He walked away from his desk to a smaller table that stood opposite his most prized samurai swords. On the table was a flat board with the map of the entire world. Pieces were laid out and areas marked for possession.

He looked down at it and finally replied. "Thank you, Mira. I'll take it."

"Yes, sir," said Mira.

Watanabe said, "Senator, thanks for taking the time."

Senator Collins replied, "I always have time for you, Watanabe. So, how's the weather in the Big Apple?"

Watanabe cringed at hearing his voice. Senator Collins was from Texas. His Southern words and drawl felt like pins and needles to Watanabe's ear. However, Watanabe remained static and never revealed how much it pained him.

"Senator, I'm sure you didn't call me to find out the chance of precipitation in the Big Apple," said Watanabe.

"Ah yes, let's cut to the chase. I've always liked that about you, Watanabe. You're so damn direct, unusual for a Japanese from my experience. But, then again, I'd rather deal with you than those damn Chinese."

Watanabe stayed silent and listened.

"Anyway," said Senator Collins, "I hear you have good news for me, Watanabe."

Watanabe said, "My English isn't so good, but I do believe there's a difference between good news and great?"

"There certainly is, Watanabe."

"Well then, I would say this is … hmm, how do you Americans say it? I'd say it's a game-changer for the human race."

"Well, those are some mighty big boots you're gonna have to fill. Don't get me wrong; I've been impressed with everything so far. Dagnabit, I'm sorry again. My memory's not what it used to be. What's the name of the pill?"

"SSP730, Senator."

"I hate when these scientists give such a complex name to this shit. I like calling it just how it looks."

"Well, it's kind of … how do you say it again? Ah, yes … romantic if you ask me how he came up with the name. The number represents the number of failed attempts before success, a nice reminder of how much work was invested in it."

The senator said, "And the SSP?"

"That's probably the least creative, as our lead scientist who came up with it just called it the super soldier pill."

The senator began chuckling on the other end, and Watanabe joined him. He coughed out a lung and apologized to Watanabe. "Oh yeah, where was I? So, when will we be testing this on our soldiers? I'm hoping it'll be sooner than expected."

Watanabe said, "We're ahead of schedule, but like I said, I have better news than that, Senator. If you will, please turn to FNN News right now, if you don't mind."

Watanabe waited several minutes as Senator Collins could be heard fumbling in the background. He could hear him mumbling and cursing technology. Then he muttered, "Fucking protestors, bitching and complaining like always. Goddamn administration is soft as hell. So, what about them?"

"It's fascinating watching them, is it not?"

"Riding a horse is fascinating, Watanabe. If anything, these damn protestors are more annoying than a fly on a horse's ass. All this bullshit about their right to protest. All these goddamn protestors mouthing off. Hmm, but then again … this is 'Merica, not goddamn North Korea," said the senator. He then paused and spouted, "Speaking of which, your employee Kirin Rise is responsible for all this bullshit, you know."

"It's America, Senator. People are allowed to voice their opinion."

"Bullshit, that's the sell, but you and I know the truth, Watanabe."

"Senator, dream with me for a second. If I asked you to tell me the kind of America you have envisioned, what exactly would that be?"

"That's simple, Watanabe. We pay off our debts to those fucking countries. Them bastards had no problem when we rescued their pussy asses in World War II, but they're hammering us with these double-digit interest rates to be their slaves, while we still make sure their goddamn country is safe.

"Second, we get control of these protesting tree huggers and get them back to working for their minimum wage. But, I'm a patriot, Watanabe. The most important thing is us regaining our status of being the number one super power in the world."

"I thought that's what you would say. Well, that's the good news." Watanabe looked down at his table and looked at where all the pieces currently lay. His vision was bigger than the senator could imagine, but he had no intention of revealing his full hand just yet.

"Don't get me wrong, Watanabe, having super soldiers is good news. Hell, I'd use them on all those bastards holding the debt over our heads. But, I don't particularly see how's that's game-changing."

"I agree. Having super soldiers is a good thing, but not even close to great. You see, soldiers are necessary when the general population has to be kept under control."

"Where you going with this, Watanabe? Now, you really caught my interest."

"Before I tell you more, be forewarned: it will cost you."

Senator Collins bellowed in laughter. "Well, damn, Watanabe, when it's other people's money, who gives a rat's ass? Besides, we can print more of this shit up."

"Very well," said Watanabe, who realized that Senator Collins was unaware that the cost had nothing to do with money.

"So, don't keep me hanging, Watanabe. I'm all ears."

"Like I said, today is a great day. We've been able to synthesize the drug and split it. So, for you ... you'll have your super soldier who can't feel pain and could fight to the death."

"Definitely like the sound of that," said Senator Collins.

"But therein lies the problem. Do you want a soldier that could fight to the death ... or would?"

"What do you mean, Watanabe?"

"You could easily sell a soldier an ideal of what they're fighting for. If you ask them the first thing that comes out of their mouths would be for 'Freedom.' And, I'm sure the general public would recite exactly the same thing. However, the problem is eventually some out there will question this. But, imagine if you didn't even have to worry about that at all."

"Go on." Senator Collins was glued on the other end, salivating with the possibilities.

"Imagine a world where you have obedient little ants that can function normally, but do exactly what they're supposed to."

The senator said, "That's the America I've envisioned forever. I mean, we've tried everything over the years to control these miserable bastards, from the products they buy, to the food they eat and the medicine they need. We got them wanting stuff they don't need, addicted to the slop that we feed them, and popping pills like it's candy. No matter what we give them or distract them with, there's a little bit of fight in them that we've never been able to snuff out ... completely."

Watanabe knew that Senator Collins was short-sighted. He could see only as far as his big belly would extend. He knew Collins was thirsting to merely control all the citizens of the U.S., but Watanabe's desire went deeper, his lust was global.

"What do you think Senator?" asked Watanabe.

"What'd I think? I think you're one God damn ambitious son of a bitch. You sound like some sick bastard who wants to make the world burn."

Watanabe pulled out the lighter he had grabbed earlier. He quickly flicked it open, and a flame appeared. He held it over his little map covering the world as he thought, *I'm the guy carrying the match.*

Meanwhile at a Charity Event

At the local orphanage in Chicago, a crowd of reporters and photographers were surrounding Kirin and Thorne. Thorne was holding a little girl and was all smiles. Always loving the spotlight, he was a magnet for attention and did his best to reciprocate. Kirin stood opposite. The flashes and reporters were the least of her problem. It was being in Thorne's presence that made things quite uncomfortable. As the event wound down, they got into Thorne's car as the photographers continued to snap away.

Inside the car, Thorne began talking to Fawn.

Fawn said, "We have another appointment in thirty minutes, right after we drop off Ms. Rise and her assistant."

Kirin was silent, and she sat as far away as possible in Thorne's limo. Angelo sat alongside her and felt the uneasiness of the moment.

"Thank you, Kirin, for joining us today for this charity event," said Thorne.

Kirin didn't respond as she looked out the window. Angelo was about to open his mouth, but decided to follow her lead.

The silence was uncomfortable, especially for Fawn, who squirmed and tried to reduce the tension.

Fawn said, "You know, Kirin, the UFMF is one of the biggest corporations for contributing to many charitable events."

Kirin glanced at him and clapped sarcastically.

Fawn snapped back, "Well, now you're just being a little bitch." He pulled out his hanky and pretended to cry, but immediately checked to see if anyone cared.

"I'm sorry. Am I supposed to be impressed with your measly donations that you give—which, by the way, is only done from your gracious heart just so you get a further tax break."

Thorne said, "Someone's a little spoiled. Several million dollars to charitable events isn't measly in my book."

Kirin said, "Considering that the UFMF is the largest corporation in the world and that once again you guys managed to pay the least amount of taxes compared to the huge chunks that the average citizen pays, I don't see how your charitable giving should be looked upon as anything but scraps."

Thorne barked back, "I'm a law-abiding citizen, Kirin, and we merely follow the letter of the law set forth by this government ... which, by the way, you the people voted for. Oh, I forgot, you don't vote."

Kirin stared down Thorne.

"Oh, or did you forget that with your little stint in the slammer?"

"The letter of the law, created and set forth supposedly by the government which is bought and paid for by the corporation. Why no one else can see this BS is beyond me."

Fawn said, "Listen, you little ungrateful—"

Angelo barked back, "Watch what you're saying!"

Fawn snarled and said, "I'm watching you … does that count?"

Angelo blushed and had nothing to say.

Thorne held his hand up, and Fawn was quick to be silenced. "Kirin, I'll give you credit for your noble cause, but many people have tried and failed in your position."

Kirin received a text on her phone; immediately, her expression hardened. She knew who it was as she pulled it from her pocket and read, "Play nice."

She looked suspiciously at both Thorne and Fawn. Neither one was holding a cell phone, but then again that would be too obvious. She thought, *It has to be them or someone they've paid who's sending this.* It was eating her up, and she had no one to turn to for help.

Angelo tapped Kirin on the shoulder and said, "I'm on the phone right now, should I tell them we're gonna be slightly late for our appointment?"

The combination of the text along with her present company pushed her past her threshold of tolerance. Kirin didn't respond to Angelo and shouted, "Let us out, right here!"

Thorne looked at Fawn, who immediately signaled to the driver. The limo driver did as he was instructed and pulled to the side of the street. Kirin got out of the car and Angelo followed; both began to walk away. As the car began to pull away, Thorne let down his window. Kirin turned around and stared at him.

Thorne said, "There are two choices in life: you either go along for the ride, or you die fighting against it. Kirin, a word of advice … whatever you started, this movement you believe will change the world, I can tell you now, there is not going to be a happy ending to this story."

Kirin stood silent as Thorne closed his window and the car rolled away.

Several Days Later

Tobias said, "Okay, I'm headed to work…. You still going to work out?"

Kirin looked sadly at Sifu and said, "Do you mind?"

Sifu laughed. "This is working out?"

Tobias approached Kirin to say goodbye, but they both paused in front of each other with an awkward exchange for a goodbye. In the end, Tobias shook his head, and he left Sifu's restaurant giving Kirin a handshake.

Kirin turned slowly to see if Sifu had been watching, but he was surprisingly on his phone texting.

Kirin said, "You know, I don't think I've ever seen you use your phone this much."

"Yeah, I know. I think I've become a slave to texting."

"I'm so surprised to hear that."

"You know Wing Chun; it's always adapting."

Kirin thought it was weird that Sifu would say that, but everything had felt out of whack the last several months.

Downstairs in the basement restaurant, Sifu and Kirin were exchanging attacks and blocks. They had been working out intensely for the last thirty minutes. Both of them had built up an ample amount of sweat, but it was Kirin who was feeling winded from their training. She went for another attack, hoping this would land, but again Sifu easily blocked it and countered as she yielded in disgust.

"You know, when I was much younger, I used to look forward to working with you alone," huffed Kirin.

Sifu said, "You're only twenty! Are you referring to sometime in the last couple of weeks?"

Kirin laughed at Sifu's sarcastic remark. "I train and train and train even harder than ever before. But, I swear I'm doing worse."

"I wouldn't say that."

"Why not?"

"For all you know, you're doing the same, and I'm the one whose improving."

Kirin rolled her eyes. The times with Sifu were special even if she felt terrible after every workout. Suddenly she heard a ding on her phone. Immediately, she excused herself, "Sorry, Sifu. Give me one second?"

Sifu nodded as he smiled and patiently waited.

She darted to the corner where her phone rested and looked at the message. She knew who it was from, but tried her best to keep a straight face. It was exactly who she feared and dreaded.

A text flashed on her phone, *Practice all you want, but the next match you'll have to lose.*

Frustration and anguish covered her face as she looked at Sifu, hoping that he could feel what she was feeling, but he seemed oddly oblivious to the situation. He had not mentioned anything about her matches this season, regardless of how bad she was performing.

Sifu said, "Anything important?"

"Uh no, it's nothing." She thought, *Come on, Sifu. You've got to be feeling that something is off. Please help me.*

"Can we practice some more?" asked Kirin. She kept a straight face as his words and reaction brought little comfort.

"Of course, you need it."

As Kirin and Sifu continued to work out, it appeared that Sifu was somehow turning up the intensity. If Kirin wasn't already looking bad, his moves seemed even more effortless, until she was being controlled like a rag doll. Attacks were being countered one after the other. He would string a succession of unusual joint locks from out of the blue, and finally when Kirin thought it couldn't get worse, he suddenly felt it necessary to show more domination as he froze her motion. Kirin tried moving, but felt herself pinned down when she should have been able to move.

"What the heck is that?"

Sifu kept his hands engaged on Kirin and asked, "What's what?"

"This…," she grunted as she struggled to squirm from their current position.

"I think it's called Wing Chun."

"I know it's Wing Chun. Why can't I move?"

"Are you trying to move?"

Kirin rolled her eyes. "Of course you know I'm trying to move."

She tried to muscle her way out, since nothing else worked. That, of course, was a bad decision. Kirin found herself losing her center of gravity. In the blink of an eye, her back was on the ground.

Kirin was gasping for air. She shook her head as she looked at Sifu, who was just to her side. "I don't know how to get better, Sifu. No matter what I do, I can't beat you."

"Hmm, interesting." Sifu stroked his chin.

"What?"

"Your goal is to beat me?"

Kirin looked confused and said, "Isn't that always the goal, to beat your opponent?"

"Beating your opponent, hmm? Interesting that you say that."

"Please not so cryptic, Sifu."

"I'm not being cryptic; I'm just wondering if you know who the opponent is?"

Kirin shook her head, as his words just left her more confused.

"I don't know what you're saying, Sifu." said Kirin.

"Oh well, maybe another time, you'll understand what I'm saying. For now, you could say your method to beat your opponent is flawed."

"How so?"

"You're trying to control me."

"What's wrong with that?"

"Hmm, maybe I can give you an example."

"I'd be happy with you enlightening me while I lie in a pool of my own sweat."

Sifu extended his hand, and Kirin accepted his generosity and found herself sitting back up. When Sifu tossed her a towel, she began drying herself off.

"To control your opponent is like trying to control the weather."

"You can't control the weather."

"I know that."

"I still don't get it. How exactly are you doing that freeze thingamajig on me if that's not total control of me?" asked Kirin.

"But it is total control of you."

Kirin shook her head. "Please, Sifu. We've been working out for several hours. Must you give me mind puzzles so late in our training? You just said you can't control people, and now you're saying you controlled me."

"To control someone is to control yourself."

Kirin squinted and tried to figure out what that meant.

"Remember that old example I used to give you of what my Sifu said about making people stick?"

"Sure, the example with the bird on the branch."

"Yes, exactly. If a bird lands on a branch I'm holding, the bird needs to push off that branch in order to feel solid ground and take off and fly, right?"

"Right."

"So, how is it that I'm preventing that bird from flying?"

"Well, from the thousands of times you've told the story, every time the bird tries to push for solid ground, you adjust the branch so it has nothing to push off."

"Right again."

"Well, at least I'm right in something."

"So, if the bird pushes down for two pounds of pressure and I move the branch down two pounds' worth and match it, he has nothing to push. So, am I controlling the bird, or am I the branch?"

"I guess you are controlling the branch," said Kirin.

"You say it, but your actions speak differently. In fact, your actions are the very same thing you are fighting against."

"What do you mean?"

"Isn't that what the corporations want? Control over the government as well as the people? I told you once, when that ball starts rolling, the power is like a drug that very few people can say no to. It consumes the individual and clouds his or her vision as the desire for more becomes overwhelming," said Sifu.

Kirin thought of Sage for a moment, as she could hear his voice say, "Dark side."

Kirin again found herself standing in silence.

Sifu said, "Let's train some more."

⋏ ⋏ ⋏

A Few Days Later

It was not how Kirin would've imagined it, as it was humble in design. From her experience, those in power often flaunted their means, but Bryce's office was situated away from the heart of the city, several miles from the downtown area, amongst everyday working men and women. Nothing fancy by any stretch of the imagination, just your standard office to get the job done.

From a distance, Kirin could see Bryce in his office staring out the window. She stood in front of his secretary and waited by the entrance. Kirin was feeling anxious about their meeting.

Bryce turned around and made eye contact from afar. He hurried his pace toward his receptionist and reached over to shake Kirin's hand. "Ah, Kirin, you finally made it." He shook it firmly, but then realized how outstretched and awkward his greeting appeared.

"Sorry, so rude of me." Shaking his head, he adjusted his suit and strolled around to properly greet her. "Come in, come in. Do you want anything to drink?" Bryce directed her to step into his office.

"Uh, no. I'm good. Thank you, by the way," said Kirin.

"Sorry about the mess. I keep telling myself to clean up, but I never get to it." Bryce made some halfhearted attempt to straighten things up.

Helen, his secretary, said, "Is there anything else you'll need for tonight, Bryce?"

"No, you've stayed late enough, Helen. Why don't you head off home?"

"Sure thing," said Helen.

Kirin watched as Helen left the room and closed the door behind them. She thought for a moment, *That was unusual. She actually called him by his first name.*

Bryce caught her reaction and asked, "Is something wrong?"

Kirin said, "No, no. Nothing."

Bryce said, "You sure?"

"Well, I thought it was just kinda strange to see your secretary call you by your first name."

"Hmm," said Bryce. "Actually, I'd feel more awkward if she called me Mr. Adams." Bryce smiled and gestured for Kirin to take a seat. "I know I may be her boss, but the way I see it, we both need each other for things to work out. Thus, respect is a two-way street and should be equally shared. Don't you think?"

Kirin smiled, as Bryce's attitude felt refreshing to hear. Her nerves began to settle as she sat down.

"By the way, you look a lot better now than your mugshot," he laughed.

"Funny," said Kirin, though she still couldn't find the humor of her past incarceration.

Kirin and Bryce had been talking for several minutes, when their conversation was interrupted by a phone call.

"I'm sorry, Kirin. I have to take this," said Bryce. Bryce's calm demeanor seemed shaken from the call; Kirin waited and pretended not to listen.

"How are you feeling...? That's good ... So, you took your medicine, like you're supposed to...? Okay, did you study hard today in school?"

Kirin observed Bryce. Whoever was on the line had his undivided attention.

"No, Daddy's working late tonight, but I promise I'll kiss you when I get home, even if you're asleep."

He paused, listening.

"Say good night to Mommy for me," said Bryce. He looked somewhat teary eyed, but quickly regained his composure.

"How many kids do you have?" asked Kirin.

"That's my one and only," said Bryce.

"She sounds adorable."

"She is.... She means the world to me, and there's nothing I wouldn't do for her," said Bryce, as he turned away and looked slightly choked up.

Kirin wasn't sure what to make off it, but quickly let it go.

Bryce snapped his fingers and turned toward Kirin. He headed for the cabinet and poured something to drink.

"You sure you don't want anything?"

"I'm sure ... thank you."

Suddenly Kirin recalled an article she had read about Bryce. She blurted, "Hey, I thought you didn't drink?"

"I don't," said Bryce. "But every once in a while, it helps calm my nerves."

"You were saying, Mr. Adams?"

"Please, Kirin, call me Bryce.... You make me feel so old when you say it that way."

"Sorry." She chuckled at the thought.

"Anyway, let me get right to the point. We all have a story, don't we, Kirin? The origin where it all began, that created that drive to bring us to this very moment. It's hard to believe I'm in politics or whatever this mess is that I got involved with. I've never told the full story of this, and I'm sure you wonder how I could stay so private being in my line of work.... But, I've always felt there are certain things you want to keep for yourself."

Kirin listened and was drawn to the tone of his voice.

"It's just like in the movies: middle class parents with three kids struggling to keep their heads afloat. My old man was a statistic, an unknown number in the world of corporate America who got the ax. Got screwed over by his insurance and was laid to the wayside by his country.

"In some ways, you want to laugh because you just don't think it's possible. They layoff thousands of employees, but the CEO gets a raise. Minimum wage workers are barely able to put food on the table, but somehow they can justify a CEO getting paid almost 1,000 times what the typical worker does. So, like any good dad, he did everything to keep the family from starving, but eventually everyone has a limit. Somehow, in his mind, he justified that taking his own life would make things better for us."

Kirin hung her head, as she knew where Bryce was going with his story.

"So, he did just that. Being the youngest one coming home from school, whether planned or not, I ended up being the first one to see my old man dead. He had a note and everything. That image is forever burned in my head." Bryce took another sip.

"Anyway, my old man's plans fell through on a 'technicality,' according to the insurance company." Bryce shook his head with a tear falling down.

"He sacrificed his life so we could get out of our hole; instead, we lost him, and the cost of the funeral and expenses brought us down even further. You know, my mom's never recovered from it. My older brothers did their best to raise me. Seems like it's my job to stop the downward spiral of the Adams family. To make matters worse, my mom's now in the hospital and...."

Bryce smashed his fist on the table. "All for a goddamn profit, Kirin. That's the world we live in, and it's gotten so bad that the rich aren't concerned with just making a profit, but seeing how far above and beyond they can stretch it."

Kirin nodded. "I totally agree." She could feel his anguish and knew exactly how he felt. "What more do you need from me, Mr. Adams—excuse me, I mean Bryce?"

"You saw what your speech did last time, but people still need to be led," said Bryce.

"Well, isn't that what you're for?"

"It is, but I can't do this alone. You've got a following that lives and dies by your words, and together we can finally get this country on the right path once again."

Kirin asked, "What are you asking?"

"I need you, Kirin. I need you with me as often as you can spare," said Bryce.

Kirin took a breath and paused before answering. "Can I at least think about it?" said Kirin.

"Okay. At least you didn't say no … so there's still hope."

Bryce stood behind her and put his hands on her shoulders. "Don't take too long to think about it, Kirin. I'll always be there if and when you need me."

Kirin looked at Bryce and tried to read him.

Bryce moved to his desk and grabbed his drink. "You can trust me," he said and looked away, taking a sip from his cup.

Kirin was left with nothing to say. She said her goodbyes and left the office.

Several minutes passed as Bryce walked toward the window and began staring outside. As the office stood silent, he muttered, "Everyone has a price to pay … everyone." With that, he pressed his head against the window and closed his eyes.

The Next Day

Kirin stared at her computer screen, feeling the burden that weighed upon her. Her every move was being watched, and constant reminders were sent to her. Whoever this was knew everything about her and her family and friends. They threatened Jim's safety overseas and dangled the possibility of Gwen being rejected for her surgical procedure. However, as important as all those matters were, the new picture of her parents troubled her the most. She thought, *Could it really be them?*

She felt alone. Even Sifu couldn't seem to help her with this, and she was desperately hoping he would be able to tell something was troubling her. The weeks tried her heart, as the words by all those around were haunting. She felt alone and, worse than that, controlled by outside forces she couldn't escape. She was about to tear up, but suddenly clenched her fist and smashed it on the table.

"I need some air." She stood up and looked at the clock. It was just past 11:00 pm.

She grabbed her coat, kissed Bacon, who was in a deep sleep and snoring, and snuck off for a late-night coffee run. Ten minutes later, walking through the surprisingly empty streets of Chicago, Kirin stumbled upon a little shop she'd never noticed before. She looked at the front of the store, and a neon light flickered a 24-hour sign. She thought, *Mmm, that's gotta be good eating.* A quick peek from the outside revealed an empty store with a single worker busy on his phone, waiting for business. Kirin took a deep breath and entered.

Perfect. One coffee … black, she thought. It was Kirin's favorite since she liked things simple and natural.

The worker was a half-asleep, skinny teenager who was more concerned with his phone than anything. That didn't matter to Kirin, as she was looking for the one thing that could bring her a little form of comfort.

"What'll you have?" he asked as he continued to text on the phone.

"Coffee, black," said Kirin with a smile. It was her brief escape.

The worker made a face and said, "You sure that's all you want? I mean … we're known for our specialty drinks. Half-calf with a sprinkle of—"

Kirin interrupted him and said, "No, just a regular, coffee … black!" She kept her head low and her hoodie on, but it didn't seem to matter, as the worker either didn't recognize her or didn't care.

The worker rolled his eyes and went to get Kirin's coffee. He was kind enough to brew a fresh batch and poured it into a cup. Then he handed it to her and went back to his phone to text.

Kirin grabbed her coffee and enjoyed the warmth. She spun around, hoping to enjoy her little drink but didn't realize someone was standing right behind her. Her wild, uncontrolled motions led her to bump into this stranger. Her coffee fell to the ground as she yelled, "Hey, watch it!"

All Kirin could do was stare at her drink that was splattered all over the floor. It was ironic. That moment pretty much summarized how her life felt.

"Sorry, miss, my apologies. Here, let me help clean it up for you."

Kirin looked at the floor to see the mess as the stranger was already down, trying his best to help out.

Kirin grabbed some napkins from the counter and noticed the worker was still texting throughout this entire commotion. She began wiping up the mess and said, "Can't you see where you're going?"

The stranger didn't reply and continued to clean the floor.

Kirin tossed several napkins on the floor and used her foot to dry it out. "I mean, there's this entire empty store, and you managed to find the one spot I'm occupying."

He continued to smile and finally said, "Uh, I hate using it as a handicap, but every so often the blindness can get in the way."

The words at first didn't compute, as Kirin was so preoccupied with her current situation. She took a second to look at the stranger and noticed he was wearing sunglasses at night.

She stopped dead in her tracks. "Oh my God." Kirin covered her mouth in shock. "You're blind."

"I prefer the term 'visually impaired' but technically you are correct," said the stranger, who continued to clean the mess.

"I'm so sorry. I ... uh, it's been a long day and—"

"No, no ... no need to apologize. Technically, you're correct." The stranger did his best to find the rest of the spill.

"Uh, can you even see what you're cleaning?"

The stranger chuckled. "I like the reference to seeing, again."

Kirin shook her head. "Uh, that's not what I meant. Oh ... here, let me help you." Kirin got down on her knees and began wiping up the mess.

"Again, let me apologize," said the stranger.

"No, don't," said Kirin.

"Seriously, you were right to yell at me, and frankly I find it kind of refreshing. Most of the time, people try to avoid me and get out of my way because of my handicap," said the stranger.

Kirin smiled and watched, as the stranger was doing a good job cleaning up. "Wow, I'm impressed."

"With what?"

"You actually cleaned it up pretty well ... you know ... uh, without seeing and all."

"I hate to sound crude, but if I can wipe my own ass, I'm pretty sure I can clean up a spill."

Kirin giggled and finally stood up. "That's pretty good. I'm sorry again for running into you."

"Apology not accepted," said the stranger.

Kirin was caught off guard and didn't know what to say.

"Look, it was my mistake for bumping into you. Let me buy you another cup, at the very least." The stranger extended his hand forward.

Kirin waited and looked around. The coffee shop was occupied only by the stranger, the worker, and her. Kirin reached out and shook his hand. "Uh, yeah sure. Uh, thanks."

He smiled and said, "Ah, my name is Quinn Michaels. Had you said no, I would've given a different name, to save me from embarrassment."

Kirin laughed again.

Quinn asked, "Uh, do you have a name?"

Kirin hesitated for a moment, not wanting to draw attention because of her status. She stammered, "Oh, it's uh ... it's uhhh."

Quinn smiled and said, "No, it's okay, I don't need a name. Besides, I can recognize you a mile away from your smell and your voice."

Kirin felt awkward as she grabbed her hair and smelled it. She thought, *What gives? I showered today or was that yesterday?* Kirin snapped back to reality and replied, "Sounds kinda superhero like."

Quinn grimaced and said, "Well, considering I'm missing my sense of sight, I only have four others to fall back on."

Kirin slapped her head and said, "Oh, jeez … I, uh, did it again."

"Look, how about for now I call you Coffee Girl, if that's okay with you?"

"Fine. I like that. Coffee Girl, it is."

For the next hour, Quinn and Kirin talked. It was the first real break from reality Kirin had in a long time. All the pressures and stress she had been facing, for a brief time, didn't exist.

"Well, Coffee Girl, I better get going. I've got work tomorrow."

"You have work tomorrow? Why'd you stay out so late?"

Quinn smiled and said, "It's not every day you get to run into a beautiful girl. Besides, no one can see the bags under my eyes with these glasses."

Kirin said, "I had a lot of fun. Thanks for hearing me out."

Quinn stood up and said, "It was my pleasure. Any chance I'll be seeing you again?"

Kirin giggled at Quinn's joke and said, "Yeah, I'd like that. I'd like to see you again."

"Power given is power that will never be returned. Very few can resist the desire to seek out more."—Watanabe

SECTION 1

Short Stories #8—Kirin's P.O.V.

<u>Just a Post—1 Year, 83 Days</u>

I dashed to my locker, as I didn't want to be late for lunch. Today was extra special, since Mom had packed me a meal and I didn't have to eat the cafeteria food. I cringed just for a moment at the thought of it, but realized I was in the minority for liking to brown bag my meals. Since Sifu had left, I looked forward to even the simplest things to cheer me up.

I placed my thumb on my locker to be scanned, and it popped out and opened. In the bottom corner, I saw my brown lunch bag, snuggled right next to my red hoodie. I had both hands ready to grab my lunch when a whimper broke my concentration.

I looked cautiously to my side to see what was happening. Just a few lockers away, I could see a girl named Lilly having a difficult time opening her locker as she tried her best to hide her tears.

I could feel right away that this wasn't a typical teenage dilemma, like boyfriend problems or clothes not matching. It was something really serious. I felt bad for her and said, "Hi, Lilly." I waved and gave a goofy smile, trying to cheer her up. "Uh ... if you don't mind my asking ... is everything okay?"

She tried to wipe her eyes to cover up her tears and said, "It's nothing." She did her best to avoid direct eye contact as she struggled with her little tissue.

From behind, I heard a couple of guys walk by and laugh. One of them said, "Are you free this weekend, Lilly?"

She tried to ignore him, but his words clearly bothered her. I watched as they whispered together, laughing some more. Lilly hung her head as the tears forced themselves out of her.

I wasn't really close friends with Lilly. She pretty much kept to herself. In high school, she would be categorized as a nerd, but I wasn't quite sure what that meant. If "nerd" meant someone who loved something that society found odd, then I guessed I would fall in that category as well. For whatever reason, people loved their little niches, and if you weren't in the right one, it made for a difficult four years of self-discovery.

My stomach grumbled as I looked back at my lunch, which seemed to be talking back to me. I thought I heard it say, *Kirin, grab me and eat me.* I shook my head and snapped out of my daze. "Quiet, you," I mumbled.

Lilly asked, "What?"

"Uh, nothing. It's nothing. Seriously, Lilly ... what's wrong?" I looked at her as she seemed lost and alone. I knew what that felt like, more than anyone.

She took a deep breath and reached into her pocket. Then she pulled out her cell phone and handed it to me.

"Just click the button," she said as she stared away.

I grabbed it and looked at the screen. It was a picture of her, and I began reading the post below.

"Who posted this, Lilly?" I asked.

"I swear, I thought he really liked me. Tim was so nice to me, and ... I didn't do any of that, but now everyone's seeing this, and I don't know what to do." She shook her head and began to sob.

Her pain became mine. I could feel it, the suffering and the helplessness, grabbing at me. I knew it all too well, when injustice ruled and good people did nothing. It didn't matter that we weren't close friends. I knew right away her suffering was genuine. I didn't know what made me snap, but I wanted to deal with it my way. "Come with me, Lilly."

"What are you doing, Kirin?" asked Lilly.

"We're gonna clear this up and set things straight," I said angrily.

"Kirin, no."

I ignored Lilly and continued walking. I didn't care if she followed. I knew where all the popular kids were hanging out, so I headed over to Tim's locker. He happened to be the star basketball player of our high school. I could see him hovering around his locker with several of his friends, laughing. As I walked down the hall, I heard the chatter of my classmates, murmuring about Lilly, who stood close behind me.

Lilly grabbed my shirt and said, "Kirin, don't. You'll make it worse."

I turned around to reassure her that things would be all right. She looked at me with a sliver of hope as we continued our walk down the long hallway.

I shouted from a distance, "Hey, Tim. I need to talk to you."

He turned toward me and asked, "Who's asking?"

"I'm asking," I said sternly as my pace increased and Lilly followed. I finally got within the proper range and then held up the phone right in front of his face.

He looked unaffected and said, "What of it?" A cynical smile followed his snide question as he chuckled like an idiot with his friends.

A huge group started circling around us. I didn't care if this was for their entertainment. I wanted the truth to come out. Lilly looked like a timid person afraid of what was going to happen next.

I said, "I want you to tell everyone the truth, that you made up these lies about Lilly … for whatever reason. Just tell the fricking truth."

Tim looked around and then at his friends and smiled back. "It's all true."

Lilly shouted, "You're such a liar, Tim! All we did was hold hands. Why are you saying this?" She started tearing up as people were jeering.

Tim made a snide comment and riled up the crowd even more.

I was tired of it. There was no need for this. A person of his stature was taking advantage of Lilly. Why did people who had so much need to squash the feelings of those who had so little? I didn't bother asking twice; it was time for action. I moved in toward Tim, grabbed him by the arm, and quickly put him in a joint lock.

He screamed, "What the fuck?"

I controlled him well as he tried to struggle, but the more he did, the more I increased the pain until I eventually planted his face to the ground.

I said, "I want you to tell everyone the truth."

"You stupid bitch, you're gonna break my arm!" He was getting angry, but not as livid as I was with his lies.

His friend started to approach as I looked at them and said, "You take one more step, and I swear I'll snap his arm." I cranked on his arm, and he screamed.

"Step back, you idiots!" he yelled.

I stared at them and said, "Good luck on your game this weekend."

He shouted again. "Fuck, it's about to snap! Aaahh!" They finally got the message and backed down as silence fell within that area.

"You've got two seconds to tell the truth, or the next sound you hear is your arm snapping. Tell the damn truth … NOW!" I tightened my grip on his arm.

He hesitated for another second and finally said, "Yes! Yes. I made that stuff up. It's not true. None of it. We just held hands."

I looked at Lilly; for the first time, she smiled.

I cranked on his arm just a little more. "One more time," I demanded.

"Fuck! Yes … it's true. I lied about the entire thing."

Upon hearing his last words, I felt satisfied with his response. I let go of my grip as Tim squirmed back to his locker, cradling his arm. The crowd murmured as I motioned to Lilly. She looked at me and gave me a hug.

"Thank you so much, Kirin," said Lilly.

I looked at her and said, "Remember, Lilly. How you define yourself is all that matters."

Monday Morning

I went to school feeling good about myself with the start of a fresh week. Monday didn't have that blah sensation that it's normally labeled for. Everything had changed; I could feel something was different in the air. From a distance, I could see Gwen. As I approached her, I saw she had a sad look on her face. Gwen strolled closer to me in her wheelchair.

"What's wrong, Gwen?" I asked.

"You didn't hear."

"Hear what?"

Gwen teared up and said, "Last night … Lilly killed herself."

"What? Why? This can't be. Everything was okay.… I thought everything was okay." I kept hearing those words over and over again in my head.

Gwen pulled her phone out and showed me some new postings. Even with the truth, the bullying hadn't stopped. People didn't care, especially Tim, who had decided to post new things about Lilly.

I cried and dropped to my knees. I thought, *Why? Why? Why did this have to happen? Why do good people have to suffer so?*

I slammed my fist on the ground and wiped the tears from my face. I looked Gwen in the eyes and began to walk.

Gwen shouted, "Kirin, don't! Don't do it, Kirin."

I could hear Gwen's voice fade. It felt like déjà vu. Once again, I saw Tim talking with his friends without an ounce of remorse on his face. What put the cherry on the top was him talking to Ripley and laughing away. A group had started following me as I neared Tim. He saw me approach and puffed his chest out.

I shook my head in disgust. I thought, *What kind of sick human being would act like this?* Even though I was filled with anger, I knew exactly how I wanted this to end. For whatever reason, I could see everything so clearly. I wanted to make sure he instigated it, that I had no choice but to defend myself.

I didn't say a word and just stared at him.

He stared at my directly and said, "I'm glad the bitch died."

I didn't take the bait. I said, "You're a coward. You couldn't leave it alone and had to push further."

"Who are you calling a coward?" He moved closer to my range.

"That's your new name from now on, Tim the Coward."

He looked around, as everyone made a noise when he took the insult.

I could see it was working and I was pissing him off. "You're upset that a little girl half your size got the better of you. You posted more lies, but everyone here knows that you're so full of it."

I could feel his rage kicking in. I needed just a pinch more to put him over the top.

"Two for fifteen last Saturday shooting. Did my arm lock screw up your shooting hand?" I stated in a cynical voice.

He finally exploded and threw a punch right at me. It was exactly what I wanted—for everyone to see that he initiated the incident. As the punch flew toward me, I formed a triangle and caught it perfectly between my hands.

Snap.

I broke his arm without hesitation as he crumpled to the floor.

"Fuck! Jeez, you broke my fucking arm!" He squirmed on the floor, but his screams echoed through the hallway.

I looked at him and said, "That pain you feel is nothing compared to what Lilly had to go through. Nothing compared to what her parents are going through right now." I turned to my classmates and pointed at each of them. I firmly looked each one of them in the eye and said, "You should all be ashamed of yourself. Do you doubt yourself so much that your insecurities make you feel better by tormenting a girl through social media? Each and every single one of you should all be ashamed of yourself. I hope karma is real, and that one day you feel the same pain."

I looked at Tim as he cowered away.

A teacher shouted, "Step aside. Step aside! What is going on in here?"

Everyone cleared a path for Mr. Gibson, and he saw Tim lying on the ground.

"Oh my gosh! What happened here, Tim?"

Tim looked at me, and I didn't even blink.

He stuttered, "I, uh … I slipped on the floor and busted my arm."

"Well, this is terrible news." Mr. Gibson helped up Tim and asked, "Is this what really happened?"

I looked straight ahead as I saw Ripley looking directly at me. Everyone began confirming that that was exactly what had happened.

Mr. Gibson said, "Let's get you straight to the nurse's office. This is horrible. Now the season's over." As they walked away, I stood exactly where it all happened. No one came within ten feet of me.

That Night

I stayed in my room, saddened by what had transpired. I grabbed my phone and decided to look through my emails. I wasn't glued to it like most teens, so there were several emails I hadn't checked yet. Suddenly I noticed one from yesterday; it was Lilly's email. I opened it immediately and read it:

Dear Kirin,

Thank you. Thank for being the only person to stand up for me. I'm sorry I wasn't as strong as you. I'm sorry that I didn't stay and fight. But even after the truth, they just didn't care.

I love you.

Lilly

"When you need to feel good by putting others down, you need to understand who it is that is really unhappy inside."—Sifu

Three Minutes Later—1 Year, 89 Days

I ran in, thinking I would be the first into Sifu's gym and realized it was the exact opposite. "Uh, sorry I'm late."

I glanced around, taking in the somber expression on everyone's face. Tobias, Doc, Big T, Ryan, Ken, Danny, and Robert all stood next to one another waiting for me to join them. "I swear I got out as soon as I could, but you know it's really difficult for me to sneak out." I tried to wipe myself dry from the pouring rain.

Tobias's voice was monotone. "Kirin, please close the door."

I did as Tobias ordered and took my time to join the others. The weather outside mimicked how I felt as well as the atmosphere in the room. My gut could already feel what was going to happen, and I wanted to delay the inevitable. I locked the door and pulled down the shades, but I didn't have it in me to make eye contact with the rest of the guys.

We all felt the awkward silence of the room, and I waited for Tobias to be the first to break it.

Tobias stepped forward and began to talk. "First, thanks for coming on such short notice. As you know, I asked only the core members of Sifu's school to attend this meeting. What we are going to talk about today is the fate of the school. I have not discussed this with anyone, and I want everyone's input on this matter."

Tobias's voice lacked the strength and conviction it normally carried. I was positive I wasn't the only one sensing his doubt.

Tobias shook his head and blurted, "I'm gonna get right to the point. Sifu's gone. I have no idea where he is or what's happened. He's simply gone. The way I see it, if he wanted to be found, he would've told us."

Danny looked up and said, "I can't believe he left us."

It infuriated me, and I shouted, "He didn't leave us! The man lost his entire family, and all you can think about is that he left us." I moved toward Danny, staring at him directly.

"He's not here, so what else would you call that, Kirin?" replied Danny. "I'm just saying what's true."

That pissed me off so much that I charged toward Danny, Big T and Doc held me back. Danny stepped back slightly, surprised by my actions.

"Enough, Kirin!" yelled Tobias. "And Danny, please shut up for now."

Danny blurted, "I'm not the only one thinking that. I'm just the only saying it."

"Quiet," Tobias said sternly. "Let me get right to the point ... again. With Sifu missing, we need to figure out what to do about the school. I've asked Doc and Robert to go over Sifu's books, and I've come to the unfortunate conclusion that we're gonna have to shut the school down."

Ken said, "Why'd you ask those guys to check the books?"

Tobias shook his head. "Ken, now is not the time."

Ken shrugged his shoulders and said, "Hey, I'm just saying the Jewish guy and bookkeeping go hand in hand."

Ken's joke didn't help lighten the mood. The group moaned and sighed as everyone feared the worst and got exactly that.

I asked, "Why do we have to close the school? Why can't we keep it running?"

Tobias looked toward Robert.

Robert stepped forward as all eyes were on him. "It's impossible to keep this place open."

"Why?" asked Ryan. "Can't we just pay our dues like before and keep it going?"

Robert looked at Ryan and said, "In theory, that would be great, but it can't be done."

"Why not?" I asked angrily.

Doc stepped forward and joined Robert. He hesitated briefly, glancing at Robert. Robert nodded as Doc faced the group and spoke. "Well, numbers don't lie. Sifu's been running this place for years at a loss."

The news seemed to stun everyone.

"Huh? How's that possible?" I shook my head in disbelief. The rest of the gang looked as confused as I was.

Doc shook his head in frustration. "We all know Sifu had a second job. He must've been using second job to cover the loss from the business."

I looked at Danny and shouted, "Do you still want to say he left us?"

Danny didn't say a word and lowered his head in shame.

"Okay, look. Why can't we just make up the difference or charge more to keep the place alive?" I asked.

Tobias said, "Even if we charged more for tuition, we still can't make up the difference of the rent. I'm the only one with a full-time job, and that's just so I can have three square meals a day."

Silence filled the room. "Come on, guys, there's gotta be a way we can make some more cash." I was driven to find an answer, and I tried to get them to brainstorm with me. I started pacing back and forth. I wasn't prepared to lose the school.

Ken said, "Maybe we could recruit more students. Sifu's never been too active promoting the school, so maybe it's just a case of more word of mouth and advertising."

Doc said, "In theory, that sounds good, but think about it for a moment. Our school's well known for winning all our challenge matches, yet have you seen an increase in enrollment?"

Ryan sighed. "Yeah … everyone's fallen in love with the UFMF schools. They're a lot fancier, state of the art equipment, and more appealing to the masses."

Tobias said, "Guys, we just don't have the time to run a business and do all the little things to keep it alive. Unless someone can come up with something brilliant, we all know what's going to happen next."

For the next five minutes, the school was silent, other than the sounds of breathing and an occasional blurb from Danny, "Wait, I got something! Forget it. Never mind."

I closed my eyes and tried to let everything flow to me. Suddenly, I snapped my fingers and said, "I have an idea."

All eyes were on me. At first, I thought it might be far-fetched, but I was desperate to keep the school open.

"It's called beat downs. I'm sure some of you have heard of it. In a nutshell, it's fighting for cash. We could join these and make money … in fact, a good amount of money."

"No. No. No! Kirin, we are not a gang. Those beat downs are dangerous. They're affiliated with the mobsters in those areas," stated Tobias.

"I'm not disagreeing with you Tobias, but if we want to keep this school alive, then I believe this is our only choice. There is no other option." I made my plea to the entire group.

"It's not gonna happen, Kirin." Tobias was trying to show his authority.

I didn't care what Tobias said, but something in me drove me to challenge him. "I understand you've always led this group, but I think this time you're wrong. You asked us all to be here, so why not as a group we vote on whether to go this route?"

Everyone stood in silence looking at one another as I tried to use logic to battle this emotional time. We all thought in a similar fashion, and the best way to sell my idea was to appeal to Tobias's sensible side. I thought, *This is my only chance; otherwise, everyone always follows Tobias.*

Tobias stepped forward and said, "Fine. Let's vote on this. T, grab a pen and paper in Sifu's office. Ryan, go get your hat for everyone to put their vote in."

Ken said, "Do we just put yes or no? Should we write our names?"

Tobias thought for a moment and said, "Just put yes or no. All in favor of Kirin's idea, just write yes down."

A few minutes passed as the group was deciding on the fate of the school.

Tobias grabbed Ryan's hat and passed it over to Robert, who began opening the folded papers one by one.

Tobias asked, "So, what's the final count Robert?"

I glanced at Robert, who looked unsure. He said, "It's a tie. Four votes to stay open, and four votes to close down."

Tobias shook his head and spoke out loud. "You guys, I'm gonna pull some weight here. Like Kirin said, I've led you guys for some time now, and you've always trusted me. I say trust me again. As much as I hate to do it, we have to close the school."

I shouted, "I'm sorry, but you're wrong this time! This school needs to stay open, and I'm not going to allow you to pull your weight on this, Tobias." Again, emotion took over as I blurted, "I challenge you to a table match."

Everyone gasped in perfect unison.

"Are you kidding me?" said Tobias, scoffing at the idea.

"No. I'm dead serious on this. Winner takes all. This shouldn't be difficult for you. And, if you win, we follow exactly what you say. But if I win, we keep the school open for as long as we can."

"Fine, Kirin. You want to be stubborn about it." Tobias walked away and motioned to the guys. "Ken, Danny, go get the table."

I walked away, and the guys who voted to keep it open—Ryan, Doc, and Big T—surrounded me.

Ryan said, "You can't beat Tobias in the table match, Kirin. You've never done it before, and as much as you've improved, he's just that much better."

I could see Doc plotting as he said, "I have an idea." Doc shouted, "Come on, Tobias! Make it fair. There's no way Kirin can hang with you."

"Well, what do you want?" asked Tobias.

Doc paused and thought for a moment. "The same three-minute rule applies. If she can push you off once, you lose." He turned toward me and winked.

Tobias thought about it and agreed quickly with confidence. "Sure. I have no problem with that. You got that, Kirin? We chi sao for three minutes, and if you can push me off the table just once, you win."

"Fine."

I knew my skills had improved significantly, but there was a reason Tobias was the leader. He spent the most time training with Sifu, so I had to find a way to beat someone who was better at everything.

Danny and Ken placed the table in the center. It was a circular table with not much ground for stepping back. It was about four feet in diameter and stood about one foot from the ground. I'd watched the other guys play this game before, and Tobias had never lost to any of them.

Doc, Big T, and Ryan were in my corner giving me some last-minute tips.

"Just do your best, Kirin," said Doc. "We believe in you." Doc caught me by surprise as he gave me a hug. I thought, *Okay ... kinda strange.*

Big T was shaking his head in doubt. "Doc, let's be realistic here. There's no way she's gonna beat Tobias in a challenge table match."

Ryan said, "Look, anything is possible. Besides, this is a chi sao challenge, and all she has to do is get him off balance once to fall off the table. The hits are all controlled and don't count for anything."

Tobias leaped on the table and struck a pose. Even though it was me, it didn't make a difference for him, he seemed to relish in this situation. I stepped up on the table and got into chi sao position with Tobias.

Tobias said, "Doc, count us down."

Tobias looked at me confidently and said, "You got three minutes, kid. Good luck."

His smugness annoyed me. I was determined to beat him.

Doc shouted, "Begin!"

We began chi saoing with one another, and quickly I began attacking. The several months I had spent working with Sifu had made a difference. I could feel the flow, and my structure felt so much stronger.

Tobias said, "Not bad, kid. You've definitely been practicing."

No sooner had he said it than I felt my center go off. He quickly loped me to the side, and I fell to the side of the table.

He extended his arm up to help me, but I refused. We got into position as the seconds continued to fade away. We began to roll again, and I held my triangle in check and continued to test his structure. He was rock solid, just like Sifu, but there had to be a way to beat someone who had more skill.

I began to press more attacks at him. From punches to palms, from every angle you could imagine, I threw it all at him. But he stayed solid within his structure, as he continued to use the force to deal with every attack.

The guys supporting me were shouting. "Come on, Kirin! You can get through. You just need to push him off."

Big T shouted, "One minute, Kirin! Do something."

Everything they were saying was just a blur. I tried throwing in kicks with my attacks, but every time I lifted my foot, he would jerk my center of balance. I forced another kick in to see if it would send him back, but he moved his leg out of the way and let me fly off the table once again.

He chuckled and looked at me.

I slammed the ground and jumped back onto the table. I thought, *Think, Kirin. Think.*

I blitzed him with combinations, but he knew the counter to each one. Each oncoming force he would meet and then turn away.

Doc called, "You got fifteen seconds, Kirin!"

Tobias said, "Give it up, Kirin."

I kept attacking Tobias and finally got him in a trap motion.

He said, "You may have my hands trapped, but there's no way in heck I'm falling off this table." He smiled with confidence just to piss me off and gave me a little wink.

Suddenly, I leaned forward and kissed him.

"What the…?" shouted Tobias.

As soon as he said it, I nudged forward, and he immediately leaned backward and fell to the ground.

The room was quiet as a sudden murmur of surprise and shock filled the air.

Danny said, "Holy shit."

Robert followed up by saying, "Well, I'll be damned."

Tobias slammed his fist to the ground, "That's total bullshit. How much time is left?"

Doc smiled and shook his head. "There's still three seconds left. Kirin won!"

I stood silently on top of the table striking a pose as I looked at Tobias on the ground.

Tobias said, "That's not fair! You can't kiss me during a challenge match."

I said, "There are no rules in Wing Chun. You, more than anyone, should know that."

All the guys looked at me in shock as I finally got the chance to catch my breath.

I scanned the room, looking at all of them directly. "The school stays open."

A Sip of Whiskey—1 Year, 95 Days

One week after the decision was made to keep Sifu's school open, we had split up into groups of twos, searching out where the underground fighting was taking place. Our jobs were simple: get a feel for how things were run and how we would take part in it. Time was not on our side, since the rent for Sifu's gym was due in just under three weeks.

I had a night out planned with Gwen, who was covering me for the next three hours. Doc and I arrived at the designated location. The underground fights paid well, for those who won, and they made sure they kept their discretion from both the police and the STDs. Finding the location was difficult. Embedded deep in the net, you had to know someone to figure out the when and where. Fortunately, Gwen was a whiz at this, and I owed her several times for helping me out.

Doc pointed in a direction and said, "We're not that late. We've only missed the first two fights."

I nodded and began walking to where the action was lively. There was a group of about thirty individuals circled around the main guy. Flanked by two huge guards, he was counting credits and preparing for the next fight.

I looked around and was glad that Doc was with me. This was not one of the better neighborhoods, and my parents would have had my neck if they knew what I was up to.

Doc and I tried to get a better view of the action, as we tried our best to blend in and be discreet. Covered with my typical red hoodie, I stood by Doc, trying to absorb what was going on.

The man in the middle began to speak. "All right, all right, who's up for our next fight? We need two." He spun around in a circle, searching for the next batch of fighters.

Clamoring amongst the crowd began as several minutes passed to see who would rise to the challenge.

Doc whispered, "So, the way it works is … it's an open invitation. There are no rules, and once you step into the ring, you have to fight."

I asked, "So, what if you step in first and some dude that's three hundred pounds comes as your challenger?"

Doc replied, "Doesn't matter, Kirin. Like I said, you have to fight. Otherwise, if you back down, they literally pummel you to a pulp and ban you afterward."

"So, aren't you at a disadvantage for being the first one to step up?"

Doc looked at me and nodded. "I would think so, but I'm sure this is to stimulate the gambling."

As noise continued to run amok, someone from the crowd took the initiative and stepped into the circle. A sudden hush set upon the crowd, but immediately the whispers began to echo throughout.

"Holy shit, it's Whiskey."

"Damn! Whiskey's gonna fight."

"I'm in. I got fifty credits on Whiskey."

My interest was already captured by the event, but now even more so with this mysterious Whiskey, who appeared to be a fan regular. I glanced at Whiskey—or what I could make out from his outfit. He looked fairly small in stature for someone who was going to fight. I guesstimated he was five feet, six inches in height, and he had a thin frame for a guy. His black hoodie was draped over his face, covering any hint of what he looked like.

A huge, hulking figure spread the crowd and stood opposite of Whiskey. He looked like a comic book figure— tall, at least two-hundred-and-twenty-five pounds, and ripped from head to toe.

"Hmm, this should be interesting," I said.

We watched a flurry of wagers between the crowd members. Hundreds and thousands of credits were being made with mere hand signals between the gamblers and the bookies. I wasn't sure how they kept track of it, but Doc had mentioned it was a flawless system. Anyone who bet got their money, or else.

I looked at Doc and asked, "Should we bet?"

"Bet? I got just enough money for lunch this week," said Doc.

"All right, fine. I just thought we should experience the entire event."

Doc replied, "I told you not to get caught up in this. We are here to observe and see all the ins and outs of the fighting system."

"We've got three weeks," I muttered. "Maybe this is worth the gamble."

Doc said, "Kirin, a good Wing Chun practitioner doesn't gamble. As Sifu taught me, know yourself and know your opponent, and you'll win 100% of the time."

I thought of what Doc said and replied with a sigh. Just hearing him say "Sifu" saddened me.

We waited for the formalities to finish, and the announcer finally signaled to both fighters to begin. As the crowd cheered on, I was particularly fascinated with Whiskey; for some odd reason, it was almost as if his energy felt familiar.

His opponent stood in a fighting stance. Once signaled, he immediately charged in. He was a freight train closing the gap and was about to make a huge impact, but Whiskey dodged the charge. The big guy stumbled and landed face first in front of the crowd.

I tried to get a better look at Whiskey, but he continued to stay cool and relaxed behind his hoodie. This definitely caught my attention.

His opponent smashed the ground in frustration and then stood back up. He pointed to Whiskey and said, "I'm gonna rip your head off."

Whiskey turned around and exposed his back to his opponent.

The crowd watched with anticipation. I thought, *Why would he do that?*

His opponent smiled and then suddenly went for a punch. With his back toward the opponent, Whiskey was at a disadvantage, but just as the punch was about to land, he dodged out of the way and evaded the force. This time, however, he grabbed his lunging opponent by the arm, spinning him around into the air and eventually landing on the ground. In a flash, the big man was out cold as the crowd went wild.

I leaned toward Doc and said, "Is that...?"

Doc filled in my sentence and said, "That's Aikido."

I said, "That was pretty damn impressive. I have to say I'm somewhat shocked."

"Why do you say that?" asked Doc.

"Because I thought traditional styles were pretty much extinct."

Doc said, "Whoever this guy is ... he's pretty skilled."

The crowd cheered as the bookies collected their money. The announcer took the winnings to Whiskey, who caught it with one hand.

And then, just like that, my jaw dropped. Whiskey removed his hoodie as my eyes bugged out in surprise. Not in a million years would I have guessed who I saw.

"Holy shoot! I can't fricking believe it. That's my classmate, Ripley Hawkins," I blurted.

She was counting her money as I watched. When she glanced in our direction, I turned away and began dragging Doc. I thought, *Oh my God, I think she saw me.*

"Hey, what gives?" asked Doc.

"Let's just go. We found as much info as we need," I said.

SECTION 2

Sifu's Journey Entry #8—The Answer

Several months had passed with Sifu slaving away from dusk till dawn under the watchful eye of Hiroshi. Every move and every detail required to make his soup needed to pass Hiroshi's stringent requirements. Hiroshi was meticulous with even the most basic of movements.

Most would find this labor of love too difficult to justify, but Sifu's years training in the art had prepared him to endure, to push beyond what one believed to be possible, and to realize the only limitation set was that which you create. Besides, while many were driven by society's norms—fame, fortune, or material things—Sifu was driven by his broken heart trying to find a way to mend itself. As difficult as the task was, Sifu never once complained or showed any signs of frustration. His desire was clear, as the goal stayed faintly in front of him, constantly reminding him. The feeling of emptiness needed to be quenched. Until the universe deemed the debt fully paid, he would not rest or be rewarded.

Trust in the timing of the universe. The words of encouragement spoken by April had haunted him every day since he'd first heard them. Those words along with perfecting the recipe had taken over Sifu's daily life. Still, he found a few scattered minutes every day for his first love. It wasn't unusual for Sifu to begin doing hand motions in thin air, in isolated areas in the restaurant, just to clear his mind as well as to maintain his skill.

Only on some rare occasion when Hiroshi needed a break would Sifu venture out of the restaurant and meet up with his friend April. The initial odd encounter between two random strangers had now been forged into a lifelong friendship. There, he would chat up a storm about nothing, just to get a breather and recharge himself for the grueling task at hand. He would also spend his time with Takashi, keeping his part of the promise to April to help this young man find his own path.

Late one night, several hours after the restaurant had closed, Sifu's work was far from done. The time was bordering close to midnight as Sifu rubbed his eyes and shook his head, staring at his soup. For the first time, he showed a chink in his armor, but before more could materialize, he took a deep breath and pulled himself back into control. Emotions ran deep, as Sifu was feeling a sense of frustration, normal for everyone else under such circumstances.

His slight hiccup did not go unnoticed by Hiroshi, who had experienced this before with his very own daughter. Hiroshi took it upon himself to ask, "What's the matter?" He stood by the table where he was just cleaning up.

Sifu didn't say a word. Then he realized he had not answered Hiroshi. He snapped out of his daze and said, "I'm sorry, Hiroshi. I'm just a little tired."

Hiroshi took several steps closer to Sifu, who continued to work on his soup. He was wise to the answer and decided to press further. "It's human nature to be upset, yet this is the first time I've ever seen you show any emotion while working on the ramen."

Sifu looked up at Hiroshi, but continued to stir his pot. Hiroshi stood silently; neither one was willing to break the silence. As Sifu stirred, he realized that his latest efforts were no different from the hundreds of other soups he had put together. He finally put down the ladle and hung his head.

Sifu spoke in a shallow voice as he said, "I'm sorry, Hiroshi. I want to get this right. I want this to be perfect. I need this to...." Sifu looked up at Hiroshi with watery eyes. "I want to taste that same soup again." Sifu's voice faded away.

Hiroshi slowly straightened up from his rickety stance and turned his back to Sifu. He walked to the nearest table and sat down. Sifu was befuddled by the old man's reaction, enough so that it broke him out of his current state.

Hiroshi gestured with a raise of his hand and authoritatively said, "Sit down for a second."

Sifu wiped his eyes and rounded the counter to get to Hiroshi. His steps were cautious, as he was unsure what Megumi's dad had in mind. He thought, *Did I say too much?*

Sifu paused as he got to the table and gently pulled out the old wooden chair. Not a sound broke the stillness of the silent room.

Hiroshi waited for Sifu to settle in before saying, "Did you find it unusual that my only request when teaching you how to cook ... was that you not taste my soup till I told you the time was right?" He laid out the question for Sifu to digest, and Hiroshi stroked his beard, awaiting Sifu's response.

Sifu nodded several times as that request had eaten into him from day one. He said, "Yes, Hiroshi, I found it strange."

"Yet, you didn't question my decision."

"I understand everything has a reason, so I was sure you had your own reason for asking that of me," said Sifu.

Hiroshi was pleased with that answer. In fact, everything Sifu had done was a pleasant surprise. Hiroshi leaned back in his seat and relished the thought. He began to laugh boisterously, so loud that it echoed through the entire restaurant.

Again, Sifu looked at him oddly, wondering what could possibly be so funny.

The sound of shuffling feet from above creaked over their heads. Both Sifu and Hiroshi looked up, tracking the sound one step at a time. A few seconds passed as the footsteps stopped and a voice followed.

"Is everything okay?" shouted Hiroshi's wife in Japanese.

Hiroshi quickly blurted out a response in the same tongue. He and Sifu looked at each other, waiting to see if they were both in trouble. Seconds passed, and no response came but the sound of his wife's footsteps back upstairs. It confirmed they had escaped any blame.

Hiroshi shook his head and seemed relieved. He said, "The man may be the boss, but the woman is still in charge."

Sifu chuckled as cultures thousands of miles away still had a universal principle that was accepted by all.

Hiroshi got hold of himself and finally revealed what was on his mind. "Did you know Megumi fought me every second of the day when I taught her?" For the first time looking back, what once was a memory of aggravation and annoyance, was somehow appreciated by Hiroshi now.

Sifu knew exactly what Hiroshi was speaking off. Megumi was not the stereotypical Japanese woman. She was strong-willed and determined, something Sifu deeply admired and loved.

"I can picture that," replied Sifu with a smile.

"Ah, I figured you would." Hiroshi pushed himself up and said, "Why don't you sit down and take a break for a moment? I want you to taste my soup." With that, he began his stroll to the kitchen.

As Sifu watched him, Hiroshi seemed to have an extra spring to his step.

Several minutes passed, and Sifu gazed in wonder as Hiroshi prepared his ramen. He had studied his movement, his every word from the very first day that he got there. But he appreciated this, as Hiroshi's skills were evident in his motion. Almost as if he was doing a form like Sifu's, but this was the creation of a soup. He moved like Sifu did when he did his Wing Chun. Skill, regardless of its intent, was easily recognizable in the eyes of others. This man had clearly dedicated his life to the Gung Fu of making ramen.

Sifu was waiting eagerly to finally taste the soup from the source. Like a little kid, he was bursting with excitement, but he hid it well, keeping it inside.

Finally, Hiroshi put the final touches on the soup and looked up. It was time. Sifu sat properly in his chair, ready to dive into the soup.

From the corner of his eye, he saw Hiroshi finally pass by him as steam trailed by like a train. He laid the bowl of ramen right in front of Sifu. The moment had arrived; Sifu was going to taste this soup.

Hiroshi waved his hand and said, "Please, try."

Sifu mimicked the exact preparation for eating ramen that Megumi did. He had seen it so many times, it was just natural for him to do the same. As his lips finally tasted the broth for the first time, he immediately smiled. However, a moment passed as he had a dumbfounded look on his face.

Hiroshi smiled, knowing he had made his point.

"You are surprised, aren't you?"

Sifu nodded and looked up to Hiroshi. "I am."

"It's different from Megumi's recipe."

"It is, but I can't quite put my finger on it."

Hiroshi motioned to Sifu. "Everything I've taught you, I am proud of. You are an excellent student and have done everything I have asked. But, you are wondering why every attempt you make to duplicate my daughter's recipe isn't quite the same."

"Yes, all the training still hasn't matched what's missing. I don't quite get it. What's still missing?"

Hiroshi said sadly, "The soup will not bring her back, but what you are trying to do is duplicate her recipe. When you do that, you'll always fail. If you notice, tasting my soup, it is different from my daughters, is it not?"

"It is," nodded Sifu.

"What you want to bring back is the feeling, not the taste. You need to be you. Don't copy her recipe. Make it your own. Only then can you achieve what you came here for."

Sifu looked at Hiroshi, as he was all too familiar with the words that were spoken. But a loss so tragic as Sifu's can cloud anyone's vision.

"You have the skill. I'll close the shop tomorrow. Start from the very beginning, and make this soup your own."

▲ ▲ ▲

Sifu woke up the next morning with the words ringing in his ears. They had never left his thoughts or his dreams. He would begin this day preparing his soup.

By the time he was ready to serve it to Hiroshi, it was close to evening. Just like he had done many months ago, it was like déjà vu as Sifu placed his ramen in front of Hiroshi again.

Hiroshi went through the same motions, but after tasting the soup, the pattern was finally broken. Hiroshi looked up to Sifu, and a small tear formed in his eyes. He whispered in Japanese, "Totemo oishii."

Sifu was still in disbelief, doubting himself as well as his eyes. He needed proof. He asked, "May I?"

Hiroshi nodded and offered the bowl. Sifu repeated Hiroshi's motions and finally placed his lips on the broth. He smiled for the first time and also shed a tear. He felt his heart squeeze as he looked at the broth. Hiroshi was right all along; it wasn't exactly like Megumi's when he tasted it. However, the feeling he got with the taste of the soup was finally it. His eyes watered as he looked Hiroshi in the eyes and whispered, "Welcome back, Megumi."

"Only when we let go of the desire of want can we see clearly the answer which we seek."—Sifu

CHAPTER 9

Twenty-One

November 4, 2033

I t was early Friday evening when Kirin found herself celebrating her birthday at her parents' home. Inside the dining room, a banner with her name was hanging along the wall, with a big sign reading "21" at the very end. In the corner lay a stack of unopened presents, and the table was set to perfection for what *should* be a joyous event. However, the mood was anything but festive, as everyone was quietly eating, enjoying the meal that her mom had spent all day preparing. The entire family attended, except Jim, who had been called away overseas. Bacon was waiting underneath the table all by himself. Even he seemed depressed, missing his longtime friend Butterscotch.

Kirin ate in silence and looked around. She was glad to see her family there for her birthday, but they were all feeling Mom's energy. She was hoping for anything to break the mood; even Bacon farting would be a blessing in disguise. She thought, *Come on, Bacon! Of all the times to be gas free.*

Kirin finally broke the silence as she put the best fake smile on her face. "Thanks again for cooking all my favorite food, Mom. It's delicious as always."

Kirin's mom forced a smile and said, "Thanks, sweetie," and continued to look down and eat her meal.

Just like that, the moment of conversation ended, and the silence grew louder with every second that passed. Kirin squirmed in her chair, trying to see if she could jolt her family out of this mood. However, she had a mountain to overcome that even she could not climb.

Kirin panicked and suddenly kicked Kyle underneath the table.

"Ouch!" shouted Kyle. "Mom, Kirin kicked me!"

"I didn't kick you. I was stretching my legs, yah baby."

Kirin's mom continued to eat as Kirin felt lost. She looked at her dad, hoping for help. Their eyes met, and he made a little shrug and shook his head slightly. It seemed almost hopeless.

Kirin looked at both Mark and Kyle. They stared blankly until Mark suddenly snapped his fingers. He gave Kirin a quick look, which made Kirin less assured and even more nervous.

"Uh, Steven, can you pass me some water?" said Mark.

"Sure thing." Steven grabbed the pitcher of water and began handing it over to Mark, who looked at Kirin and winked. Kirin gritted her teeth and was afraid of what Mark had planned.

As Steven began handing over the pitcher, Mark reached out for it, knocking over his glass and spilling water. "Oh, shit!" shouted Mark as he began to flail and reach out in panic to clean up the spill. Everyone reacted to the spill, but Kirin's mom stayed just continued to eat.

Kirin stared across from the table as the chaos separated them. Kirin's mind was racing. She was being forced to fight. There was something greater at stake that no one knew about. She wanted to scream and tell her mom the truth, but she couldn't. Kirin stood up and began crying. "Mom, please stop doing this. You're killing me inside." She slammed both her hands on the table. All the men had that petrified look of fear on their faces.

Kirin's mom stopped eating and wiped her face with a napkin. She stood up, and everyone froze in place to stare. Her voice crackled as she looked directly at Kirin. "Now you know how I feel." Just like that, she walked away from the table as tears started rolling down her face.

Kyle looked at everyone as this night turned out as bad as one could imagine. "Uh, the food's gonna get cold."

Dad and the rest of the brothers threw their napkins at Kyle. Kirin, still in tears, stood at the head of the dinner table and was unsure what to do next.

Her dad said, "Guys, clean up the mess."

He began to walk toward her as he gently wrapped his arms around her. He slowly kissed her forehead and whispered, "Hey, Princess."

"Daddy, I'm so sorry. I don't know what to do anymore."

"First, you're gonna wipe those tears from your face," said her dad.

Kirin continued to squeeze hard, as she felt lost.

"I know this is gonna be tough, but I want you to speak to your mother, okay?"

Kirin nodded as she still held onto her father. She felt afraid and lost, like when she had first met her parents to go to the States. Dad pulled out his handkerchief and was about to wipe Kirin's face when she quickly snatched it from his hand.

"No, uh … it's okay. I'll do it myself and talk to Mom." She kept her face down as she quickly dashed to the bathroom to fix her makeup first.

Kyle looked at everyone and asked, "Now can we eat?"

Both Mark and Steven rolled their eyes and simultaneously shook their heads.

⋏ ⋏ ⋏

Kirin searched the main entrance of the house, but couldn't find her mom. All the men were still in the dining room, while the rest of the lower floor was empty. She looked up the stairs and saw light in her room. She took a deep breath and began walking up the stairs. Her heart was racing, as she was afraid to confront her mom.

As she slowly walked toward her room, she hesitated at first to peek. Facing reality wasn't something she wanted to do on her birthday, but she forced herself to look through the crack in the door. Inside, she saw her mom, who was oddly sitting on her bed. She paused for a moment and wondered what her mom was holding in her hands.

She opened the door as it creaked with each push. "Can I come in?" she said in a timid voice.

Her mom looked up and put the item in her hand by her side. "It's your room. You don't need to ask to come in."

Kirin nodded and then approached her mom, who was staring sadly at the floor. She sat next to her and stared as well, unable to find the words she needed.

As she was about to break the silence, her mom spoke. "I'm sorry I ruined your birthday."

Hearing her mom apologize crushed her from within. Kirin began to cry as she struggled to reply. "Mom, you never have to apologize. This is my fault, not yours." She leaned into her mom's shoulder. Just like any good mom would do, Diane cradled her daughter and tried to comfort her.

"Kirin, baby … what's wrong?"

Kirin remained silent and continued to cry on her mother's shoulder.

"You know you can always tell me anything," said her mom.

The words tore into her as the truth weighed heavily upon her. If she could just open her mouth, everything she was holding back could finally be set free. But, there was too much at stake. She knew the price of getting her parents further involved. This was a burden she would have to deal with on her own.

Her mom squeezed hard, trying to comfort her daughter as she brushed her hair. She waited several minutes, but Kirin would not say a word. With each squeeze, Kirin made sure it remained bottled within. Diane was torn as she knew her daughter was keeping something from her.

"Look, Kirin … when you're ready to talk. I'll be there to listen." She reached behind her and grabbed a small package. She placed it on Kirin's lap, hoping this would help break her silence.

Kirin sat up and stared at the package. "What's ... what is this?"

"It's your birthday gift, of course."

"Mom, you didn't need to get me anything."

"It's my daughter's twenty-first birthday. Of course I needed to get you something."

"What is it?"

"Well, you're going to have to open it, silly."

Kirin began removing the wrapping from the item. As she carefully undid the perfectly wrapped gift, she saw a plain rectangular box, about the size of a frame. She removed the final layer and opened the box.

"Oh my god. How'd you get this?"

"Honestly, I can't take the credit. Your father took this picture."

"Wow. This is ... this is just incredible."

Both Kirin and her mom stared at the picture.

"When? How? I can't believe Dad got this! I don't even remember him ever taking this picture."

"Yeah, I had no idea. In fact, I don't think he remembered either. He was sorting through old pictures, and he found it just a month ago."

Kirin touched the picture and remembered that exact moment in time.

Diane said, "It was just like yesterday. We landed for our layover, and I remember holding your hand in the airport in Narita. The noise and the crowd probably scared you, and you ran off. Kevin and I scrambled to find you. We panicked. You ran so quickly; in a blink, you were gone."

Kirin smiled as she recalled that day. "I can't believe how much you remember."

Kirin's mom kissed her on the head. "Of course, I would remember that moment well. I finally had a daughter I had always dreamed of, and you were my light the moment I met you."

Kirin shook her head, as the picture brought back so many memories.

Her mom said, "I honestly don't know how we found you. It was so crowded that day, and I had no idea where you scampered off to. Do you remember?"

"Yes."

"And, just like that ... I remember it. I can picture it perfectly. I felt almost drawn to go in that direction, and there you were in that store, hiding underneath the huge neon lights of that famous beer." Diane giggled.

Her mom held the picture with Kirin and looked at it. She shook her head.

"What, Mom?"

"I'm afraid to think what would've happened had you gone under a different sign. You were so dead set not to keep your original name. For whatever reason, you had it ingrained to use Kirin as your name."

Kirin giggled. "Mooom." Kirin smiled, as the memory was warm. The sign was the first word she had learned.

"I love you, Mom." She looked at her mom and squeezed her, just like in the picture.

"I love you, too."

Her mom stared at her and said, "Kirin, you're terrible at putting makeup on. Here, let me clean it up." She grabbed a tissue and began to wipe her daughter's face.

"No, Mom, it's okay." She tried to wave her mom away.

"Hold still, Kirin." Kirin's mom brushed her face and then saw the makeup was covering a bruise on her face.

"No, Mom ... please don't do that."

"Oh, my gosh, Kirin ... your face!"

Kirin's mom saw the damage from the last fight. It crushed her instantly. She hugged her daughter and began to cry. She muttered, "Oh my God, my poor baby."

Kirin's moment of happiness slipped away.

▲ ▲ ▲

Several Days Later

The gang was all there at Tobias's apartment.

Robert said, "Tell me again why we decided to meet here."

"Hey, nothing's wrong with my place!" shouted Tobias.

Doc said, "We're meeting here so we don't have a crowd of people stalking Kirin at her place."

Ken said, "All right ... so where are we going tonight?"

Danny said, "Don't you guys check your emails? Like I said earlier, we're going to Club G.G.G."

Ryan said, "I've never heard of this place. Is it any good...? Anyone?"

One by one, everyone said the same thing. "Never heard of it."

Kirin asked, "Who booked this place?"

Big T said, "Danny."

Robert said, "Good lord. We've entrusted Kirin's birthday to Danny."

Danny shouted back at Robert. "Geez, I'm telling you this is a new place, and I'm hearing it's the talk of the town. Trust me, guys. I know people."

Kirin said, "I recall the last time you told me to trust you."

Danny said, "Must you bring the past back every time?"

Ken rolled his eyes, and Robert said, "Yeah, I know people, too—the names of my mailman and garbage collector, but you don't see me bragging about it."

Tobias shouted at Ryan. "Will you stop feeding my fish?"

"I can't help it. He looks hungry." Ryan didn't pause, dropping in more fish food. "By the way, what's his name?"

Tobias said, "Fish." Everyone turned toward Tobias and stared. "What? It's a fish, not a dog. I'm not five years old."

Sifu said, "Let's head out. I'm the old man here. Once we hit 9:00, that's my bedtime."

Kirin laughed. "Nine o'clock?"

"Yup," said Sifu.

Robert pulled open one of Tobias's kitchen cabinets and said, "Holy shit."

The gang stared.

Tobias replied, "What? What's the big deal?"

Upon opening his pantry, Robert revealed a huge collection of cereal boxes, lined up from one end to the other, top and bottom.

Big T said, "Damn, Tobias. You got, like, every single cereal on the market."

Tobias said, "I wouldn't say 'every.'"

Ken said, "Ah, you even have my favorite! Ho Ho cereal."

Doc said, "Wasn't that the name of your last girlfriend?" He turned to Sifu and asked, "Sifu, do you remember?"

Sifu stopped and pondered. "Can't say I remember. All I remember was that one girlfriend with that odd name. What was it…? Oh, yeah." Sifu snapped his fingers and said, "That's it, Dee-anne. For a couple of months, he brought her to the school. It would drive me crazy every time I said hi. Why was it Dee-anne, with the emphasis on the *D*, when it was spelled 'Diane'?" Sifu continued to mumble to himself, walking away from the group.

Ken said, "Shut up, Doc."

Robert began to laugh. "See, Ryan, this is why bachelor life is good. Look at Tobias. He's living the good life. Tons of cereal, bread, and milk."

Ryan replied, "That's the good life?"

Tobias looked at Ryan and asked, "When was your last date?"

Ryan sulked, pulled out his phone, and began searching for love online.

Danny looked outside. "Ah, here it is, the limo."

Big T said, "Damn, a limo? How'd you afford that?"

Danny said, "I used Kirin's credit card."

The guys laughed and ran to the window to see outside. Just as one would expect, it was a decked-out, long stretched black limo, enough to accommodate the entire gang.

Robert said, "Nice job on not attracting attention, Danny."

Danny gave Robert a look and then replied to everyone else, "Didn't I tell you I planned this out well?" He sounded overly cocky.

Tobias said, "I'm sure it's a lot easier when you're using Kirin's credit card."

Angelo interrupted and said, "By the way, Danny ... you still haven't given me Kirin's credit card back."

"Oh yeah, I forgot.... Anyway, she's the celebrity with the big bucks," said Danny.

Kirin said, "I'm not a celebrity, nor do I have big bucks."

Doc said, "Kirin, you're not gonna be able to convince anyone of that."

Sifu interrupted. "Okay, let's go before I fall asleep. Besides, I'm getting claustrophobic in here."

Tobias shouted, "Hey!"

Sifu quickly replied, "Uh, that's what Danny told me."

Danny shouted, "Why does everyone blame me?"

The guys and Kirin started packing up, and Tobias closed the door to his apartment.

Ken said, "I have a feeling we are in for one hell of a night."

Big T and Danny immediately looked at each other and said, "Do you want to bet?"

Twenty Minutes Later

The limo pulled up in front of the club as the bright neon lights sparkled in the night. There was a huge line waiting to get in, and a door man reached out to help everyone out.

Tobias leaned outside to stare and said, "Kirin, you should go last."

"Why?" she asked.

Ryan said, "Kirin, whether you like it or not, you are the main star. You're the celebrity."

Doc said, "Uh, somebody wake up Sifu."

Everyone turned around to Sifu in a deep sleep, snoring.

People started wondering who was coming out of the limo. As each guy stepped out, the crowd continued to wonder and look. Finally, Kirin stepped out as the gang waited around her. Suddenly, the crowd shouted, "It's Kirin Rise!"

"Holy crap."

"Kirin!"

"Over here, Kirin! I'm your number one fan."

Several of the bodyguards started pushing back the crowd as they helped escort her into the club. Photographers and fans tried their best to snap pictures. Kirin was humble as always as she took some time to wave at the crowd and sign autographs. Once inside the club, the gang was in awe of the main entrance. Inside, the group stood in a circular complex. Massive in design, and expensive in taste, it made for quite a first impression.

Danny was extremely proud of himself as he said, "Huh, VIP treatment. Nice. Yes!" He nodded his head with a huge smile on his face, rocking back and forth in his stance.

Angelo looked at Danny and said, "You know, I should be in charge of all her outside affairs."

Danny replied, "Oh, chill, Angelo. It's just this one night."

Robert said, "Uh, what kind of place is this?"

Danny said, "I was told they have everything. Games and gambling."

Ken said, "What's the last *G* stand for?"

Tobias said, "This place smells funny, like somewhere I've been before."

An elderly gentleman in his early sixties with silver hair and distinctive glasses introduced himself. He was dressed from head to toe in a slick tuxedo. "My name is Ray, Ms. Rise. I'll be your host for the evening. Anything that you need, I'll get for you. I'm so glad you can celebrate your twenty-first birthday with us along with your friends."

Kirin shook his hand and said, "Thanks."

Ray asked, "Is this your first time here?"

Everyone nodded, still admiring the main lobby.

"Great. I'm sure you'll enjoy this evening's festivities. Now, we have a room reserved for you, but you're free to go anywhere you want right away. If you don't mind my asking, do you prefer starting the night off with games, gambling, or girls?"

The gang looked somewhat confused—and curious—at the last word.

Ryan stepped forward and asked, "Girls?"

Ray said, "Yes, sir, Club G.G.G. is known for its triple fun, and we also have the most gorgeous girls dancing."

Doc said, "Um, by 'girls,' do you mean this is a … um … strip club?"

Ray said, "We prefer to call it adult entertainment."

Ken turned around and looked at Danny. "You…," Ken pointed directly at Danny, "booked Kirin's birthday party at a strip club!"

Danny's confidence quickly disappeared as he staggered to form a clear sentence. "Strip club…? I, uh …. What the…? I mean, I had no idea this was a strip club."

The gang started taking swipes at Danny.

Tobias shouted, "You dumb ass!"

"I swear, I had no idea this was a strip club."

Angelo stepped in and said, "Had you allowed her personal assistant to handle her birthday activities, this would've never had happened."

Ryan said, "Nice fail, Danny!"

Danny raised his voice and pointed back at Ryan. "If you think about it, I was two for three…. In any sport, that's pretty impressive. I mean, isn't that 66%?"

Ryan said, "So, 66% of the time you're 100% right?"

Danny shouted, "Exactly!" Even so, he looked confused.

Tobias looked back. "In the human race, yah still failed." He punched Danny in the arm.

Kirin surprisingly was laughing at how odd her birthday celebration was beginning. It had been a year of unpredictability, and this seemed almost fitting.

Robert said, "This is so fricking awkward."

Ken looked at everyone and asked, "So, what are we going to do? It's too late to book anything else with this size of a group."

Tobias looked at their mentor. "Sifu?"

Sifu was calm and cool. He shrugged his shoulders and said, "If Kirin wants to stay here … what can I say? When in Rome…."

The guys looked at Kirin, who said, "Well, they do have other things inside besides strippers. We could play games or gamble, right? Anyway, I'm fine with it."

Big T said, "Yeah, yeah ... I'll be, uh, gaming and gambling."

Robert shouted at Ken, "Tuck in your shirt."

Ken gave Robert the finger as they both laughed.

Ryan looked around and said, "This is definitely gonna be awkward."

"So, why again are we doing this, Sifu?" asked Ryan.

Sifu smiled. "No one is ever gonna believe you went to a strip club with your teacher."

Robert said, "I'll make sure this goes in the director's cut, if this story ever becomes a movie."

"So, where should we go first?" asked Ken.

Kirin said, "I thought we'd start at the gaming area first."

Everyone turned around to see Tobias at the girls' entrance.

Tobias looked at everyone and said, "Oh, I thought this was the gaming area."

Kirin shook her head as the gang was ready to go to the gaming area.

Doc said, "Sifu, where are you going?"

Sifu said, "I'm going to gamble."

Kirin said, "You don't gamble."

Sifu laughed and said, "Exactly."

An Hour Later

"Okay, I'm gamed out," said Kirin. "Besides, I'm terrible at these games."

Ryan said, "I agree. Let's go find Sifu."

Robert said, "Wait a second, I still have one more drink I bought for myself and Kirin."

The waitress delivered the drinks, but Robert said, "Uh, this isn't what I ordered."

The waitress apologized immediately, confused about her mistake.

Tobias said, "What's your name?"

The waitress said, "Feather."

"It's not your fault, Feather. Robert doesn't speak the best English. I'm actually his translator."

Robert began to laugh uncontrollably at Tobias, who began speaking in gibberish. Robert bowed his head in acknowledgement and said, "Hai."

Feather giggled and said, "I'll get you some new drinks, my apologies."

The gang began to laugh, and Kirin was amused by Tobias's humor.

Kirin said, "You used Japanese and Tagalog for your translation to the Korean guy?"

Tobias laughed, as the moment was one to be remembered. The gang was in a good mood, despite the initial shock. Angelo then gathered the gang together, as they were in search for Sifu. As they entered the other room they saw a huge crowd cheering. They all looked at one another.

Danny said, "Let's see what's going on over there."

Tobias looked at Kirin as they walked toward the crowd. "So, are you having fun?"

Kirin said, "Strangely, I am." It had been a while since Kirin and Tobias had been normal with one another. Their relationship was somewhat strained, where neither one knew exactly how each one should behave.

Big T said, "Danny, twenty credits that it's Sifu in the big crowd."

Danny said, "You're on."

As the gang approached the action, they saw who was the center of attention: Sifu. The crowd was excited by the huge pile of chips right in front of him.

Robert said, "Holy crap, it *is* Sifu!"

Danny shook his head and passed Big T twenty credits.

The gang snuck through and stood behind Sifu.

Kirin asked, "Oh my gosh, Sifu, how much money have you made?"

Sifu said, "I'm not really sure, maybe about ten thousand chips. I need an Asian guy to calculate this … Robert!"

Robert said, "Sifu, ask Ken. I'm pretty sure the Jewish guy is better at counting money than I am."

Ken said, "You know you're totally being racist."

Robert said, "Whatever … besides, are you Jewish?"

"Yes."

"Are you good with money?"

"Yes."

Robert laughed, "Well, you see, it can't be racist if it's true."

Ken replied, "It's actually 11,525 chips."

Tobias said, "I thought you said you don't gamble."

Sifu said, "It's roulette. It's not gambling. I'm using Wing Chun theory."

Kirin's face cringed as it often did when Sifu said something unexpected. She asked, "So explain to me how you are using Wing Chun theory."

Doc said, "You never cease to amaze me."

Sifu turned to Doc and said, "When I cease to amaze you, that's when I'm pretty sure I'll be dead."

Kirin said, "No, seriously ... explain, Sifu."

Sifu said, "Okay, there's a universal balance to life. Whether one believes it or not, it just happens. So, for example, the number 13, I put a single chip of ten credits. If I lose, I'll double down on that and continue to do so. It's a somewhat tedious process, but eventually I know I'll win. It has to come back."

Kirin peeked over his shoulder and said, "So, that's how you won all this money."

"Yup. Let's end this." Sifu shrugged his shoulders and took all his chips and placed them on a random number and color.

Tobias said, "Holy shit! What are you doing?"

Sifu said, "This game bores me." He turned around and walked away as the gang's jaws dropped. The dealer spun the wheel as the entire room looked to see the outcome.

The crowd watched as the dealer said, "Red."

Robert said, "Did he just blow 10k?"

Ken whispered, "It's 11,525, to be exact."

Kirin said, "I can't believe what he did," as she held her hands up in disbelief.

Tobias said, "What's the big deal? You gave away 25 million credits."

Kirin gave Tobias a look.

The gang chased Sifu, who was walking away.

Danny got in front of Sifu and said, "You just blew 10k, Sifu." He shook his head and said, "What gives?"

Sifu turned around. "No matter. You win some, you lose some. It's just money. Anyway, a fast win leads to a fast loss. I decided to create the balance immediately so it doesn't catch me by surprise.... Besides, I'm old and tired, so I'm gonna head home." Sifu reached into his pocket and tossed a chip up in the air for Tobias.

Tobias said, "What's this?"

Sifu said, "I believe it's a—"

Ken shouted, "Thousand-dollar chip!"

Tobias looked at the group and said, "This could get interesting."

Sifu said, "Be good, and watch over Kirin."

Kirin was holding her drink as she said, "I think I'm feeling the effects of my second drink."

Big T said, "Little sista, those two drinks barely have any alcohol."

Robert said, "She's also tiny, so it'll hit her harder."

Ken said, "Maybe we should call it a night and get Kirin home."

As they were headed to the door, Ray stopped by and said, "Are you guys leaving so soon?"

Robert whispered into Ken's ear, "I think the devil wants us to stay."

Ken leaned back and said, "I'm Jewish. I don't believe in the devil."

Robert made a slight gesture toward Ray, "Uh, there's your proof."

The gang wasn't sure what to do, and Tobias took the lead and suggested. "So, should we go to the 'girls' room'?" All eyes looked toward Kirin to see what was going to happen.

Kirin was feeling a little tipsy from all the night's drinking and said, "Sure, why not? Let's go." She waved her hand at the guys and began walking toward the entrance.

Angelo leaned forward and said, "You sure about this?"

Kirin whispered, "Angelo, just chill. You're my friend. Stop with the personal assisting for one night."

The guys looked at her, and then hormones took over. Tobias shouted, "Well, it's Kirin's birthday.... Let's go in."

Danny said, "What?"

Tobias replied, "Uh … never mind … you know what I mean." He then took the chip Sifu had given him and flipped it to Ray.

Ray grabbed it in the air and, with a devilish smile, muttered, "Seguir el diablo."

Kirin said, "Uh, what was that?"

Ray said, "Oh, nothing, Ms. Rise. Please follow me."

As he approached another area, there were two guards waiting by the door step. Ray motioned to them, and they swung the doors open. Inside the room, the music and mood changed immediately, as the guys looked like little kids in a candy store. Several stages across the way held beautiful women who gyrated and performed acrobatic moves.

Ray motioned to his helper as Kirin and the guys got the best seats in the house.

Danny said to Big T, "Want to bet who gets the first dance?"

Big T nodded and said, "I'd love to. Problem is Doc's already getting a lap dance."

Everyone turned in surprise, as Doc was enjoying himself with the comfort of the dancer. It appeared he was no stranger to this environment, as he was striking up quite an interesting conversation with one of the ladies.

Kirin listened in, and she overheard some of the conversation.

Doc said, "You seem nervous. Is there something wrong?"

"Uh, no." The stripper looked around, confirming Doc's initial impression.

Doc said, "Look, my name is Danish, but my friends call me Doc. What's yours?"

"Candy," she said.

At Doc's flat look, she broke down and gave her real name.

"Actually, it's Alexandra," she said with a nervous voice.

"Let me guess … is this your first time doing this?"

She hesitated and gently nodded her head.

Doc said, "Look … I'm gonna help you out. Is that okay?"

She smiled, as Doc's gentle personality seemed to put her at ease.

"First of all, nothing else matters than the person you are with. So, look at me, and keep eye contact at all times."

She nodded and sat in a seductive position on Doc.

"You have to remember this is the game and you are in charge of it."

Robert began to chuckle as he was listening in on the conversation, too.

"Guys, I have a new name for Doc. Let's call him 'The Professor,' because class is in session."

Kirin shook her head and suddenly noticed that Ken was seated on his chair, getting a massage from behind. The guys and Kirin watched in surprise. Several minutes later, the girl left as Ken smiled.

Danny said, "What's up with the massage?"

Ken said, "I'm not gonna pay twenty credits a dance so some chick can put me in blue balls heaven. At least this way, I'm in control."

Danny laughed and said, "Man, that makes sense."

"Damn straight," said Ken as they ended up high-fiving one another.

Kirin scanned the room to see what the other guys were doing. Ryan was paying no attention, hunched over something on the table. She wondered what he was busy working on, so she tapped him on his shoulder to get his attention.

"One second, Kirin, almost done," said Ryan.

Kirin waited, curious to see what Ryan had to showcase from the fruits of his labor. He held several credits which had transformed into origami: butterflies and birds and a single heart.

Kirin replied, "Oh wow, that's so cool!"

Ryan said, "I thought a little loving touch would be appreciated by these ladies who work so hard." Ryan approached the stage and handed one lady several of the origami credits. She was genuinely surprised by the little gift. She gave Ryan a huge hug and a kiss on his cheek—and a gyration of her chest on his face. She did several complex yoga-like poses, and Ryan's eyes opened up and he leaned in further. Suddenly, she thrusted back onto his chest as he flew back and fell into his seat.

Robert said, "Uh, your center needs work."

Kirin covered her eyes in embarrassment as she said, "I can't believe you guys."

Kirin looked to see that Big T was having quite a bit of fun. Then she took another look at the dancer. She leaned over to Ken, who shared her expression. "Uh, Ken?"

"Yeah, what's up, Kirin?"

Kirin leaned forward and said, "That's a girl, right ... dancing for Big T?"

Ken looked closer and squinted in his direction. He cautiously replied, "I ... think ... so."

Even as she scanned the other guys, Kirin's eyes kept returning to Tobias. He had refrained from any dance and seemed to be on good behavior, unlike the rest of them. It surprised her; she wondered if he would be getting a dance.

She was about to bother Robert, but then was surprised to see a well-endowed, extremely large, and probably the least attractive dancer working her magic on top of him. Knowing Robert, she found this quite unusual, but she then saw Ryan and Doc laughing out loud.

Kirin asked, "What did you guys do?"

Doc said, "I just bought Robert that dance."

"Why?"

Ryan laughed, "I thought he deserved the prize dancer of the evening."

Kirin looked again and said, "But she's quite ... big and...." It finally dawned on Kirin why they had done it. "Ugh ... oh, my gosh. You guys are so mean."

Ryan and Doc watched as Robert looked back and gave them both the finger.

Twenty minutes and several liters of alcohol later, the entire gang was feeling a bit more jovial than normal.

Robert said with a slight slur, "Okay ... okay ... all these chicks are gorgeous, but which one would you date?"

Tobias said, "As in race wise?"

Doc commented as he took a sip, "I thought we didn't care about race."

Tobias replied, "I know we don't, but we still need to categorize them."

Kirin said, "You guys are terrible. Why do I hang out with any of you?"

Robert replied, "Our warm personalities."

Kirin rolled her eyes and took another sip of her drink.

Danny said, "Okay, let's start with white girls."

Ryan said, "What about?"

Doc said, "We need a code name for all the girls, so they don't know we're talking about them directly."

Big T said, "I love all the girls."

Kirin looked at Big T and wondered, *Hmm ... that last dancer didn't look like a girl.*

Ken said, "Strangely that's still higher than Danny's standards."

Danny said, "Yup, all I need is a breathing counterpart."

Kirin asked, "So, you guys actually have code names based off the girl's race? I know I'm going to regret this, but I have to ask."

They looked at each other and eventually back to Kirin as they nodded their heads to confirm.

"So, what do you call white girls?"

Tobias looked around and said, "Milk?"

"Why milk?" Kirin had a confused look on her face.

"Coz their good looks expire really quickly."

The guys chuckled, and Kirin said, "That's so bad! No wonder you guys don't have girlfriends."

Robert said, "I don't have a girlfriend by choice. Don't be mixing me with the rest of the guys."

"I have a girlfriend," said Ryan.

Ken shouted, "Your hand doesn't count!"

Kirin asked, "So, what about Hispanic girls?"

Tobias said, "Easy, volcanoes."

Big T said, "Crap, I forgot. Why'd we call them volcanoes?"

Doc said, "T, that's simple. Guys always end up screwing up, so with Hispanic girls it's like pent-up rage till they explode."

Tobias said, "Check out the tornado at three o'clock."

The gang turned around as they stared at the black girl who was dancing from afar.

Kirin said, "Dare I ask why they're called tornados?"

Tobias answered, "Considering the fact that I've dated some ... black girls are tornados, unpredictable and destructive."

Kirin rolled her eyes. After a minute, she wondered, "Wait a second. Now you got me wondering what you say about Korean girls."

Tobias said, "Oh, we don't have a code name for them yet," as he looked away with a guilty expression.

Kirin smiled, "Good. You better not. Crap, I'm off to the little girls' room. Make sure you guys behave."

As Kirin got up and went to the restroom, the guys waited until she was out of earshot.

Danny said, "No one tell her the code name for a Korean girl is museum."

The guys all shook their head as they continued to drink. A few minutes later, Kirin returned and sat back down. She looked at the guys, who were still mesmerized by the dancers.

Kirin said, "I was thinking about it while in the girls' bathroom. . . . I know you guys too well. There's no way you don't have a label for Korean girls."

Danny looked at Kirin and squirmed in his seat. Kirin pinned him in place with her gaze as he tried to shy away. She stretched out Danny's name and pulled him by his shirt. He swallowed as Kirin leaned in face to face with him.

"Tell me what you call Korean girls."

The guys looked at Danny in a panic as the mood suddenly changed. He looked toward the guys for help. He could see them shaking their heads not to say anything.

Kirin said, "Answer me, Danny."

Danny stammered, "Umm ... umm. . . ."

Kirin counted, "Three ... two. . . ."

Danny shouted, "Museum! Museum ... don't hit me." He cringed in fear for his life as he looked away.

Kirin loosened her grip slightly as she thought about the code word. She began muttering to herself, "Museum … museum? I don't get it. Explain."

Danny fixed his shirt and said, "Jeez, Kirin, you don't have to be so violent. Okay, I'll explain."

Danny looked at the other guys and said, "She knows already. If we don't tell her now, she'll keep hounding me nonstop … or worse, beat me up."

Robert said, "I can live with that."

Kirin waited, as the chaos of the nightclub around her didn't seem to matter.

Danny said, "We call them museums because they're extremely pretty … but, like things in a museum … uh, you can see but you can't touch."

Kirin began to lower him after hearing Danny's pitiful explanation, but then she saw something that caught her eye.

Tobias had been talking with one of the waitresses for quite some time. She finally moved within hearing range of Tobias and listened in.

"You're Tobias, aren't you?"

"That I am."

The waitress said, "So, what brings you here tonight?"

Tobias said, "You could say, I'm looking for my future ex."

She laughed at Tobias's joke and asked, "Can I get you a drink?"

"I'm okay, but you look a little tired."

"It's been a long night, and my feet ache."

"Well, they say my lap is extremely comfortable."

The waitress took the hint and decided to rest on Tobias. He peeked from the corner of his eye, as he had a feeling that Kirin was watching his every move.

As Kirin watched, she began to get jealous. Their short conversation soon turned into several minutes. She was about to get up when someone called out her name. Kirin turned around to see several men approaching her.

One of the guys said, "Hey, baby, how about you come over to our table and dance?" He pointed over to his area where a dozen of his friends were sitting down.

Kirin smiled and said, "Uh, thanks, guys … but I don't work here." Kirin turned around and was about to go toward Tobias when the guy grabbed her arm.

"No, seriously," said the stranger as he spanked Kirin on the butt.

Kirin reacted naturally, putting the guy in a joint lock. She didn't find it amusing at all. Within the blink of an eye, the guy was thrown across the room and onto the stage. The girl dancing screamed, and chaos suddenly erupted.

The entire gang stood up as the girl sitting on Tobias's lap ran off.

Tobias shouted, "What the heck is happening?"

Kirin said, "If you weren't so busy trying to get a lap dance from that girl, you'd know. This jerk just decided to grab me."

Tobias shouted, "She's a waitress, not a dancer."

Doc stood next to Kirin, and Ryan covered her other side.

The guy on the stage recovered from the throw and shouted, "Get that bitch!"

His two nearest companions closed the gap on Kirin as the rest of his friends began rushing in.

Danny said, "Oh, shit ... guys."

The rest of the guys snapped out of their dream as they realized what was about to go down. Angelo huddled next to a table and screamed, "I told you we should've gone home!"

For the next several minutes, chaos ensued as Kirin and the guys dealt with business. Even in their intoxicated state, they easily handled the other guys attacking. The problem was the amount of damage: the area looked like a war had taken place.

Tobias tossed the last guy to the ground as Kirin looked at what they'd all just done.

The doors flew open as the police arrived at the scene. Kirin approached the officers and said, "Finally, I'm glad you came! Those bouncers didn't even help us."

The officer shouted, "Get on the ground ... all of you!"

Kirin said, "Wait a second! We didn't start the fight—"

"Get down. Now!"

Kirin and the others got on their knees. She watched as things were unfolding from bad to worse. Kirin looked on suspiciously as Ray whispered into the lead officer's ear.

Kirin felt her phone vibrating and checked it. A message popped up on the screen: "We can do whatever we want." She closed her eyes, as she realized what had just happened.

Robert yelled, "This is total bullshit! We didn't do anything."

Big T looked at Robert, "See, this is the shit that happens to me all the time."

Tobias looked at Kirin and said, "Are we getting arrested?"

Kirin said, "Pluck a duck." She thought, *I got set up.* She watched as her friends one by one were being handcuffed by the police. Across the room, she saw Ray with a smile on his face.

"Cause and effect explains the rhyme to the reason."—Sifu

SECTION 1

Short Stories #9—Kirin's P.O.V.

<u>Training Time—1 Year, 109 Days</u>

As I opened the door to the school, I saw Tobias was already inside working on his forms. I knocked first to let him know I was there and then quickly entered.

I waved. "Hey."

Tobias stopped his practice and said, "Thanks for coming thirty minutes early."

"Yeah, it's no problem."

"So, the reason I asked you to come here earlier is so I can work with you personally in street fighting application. I figure at some point everyone's gonna have some opportunity to get some credits on these fights," said Tobias.

"You do know that I pulverized the last opponent in the challenge match, right?"

"Yeah, I'm well aware of that. And, from Robert's account of the fight, you lost control."

"Lost control? What do you mean? I had him down, and he was out," I said sternly.

"That's not the issue, Kirin ... but you lost control. Had the guys not pulled you off him, who knows what could've happened?"

"So what? It was either beat his ass or lose the school."

"You still don't get it." Tobias raised his voice.

"I get that I did what I had to do to make sure this school never closes."

Tobias sighed. For the first time, he actually held back and controlled his temper. "The art ... is all about control, Kirin."

I was angry and shouted, "You're not Sifu, so stop trying to sound like him."

"Kirin, I'm telling you … your recklessness will get you and this school in trouble."

I scoffed at him. "You're giving me advice on being reckless? Talk about the kettle calling the pot black."

Tobias said, "I'm pretty sure it's the pot calling the kettle black."

"Whatever, you know what I mean."

"Jeez, Kirin, you are so stubborn."

I rolled my eyes and stared back at him.

He raised his hands and said, "Seriously, you better hope I'm not around when you screw up."

I shook my head and didn't utter another word.

Tobias said, "Look, everyone knows you're the most talented student to enter Sifu's school in years, but there's still so much you have to learn. Your fighting is being fueled by anger and hate. When you let that take over, you'll end up on the wrong side of a fight."

I didn't say a word; I was just stunned that Tobias said those words about me.

Tobias asked, "What?"

I said, "Seriously, everyone thinks I'm the most talented student Sifu's had?"

Tobias said, "Don't let that comment go to your head."

"What comment?"

He shook his head and said, "You're gonna be the death of me, Kirin."

"Don't say that. I'm pretty sure your own craziness will lead to your early demise."

Tobias smiled and messed up my hair as he patted me on the head like a little kid. "Come on, let's roll."

For the next fifteen minutes, I worked with Tobias. We did several drills together, and he took the time to explain certain things to me.

Tobias said, "You've got to learn how to control your ego, Kirin. Anger and hate can't be the driving source for your skill in fighting. If you rely on that, you'll get caught up in the moment."

I listened as he continued to give me a lecture.

"The art goes further than you can imagine, but if you don't control the ego, you'll always be second best."

"I don't get it. If I see the center, target it, and decide immediately that I should own it … is that not Wing Chun?"

"From the outer shell, it is, but if you're not controlling your emotions, then your emotions are controlling you. In the end, it's how well you can control yourself. Let's practice this: you attack, and I'll just block."

I began rolling with Tobias and did as he asked. I kept flowing my attacks upon him, but he was doing an incredible job of blocking each one. I was focused on trying to see if I could contain my emotions like he said, but suddenly he stopped.

I said, "Hey, what gives? I was working on what you said."

Tobias said, "I can tell you've spent a lot of time working with Sifu. I can feel his roll within yours."

I was surprised by his words, and the thought saddened me.

"Thanks, I …," I said with a somber voice.

Tobias said, "You know, Kirin, I never see you smile like you used to. You haven't been yourself since—"

"I'm fine, okay? Can we just continue our training?"

After several more minutes of chi saoing, I decided to break it up. "So, let me get this straight … it's all about controlling your emotions, right?

Tobias said, "Yes. It always is."

"So, when we battled on the table during the chi sao, what happened there?"

Tobias cleared his throat and looked away. He said confidently, "It was a fluke. You just caught me off guard."

"So, you're suggesting it was just luck on my part?"

Tobias replied, "I never said that. It was you who just said it now."

Tobias approached me to continue rolling again, but before I connected with his hands, I had another question that I wanted to ask him.

"So, I'm curious … did you like the kiss?"

"What do you mean?"

"Do I have to speak slower? How … was … the … kiss?"

Tobias shook his head and thought about it for a moment. "Uh," he had a serious look on his face. "How old are you?"

"I just turned seventeen," I said.

Tobias replied, "Then the answer to your question is … no!"

"By the way, that was my first kiss," I said.

Tobias looked even more confused and was about to speak. Suddenly the door flew open as the rest of the gang interrupted our conversation. Class was about to start, but neither Tobias nor I had any questions answered.

5239 Credits—1 Year, 148 Days

It was going to take some serious credits for us to pay off Sifu's monthly bill for the gym. Tonight was the first time we were going to one of those underground fight clubs. We gathered first at Sifu's school to finalize our plans.

The core arrived at Sifu's at the exact time Tobias had requested.

Tobias said, "Okay, guys, do we have to go over any last-minute instructions?"

Danny said, "So, who's gonna enter first for this fight?"

Tobias rolled his eyes and said, "Carlos and Rico."

Danny yelled back, "They aren't even here, and they both have less than a year of Wing Chun!"

Tobias shouted, "Will someone hit the stupid out of Danny's brain? Of course, I'm gonna be fighting the first match."

Tobias pointed to Doc and said, "Doc, give us a rundown."

Doc stepped up and took over. "As Tobias said, this is our first fight, so it's really to get a feel of how things work. Now remember to stay separate from one another so we can all make individual bets when Tobias is up for the fight."

Robert pointed at Danny, "So that means don't be stupid and talk to Big T or make ridiculous gestures in his direction … Danny!"

Ryan said, "So, between the eight of us, how many credits do we all have to bet?"

Doc said, "Let's do a countdown on numbers."

Ryan said, "I've got twenty-five credits."

Big T added, "I've got ten credits."

"I've got thirty-five credits," was Danny's response.

I said, "I've got forty credits."

Tobias said, "I've got one hundred twenty-five credits."

Ken said, "I've got twenty credits."

Doc ended it by saying, "I've got thirty credits … so, adding that all up, how much is it, Robert?"

Robert said, "I believe that's about two-hundred-thirty-nine credits for us to bet."

I said, "Well, that's perfect! Now we just need another 5,000 credits, and we're home free."

Tobias said, "Remember: we're less than two weeks away from Sifu's rent being due. If we play this correctly, we should be able to fill in half the amount with just this fight night alone."

Doc kept giving instructions. "Try to wait till the very last moments to place your bet."

Ryan said, "So, in the very unlikely chance that Tobias loses ... what then?"

Tobias shot Ryan a look.

Ryan said, "Hey, anything's possible. I'm just trying to be realistic."

Tobias stepped forward. "I won't lose."

Doc confirmed and said, "Tobias won't lose."

Danny said, "So, technically, are we officially a gang right now or more of a team?"

Robert shook his head, "We are not a gang, you dumb ass."

"I'm sorry," Danny said, sounding offended, "but we're doing everything a gang does, so naturally I assumed that we were one."

Ken stepped in. "Okay, just for the sake of argument ... if we are a gang, shouldn't we have cool matching outfits?"

Doc and Tobias turned to Ken, "We are not a gang—and please stop amusing Danny into la-la land."

Danny pressed on. "Hmm, I mean, by definition, a gang is a group consisting of three or more members who share a common cause, so I thought we should have some kind of unified identity, maybe a mascot or a cool name."

I asked, "Now I'm curious, what did you have in mind?"

Tobias put his hands on his hips and said, "Guys...."

"Thank you, Kirin. Not that I did much research into it," said Danny.

Tobias said, "Well, that's a news flash."

Danny continued, "Anyway, checking on comic books, other gangs, universities, and so forth ... I thought it would be cool to find some kind of creature that represents Wing Chun."

Doc said, "Well, technically, I'm pretty sure it's based on a crane and a snake fighting."

Danny blew Doc off and said, "That's all great, Doc, if we're talking hundreds of years ago. Now, I wanted something modern, yet a creature that truly encompassed who and what we are."

I said, "Go on already. Spit it out!"

Danny said, "I give you the ... ta da! Honey badger."

Ken said, "Why the honey badger?"

Danny replied, "I'm glad you asked that question. Because, unlike other creatures, a honey badger just doesn't give a shit."

Tobias shouted, "Okay, can we worry about this some other time?"

Danny said, "Fine. Can you guys at least do me the favor of letting me come up with a secret handshake?"

Robert said sarcastically, "Someone's been on the internet way too long."

"Will you shut up if I say yes?" Tobias muttered.

"Duh, of course," said Danny.

Tobias replied, "Okay then, I'll give it some thought. No promises."

Big T said, "I'd prefer we forget the honey badger and go for outfits with a cape."

Ryan said, "Well, if we go with the cape, my vote is that we add a mask."

Robert said, "Ryan, what do you think would happen if the cops saw Big T … a two-hundred-eighty-pound black guy in a hood and a cape?"

Big T stopped to think about it and said, "You have a good point, Robert."

Nearly in unison, Tobias and Doc shouted, "We are not a gang or some kind of superhero team!"

I said, "Okay, guys, just keep in mind that, besides betting, we have to watch each other's back, okay?"

We all nodded and headed out to our first underground fight.

Two Hours Later

The school door flew open as we were all celebrating. This was the first good time we'd all had since Sifu had gone missing. Big T was carrying a stack of pizzas as we entered the school.

Robert said, "Damn, Tobias! It never gets old watching you kick ass."

Tobias said, "Someone lock the door. Let's celebrate."

Ken patted him on the back. It was the first time I'd seen all the guys smile in a while—what's more, I was smiling, too.

I asked, "So, how much did we pull in for the fight?"

"Well," Ryan paused, doing some calculations, "tonight's winnings came out to a grand total of 1,750 credits."

Everyone looked toward Robert and waited.

Robert said, "Hey, I'm not the only Asian guy here."

We just waited for an answer.

Robert finally gave in and put his hands on his waist. "Fine. We need another 3,589 credits."

Tobias said, "Okay, good job, everyone. We still have some work to do to keep this school open, but tonight ... let's enjoy ourselves and eat."

"The strength of a team is not its uniformity, but the gelling of all personalities to work for a common goal."—Sifu

Allies—1 Year, 155 Days

Since the curfew had been lifted a few weeks ago, moving around was much easier. The streets of Chicago didn't look like the city was on lockdown, but it did have a different feel from what it used to be. The most noticeable difference was all the drones hovering around the place to aid in stopping misbehavior from the city's own citizens. The government had added checkpoints for certain areas, but they were only placed for those who were extremely well-to-do. All this somehow was justified and sold to the people as safety for the citizens. Everyone knew otherwise, but had no choice other than to follow.

It was an eerie feeling as we met at an abandoned building. The place looked right out of a horror movie, but it was a good choice since it didn't look like anyone had been here for years. It certainly wasn't a place that the police or the STDs would venture to for patrol.

I sat in between Doc and Robert, as we were surrounded by unfamiliar faces. Usually a gathering of this size would lead to some kind of fight, but this was different. Tobias felt we were in need of allies, and he had invited the handful of the remaining schools that hadn't been shut down to meet.

I asked Doc, "Do you know who these guys are?"

Doc scanned the room, calculating and thinking as always. He never spoke without thought. "Some of them ... not all."

Robert said, "I don't see why we need to team up."

"That's because you're antisocial," I countered.

Robert frowned. "I'm a social butterfly. I have no idea what you're talking about."

I laughed and punched Robert on the arm. He looked at me and mumbled something in Korean.

I leaned over to see Ryan chomping on a snack, while Ken and Big T were discussing something out of my range.

"Hey, where's Danny?" I asked Doc.

Doc rolled his eyes and said, "Robert, can you fill Kirin in on the location of wonder boy?"

Robert nodded and leaned forward. "Guess who's in love?"

I said, "Wait, has it been fifteen minutes already?"

Both Robert and Doc raised their hands and gave me a high five. We all had our inside jokes, but it was always easiest with Danny.

"Anyway, are you telling me he missed our meeting for a girl?"

Robert face palmed himself and then whispered, "Yup. Some new girl he's met, that he's head over heels for."

"I can't believe Tobias allowed this."

Doc said, "You know Tobias … he's a softy for love."

"Really?"

Then I saw Robert tap Doc on the arm as Doc said, "Uh … forget I said that."

As everyone finally settled in place, the meeting was about to begin.

Tobias stood up and spoke. While he was reluctant to take the role of the leader of the school, his actions showed otherwise. He had a commanding presence that I admired, and even he wasn't aware that it had nothing to do with his ability to kick ass.

Tobias said, "First, thank you…. Thank you to everyone who showed up tonight. As you know, there are fewer than twenty existing martial arts schools in the Chicago area that have not been over taken by the UFMF. I'm glad that at least three of those schools agreed to join up with us tonight. I'm hoping eventually more will come around, but I appreciate you taking the time to come. So, why don't I begin with the introductions?

"My name is Tobias, and I'm with Sifu Kwan's Wing Chun Gung Fu School. My Sifu sends his apologies for not meeting with you tonight, since he's been under the weather. He said I could speak for him as well as for the school. Tonight, I brought several of my brothers and our sister in the art with me."

One by one, our group introduced themselves. Tobias eventually stepped back and left the floor open for the other schools to do their introductions.

I watched as a thin and lengthy guy stood in front of the circle. "Hi, my name is Trevor. I'm with the Suguwashi Aikido School, near the South

Side. I'm speaking on behalf of our group, since our lead student couldn't make it tonight." He then introduced several of the other students who had accompanied him.

"Hi, my name is Freddie. I'm with the Filipino Arnis and Kali School, located on the west side of Chicago. I'm also accompanied by several of my brothers and sisters. I'm glad you invited us to this meeting."

"Hi, everyone, I'm Chen with the Tai Chi Martial Arts School, also on the west side. Happy to be here. Actually, I'm glad we aren't the only ones left."

Tobias waited until all the formalities and introductions were done. He decided to take control again. "Like I said, I'm glad you guys and gals could make it. As you know, we are the few that remain. And, it's quite obvious that the UFMF won't stop till all our schools are shut down. Thus, I thought it would be wise for the few remaining schools that have survived so far to ally together in some shape or form."

Freddie asked, "Okay, I'm glad to do that, but what exactly are we gonna do against all these challenge matches?"

Trevor responded, "I'm all for allying with you guys, but Freddie's right: what does all this involve?"

Chen sat silently in his corner and did not speak a word.

Tobias spoke up. "Technically, when challenge matches do occur, there's nothing we can do for each other than win the fight you are in. But at the same time, I wanted to bring to everyone's attention that, whenever we win a challenge, the UFMF just closes the school that lost and then reopens it with a different name."

Both Trevor and Freddie were in shock. I guessed they were unaware of some of the underhanded dealings that the UFMF schools were up to.

Tobias said, "The way I see it … is that we are all buying time. No one can win forever, and if they don't beat us in a challenge match … I'm sure they'll find some other means to close us down. These guys have unlimited funding to back them, and by whatever means, they're going to push till we all close and have to go into hiding."

Chen asked, "What else have they done?"

Tobias shook his head and said, "Not sure if any of your teachers have been approached, but they did try to buy our school. Fortunately for us, our Sifu said no."

Trevor added, "It seems you're right. Who knows what else they are willing to do?"

Freddie said, "If that's the case, there really is no stopping them."

Doc stepped in. "History has shown that, when evil has risen, good men and women gather to stand up against it."

Tobias put his hand on Doc's shoulder. "Doc's right. If we stick together, we have a chance. Maybe we can brainstorm some other way to deal with it. But, whatever it is, we better think of it fast. Time, resources, and statistics aren't on our side."

I considered his words. I feared that, if Tobias was right, maybe it was just a matter of time.

SECTION 2

Sifu's Journey Entry #9—Farewell to Japan

December 2030

T he task had been completed, and the goal achieved. The last several months had been used to work on his craft. Sifu was ready to head back home to the States. But before that, he wanted to stop by and say a final goodbye to his close friend April.

Outside April's store, he stood. The winter air had made it thick and chilly, but to Sifu, who had been encased in his work for months, it was literally a breath of fresh air. He looked around the store and wanted to admire it one last time. He allowed all his senses to absorb and relish the moment. Sifu knew it would be a while before he would return. He smiled and was slightly choked up, but he grabbed the knob and opened the door to her store.

He was a good hour before the crowds would show up, and he was hoping to catch her before it got busy. Instead, his eyes fell upon Takashi, who was busy mopping the floor.

Before Sifu could open his mouth, Takashi smiled, stopped his work, and cheerfully said, "Morning, Sifu."

"Ah, hey, Takashi," he said gleefully. "Where's April?"

Takashi's demeanor had changed significantly over the last several months, as both Sifu and April had finally helped him to find direction and purpose. Takashi took several steps closer to Sifu and said, "April's on her usual food run."

"Food run?" Sifu looked puzzled. "I've been here for almost a year, and I've never heard of her doing a food run before."

Takashi approached and spoke apologetically on behalf of April. "Sorry, Sifu. It's my fault, but I think it's because you've never come on an early Sunday morning."

Sifu thought about it for a second and didn't bother to search the depths of his memory. He decided to let his own oversight pass and said, "You know what? You're right. No worries. Anyway, can you tell me where I can find her doing this food run?"

"The usual place, Sifu. It's just off the main district of Shibuya, about a ten-minute walk from the station," remarked Takashi.

Sifu asked, "You said by the Shibuya district, right?" Sifu thought for a moment and recalled a segment of that area where the homeless congregated.

Takashi nodded, "Yes, that's right, Sifu. I could take you there if you like."

"No, no ... it's okay. You have to get ready for the opening. Besides, I can figure out how to get there."

Takashi nodded and said, "Well, I better get ready for the opening."

"Is she gonna be back before that?" asked Sifu.

"You know April. She may or may not. But, lately she's given me more responsibilities, and I've been handling a bit more of the openings."

Sifu took a sense of pride from that statement, realizing that his words and teachings had finally sunk in. "Well, have a good day, Takashi."

Sifu said his goodbye and began to search for April. Just as he left April's place, Takashi busted out the doors. Takashi said, "Oh by the way, Sifu. Good news."

"What?" asked Sifu.

Takashi opened his mouth and was about to speak, but immediately shut it. "Uh ... I don't want to ruin the surprise. I'll let April fill you in on it." Takashi smiled and waved goodbye again.

As Sifu spun around to leave, Takashi realized something different about this goodbye. Takashi reached out and shouted, "Sifu, are you leaving? I mean ... uh, leaving back for the States?"

Sifu stood fixed with his back turned to Takashi. "I'm not too good at saying goodbyes." He lowered his head. "I thought I'd leave remembering you as you were."

Takashi inhaled deeply, but he understood. He began to search for some words to express his emotions, but staggered at the thought. "Uh ... I, uhhh...." He quickly edged forward to Sifu and bowed horizontally all the way. With determination and grace, he uttered in Japanese, "Honto ni, domo arigatou gozaimashita."

Sifu realized that expressing one's feelings in Japan was a difficult task. Takashi had shown his appreciation toward Sifu.

Sifu spun around and bowed. He did not speak another word and began walking away.

Thirty minutes later, Sifu found himself in the odd part of town, where the few had been forgotten. Every place, no matter where you go in the world, always has its dark side. Unfortunately, globally, the impact of the economic downturns had affected a larger portion than ever before. Japan was no different. The culture shunned them, and they in turn accepted it.

Sifu emptied his mind and then went with his initial feel. He went with the flow like always and began walking in one direction. After only a short walk, he stopped in his tracks and stared straight ahead. In the distance, a puff of hair was bouncing about several meters down the street. He thought, *Only one person in this part of town could have hair like that.*

Sifu began heading in the hair's direction, and he finally confirmed that it was indeed April. She was busy spending some time talking as well as distributing food to the homeless. He stood behind her and did not interrupt, as he was sure April already knew he was there.

Without turning around, she spoke. "I had a feeling you'd be looking for me."

Sifu remained silent as April continued to do her work.

"I'm guessing it's time for you to head back."

Sifu said, "I was going to say that, but I had a feeling you already knew that."

April sprung up and turned around. "I'm going to miss you."

"Same here."

Both smiled and realized that this was goodbye, for now.

"Aren't you going to ask me what I'm doing or why I'm doing it?" asked April.

"I would, but I figured you already know that I do something very similar back in the States."

"Hmm, I guess the question is: who started it?"

Sifu said, "Does it really matter? I figure we're both doing it for the same reason."

Both April and Sifu snickered, as their bond was unlike any other.

"So, how often do you come out here and do this? asked Sifu.

"As often as I can."

"Hmm, I'm kinda torn on whether you're helping them or trying to kill them slowly with chicken and waffles."

April snickered an evil laugh. "Bwahahaha ... the master plan."

Sifu said, "You don't have a master plan, do you?"

"Nah, I don't." She shrugged her shoulders and continued to go to the next needy person and handed them a meal. "So, when are you taking off?"

"Tomorrow, early in the morning."

"Hmm, that soon."

"I don't know if I'd say that soon. I have been her almost a year now," Sifu scratched his head.

"You know what I mean." She raised an eyebrow, looking at him.

"I do."

"So, did you finally get what you came for?" asked April.

"I guess you can say that." Sifu reached into the cart and passed another meal to April.

"What did I say about trusting in the timing of the universe?" said April.

"It's not like I didn't know that.... I just needed a reminder."

April nodded and smiled. She turned her focus to Sifu and said, "I'm gonna miss you stopping by the shop."

"Same here, you've been a good friend," said Sifu as he stared into April's eyes. Both remained silent after that statement and more than likely were thinking the same thing.

Sifu broke the silence and said, "Chicago's only thirteen hours from Japan, you know."

"I know." April approached Sifu and gave him a hug.

"My god, you're going to squeeze the life out of me!" He gasped for air.

"Oh, don't be a baby."

Sifu struggled to speak, "No I'm serious. I think you cracked a rib."

"Now I know you're lying because hugging you is like squeezing a rock."

Sifu said, "Have you squeezed that many rocks?"

"Funny," said April. "You're not going to say your goodbye now, are you?"

"Why wouldn't I?" asked Sifu.

"I figure you can help me distribute the last of the food for the next hour ... and we can spend your last night hanging out."

"That sounds like work," said Sifu.

April squeezed Sifu harder.

"Okay, okay … I get the hint." Sifu gasped for air.

April released her hug and let go of Sifu. "Now that's more like it." She reached in for another meal from her cart and said, "Anyway, you never know … one day, I may return the favor."

"By 'return the favor,' does that mean I won't have to eat your food so my cholesterol level drops?"

April looked devilishly at Sifu. "Hmm, you're always so quick-witted with your jokes." She placed her hands on her waist and said, "Well, you don't have to help out.… I guess you wouldn't be interested in what finally got finished." With those last words, she turned her back to Sifu and waited.

Sifu thought for a second what she meant by that, and suddenly his eyes lit up. "No way."

April didn't respond.

Sifu uttered the same words again, but this time louder. "No way!"

April turned her head slightly and said, "Way."

Sifu's mouth dropped as he said with a loud bark, "Takashi's father finally finished it?"

"Yup. It's sitting back at my place," said April as she began to walk away from Sifu. "You know, this was the most challenging project for him. Since he's never made blades like this, it took him forever, but he said that, even though they are butterfly swords, the blades are true."

Sifu said, "I'm still in shock he was able to pull it off."

"But, if you're not interested in staying to help, well … you can go right ahead and head back to the States now."

"Okay, okay… I'm helping." He laughed out loud. Sifu grabbed April's cart and began helping her finish her work.

Sifu leaned over and said, "You know I was going to help you, right?"

April said, "I know, but it's more fun when we play these games."

"By the way, that reminds me." Sifu reached into his pocket and pulled out a little trinket. "This is for you."

April reached over and grabbed the item. "A key?"

Sifu placed it safely in her hands and pressed his hands over hers. "I figure you'll know when this is needed."

April said, "That's a lot of trust in the universe."

Sifu looked at her and said, "I trust in you."

CHAPTER 10
The Battle Royal

November 6, 2033

At Sifu's restaurant, the crowd was buzzing as Kirin decided to make an unexpected appearance. It had been a troubling two days, and she needed some stability in her life. Her youth showed as her training could not silence the noise streaming from the outside world. Because Kirin always came to Sifu to bring her balance back, she decided to help Sifu and Lance in the kitchen.

Kirin didn't seem to mind being in the public eye at Sifu's place. It could be that Sifu was always the safety net for all of Kirin's insecurities to fall back on. The crowd there seemed to be more understanding of her situation. As Sifu had taught her, one's energy attracts like individuals, and everyone gathered felt like Sifu.

Sifu was in the back room preparing his soup. He could tell Kirin was preoccupied with her thoughts.

When her phone rang, she answered it.

"Hey, Coffee Girl, can you talk?"

"Hey, Quinn. I'm glad you called, but your timing is terrible."

"Tell yah what … I'll call you later tonight, okay?" said Quinn.

"Sure thing." Her expression softened.

Kirin hung up the phone, relieved it had been Quinn. For the last two months, she had grown closer to Quinn, as Hunter was away at school and her relationship with Tobias continued to be strained. It was easier for her not to deal with those pressing issues and escape from her reality. Kirin's relationship with Quinn was somewhat unusual. She hadn't told him her name—and he was fine with that. Quinn didn't bring about the pressure she normally felt with others. Kirin liked the anonymity and enjoyed being treated just like a regular person.

"Kirin, can you deliver this to table number three?" asked Sifu.

"Uh, what, Sifu?"

"Table three, please."

Angelo said, "I could help you, if you like, Kirin."

"I'm fine, Angelo. I told you to take a day off."

Angelo pouted, sat back in his chair and took out his phone.

Kirin looked back at Sifu and nodded, she grabbed the tray and headed toward the main dining area. As she passed the kitchen and made her way into the crowd, they clapped every time she made an appearance. She smiled humbly and began looking for table number three.

One customer yelled, "You rock, Kirin!"

Kirin said, "Thanks! Uh, a little help. Which one is table number three?"

From several feet away, a couple raised their hands, waving Kirin down.

She said, "I believe this is yours."

The girl said, "Yes. It is."

The guy hesitated briefly and asked, "Uh, Ms. Rise, do you mind if we take a picture with you?"

Kirin set the food on the table and moved to stand beside the couple. The guy pulled out his phone and took an "us-ie."

"Thanks again," said the guy.

"It's no problem."

Everyone was having a good time, and the large-screen TV was blaring out the news. A local smash magazine show popped up, and a voice said, "Kirin Rise's latest arrest and the controversy behind the superstar coming next."

Heads turned, as this caught the crowd's attention.

Sifu, who was always aware, ran to the front and said, "Change that channel."

Kirin raised her hand and waved down Sifu. She stared at the TV and said, "It's okay, Sifu. I'm fine with it."

Kirin stood there and began watching the report with everyone else. She had been laying low for the last several days and was far from the online grid, so she was clueless about what they were planning on saying.

A VRAI TV reporter named Rose Stevens began to speak. "Reporting the latest troubles of the mega superstar, I'm her with my co-host Celine Michaels to go over all the unusual activity with Kirin Rise. It has been an unusual year for Kirin Rise, and now it's jumped from weird to down-right bizarre. The superstar is a magnet for controversy, and this weekend was no different. She celebrated her twenty-first birthday at a well-known strip club, which is … well, odd, to say the least, don't you think so, Celine?"

Celine said, "I agree. For someone who's a proponent of woman power, going to a strip club is something I find highly questionable for the young role model."

Rose added, "And, now we've got further controversy…. It appears that Kirin Rise might have a new love interest."

Kirin looked surprised by that announcement. She waited as the screen flashed an image of her and Danny face to face. Someone must have snapped a picture of her grabbing Danny at the club during her discussion with him. She began rubbing her temple as she thought, *Ugh. These are all lies.*

Celine added, "We're not quite sure who this Latin lover is, but you can see from this picture that they seem to be extremely close."

Rose said, "If that wasn't enough, a fight broke out as sources said the superstar refused to take an autograph with fans."

The clip showed them interviewing one of the gentlemen, who said, "I just wanted to get a picture with her and an autograph. She was all snippy and bitchy, and the next thing I know, she's throwing me up on the stage."

Kirin floundered in embarrassment. She raised her voice, saying, "That didn't happen at all! He grabbed me from behind and...." She shook her head. *What the heck is going on? Could things possibly get any worse?*

Unfortunately, her question was answered, as the doors smashed opened. The cops, all dressed in Chicago blue, burst into Sifu's establishment as heads turned and chaos ensued. The crowd's attention was taken away from the screen, fixated on this new development. Kirin watched things unfold as her body tightened. She wondered what was happening.

Sifu calmly approached the policemen. "What seems to be the problem, officers?"

The officer was belligerent from the start. "Sir, don't you dare get any closer! Stay exactly where you are and turn around."

Sifu did as he said, moving slowly to follow the officer's orders. The patrons of his restaurant began pulling out their cell phones.

The lead officer shouted, "If anyone records this, you will be arrested immediately." His tone struck fear as more officers poured into the room. One by one, the customers lowered their phones and did as they were told.

Sifu said calmly, "Officer, maybe you didn't hear me. Can I ask you, again, what seems to be the problem?"

One patron refused to stop taping, and the officer made a motion.

Several of the officers rushed toward him and pinned him hard to the ground. He shouted, "You can't arrest me for taping this!"

The tension grew, as everyone was fearful of the force being demonstrated by the officers. The man's phone fell to the ground, and one of the officers stepped on it, crushing it to pieces.

Sifu turned slightly to see what was happening.

The lead officer took out his taser and said, "You make another move like that, and I'm going taze you right where you stand."

Kirin got upset and was about to approach the officer, but Lance grabbed her and said, "Don't. Sifu knows what he's doing." Anger seared through her as she clenched her fist.

Several officers surrounded Sifu, and more tasers were drawn and aimed directly at him.

"Mr. Kwan, get on your knees!"

Sifu said, "Am I being charged with something?"

"Shut up!" The officer motioned for another to restrain Sifu.

"Cuff him down, boys, and read him his rights,"

Kirin reached out and said, "Sifu!"

Sifu winked at Kirin and said, "It'll be okay."

The two officers rushed Sifu from behind, pinning him to the floor. They were far from gentle and began handcuffing him. Sifu did not fight back. Their actions brought fear to the entire room. People were in a state of shock, but feared doing anything in return.

Upon seeing this, it was Lance who now lost his cool. He shouted, "I will beat you like a drum … and I only know how to play a guitar." He let go of Kirin and was about to rush in, but she held him back. One of the officers saw this and raised his taser aimed right at Lance's face.

"Try me!" he taunted Lance.

"Anything you say may be used against you in a court of law. You have the right to consult an attorney before speaking to the police and to have an attorney present during questioning now or in the future. If you cannot afford an attorney, one will be appointed for you before any questioning if you wish. Mr. Kwan, you are being charged with illegally gambling. As per regulation of the UFMF bylaws, no assistant associated with the fighter can place bets."

Kirin frowned as she listened, mumbling, "I never had Sifu linked as my own personal trainer or even part of my camp."

Lance looked at her; they were both concerned.

Kirin shouted, "Sifu was never associated with my training camp in any shape or form!"

The officer said, "Ms. Rise, stand down and step back. We have proof that you wrote his name and confirmed that he was part of your entourage. His gambling is against UFMF code as well as illegal gambling violation under section 37–49. Seems like he was making money off your bets."

"I never signed that! I know for a fact that I never signed that." She looked back at Lance.

Lance grabbed her as the same officer switched targets and aimed the taser at Kirin.

"Not another step, Ms. Rise."

Sifu said, "It's okay, Kirin. Please, do as they say. Contact Mike, my attorney, and we will sort this entire mess out."

The room felt like it was spinning. Kirin didn't know what was happening. Her phone began vibrating as she stepped back and did as Sifu had told her. At first, she ignored it, but it continued to press on her. She looked at her phone as a message appeared, "We have the power to do what we want." Another message flashed: a picture of what was happening in the restaurant that very moment. She looked around, trying to figure out who had taken this picture.

Four officers escorted Sifu out of the restaurant as the room went silent.

Kirin immediately turned to Lance. "Do you have Mike's number?"

"Yeah, I'm on it. Let me just make an announcement."

Lance waved to the customers in the restaurant. "Please, everyone, finish eating. We're closing for the night."

Kirin began contacting the gang to frantically explain what had happened.

Several Hours Later

Kirin was busy talking to Mike, who was explaining the situation to her. They had all gathered at the Chicago precinct to see what would happen to Sifu. The entire gang was there, except Tobias. She had called and left several text messages, but he did not respond. Outside news had spread that Kirin was involved in another controversial situation, but she didn't care. Her main concern was Sifu.

"Mike, this can't be happening," said Kirin. She was pacing back and forth as that feeling of helplessness found its way back into her life.

"I'm afraid it is. These are some serious charges against Sifu."

"I can't believe this is considered serious. Just last week, I saw more police brutality on the news. That should be headline news, not this crap."

Mike replied, "I agree with you 100%, but you know the UFMF's business is wrapped around gambling. If word spread that it was somehow fixed, that could topple their entire industry."

Kirin smashed her fist against the wall. "I'm telling you, Mike. I never did anything to link Sifu with my camp. That signature isn't mine.... Why would I ever do that?"

Mike said, "I believe you, Kirin. You know I'll do anything and everything for Sifu, but we have to prove that your signature was forged."

Kirin said, "Can't we make bail and get him out of here for now?"

Mike said, "The amount of bail is ridiculous, Kirin. I'm trying to get it lowered, since he's not a flight risk, but someone's definitely pulling the strings to keep Sifu inside for a while."

Kirin pulled her hair and was upset. "I can't believe this is happening."

Mike put his hand on her shoulder. "Kirin, go home. Get some sleep. There's nothing more you can do here."

Doc said, "Wait ... what if we pool our credits?"

Ryan said, "How much is bail set at?"

Mike looked at the gang and said, "His bail is 10 million."

Danny said, "Are you kidding me?"

Big T said, "Kirin, don't you have the credits to cover this?"

Kirin shook her head. "You know I donated all my money. I've only kept what was needed to survive. I don't have that kind of cash on me."

Ken said, "Any chance we can look for donations?"

Robert said, "Frick, we're screwed."

Kirin was tearing up. "Dammit ... somebody text Tobias again. Where is he?"

Angelo replied, "I've tried calling him as well. He's not picking up."

Kirin was flustered and decided it was better to move than sit around.

Outside the police station, reporters had gathered. Her fan base was wondering what was going on. Kirin was tired of waiting and needed to do something. She ducked away from the big crowd, as she had decided to head to Tobias's apartment and look for him herself.

Twenty minutes later, Kirin finally arrived outside Tobias's apartment. She scanned her phone for a final time, but still no text or call from him. She needed a friend. She needed someone to lean on—and, for whatever reason, he wasn't responding. So, she gambled that this was the best bet to begin to search for him.

She was surprised to see his motorcycle parked in the front of his apartment.

She thought, *He's here ... he's gotta be.*

Several flights up, she got to his apartment. She knocked and waited. She continued to bang on the door before it suddenly opened.

Tobias was half-dressed and surprised to see Kirin.

"Hey, what are you doing here?"

"What the hell!" shouted Kirin. "Why aren't you answering your phone? I've been calling and texting you for the last several hours."

Kirin was about to walk in, but Tobias blocked her from entering.

"Uh ... this is not a good time." He looked nervously around.

"Not a good time? Sifu's in jail! How's that for timing? The entire gang was there, but you were nowhere to be found."

Tobias said, "Sifu's in jail?" The news rocked him back to reality.

"Yes! That's why I've been trying to get a hold of you. I need you now more than ever and—"

Suddenly a voice from inside Tobias's apartment called, "Tobias, who's there?"

Tobias's face froze as Kirin's eyes widened.

Tobias said, "Look, uh ... give me a minute, and I'll go down there with—"

Kirin kicked the door open and walked through. She saw a beautiful girl wearing only Tobias's T-shirt. Kirin stared at her for a moment and stood there in total shock.

"You look familiar," she said angrily. A few seconds passed before she realized that this was the same girl who had sat on Tobias's lap. Her spirit fell, and she spun around to walk out. Tears began streaming down her face.

Tobias blocked her path and said, "Look, I can explain."

"Get out of my way," said Kirin as anger swelled up inside. The tears continued to roll down her face as she pushed Tobias to the side and bolted out of his apartment.

Tobias watched as Kirin left. He dashed back to his room and rushed to get dressed. He couldn't let her go. He needed to explain to her what was going on.

Kirin was halfway down the stairs when Tobias reached for her arm. "Look, I'm sorry. I can explain."

"You're sorry."

"Hey! I didn't do anything wrong."

"If you didn't do anything wrong, then why do you look so guilty?" She looked down, unable to look at him anymore.

Tobias was taken aback and didn't know what to say.

When Kirin began walking away, he shouted, "You're the one who said you were unsure of our relationship! You didn't say we were going out or anything."

Kirin turned around and yelled, "You don't get it! That's your problem. You don't know the first thing about love. Love isn't about you, Tobias. It's about the other person. So, our relationship isn't so clear … fine. That's my fault, but you don't see me going around banging a stripper."

"She's not a stripper!" yelled Tobias. "Will you just listen for a second? She's a waitress."

"Whatever," Kirin spat. "Do whatever you want—coz that's what you're really good at, isn't it? Taking care of yourself." Disgusted, Kirin shook her head and ran down the stairs and out the door. Tobias stood there in silence, wondering what to do next.

At Kirin's Loft

It was close to midnight. Kirin was having the most terrible night she could've ever imagined. She needed someone, and she knew just who to call. It had been a while since she had spoken with Hunter, but if anyone could help her through this time, it would be him. He was always there for her, and she desperately needed him.

She picked up her phone and dialed. Still in tears, she waited. She clung to a glimmer of hope as the phone rang. Finally, someone picked up the phone.

"Hunter, it's me, Kirin."

She waited, expecting to hear Hunter's voice, but a girl responded instead.

"Hi, this isn't Hunter," said the soft voice.

"Who is this?" asked Kirin.

"Is this Kirin? Kirin Rise?"

"Yes, who is this?" Kirin demanded an answer.

"Oh my gosh! It's a pleasure speaking with you, Kirin. This is Olivia."

Kirin was confused as she thought, *Who's Olivia, and why is she answering Hunter's phone?*

"I'm sorry. Who is this?" asked Kirin.

"I'm sorry. Hunter's told me so much about you. I'm a huge fan, Kirin. Oh, uh … is it okay to call you Kirin?" said Olivia.

Kirin remained silent, her heart was racing.

"Where's Hunter?"

Olivia replied, "He's sleeping right now. Would you like for me to wake him up?"

Kirin said, "Why are you answering his phone?"

Olivia said, "I know you've been busy, but I'm not sure if Hunter's told you that I'm his girlfriend."

The news just shocked Kirin. It was more than she could bear. That was the final straw that broke her from within as she just sat there, dazed.

Olivia said, "You know what…? Let me wake him up. I'm sure he wants to—"

Kirin hung up. She sat there, alone on her bed, and began to cry. She thought, *Why is this happening to me?*

For the next several minutes, she just stared into space, wondering when this night would end. It was almost as if she were mentally broken beyond repair. Suddenly, the phone rang, breaking her out of her trance. She forced herself to look down at the ID, thinking it must be Hunter. To her surprise, it was Quinn calling her.

She wiped her tears and answered, "Hello?" Her voice cracked, struggling to form the word.

Quinn said, "Hey, Coffee Girl, I hope it's not too late. I promised I'd call you and—"

Kirin said in a shaky voice, "I'm not okay."

Quinn asked, "What's wrong? Talk to me."

Kirin failed to answer as she began to sob over the phone.

Quinn's words tried to reach out to Kirin. "I know it's late, but I can be over there in about ten minutes. Everything will be all right."

Kirin hung up the phone, feeling lost. For the next fifteen minutes, she didn't move. The events that had unfolded were just too much for her to handle. Pity, doubt, every negative emotion one could imagine was consuming her.

The intercom buzzed several times with no movement from Kirin. She finally managed to moved lifelessly toward the door. Nothing seemed to matter. Kirin didn't even bother to ask who it was. She simply pressed the button to allow whoever it was to come in.

Knock. Knock. Knock.

Kirin opened the door and saw Quinn standing there.

Quinn opened his mouth, breaking the silence. "I'm so sorry I'm late, Coffee Girl. I—"

Kirin rushed toward him and held him tight as Quinn's walking stick fell to the ground. Her eyes began to tear. His touch was the first thing that helped relieve her pain. Quinn held her tight and did his best to comfort her. Kirin whispered into Quinn's ear. "Stop calling me Coffee Girl ... It's Kirin."

▲ ▲ ▲

The next morning, Kirin was sound asleep on her bed. The night before had been draining, and she'd found comfort in the company of Quinn.

Quinn leaned over and kissed her on the lips, murmuring, "Sorry to wake you. I gotta get ready for work."

Kirin opened her eyes and smiled. "I'm glad you came over last night. I needed you, and you were there."

Quinn was all dressed as he pulled out his walking stick. He went over the bed and kissed Kirin on the head.

"You're leaving? Can't you stay for a pinch?"

"I'd love to, but I can't. Today is a work day for us regular guys.... I promise I'll call you later. Maybe you can come and meet me for lunch? Okay, Coffee Girl?"

Kirin sat up and used bed sheets to keep her naked body from being exposed. She laughed and realized how unnecessary that was with Quinn. She said, "You don't have to call me that anymore."

Quinn laughed. "Sorry, it's just habit now. Anyway, promise me you'll see me later."

She murmured, "Hmm," as she hunched over and pouted, hoping that Quinn wouldn't leave.

Quinn replied, "I may be blind, but I can feel when someone's upset."

"No, no, you have work. I understand."

"I'm sorry. Yeah, you know how it is. They work me like a dog at the UFMF."

Kirin's face quickly changed as she asked. "Wait … what did you say?"

"I said they work me like a dog," said Quinn.

"No, not that part … who do you work for?"

"With the UFMF, of course," said Quinn.

Kirin shouted, "You work with the UFMF, and you didn't tell me?"

"Why? What's the big deal, Coffee Girl? Oh, sorry … I mean, Kirin."

Kirin grabbed her phone and looked at the text. Then her head began to race. "What's the big deal? Did they put you up to this? Have you been the one sending me the texts?"

"Who put me up to what? What texts?" asked Quinn.

"I can't believe it," shouted Kirin.

"Talk to me." Quinn approached her, confused and puzzled by Kirin's reaction.

Kirin shook her head as she thought, *How could I be so stupid?* She raised her hand and hissed, "Don't come any closer."

"What's the matter?"

"What do you mean 'what's the matter'? You know how I feel about the UFMF!"

"Why do you care about who I work for? And no, I don't know how you feel about the UFMF."

"You're telling me you haven't the slightest clue?"

"Honestly, I have no idea what you are talking about."

"Kirin, dammit! Kirin … you know Kirin Rise. I'm Kirin Rise!"

Quinn suddenly pieced it together. He looked startled, nearly in shock. His surprise seemed genuine, but Kirin did not care.

"I swear. I had no idea." His voice sounded staggered in the moment.

"Just go. Get out of here, Quinn."

"Kirin, I honestly had no idea … I swear. You have to believe me."

"Get out of here, Quinn. I'm not gonna say it again."

Quinn reached for his walking stick and walked out of Kirin's loft. The door closed as silence filled the entire room.

Kirin sat on her bed and began to cry.

The Next Day

Kirin was in the kitchen, helping Lance. She was washing dishes when he shouted, "Kirin!"

She continued to wash the bowl and ignored Lance. As water poured over, Kirin was lost in thought.

"Kirin!"

"Oh, sorry, Lance." She turned off the faucet and snapped to attention.

"You've been washing the same bowl for the last five minutes. I'm pretty sure it's clean."

She chuckled and put it on the side to dry.

"Kirin, like I told you earlier, I'm fine. I can handle things myself tonight." Lance looked at the watch that hung over the oven. He said, "Come sit down for a while. Let's talk."

Kirin dried her hands and did as Lance asked. She sat down and slumped over.

Lance said, "Listen, kiddo … I'm not like the old man, filled with wise quotes and pick-me-uppers … but I've got a pretty good ear that's pretty clean for the listening."

Kirin took a deep breath but didn't say a word.

"Look, I know you're worried about Sifu, but I'm not."

Kirin looked up in surprise.

"If there's one thing I know about the old man, everything he does is calculated."

Kirin snapped, "How can you say that, Lance? He's stuck in prison right now, and we can't seem to figure out how to get him out of there. Do you honestly think he wants to be there?"

"No … but…." Lance rubbed his beard and finally sat down across from Kirin.

"I know Sifu's situation is bothering you…. I've been around for a while, and I can read people. There's more to this … isn't there?"

Kirin began opening her mouth but caught herself. "Lance … I remember you saying something about believing in something…. What was that again?"

"I think I know what you're talking about. Having served and lost men doing things you thought were for the right reason…? What I said was that your true conviction … how much you honestly believe in your cause … isn't put to the test till you've actually lost something."

Kirin looked away, deep in thought.

"Lance, can I ask you something?"

"I'm all ears."

"How do you know if what you're doing is the right thing? How do you know if the price to pay is too great?"

"Only you can answer that, Kirin. Most people break at the first sign of trouble. That's why I don't think you know until you've sacrificed something. Just remember, there's what you can lose and what could be lost. Both seem about the same, but they aren't."

Kirin sat there as those words hit home.

"Shouldn't you be training? You've got two fights left."

Kirin looked at her phone and the constant reminder that hung over her. She clenched her fist and said, "Enough is enough."

A Few Weeks Later

Linkwater and Connor were explaining to the audience how the battle royal functioned.

Connor said, "This is the last slot that needs to be determined for the Dome. The three champions from outside the US have already qualified."

Linkwater asked, "To me, Dryden is still the favorite. He's been dominant throughout the entire year."

Connor replied, "I do agree, but all eyes are now watching Kirin Rise. Last year's champion seems to be the dark horse. For most of the year, she's been struggling, and many have questioned whether she would even survive, let alone qualify."

Linkwater said, "That's true, but her last two matches reminded me of the old Kirin Rise. Not only did she seem like a changed fighter, but she put an exclamation point on her last fight by knocking out her opponent in less than three seconds. That broke her record!"

In Kirin's Loft

One by one, the contestants for the battle royal were being announced. Kirin was halfheartedly listening to the comments made by Linkwater and Connor.

Sage said, "This is pretty crazy."

Kirin was too preoccupied with other burdens to be too concerned. Sifu was still locked away, and Mike was having a difficult time trying to get him out.

Gwen asked, "Hey, where's Tobias?"

Kirin ignored her question and continued to stare out the window of her building.

Linkwater finally called out the last name, and Kirin jerked toward the TV. "What did he say?"

Sage asked, "What did who say?"

"The TV? Who did he just announce?"

Sage said, "TV rewind ten seconds and volume up."

Kirin approached the TV, listening to Linkwater announcing the twentieth contestant to the fight. "And our last contestant hails from …." The moment was surreal, as she could hear the sound, but not process the information. She looked at the figure on the screen and heard, "He is Justice—"

Kirin's jaw dropped and shouted at the screen, "What? What did he just say?"

She waited, seeing flashbacks as she stared at the face plastered across the screen. "TV pause."

Kirin stared at Justice, Thorne's personal bodyguard who was now entered into the UFMF battle royal.

Both Gwen and Sage said, "Isn't that…?"

"Yes … it's him."

For the next ten minutes, the gang was glued to the TV screen. There, they witnessed total brutality, as a lone fighter stood amongst the many fallen. It was a display unlike anything anyone had ever seen before. Amid the carnage, the referee held his hand up high. Justice was victorious, covered in blood, and had earned the right to join the Dome.

Kirin had seen enough. Watching him fight had confirmed what she had already felt.

Kirin grabbed her coat and yelled to Angelo, "I'll be back soon!"

Angelo's typical witty remark died on his lips at the determination on her face. He decided it would be best if he remained silent. Seconds later, Kirin slammed the door shut as Sage, Gwen, and Angelo were left sitting in Kirin's loft.

An Hour Later

Kirin finally got a chance to see Sifu, who approached the glass separating them. Kirin flashed her phone, holding it up for Sifu to see.

"Who is he?"

"Not even a hello?" said Sifu.

"Sifu, I'm not trying to be rude."

"Yet ... you are," said Sifu.

"I'm sorry, Sifu, but you know who this is, don't you?"

"Yes."

Kirin shook her head in frustration. "Please, Sifu. Please don't say ... you didn't tell me about him because I didn't ask."

"I didn't tell you about him because I've had no idea what he's been doing." Sifu kept a calm face.

"I can tell you what he's doing. He's qualified to be in the round robin tournament of the Dome. Tell me everything you know about him.... Who is Justice?"

"There's not much to say. Justice was one of my earlier generation students that I taught back in the day. If anything, Phil worked with him quite a bit. He knew him more on a personal basis."

"Did you teach him the complete art?"

"Yes, I did."

"How could you do that, Sifu?"

"I teach everyone who wants to learn the art openly, Kirin. You know that," said Sifu.

"How good is he?"

"He's extremely talented."

Kirin shook her head ... suddenly a question arose that needed a definitive answer. "Sifu ... does he have the skill to freeze motions like you?"

Sifu looked away and said, "Yes...."

"The past can always be forgotten, but never escaped."—Sifu

SECTION 1

Short Stories #10—Kirin's P.O.V.

A Book by Its Cover—1 Year, 169 Days

I found myself standing alone, late at night as a last-minute match was secretly posted. I didn't have enough time to contact the guys, and the money that was being offered was too good. I hid behind most of the crowd after several fights, just to catch a feel of where everyone was. I knew this was stupid to do on my own, but I was driven to do whatever was necessary to keep the school open.

The head guy stepped into the area and said, "Our next match is against a very high-flying capoeira fighter." He directed everyone to the corner as an acrobatic guy flipped into the fighting circle. "He is Gabriel from the South Side ... with an eight-game winning streak! Who amongst you dare challenge him? Opening bets begin at five hundred credits."

The crowd cheered, looking for a volunteer, but all I heard was the five hundred credits, which I knew would help pay the school's rent.

I stepped forward and took my hoodie off. "I'm in."

The wall of bodies separated before me, clearing a path to the center of the fighting area.

"We have a challenger! And what's your name, little lady?" asked the ring leader.

"I have none. Let's get to the fight."

"Wow, this little lady, who wants to remain nameless, is ready to go."

With that, the group of individuals who surrounded us began to exchange bets. It was chaos—and I was sure they were all betting against me. The guy in the middle checked me out from head to toe; just as I expected, he laid out favoring Gabriel.

"Remember the rules: anything goes, but you have to stop once the opponent bows out or can't respond. Do you both understand?"

I nodded my head along with my challenger.

Unlike the challenge match where I had been nervous, I didn't feel anything. I was just too focused on the result. I wanted those credits regardless.

Gabriel bowed before me and did several flips backward to begin the match. He flashed me a smile, which didn't matter to me one way or another.

He lowered his hands, and the crowd of about thirty began shouting, with a mixture of cheers and swears. I could feel their energy. Gabriel was dancing from side to side, which I assumed was part of the style. But I didn't care. I knew what I was gunning for—as long as his center was in sight, that was all that mattered.

He did a spinning kick to charge in, which totally exposed him once he was in the air. I shifted and flanked him, dodging his attack. Our eyes met for a split second as I returned his smile.

Whack. Smack. Thud.

Thump!

Just like that, I released a chain of attacks as he went down. It was over.

I quickly collected my pay as many of the people were busy exchanging credits. I was so excited by how much I made that I couldn't wait to tell the gang. However, for a moment, I thought about Tobias and what he would say. *Kirin, are you crazy. I told you not to go on your own.*

As I was basking in the excitement of my victory, someone grabbed me by the arm and started dragging me away. Caught off guard, I was pulled momentarily before I said, "Hey, what's going on?"

"Come with me," the stranger insisted.

"Why should I?"

"I'm trying to save your stupid ass," said the stranger in a weird voice.

The voice sounded somewhat oddly familiar, and I went with my gut feeling, following the stranger. After running for a block, I finally said, "Okay, enough. Stop! Who are you, and where are we going?"

My eyes popped open as the stranger in the hoodie finally revealed herself to me. I gasped, "Holy crap ... Ripley?"

I stood across from my hated nemesis as she removed her hoodie. I continued to stare at her, as if I had just seen a ghost.

"Ripley Hawkins?" My lower lip trembled.

At first I couldn't believe it, but when I said her name, Ripley rolled her eyes and gave that annoying smirk. In typical fashion, she confirmed her identity with those gestures.

"Hey, what gives?" I asked.

"Oh, don't play so innocent, Kirin." Ripley seemed preoccupied with her surroundings.

"What are you doing here?"

"Please. I've seen worse acting on a Korean drama. I know you saw me in a fight several weeks ago when you and your friend scouted out the area."

Ripley had me dead on. I had nothing to counter her remarks.

"Look, Kirin, you're a noob to this underground fighting. You may be able to fight, but these seedy places.... Well, if you go by yourself, once they lose their money, they'll try to hunt you after the fight and get it back," said Ripley.

"How do you know all about this?"

"I know this because I've been doing it longer than you have." The sound of a police car jolted us both. Ripley was on edge.

"Now either come with me and believe me, or stick around and see if I'm lying."

The illusion of choice, I thought. Even though I despised everything about her, my gut feeling was to trust her this moment. I had to go with the lesser of two evils. "Fine. Lead the way."

"Okay, it's just a block away. We'll hide out there for about fifteen minutes, and we should be clear afterward," said Ripley.

We ran another two blocks and hid underneath a porch area. Ripley squatted in the corner with me as she signaled to not make a sound. A few minutes later, we heard a bunch of guys run past that area.

"Dammit, where could that bitch be? She took all our money."

"Fuck if I know. She ran right away, and no one got a good glimpse of where she headed," said the other strange voice.

I held my breath as Ripley looked at me in dead silence. She slowly lifted her index finger to her lips as if I didn't realize the gravity of the situation.

My heart was racing as I began to focus on a single thought to control my breathing. After several minutes, silence kept us company, and the tension that surrounded us finally eased.

"Okay, the coast is clear," said Ripley.

"Hey … um, thanks again," I said.

"Don't thank me," said Ripley. Suddenly my stomach rumbled, interrupting our little conversation.

She looked at me and then my stomach. I look at her and asked, "I owe you one. Let's go out to eat. There's a place several blocks away that no one really goes to."

"Is this one of your dives, Kirin?" said Ripley.

"Look, I'm only going to ask you once."

"Fine, let's do it," said Ripley.

Fifteen Minutes Later

We arrived at one of the few late-night restaurants. It was close to midnight, and Ripley appeared to be just as hungry as me.

I turned to her and asked, "Is this place okay? It's kinda a hole in the wall that not many people know about, but the food is good."

"I guess I have no choice. I'm starving…. This will have to do," said Ripley.

We sat down across from each other and ordered our meal. It was awkward for both of us, and we spent much of our time disrupting the silence by taking sips of water.

"Why are you staring at me?" asked Ripley.

"I can't believe I'm eating dinner across from you," I said.

"Well, that goes for two of us," replied Ripley.

I wanted to get to the point. "So, what gives, Ripley? What's with this double life?"

Ripley fired back. "I could ask you the same thing, couldn't I?"

I didn't open my mouth. I didn't want anyone to know that Sifu was gone, and that this was the only way we could keep the school open.

"How long have you been doing this?" I asked.

"For a while now," said Ripley.

I thought, *Well, that didn't answer anything.* She was keeping things from me, but I wanted to dig.

Ripley asked, "So, how about you? Why are you doing this?"

I answered with a lie, "I find it beats having to do homework on a Friday night."

We stared at each other like we were playing a chess match without the pieces.

"Well, at least answer me this: what's with the nickname, Whiskey?" I didn't think she was going to answer, so I tried to bait her emotionally. "Let me guess … you love to drink."

She rolled her eyes and pouted her lips again. "Typical, Kirin. You're so wrong."

"I'm listening."

"Long story short … in my first fight, I got tossed to the ground, and the guy was charging into me. I grabbed the nearest thing available and smashed him on the head with it." She stared directly at me. "Guess what it was?"

I answered, "A whiskey bottle."

Our food finally came, and we both gorged ourselves, like we'd never eaten before. Little was spoken during that time as we tolerated each other's company.

"You know … you're right; I did see you fight. You must've learned to fight from somewhere around here?"

"Stop digging, Kirin. You're no good at it. If you must know, a handful of us exist, and I'm willing to do whatever it takes to keep my school around," said Ripley.

I leaned back in my chair as I looked at Ripley. Without saying another word, I knew she was going through the same thing I was.

The Christmas Wish—1 Year, 187 Days

It was Christmas morning, and I heard the guys scamper downstairs, waking me up. I sprang out of my bed, but I immediately ran to Jim's room to see if he'd made it back. I swung open his door, hoping to see his face, but instead I saw an empty room. I sulked for a second and then realized that he might be downstairs with my parents eating breakfast already.

Emotions were swinging quickly from highs to lows as I changed gears and began running down the stairs. I bypassed the tree, unlike my brothers, who seemed like they were little five-year-olds waiting for Santa's gifts. I was a blur as I slid into the kitchen, yelling, "Morning!"

Both my parents smiled at me, having their morning coffee, but Jim was nowhere to be found.

"Jim's not here?"

Dad said, "Not yet, Princess. You know his schedule isn't set like ours."

Mom said, "Come on, sit down, and have breakfast. And, Kirin … Merry Christmas."

I smiled at my mom and moved toward them as I gave them each a hug and a kiss.

I ate breakfast, but I wondered if every little sound I heard was Jim. While I was close with all my brothers, Jim from the very start had watched over me. From the time I first came to the States, he was always there to give advice and cheer me up. However, our time together was so short, and when he decided to enlist, the next thing I knew he was gone.

Jim would do his best to write to me all the time and call me to see how I was doing. But, the last several years he was more in the dark, rising quickly up the ranks and doing more covert missions. Our time, even digitally, was thin.

This Christmas day had been planned according to the same tradition: morning mass followed immediately by our Christmas lunch. We didn't have any friends or relatives who were gonna stop by this year because my mom wanted to keep it simple.

As the day passed by, I kept wondering if Jim was coming home. His last message to the family had said he would be home early on Christmas, but it was already late afternoon and still no sign of him. I looked outside, and the weather was just right with a slight skiff of snow, making for a picture-perfect scene.

Christmas was nearing its end, and we were all stuffed. We played board games, watched TV, and opened gifts from one another, yet as each minute passed, our awareness that Jim hadn't shown up grew. Even my mom seemed somewhat disappointed; unlike me, she hid it a lot better.

At 10:30 pm, everyone began heading up for bed. Mark, Steven, and Kyle looked exhausted from gaming all day and surprisingly didn't pull an all-nighter.

My mom asked, "Kirin, aren't you going up to bed?"

I said, "Mom, if you don't mind, I'll just sit by the Christmas tree."

My mom came near and kissed me on the head. "Don't stay up too late, sweetie."

Dad did the same thing and said, "Make sure you turn off the lights, Kirin."

I looked up and said, "Sure thing, Dad."

I sighed and stared at the lights on the Christmas tree. They were blinking on and off, and I enjoyed the decorations. Butterscotch and Bacon came by me and sat by my feet.

"Good girl," I told Butterscotch as I pet her on the head. Bacon looked at me all jealous, so I gave him his favorite belly rub. They had been chasing each other all day, and they looked all tuckered out. Butterscotch stayed with me for several minutes. Then, like the rest of the family, she headed up the stairs to sleep in one of my brothers' rooms. Bacon, on the other hand, feel asleep by my feet.

As I looked out the window at the snow falling, I saw not much was happening on the roads. Every so often, a beam of light would come, and I thought it might just be Jim. But thirty more minutes passed, and with each tick of the clock, I knew my wish for Christmas wasn't going to happen.

While many people look forward to getting things for Christmas, my wish every year was always the same. Having the entire family together on this day meant more to me than anything you can buy in the store. The last several months had been difficult for me since Sifu had left and I had no idea where he was or how he was doing.

I started to cry silently and soon fell asleep.

11:49 pm

I was in a deep sleep when I felt a kiss on my forehead. At first, I was in a daze as I looked up and couldn't quite make the figure. It took my eyes a few seconds to get used to the light.

The stranger said, "Hey you, don't tell me you waited up for me."

I rubbed my eyes and finally realized who it was. I jumped out of my chair and screamed, "Jim! You're home."

Jim said, "Shh, you'll wake up everybody."

I jumped up and gave him a big hug, squeezing him so tight. I started to cry and said, "You made it...."

Jim said, "Didn't I tell you I'd make it in time for Christmas?"

I asked, "What time is it?"

He looked at his watch. "It's 11:49 pm.... Sorry, kiddo, I know I came late, but I still kept my promise."

"Yes, you did, and you made it just in time for Christmas."

Suddenly, I heard a commotion upstairs. Butterscotch came running down the stairs, and then one by one my parents and brothers followed.

Everyone hugged Jim, and I got my wish for Christmas. We were all home safe and sound, and we were all together.

"We can live without material things, but we cannot live without each other."
—Sifu

Roll the Dice—1 Year, 191 Days

Tobias looked down at me and asked, "So, how many do you have left?"

"I've got twelve arrows left," I replied.

Hunter snapped around and said, "Only twelve?"

"Hey, it's not my fault! The last fight we got into, we used up all my supplies. Besides, the goal is to stay alive, right? Not save arrows."

Tobias said, "Well … then, make sure every shot counts."

Sage was busy dealing with our obstacle. Several huge pillars had collapsed in the room, blocking our way into the entrance. He said, "Well, at this point, we either figure a way to move this, or we have to go around."

I said, "As our strong men, you guys are telling me that Tobias the Barbarian and Hunter the Guardian can't lift them?"

Sage said, "Hey, how come you left me out?"

I replied, "Last time I checked, thieves were designed for sneaking around, not lifting huge objects."

"Okay, okay. Everyone, settle down. That's why you guys have me in the party. I'll conjure up a levitation spell, and the problem will be solved."

Gwen was on top of her battle-armored giant hamster, Scrambles. He was busy grazing on food and stuffing his face, while Gwen began searching through her book of spells.

Gwen said, "Ah, I found it!" She began chanting her spell and waving her hands around, finishing with a flourish. "Leviasa!"

We all looked at her, but none of the pillars moved.

Sage said, "Don't you mean Leviosa?"

Gwen snapped back at him and said, "It's Leviasa…. Do you want to get sued?"

We waited as she said the spell again, and this time a magical sparkle surrounded the pillars. They began to shake and then slowly float before crashing back to the ground.

"What gives?" I said, as a general moan of disappointment soon followed by the rest of our team.

"Dammit!" Gwen crossed her arms and pouted. "I can only levitate objects based on my current level."

We were exactly where we had begun several minutes ago. It appeared we had exhausted our options. But, I knew that there was always a way, and the answer was often right in front of you. I snapped my fingers. "I've got an idea."

Scrambles was carrying all our supplies as I pulled out his favorite food. I hid it from his view and walked toward the pillars.

"Hey, Tobias, can you help Gwen remove the supplies from Scrambles?"

I waited as Tobias showed off his strength by lifting all the supplies in one swoop.

I said, "Gwen, can you get off the battle hamster for a second?"

Scrambles was no longer encumbered with our supplies.

"Okay, everybody, get out of the way." The guys moved to the side, clearing a path to the pillars. From behind my back, I whipped out Scramble's favorite treat. He stopped chewing on his food, and his eyes popped open. He began to drool as I continued to wave the food from a distance back and forth. He was hypnotized by every move of his treat. Scrambles started shaking and then came charging toward me. He curled up into a ball and spun at full speed in my direction. I jumped out of the way, dodging his attack.

Crash!

As the dust and smoke settled, the pillars were smashed into pieces. I smiled at the result and dusted myself off. Scrambles approached me and waited for his reward.

"Good job, Scrambles," I said as he began stuffing his face with his treat. He looked cute and a little disgusting, and I decided to leave him alone.

"Way to go, Kirin!" shouted Gwen.

I said, "Tobias, Hunter, can you both put the supplies back on Scrambles?'

Gwen said, "Wait one second. That amount of weight, I can move." And, with that, Gwen said her little spell and was able to transport all the supplies to their original spot.

A huge double door entrance revealed itself in front of us. It was carved with ancient writings, and we wondered what it all could mean.

Sage said, "I don't like this one bit. These doors dwarf Scrambles, and you know what that means."

Hunter said, "Yeah, we need a bigger key."

Sage yelled, "No, you dumb ass! Big doors mean big creatures."

Hunter replied, "Yeah … yeah, you didn't let me finish."

Gwen said, "So, how do we open the door? Should I try an unlock spell?"

Sage said, "I could try picking the lock."

Tobias said, "Hunter and I can try to ram it down."

I walked up and turned the knob. When the door immediately opened, I turned around and gave everyone a funny look.

Gwen pointed at me and said, "Don't you dare say a word."

I giggled and bit my lip.

Tobias said, "Remember the goal. We beat whatever monster is in our way. Then we rescue Sifu and split the treasure."

Everyone nodded and prepared for the fight.

Tobias took a moment and began sharpening his axe. Hunter warmed up by swinging his sword and bashing his shield several times. Sage was spinning his double knives, ready for his sneak attack. Finally, Gwen was preparing chants to read for our fight. And I made sure I had enough arrows to unleash if necessary.

Tobias said, "Okay, everyone ready?" We all nodded and drew our weapons. "On the count of three, we all charge in. Got it? And remember your spacing."

We swung the door open, and we all charged in. We entered a huge, domed room with a white marble floor. Sage tapped my shoulder and pointed. "There's the treasure on the other side. It's so shiny."

I asked, "What about Sifu?"

Sage replied, "Oh yeah, he's here, too."

I said, "Quiet and concentrate."

Hunter said, "I don't like it. It's too easy. It's gotta be a trap."

"So, what should we do?" I asked.

Sage winked at me and said, "Let's spring the trap."

We began walking cautiously toward Sifu and the treasure. Suddenly, the room began to darken.

Gwen shouted, "Everyone scatter! Above us!"

We all jumped out of the way and then watched in horror. The ground shook, and the air smelled of wretched grease. The creature was unlike anything we could imagine.

Tobias said, "It's a burger?"

Sage said, "A colossal triple patty burger at that."

I thought, *God, I hate burgers.* It looked angry, growling at us and slamming its fist into the ground as it shook the very earth beneath us. Both Tobias and Hunter fell to the ground, but I was able to maintain my stance.

Sage turned to me and said, "Light him up!"

I grabbed two arrows from my quiver and launched them at the giant burger. They sailed through the air and penetrated its buns. The burger let out a huge roar, but it seemed to do nothing.

"Crap!" I shouted.

Tobias yelled, "Time for some ass kicking! Come on, Hunter. Let's rush this bitch."

"How do you know it's a girl?" asked Hunter.

Tobias shrugged as he held out his axe and began charging in. Hunter quickly caught up and did the same.

I prepared another arrow and said, "Sage, you know what to do." Sage nodded and quickly disappeared into the shadows.

Both Tobias and Hunter were swinging at the burger, sending chunks flying through the air.

"It's not doing any damage!" yelled Hunter.

Suddenly, the burger took a huge swipe, knocking both of them back to the ground.

I fired another arrow right into its face—or what I thought to be its face—and it yelled out again.

"Crap, it's not doing anything!" I decided to climb up and see if I could get it at a better angle.

The burger let out a huge scream and swung around, revealing Sage on its back as he went for his backstab. Sage smiled, and then the burger grabbed his leg, yanking him into the air.

"Oh, shit!" said Sage.

The next thing I knew, Sage was flying right into me, and we both hit the floor.

Hunter said, "None of our weapons are doing any damage to it. Gwen, do you have something?"

Gwen smiled and said, "Finally! I was hoping you'd ask."

I pushed Sage off me and said, "Whatever you're gonna do, do it fast."

She began chanting words from her book, "Dwarnuveous buffetaus." A huge cloud appeared in front of Gwen as a dozen dwarves popped out of nowhere.

Tobias shouted. "Dammit, Gwen, you low-level wizard! Couldn't you summon an army of dwarves with weapons at least?"

Gwen had an evil grin on her face as she then pointed the dwarves at the burger. She shouted, "Lunch time, boys!"

The dwarves looked ravenous. They were drooling and didn't hesitate to move in on the burger. We watched in amazement as twelve dwarves quickly began consuming a giant-sized triple burger right before our eyes.

Several minutes later, they were on the floor, picking their teeth, licking their fingers, and making nasty sounds from various parts of their bodies.

Tobias was checking on the other party members when I spotted Sifu in the distance.

I said, "I'll get Sifu."

As I began walking toward Sifu, he began to fade further away with each step. I decided to run toward him, but he kept drifting away from me. I screamed, "Sifu? Sifu! I'm coming to get you."

Sage shook me, "Wake up, Kirin!"

My eyes opened. Inches from my face were a pair of dice and a half-eaten burger. I quickly sat up and wiped the drool from my mouth.

"What's going on?" I mumbled.

Gwen said, "We got bored playing the game, and you ended up passing out. What gives? You've been so tired lately."

I said, "I've been training a lot."

Sage looked at me and said, "Uh, are you gonna eat the rest of your burger?"

I looked down and cringed. "Nah, you can have it."

Hunter said, "Rock, paper, scissors for the burger."

Sage said, "Two out of three?"

Hunter nodded and said, "Deal."

Gwen whispered into my ear, "You were mumbling all kinds of stuff in your sleep, Kirin." She giggled and said, "Pretty sure I heard you say Tobias and Hunter several times?"

"Oh, be quiet. What time is it anyway?"

Sage said, "It's only 9:15. Come on; let's finish the rest of this D&D session."

I looked at the guys and said, "I'm gonna call it a night." I couldn't believe that was all just a dream.

"A way will present itself, if you never stop trying."—Sifu

SECTION 2

Sifu's Journey Entry #10—Universal Harmony/ Come Talk to Me, Part 4

Mid-December 2030

For almost a year, Sifu had been in Japan. His training with Megumi's father was complete, and he said his goodbyes to her parents. It brought some relief to his aching heart that was still far from ever feeling closure. It had been a difficult journey, but a necessary one, filled with self-discoveries as well as the creation of lifelong friendships. He found it difficult to say farewell to his friend April, who had helped him along his path. Still, the time had come to say his goodbyes, as he was headed for the plane. Deep down, he was sure this would not be the last time they would be seeing each other.

On the Plane

Sifu did not dread the long flight back. He felt some sense of accomplishment as he looked forward to seeing Lance and his progress. Good fortune smiled upon him as the seat next to him was empty. It was only a matter of time before Sifu fell into another deep sleep.

⋏ ⋏ ⋏

Dreaming (continued)

Sifu was sitting at a restaurant with Megumi, enjoying their meal. She had been acting aloof all day. He watched her as she was eating her meal and could tell something was wrong.

"Megumi?" he asked, hoping that his timing was right.

She looked up slowly and forced a smile. "What is it, Bing?" she said softly.

Sifu hesitated and stared at her directly. "What's wrong, Megumi? You've been so distant today." He reached forward to hold her hand from across the table, but she pulled away before he could touch her. Her reaction confirmed his feelings. He looked slightly away and remained silent. He waited passively to see what Megumi would do next.

"Bing…." Her voice carried a tremble.

"Just talk to me, Megumi. What is it?" said Sifu.

"Bing, you know why I came to the States…?"

Sifu nodded and continued to look cautiously at Megumi. He was wondering where all this was leading.

Megumi cleared her throat as she said, "Well, you also know I wasn't supposed to stay here permanently."

"What are you trying to say?" Sifu leaned forward, knowing the answer to his question.

"I have to go back. Father's been hounding me to return." Her voice cracked.

Sifu shook his head, as his world suddenly felt like it was crumbling around him. "You can't go back…. You have to stay here." He blurted it out without hesitation or even thought.

"Bing, I was supposed to go back months ago. I kept giving Father excuses to prolong my stay, but it's come to the point where he's demanding that I go back home."

Sifu had no idea that Megumi had been prolonging her stay. He felt bad for a moment, but selfishness kicked in. He asked, "When do you have to go back?"

"Next week." Megumi bowed her head further. "Next Saturday, in the morning." Tears began rolling down her face.

Sifu's jaw dropped as the news caught him fully off guard. "I can't believe you didn't tell me about this. You're leaving … and you're leaving so soon." Sifu pulled away and began to choke up as well. He was hurt, confused, and lost as every emotion he was unfamiliar with attacked his heart.

Megumi felt heartbroken, as she could see and feel that the news was painful for Sifu to bear. Unsure what to do next, she sat quietly. Sifu felt lost as well. He sat there as they wept. Sifu then grabbed his wallet and placed some credits on the table. He got up from the table without saying a word and left for the exit.

Megumi began to tear up even more as she sat by herself. With all her effort, she finally got up from the seat and ran after Sifu. As she swung the door open, she looked around and finally spotted him walking away. She chased after him and cut off his path.

"Bing. Bing! I'm sorry, but there's nothing I can do," she cried hysterically. "I have to go back."

Sifu couldn't look her in the eye. Even though they were just inches away, he felt so withdrawn. He could hear her voice coming from her mouth, but he was silent.

Megumi said, "Bing. Please, don't be upset. Please, say something…. Come talk to me." She tried to force Sifu to make eye contact, but he refused.

Sifu's heart squeezed, as it pained him to see her suffer. But, for whatever reason, he couldn't say a word. The surprise devastated even Sifu, and he was unable to control his emotions for the first time.

Megumi began to weep in the middle of the sidewalk. Still without any eye contact, Sifu began walking away.

One Week Later

It had been a troubled week since Sifu had his discussion with Megumi. He had not called her this entire time, and was well aware that today she would be leaving for Japan. The night was restless as the break of dawn was nearing. Sifu had remained awake, as the uneasiness continued to press on him.

He stared at his phone and saw the time. The sight of the numbers made it surreal, yet it suddenly hit him that she would be gone. He shook his head to snap out of his week-long daze as he realized that the answer was simple. It always is. He thought, *I want her. I need her. Go get her.*

He sprang out of the bed and figured out what he wanted to do. He ran to his closet and opened his safe. There, he found it, untouched for years. He reached for it and opened a small container. His mother had said that, one day, when the time was right, he'd know when to use it. He smiled briefly, as the memory felt fresh, and he got dressed and ready to see Megumi.

Sifu ran like he never had before. The motivation was great to see her face once again. He was several minutes away from her, and it was the darkest moment before dawn. His exhaustion from the run was overcome by desire as he finally got to Megumi's apartment and took a moment to catch his breath.

"Holy crap," he said. "I never realized I still had it in me to run that far and that long." He took several deep breaths to try to stabilize his breathing.

He went to the front of the door and hit her buzzer. Several quick impatient pushes later, there was still no response from her. He panicked and wondered if she might still be asleep. He reached inside and pulled out his phone, and he began to call her and text.

What's going on? Why is she not answering? Is she mad at me? Sifu thought.

Sifu reached into his pocket and pulled out a deck of cards. He began slinging them one by one toward Megumi's window. Each hit the target and immediately bounced off. After emptying his entire deck, the results were no different. Her whereabouts were still unknown, and the street was littered with cards.

"Dammit, where could she be?" he said, frustrated. He began to pace back and forth.

Wondering what to do next, he thought, *It's possible she already headed off to the airport.* He snapped his fingers and quickly turned around. Suddenly, he bumped into a stranger who was accompanied by two companions.

"Oh, excuse me," said Sifu apologetically, still focused on his goal—seeing Megumi.

"You're excused," said the stranger as he quickly pulled out a knife and flashed it toward Sifu's face. His companions began to laugh as they surrounded Sifu.

"China man kinda early … all alone, I see," the stranger snickered.

Sifu said, "Look, this isn't really a good time, guys."

"Damn straight, it's not a good time for you," said the stranger as he waved the knife in front of Sifu's face.

"No, guys, you misunderstood me. I meant it's really, really not a good time for you. Tell yah what, I've got some spare credits in my wallet. You can have it all, and we can pretend this never happened." Sifu tried to negotiate a peaceful settlement to the situation.

"Don't you move," said the stranger. "Tell yah what, my companions are gonna take your wallet and anything else you got."

Sifu was trying to figure a way to resolve things peacefully, but he knew his time was limited if he wanted to find Megumi. The companions began searching through Sifu's stuff and got hold of his wallet. After a moment, one of the friends found something in Sifu's inner jacket.

"Well, well. What have we here?" said one of the companions as he began opening the little container.

"Don't touch that," said Sifu, who showed a hint of annoyance building up.

"Fuck you, man. Don't ya tell me what to do. I'll cut your bitch ass up," he said forcefully. The other guys still were circling close to Sifu as one of the companions gave his wallet and the container to the head guy.

"Guys, I totally want to apologize," said Sifu.

"Shut the hell up. Apologize for—?" said the stranger.

Just like that, Sifu sprang into action. The nearest guy happened to be the ring leader. Within a second, the knife was out of his hand, and a chop to his neck ensued. The force was just enough to stun him and drop him to the ground.

His two friends were in shock, and Sifu quickly turned around and blazed them both with several attacks. He made sure that the companions were out cold, but he did not end their time on earth that day. The speed and skill with which Sifu delivered his defense was mind-blowing. Within the blink of an eye, Sifu was in control of the entire situation. He had broken his own rule on self-defense but was more focused on the goal at hand.

Sifu went to grab his small container as well as his wallet. He opened it to make sure it was okay. He sighed in relief and placed it back in his sweater pocket.

"Dammit! You know you should've taken the offer. Now you've annoyed me, and I'm gonna give you nothing," said Sifu.

The guy was still gasping, holding his throat as Sifu looked around. Still, no one was in sight. Sifu thought for a moment that it was going to be difficult to find a taxi so early in the morning in this part of town. A strange idea popped into his head, and he went to the leader and grabbed his arm from behind, putting it in a lock.

"Oh shit, that hurts!" said the stranger, coughing the words out.

"I'm pretty sure you'll change your mind if I decide to break this arm of yours," said Sifu. Still pressed for time, Sifu checked his phone again and stared at the clock. As he kept the lock on the stranger and stared at his two companions who were knocked out, he quickly re-examined his crazy idea.

He squeezed the lock on the stranger and said, "Do you have a car nearby?"

"What? What's it to ya?" he yelled back at Sifu angrily.

Sifu put a pinch of extra pressure on the joint lock on the stranger, whose face was on the ground. "Do you have a car nearby?" The pressure grew greater than he could bear, and he screamed.

"Yes! Yes, I have a car. It's just around the corner…. Shit, don't break my arm!" He squirmed.

Sifu kept the lock on and searched the guy. "Is this your car key?"

"It's your mama's key."

Sifu shook his head and put extra pressure on the lock, asking no further questions.

"Yes! Yes, it's my goddamn car keys," shouted the stranger.

"Okay, I'm gonna take your car. Actually, I should say, I'm gonna borrow it for just a pinch," said Sifu.

"What the fuck are you talking about? You're gonna steal from me?" The man tried to squirm, but couldn't free himself from Sifu's lock.

"Steal? I clearly said 'borrow.'" Sifu chuckled at the suggestion. "Today's youth are just terrible listeners."

Sifu said, "If you get up after I let go of this lock, you are gonna be joining your two friends who are fast asleep. I want you to count to one hundred and then move. Nod your head if you understand."

The stranger nodded as Sifu cautiously let go and stood up.

"Let me hear you!" demanded Sifu.

"Uh … one, two, three…," said the stranger.

"Slower," said Sifu.

"Four … five…."

And with that, Sifu took the keys and began to run to the stranger's car. A minute passed as Sifu screeched by with the stranger's car. Still lying on the ground, counting, the stranger watched him pass. His scream faded into the distance.

"Myyy caaar! Fuuu…."

Twenty Minutes Later

Sifu disregarded the speed limit and every other rule of the road one could imagine. He came to a screeching halt at the departure area at O'Hare airport. He jumped out of the car and left it running in the no-parking area. The attendant shouted, "If you leave that car here, it'll be towed!"

Sifu smiled and said, "You should give me two tickets, just so I learn my lesson," and with that ran into the airport. It was busier than he expected, but he fought through the crowds to check out the boarding times. He began scanning through flights to see which one Megumi would be on. She had told him that it would be the early flight back to Japan. Finally, he saw the flight and began heading toward it.

Sifu quickly realized that there was no way he could go further into the airport without a ticket. He went to the counter and purchased a ticket. He was checking his time as he felt the pressure of it.

"Dammit, thirty minutes till they take off. They gotta be boarding by now." He thought, *Hurry! Hurry already.*

Sifu waited in line, going through the hassle and safety protocol at the gates. Even without any luggage, that venture ate up around twenty minutes. The slow, un-attentive guards and clueless passengers led to a longer-than-normal walk through. Once through, Sifu began running for the gate. He was moving from side to side, controlling his center with grace. He looked like he was floating through the heavy crowds that were unaware of his desired goal.

By the time Sifu got to the gate, he could see the plane pulling away.

"No ... no. No!" he shouted.

He ran up to the attendant and begged, "You have to stop that plane; I need to speak with someone on it."

The Japanese attendant held her composure and said, "Sorry, sir. That's impossible. Once it pulls from the gate, no one can stop it." She smiled, trying to ease the situation.

Sifu realized there was no arguing, as his face hugged the glass and watched, hoping that Megumi would see him one last time. He banged his head against the glass as his stomach sank. The realization of failure struck him deeply.

Why did I hesitate? he thought. He watched in sadness as the plane began its preparation. Several minutes later, it began its take-off. Each second was filled with agony and regret. He watched sadly as it left the ground and climbed into the air and quickly flew away from his sight.

Depression greeted Sifu as he walked away from the glass and sat on a chair. Minutes felt like hours. With his head hung as he slouched over, he reached into his pocket and pulled out the container. He stared at it, recalling what his mom had told him—that when she had passed away, she'd wanted Sifu to have this; that if he ever found someone who captured his heart, this would one day help him out. He stared at the tiny container as a tear fell from his cheek onto it.

He sighed and wondered if there was anything he could've done differently. He was in pain, wondering how things could change from happiness to pure dejection within a matter of a week.

He closed the container and hid its contents. Guilt joined him in his solitude. "Why?" he muttered as the crowds of people passed him by while he sat there lost in his own thoughts.

"Bing," a soft voice pierced the grumbles of the crowd and quickly eased the pain in his heart. He closed his eyes, pressing the tears to fall to the ground. Sifu was afraid to seek out the voice. He felt guilty for the way he had behaved and only turned toward its direction.

"Bing," the voice called again.

Sifu gathered his strength, breathing out slowly as he put the container he was holding back into his pocket. He looked up to see Megumi's face. She looked as surprised as he was.

He got up to approach her, and they both said, "What are you doing here?"

They shuffled awkwardly as Sifu made small talk.

Sifu said, "I thought I missed your flight."

Megumi's voice was soft as she said, "There were two morning flights. For some reason, something made me switch it at the last minute."

"Oh…," said Sifu as silence formed between the two, creating some tension. Sifu's heart was racing. He squeezed his fist and took the initiative, shaking himself out of his funk.

"I'm sorry. I don't know why I behaved that way," he said, trying to find the words to ask for forgiveness.

"Why are you here, Bing?" asked Megumi.

"All week long, I've been moping around, drowning in my own self-pity, and I realized how selfish I was being. I was asking you to stay just for me," said Sifu.

"I just wanted you to talk to me. I'm sorry I didn't say anything sooner. I was afraid how you might feel…. I, uh, I was afraid you might leave me," said Megumi as she hung her head in shame.

Sifu reached for her chin and lifted it up. "You have nothing to be sorry about. It was all me. I was afraid…. I was just too afraid to just … talk to you and tell you what's truly in my heart."

Megumi stared at Sifu as he gently brushed the tears from her face.

"When I walked out of the restaurant, I was lost. Every time you asked me to talk to you, it wasn't that I didn't want to. The reason I didn't speak is because I couldn't find a reason for you to stay that wasn't about me." Sifu then reached into his pocket as Megumi stared at him with loving eyes.

"I came running down to the airport because I finally realized that the simplest answer was right in front of me."

He smiled with his heart beating uncontrollably as he said, "If you need a reason to stay, I want to give you this one." He held the container in front of Megumi and opened it.

Her eyes widened in surprise as she was staring at a ring. The lights hit the diamond perfectly, and it reflected upon her face.

"Bing," she gasped as she brought her hands to her mouth to cover it.

Sifu held the ring steady, watching Megumi's reaction. She did not speak another word, and the moment of silence had Sifu unnerved. Suddenly, she leaped up toward Sifu, who caught her and felt her warm embrace. Sifu's senses were overwhelmed as her smell, her touch, her sight, and her sound surrounded him.

Sifu whispered in her ear, "Stay with me, Megumi. Let's begin a life together. I want to have kids, get a dog, buy a house, and grow old with you … and of course, love you forever."

Megumi hugged Sifu tightly and whispered, "Promise me."

Sifu said, "I promise."

"Life is short, like a dream. In just a blink, it can all be gone."—Sifu

CHAPTER 11

Haunting Past

Friday Afternoon, the Day Before the Dome

Watanabe looked outside as a mass of speckled dots were marching to the front of the UFMF building. He was in the middle of a phone conversation with Senator Collins. The protesting had increased over the last several months, much to Watanabe's liking. He smiled as he watched the chaos unfolding before his eyes.

"Watanabe … Watanabe, you still there?" said Senator Collins.

"Yes, Senator … of course." He continued to stare outside, cringing a bit as Collin's thick Southern accent sounded like fingernails scraping the chalkboard.

"So, you said you'd have something special for me several months ago, and I've been very patient."

"Ah, the beauty of the American culture, patience."

"Don't patronize me, Watanabe. You know how us Americans are…. Anyway, you can't tease me with a product and make me wait this long. Feels like forever waiting for that dang Chinese food to be delivered, don't it?"

Watanabe replied, "I'm Japanese."

"Yeah, yeah … whatever, yah all like rice, don't yah?" Collins bellowed a laugh.

Watanabe let Collin's ignorance slide by, as he found it amusing. He had bigger things on his mind and would tolerate it for the time being.

Watanabe said, "You're correct, Senator. Maybe a demonstration is in order."

"Now we're talking, Watanabe. I have my doubts that anything can be more impressive than your super soldier pill."

"Senator, I expect you to be pleased."

"So, what yah got for me?" asked Senator Collins.

"At this very moment, there's a demonstration taking place in front of our UFMF building…. My secretary has sent you a video feed for you to see."

"Yeah, I got it. Shit, these tree huggers are popping up everywhere. I'm telling yah, the new administration is soft, pandering to these bastards like they're in charge. At least when we first introduced the gun bill, we squashed these protests right away. But now, your employee Kirin Rise seems to have the country in a tailspin."

"Ah, yes ... anyway..." said Watanabe.

"I'm telling you, if I had it my way, I'd just get rid of the entire 'democratic' process and clean this mess up with a tank," said the senator. "Oh yeah, remember back in the days ... what was that, Tiananmen square?"

Watanabe ignored his comment and said, "Are you watching your screen right now, Senator?"

"Why yes, sir, I am."

"Can you see that main group of about twenty leading the mob into a frenzy?"

"I see it."

"Keep your eyes on the show. I'm sure you'll find it very ... uh, what's the word I'm looking for? Entertaining." Watanabe pulled out his lighter from his pocket and flicked it. He so enjoyed watching the flame wave around in the air.

As both gentlemen watched the screen, things were unfolding with the unruly mob just outside of the UFMF Tower. One of the STDs moved toward the front of the mob, while the rest of the STDs remained in a uniformed line. A handful of protestors were hurling rocks at him as he hid behind his single shield. Suddenly, he threw a canister in their vicinity, and they quickly dispersed. The group of twenty ran, thinking it was tear gas, but they quickly returned, laughing as nothing came out of the can. A minute passed as the lone STD lowered his shield and approached the unruly mob. The group of about twenty men and women surrounded him as the cameras continued to focus on this bizarre event. A minute passed, and the once-rambunctious crowd seemed to be talking to the STD patrol. He waved his hand, and the rest of the group began to file in a line and disperse in an orderly fashion.

Senator Collins replied, "Well, I'll be a son of a bitch."

Watanabe said, "That you are."

"Yah got me there, Watanabe.... Yah got me there. Anyway, did I just see the American dream?"

"I believe what you just saw is the dream of any governing institution ... law and order.

Senator Collins said, "Damn, yah Asians are just unbelievable. Yah darn right outdid yourself, Watanabe.... Like I always said, yah want something done right, yah do it yourself. Yah want something done great, get an Asian guy."

Watanabe placed his lighter into his pocket and went back to looking outside.

"I didn't think you'd come up with something better than a super soldier, but yah did."

"This is going to cost you, Senator."

"I'm fine with that.... Besides, I can live with giving away money and signing a big ole fat check to the UFMF. It's just the goddamn tax payers' money, so who cares?"

"It's going to be much more expensive than that."

The senator stopped his laughing as the mood turned serious. Collins spoke, "More expensive than money?"

Watanabe said, "You see, Senator, I've been around and have seen the world. There are places that exist where money doesn't mean anything.... What I want is far greater than the almighty dollar."

Senator Collins did not respond right away. When he did, his voice intensified over the air. "Now yah see, Watanabe ... everything was going so smoothly between us, until you got darn right greedy."

Watanabe listened in.

"You listen to me now, yah son of a bitch. I don't care what the hell kind of super drug you've created. Once this drug is in full effect, we're gonna do it my way. You'll hand it over to me, and I'm gonna write you that darn hefty check. It's win-win, as long as you play the game.

"I don't care how big the corporations are.... Perception is still reality, and you'll never be able to sell that companies can rule over the people directly. You still have to go through the government."

"Hmm," said Watanabe.

"Do we see eye to eye on this, Watanabe?"

"We're clear, Senator."

"Eye to eye." Collins chuckled. "Yah Asians can do that?"

Watanabe hung up, feeling a sense of relief at not having to hear the senator's voice. He walked over to the desk and stared at it. Atop the desk was a map of the entire earth. A total of five sets of color with different pieces spanned the board, with his red pieces blanketing the most—yet not enough to cover the entire map.

Watanabe spoke to himself, "We are definitely clear, Senator ... Eye for an eye."

Later That Night

It was late at night, and only two people could be found working at the main headquarters of the UFMF. The huge TV screen was projecting highlights to watch for this weekend's event, but neither Kristen nor Watanabe showed any concern.

Kristen was busy on her pad as she worked across from Watanabe. She looked up to see him staring outside for the first time. Kristen, like many others, admired Watanabe. There was something about him that stood out from everyone else. She removed her glasses and took her first break.

She spoke, "Sir…."

Watanabe spun his chair slightly and looked at her. "Yes, Kristen."

"Sir, you sure you don't want to fly down for the match tomorrow?"

Watanabe rubbed his chin and said, "I guess I'm a little superstitious, but the truth is I've never seen it live."

Kristen's eyes perked up as that news came as a surprise. "Sir?"

Watanabe chuckled. "I'm wondering what's more surprising to you, Kristen. Is it the fact that I've never gone or that I'm a bit superstitious?"

Kristen thought about it and answered, "I guess both, sir."

Watanabe grabbed a drink and poured one for himself as well as for Kristen. He motioned to her to have some. He spoke in Japanese, "Nonde Kudasai."

Kristen bowed slightly and replied, "Domo."

Watanabe lifted his glass as he said, "Kanpai!" He took a sip of the drink and enjoyed it. Then he shifted his eyes to stare at Kristen.

"I hate to be rude, sir, but you don't seem to be the superstitious type."

"Very good, Kristen…. Like always, you've got a keen eye for the truth."

Kristen nodded and waited for the answer.

"I never venture too far away from what's most important. Watching the fight is a mere distraction, as the value of all our work lies right here in this very building."

"Sir?"

"Protect what is yours at all cost. The work being done here in this facility is my prized possession. It is the source of everything that we do." Watanabe poured another drink for himself and motioned to Kristen to see if she'd like another.

"No, thank you, sir."

He said, "Kristen … were you upset when I decided to give the position to Thorne, instead of you?"

Kristen was still drinking and remained calm. She lowered her cup and wiped her face before answering Watanabe truthfully.

"I was, sir, but I believe the correct word to describe it would be 'disappointed.'"

"You know, the decision was a difficult one since you and Thorne share many of the same characteristics."

Kristen struck back, "Do you still believe you made the correct decision?"

Watanabe smiled and said, "I like that about you. You have always been … fearless. Even when talking to your superior, you don't back down."

Kristen smiled and sat up. "Most men would call a woman with that kind of attitude a bitch."

"Mmm, I'm not like most men," said Watanabe.

"No, you're not," said Kristen as she took her last sip from her cup.

Watanabe said, "Kristen, I believe I owe you an answer to that question."

"Fair enough, sir."

Just as he was about to speak, the TV screen flashed the mob demonstration that had occurred that morning. Reporters were speculating on what they had seen, but all were clueless to the truth.

"Seems that was a success, sir," said Kristen.

"Caution, Kristen. Be very careful how one defines success."

"Wouldn't you, sir? You have Collins nibbling at the bait, and he's being led like a lamb to the slaughter."

"I don't take much pride in this battle, Kristen. Collins is a typical senator, short-sighted and filled with lust for greed and power. This type of game somewhat bores me, since they fall over just as you expect."

"What is the game, sir?"

"That is the billion-dollar question, is it not, Kristen? What is the game? You see, I envision a world that goes beyond the greed of the leaders of today. Take, for example, all these pharmaceuticals and corporations racing to find cures to diseases…. Can you imagine if the day ever came when they discovered how to deal with this? Like animals, they would lose control of such a gem, and prioritize in regard to how they can maximize the amount of profit to the hilt."

"Sir?"

"Ask yourself: if they did find a cure to, say, anything, would they ever give it out? Or, would they leak it out to the point where it helps the individual but he or she would forever be a lifelong customer?"

"The latter, sir."

"And therein lies the problem: the infinite repetition that has continued to occur since man became aware of his own power. The world I see needs to be controlled by the right person ... who has an interest in something greater than lining his or her pockets. So, when the time comes, we can create that society that goes beyond its own pettiness."

He turned to look at her and added, "And, that's where you come in."

"Sir?"

"I won't be around forever ... but I'll need someone who shares the same vision as I do ... and, thus, Kristen, the answer to your question."

Kristen was caught off guard and had a puzzled look on her face. She stared at Watanabe and waited for the answer.

"I believe you are the one who can take my place."

Kristen looked surprised, and her hand twitched, spilling some of her drink. "Sir ... I ... don't know what to say."

"I guess there's a first time for everything." Watanabe chuckled and drank again.

"Sir, do you mind ... what about Thorne?"

"Ah, my dear friend Thorne ... I love him like my own son, but his error from last year can be forgiven, but not forgotten."

Kristen looked away and thought about Watanabe's words.

Therein lies the difference between the two of you....

"Anyway, is everything in place for tomorrow's fight?"

Kristen replied, "Justice has been doing exactly as he's been told. He's been toning down his fight till the time is right."

Watanabe said, "Will you be making that decision when to unleash him?"

"He's skilled at only one thing. I'll do my job, and he'll follow it. It's very simple."

"How about our insurance policy?"

"I've spoken to Thorne, and he's got his man on tight strings like a puppet."

Watanabe said, "And there you have it, Kristen. Thorne's error was banking on the will of others, believing that Diesel could do the task set forth. Thus, why have one insurance policy when you can have two?"

"Excuse me, sir, but aren't we doing the same thing, banking on Justice and Thorne's puppet?"

"Almost ... but I'm betting that, in the end, our little rising star will find a way to lose on her own."

Kristen said, "Well, she's deviated from the plan and has been tearing into her opponents."

"Oh, Kristen ... that's a good thing."

"Sir?"

"I would be most disappointed if she had not. In fact, I quite enjoy that little fight in her.... Predictability is a most defining characteristic. Never forget that, and cherish that challenge. Kirin straying and creating a bit of chaos is most refreshing."

"Still, sir, you seem quite confident that everything will go exactly as planned."

"In the end, it is not the control that you have over others, but ultimately the control you have over yourself.... That is how I know it will all work out."

The Semifinal

Linkwater was hyping the match; he and Connor seemed like fans, excited for the battle to begin. Their emotions couldn't be contained and was contagious to all. The same team from the previous year had assembled again with Krenzel, Stabler, and Grandmaster Chang rounding out the panel of experts.

Krenzel said, "The crowd here in L.A. seems to be as surprised as we are gentlemen."

Connor said, "The odds maker would've never predicted that the three-time champion would be going head to head against a reality-based fighter who qualified for the wild card."

Stabler said, "Well, the odds maker couldn't have been more off than last year with Kirin Rise."

Krenzel said, "Agreed. I bet Vegas is scrambling right now."

Linkwater said, "Regardless, we all are waiting to see who will fight Kirin Rise for the championship. It would appear the three-time champion Dryden Rodriguez should have an easy time with this wild card, but after last year, you just never know."

"While Justice was impressive to win the battle royal, his run through the round robin hasn't been entirely dominating," said Krenzel.

Stabler said, "That's true, but a win is a win, and he still ended up beating the UFMF champion from Japan and the highly favored fighter Chapman in his draw."

Connor said, "On the other hand, the champion has been more dominating than ever; he's managed to finish off his matches in under a minute. I'm going to have to go with the champion. This may be a difficult fight, but he should be able to bring it home by the third round."

Linkwater asked, "Grandmaster Chang … Justice has declared his style of fighting is mixed. However, many people are saying his fighting looks surprisingly much like Kirin Rise's. Do you agree with that?"

Grandmaster Chang replied, "For the average couch potato Joe watching the UFMF fights, it would seem to be the case… but having trained in the art for almost half a century, I can tell you that their styles are totally different from one another."

Stabler said, "And the moment we've been waiting for…. the second half of the semifinals to see who will fight for the Dome Championship here in L.A.!"

The next thirty minutes were filled with introductions from both sides. Justice stood across from Rodriguez as the crowd continued to shout out the champion's name. Rodriguez was old school and one of the few to wear the traditional uniforms that he trained in. He stood only a few inches taller than Justice. Rodriguez was in great shape, but did not have a daunting figure like most of the UFMF fighters.

Kirin was with Bryce and most of the gang watching on the TV. Like everyone else, they were glued to the set, waiting to see who her next opponent would be.

Gwen and Sage sat next to each other. Gwen said, "Is it just me, or is Justice kinda cute?"

Sage looked at her and said, "Hey!"

Gwen quickly turned toward him and pulled him by his tie to give him a kiss. Sage blushed and turned around to the group and said, "Yah see, brains over brawn."

Danny shouted, "You! Down in front. I'm not here to watch a love story."

Ken said, "Yeah, because we saw that on Kirin's birthday party that you set up."

Doc turned around and said, "Guys … seriously, we made a vow never to speak of that night again."

Robert replied, "You may not need to speak of it, but I've been showering several times a day to get rid of the stink."

Big T said, "Not sure what you're all complaining about. I had a good time."

"That's because you're used to that sort of thing!" Danny shouted toward Big T.

"What yah talking about? I've never been arrested," said Big T.

"Oh," said Danny.

"Yeah, that's racist, Danny," said Ken.

"Seriously, Big T, you've never been arrested before?" said Robert.

"Dick!" said Big T.

Robert replied by raising his hand. "Present."

Kirin waved down her friends and said to Bryce, "You see what you signed up for?"

Bryce laughed and said, "It's all in fun, Kirin."

Ryan said, "Quiet, everybody! They're doing the stare-down."

The referee called both Justice and Rodriguez to the center of the ring. He said, "Now, both of you know the rules."

The two men seemed to have mutual respect as Justice extended his hand and Dryden shook it firmly. Justice smiled at the champion and said, "Good luck." The champion acknowledged his statement with a simple bow.

The crowd continued their boisterous cheers, knowing the winner would fight Kirin. They had been waiting to see the three-time champion go against last year's champ for the ultimate rematch. While many had been impressed with Justice's success, only a few gave him the chance to win this fight. The champion had displayed a dominating performance for the entire season.

Justice stood silently awaiting the call, eerily resembling Kirin just before her matches. Dryden, on the other side, was confident and was hopping around.

The level of intensity was at an all-time high. The referee waited for the bell, and then waved both fighters to begin. He shouted, "Let's get it on.... Fight!"

Justice moved slowly forward and paused in his stance. He looked like ice with no emotion. Suddenly, Dryden went for a shoot to the legs. Immediately, Justice closed the gap, and managed to time it perfectly as the champion ate his knee on the way down. That move caused Dryden's head to pop up, and Justice took advantage of it.

Kirin watched and was the only one to scream. "No!"

In a blink, Justice snapped Dryden's exposed neck like a twig, and the champion fell to the ground and lay limp.

It happened so quickly that no one was aware of what had just happened. The crowd was cheering, and suddenly the noise began to dwindle down.

Justice turned around and walked away. The referee finally went to see if Dryden was okay. As he kneeled by Dryden, he had a look of panic on his face as he tried to wave down the medical staff.

Bryce said, "What's going on?"

Sage added, "He's not moving. I didn't see what happened. It was too quick!"

Kirin turned toward her friends and said, "He killed him."

Linkwater and Connor began trying to assess the situation.

Connor said, "The champ is not moving."

Stabler chimed in and said, "Let's replay that again in slow motion."

As the world watched and the crew looked on, there was steady silence throughout the broadcast. Even the crowd was stunned and unsure of the moment.

Krenzel said, "My god."

Grandmaster Chang said, "He might just be knocked out cold."

As the rest of the crew was recovering from the shock, Stabler took over and continued to announce. "The UFMF has the best medical staff ... and I don't want to assume what's happened out of respect for the family involved."

More crew began piling into the ring, and Dryden's entourage was clamoring back and forth between one another. Justice stood before the crowd and raised his hands. They began chanting his name, even after the viciousness he had just inflicted.

Kirin watched and shook her head. She thought, *That monster ... he needs to be stopped.*

Saturday Evening, at the Weigh-In

Kirin watched from the shadows as Thorne called out Justice for the initial weigh-in. He walked in confidently, going directly toward Thorne without making any motion to acknowledge the screaming fans. They, however, did not appear to care as his intensity was mesmerizing. Justice had quickly amassed a huge following. From behind, the sponsors were salivating and taking advantage of this newfound hero.

Kirin felt sick to her stomach. She had just witnessed Dryden's life be quickly snuffed out at the hands of Justice. He appeared to have no remorse at the time, like he had planned it all along. Kirin waited for them to call her name and stared down Justice once she heard it.

Thorne said, "And last year's defending champion of the Dome, the ever beautiful but deadly Kirin Rise!"

Kirin was still a star as the fans chanted her name and screamed. However, she was focused on Justice and was able to silence the distractions. From a distance, she noticed the moment he moved. Justice did not take his eyes of her. They began a stare-down the moment she moved and continued to do so till they were a mere foot apart from one another.

Thorne smiled as the crowd waited in anticipation. He waved them down so he could speak. He was the center of attention as always, and the lights glistened upon him, as if he were a god. He began to speak. "If you believed last year to be the most stunning fight in UFMF history, be prepared to do it all over again. Tonight's fight is going to be the greatest—"

"Shut up!" said Kirin.

"Excuse me?" Thorne looked at her with surprise and then contempt.

She kept staring at Justice and said, "You heard me," as if Thorne was of little concern to her. Justice remained silent as usual and continued to stare her down. The intensity between the two fighters wasn't just for show.

Kirin finally broke her silence and said, "You're a disgrace ... you know that? You're a disgrace to the school and everything that it stands for, and I, for one, will never ever call you my Si-hing." She shook her head in shame and clenched her fist, as her heart was racing and her rage was about to explode.

Kirin's comment finally provoked a reaction from Justice, and he cracked smile. "So ... the old man finally told you about me." His voice was that of nightmares, low and scratchy.

"So, the dog can talk?" said Kirin.

The snide comment made Justice cringe. He felt it and reached within to calm himself down. He continued to stare down Kirin and took a small breath before speaking. "Patience, Kirin ... a lesson I'm sure the old man will reveal to you one of these days."

"You make me sick."

Justice chuckled. "To make is to control. If that is the case, you still have much to learn.... You'll find out soon enough when we meet in the Dome tomorrow." He paused and said, "The old man's holding back on you, Kirin."

"Show some respect.... It's Sifu."

"He's gotten soft and has bowed down to tradition, instead of adapting to the future.... You know that was his problem." Justice shook his head in disgust. "What's the point of all this training if you have all this power and never use it?"

Kirin snapped back. "Power, control ... you're no better than this million-dollar-suit buffoon standing next to me, who would rather see this world burn in front of his eyes."

"Careful, Kirin. Sifu's karma isn't as clean as you think."

His comment caught her slightly off guard, making her wonder.

Justice noticed her reaction and said, "I can tell the old man hasn't told you everything."

Kirin hated the disrespect. It annoyed her when anyone called Sifu something other than his proper title. She said, "He's told me enough. He's taught me what happens when you don't know how to control the skill that was given to you.... You end up like yourself ... a monster just like Thorne."

"You see, again with the talking.... Unlike the old man, I'm at least using my skill. Let's face it: all his skill didn't save his family's life, did it?"

Her eyes widened as the emotion swelled from the inside and could no longer be contained. Kirin teared up as the faces of Simo and all the kids burst in front of her. She took a swipe at Justice.

Swoosh.

Justice immediately blocked it and controlled her hand. She trembled in anger as Justice said, "See, Kirin? Unlike you, I know the entire art. Let's face it ... I'm better than you in every way."

He slapped Kirin with his other hand, and the impact spun her around and sent her flying back. Chaos was about to ensue, but several handlers grabbed Kirin, preventing the situation from exploding. Two other handlers blocked Justice from Kirin, hoping to calm the situation. The crowd was on its feet, and the cameras zoomed in to the action.

Kirin wasn't having any of this. There was no way Justice was going to have the edge on her again. She was being held back by two of the handlers when she went with the force and broke their grasp. She did her best not to hurt them since they were just doing their job. Kirin tossed one of the handlers into the other to run interference. Though the man was bigger, Kirin threw him as easily as a rag doll. His center was off balance, and he tumbled into his partner. Her attention quickly snapped back to Justice.

The crowd, both in person and on TV, was in shock. This moment was unplanned, onstage, and completely raw. It was surprisingly quiet as most of the noise was being created on the stage below.

Justice wanted to end this moment now, even before the fight. Unlike Kirin, he did two quick attacks and knocked the handlers, in his way, unconscious. The speed was a mere flash as neither one of the handlers knew what was coming.

Thorne shouted, "Justice! No!"

The path was clear for both Justice and Kirin, and their training kicked in. They closed the gap without hesitation, as a switch flipped in each of them. Kirin's emotion took control. She wanted a piece of Justice, for their last encounters as well as everything that he stood for.

Thorne motioned to the rest of the handlers to try to contain the situation. He stepped back, out of the way, and could do nothing else but watch.

As they both entered kick range, Kirin lacked the patience and threw out the first attack. Justice had the experience and quickly countered it. She exposed herself right away, as she was going for the kill and invested heavily in her first attack. Justice made her pay the price, landing several combinations and sending her crashing back.

Kirin flew to the ground and wiped the blood from her mouth. She was tenacious and went in for an attack again before the pain could even set in. The speed at which she got back up and closed the gap seemed almost super human. Her emotions were her fuel, but they were blinding her from the control needed to deal with her opponent.

Thorne shouted again, "Justice!"

The handlers came one by one to try to stop the fighting. Anything and everything in Justice's way was being destroyed. As each handler approached within his range, he laid down a path of destruction. Justice quickly launched several attacks and sent them flying from all directions. Soon, even the handlers were hesitant to try to deal with Justice.

Kirin, on the other hand, evaded their attempts. Each move of her center was to get to Justice. Those in her way were stumbling out of control, unable to get a grip on her.

Thorne looked at Fawn and said, "Get security in here, right away! Tell them to send everyone."

Fawn said, "Everyone?"

"EVERYONE!" Thorne had lost his cool and shivered from anger.

Fawn's eyes bugged as he dropped his walking cane and ran away. "Yes, boss!" He screamed it from a distance with his hands flopping around in a panic.

Kirin closed the gap while Justice was busy dealing with one of the handlers. His back was turned for a split second, giving her the perfect opportunity. She went in for another punch and launched it with no restraint. Justice snapped around and caught Kirin's arm in a trap.

She was in shock. How could he tell? How did he time it so perfectly?

He smiled at her and said, "You're lucky I don't break this."

His brief monologue gave her the opportunity to counter the trap. As soon as she saved her arm, she threw a blur of attacks at Justice, hoping that one of them would connect. Justice was smooth and calm. He allowed each of the attacks to get closer and closer, but at the last second he would change angle and avoid the impact.

They were exchanging attacks and blocks between one another. Justice started to attack heavier, and Kirin found herself on the defensive. She was blocking lightning-fast attacks one after another. The quick shift and angles of her hands made her dodge the attacks just out of harm's way. They were applying Sifu's training with precision, and all those watching were in awe.

After several exchanges, they found themselves at a stalemate, as each one was neutralizing one another. Kirin looked at Justice and said, "Your skill is far from Sifu's."

Justice took offense at the insult. His eyes lit up as he looked past Kirin's gaze and stared directly into her soul. He suddenly smiled at her. Kirin was matching his force when she felt a change in what she was feeling from Justice. It was a technique that Sifu had used with her before, which she recognized right away. Justice sneered and said, "Are you sure, Kirin?"

The look of panic ran through her as she thought, *Crap*.

Her hands felt frozen for a split second as the force surged through her entire body. She knew an attack was coming but could not react in time to counter it. Suddenly Justice pulled her toward him and then launched a kick to her chest. She flew backward, knocking over several handlers. Kirin sprawled on her knees as she rubbed her chest in pain. She was about to get up and attack again, but over a dozen security officers pinned her down.

Several security guards pulled out their tasers and aimed them at Justice. He held his hands up and smiled as he stared at Kirin and taunted her further.

Fawn was scrambling like a chicken waving his hands in the air as he screamed, "Stop fighting. Stop fighting!"

"When you allow greed and anger to take over your spirit, then stupidity will surely follow."—Sifu

SECTION 1

Short Stories #11—Kirin's P.O.V.

<u>Team Work—1 Year, 216 Days</u>

T obias was barking out orders and positioning the group exactly where he wanted. He was pointing to the other group that stood from afar and making sure everyone knew their assignments. He shouted, "Just remember to follow my lead!" Watching him was humbling, since he had finally assumed the responsibility of the school leader in Sifu's absence.

One by one, the guys confirmed with a response as we prepared to go into battle.

He turned to each one of us and said, "What's the number one rule we don't break?"

Danny responded, "Stick together. Period."

Tobias said, "Did everyone hear that?"

I nodded my head, but it was difficult to hear as the crowd around us was extremely loud. I figured, *If he's not on my side, punch him.*

I looked around as everyone was placing their last-minute bets on the fight. This was our third gang fight that we ventured into. We were forced to do this instead of the usual solo challenge matches, since we were barely able to pay for the school's monthly rent.

Our reputation had grown even more. Not only had we won challenge matches and kept the school open, but we were dominating the underground fighting circuit.

I looked across, seeing that the numbers were not in our favor. In fact, the other group outnumbered us by five. However, the uneven number meant a higher return on the bet. While our skills weren't affected by the size of an opponent, the guys we were going to be fighting looked like they were juiced up on roids.

Danny said, "Not that I wasn't paying attention, but we have an uneven number to deal with. Do we just close the gap like always?"

I said, "What about Ryan? He's still not here."

Ken said, "We can't worry about him right now. It's up to us."

Tobias said, "We stick to my strategy. I'm gonna move in first and draw as many of them as possible. While they are busy dealing with me, you guys pick off the stragglers."

Robert said, "You're gonna go in first solo?"

Tobias nodded, "That's the plan," and winked at me.

Big T asked, "This is Wing Chun strategy, how?"

Tobias said, "I'll get them to react to me, and you guys counter it."

Robert said, "Uh ... isn't that a bit reckless?"

Tobias said, "No. I'm sure they won't expect it, and that'll give us the edge."

I turned to Doc and said, "Doc, does this make sense?"

Doc nodded and said, "In theory, I get it."

Ken shouted, "Just make sure you leave me some guys!"

With one raised eyebrow Tobias turned around and looked at Ken.

Ken pointed at him. "Don't.... You know what I mean. Not that there's anything wrong with it."

We all waited for the guy to signal for the fight to begin. My heart was racing even though I now had several fights under my belt. I thought, *Mom and Dad would kill me if they knew this is what I was doing tonight.*

Suddenly, we heard laughter break out from the crowd, as an opening revealed the joke. There was Ryan, dressed up in a Godzilla suit as he finally came to join us for the fight.

I said, "Uh, what the heck is going on?"

Ryan came running up to our group and was out of breath. "Sorry, guys, I tried to come here as soon as possible, but they kept me later than I expected at work."

Robert burst out in laughter. "Jesus, what the fuck is with the Godzilla outfit?"

Ryan said, "What? I work at Godzilla pizza.... I'm the dude who holds up the sign to bring people in."

I couldn't help but crack a smile. Only Ryan knew how to break the tension quickly.

Danny said, "Dude, aren't you going to remove your outfit for the fight?"

Ryan replied, "Unless you want me to fight in my underwear, then the answer is no."

Robert said, "Are you sure you can fight in that?"

Ryan smiled. "Hey, this is more comfortable than my kicking jeans."

Tobias waved everyone down and said, "Okay, okay. Everyone stay focused and remember what we are fighting for. We win this, and we can pay for this month's rent on the school."

I looked at each one of the guys. Their game faces were definitely on. Tobias turned around as I stood by him. He looked at me and said, "Kirin, stay by Ryan at all times!"

"I can fight!" I shouted back.

"You don't have the experience, Kirin. Just do as I say, will you?" Then he snapped back to prepare for the fight.

Both sides waited for the main guy to initiate the fight. He looked to the left and then to the right, as he raised his hand up and swung it down to begin the battle.

I checked our group out one last time as Tobias stood in front. Just like he said, as soon as the signal was given, he moved in first by himself. He walked casually toward the other group, but I saw him make the sign of the cross before the fight began.

One of the guys shouted, "God's not gonna help you today, my friend!"

Tobias continued walking toward them and replied, "Oh no, you have it mistaken. I'm asking God for forgiveness in advance."

I said to Ryan, "Geez, he's crazy."

Ryan pointed at himself. "You sure about that?"

Doc was keeping watch as the other guys started surrounding Tobias. Doc shouted, "Now! Everyone move in now!"

We all rushed in and were picking off the scraps that Tobias was tossing to us. I stuck by Ryan, initially just as Tobias had asked me to. It was total chaos. Whenever a battle starts, all the plans go to hell. I was busy rearranging this guy's face when I caught sight of Danny fending off three individuals.

I shouted, "Danny!"

I heard Tobias yell, "Stay with the group! I'll help him," but he was busy fending off several of the attackers and so was Ryan.

It was too late. I was determined to do the deed and ran off to help Danny. He had gotten separated from our group and was taking a pounding from three guys. He was doing his best to block their attacks while on the ground. However, several got through, and the pounding continued. I shook my head and thought, *Danny's always the first one not to listen.*

As I got there, the biggest guy was busy using Danny's ribs as a welcome mat. His legs were spread open, and my adrenaline was pumping. I thought, *Let's hear him sing.* With a quick rush and no hesitation, I sent a kick flying from behind and into his groin. I connected and waited to see him crumble, but he didn't. He slowly turned around and looked down on me; I was shocked.

I looked up and ate a slap that sent me flying. I quickly shook it off and closed the gap again. There was no way my kick hadn't connected, so I thought the second time should be the charm.

As he was distracted beating on Danny, I gave it my all and hit him again at the same spot. This time, I gave him an upper cut and the result was immediate as he fell to his knees and rolled over. He looked up to me from the ground, and I greeted him with a foot stomp to the face. I said, "Good night!" He was out cold, but the attention of the other two guys quickly shifted to me.

They hesitated, taking a break from pounding on Danny, and I moved in right away. The closest guy went for a wild swing as I focused all my efforts on his center. He quickly crumpled to the ground. His hit never even reached me as the impact of my fist was true. Suddenly, I felt myself being grabbed from behind in a bear hug. I tensed up for just a second, which allowed him to lift me off the ground.

I remembered my training and relaxed my entire body, making it difficult for him to control me. As he struggled to find his grip, I landed on his foot, breaking his grip. I quickly spun, swinging my ponytail at his eyes to distract him further. I thought, *What the heck? That actually worked!* Once he was stunned, I sent a combinations of elbows to his face. He dropped like a rock while the other guys were busy with their own opponents.

I had a moment to breathe as I hovered over Danny to see if he was okay.

"Dammit, didn't Tobias say stick together?" I shouted at him, trying to help him get up.

Danny said, "It's not my fault, I was covering our flank, and I got drawn away from the group."

"They were baiting you to separate, Danny!"

He grabbed his ribs and sat back up. "Ouch."

I checked on him and was about to stand up when—

"Duck!"

I did just as I had heard. A body flew right over our heads. Moments later, the dust settled, and chaos quickly changed to elation, as the fight was completely over.

Tobias came running over to me as I smiled. The rest of the gang was celebrating as they came to see if Danny was okay. As I was about to open my mouth, he shouted, "What the hell was that?"

I was surprised that he was upset and said, "What do you mean?"

"What did I tell you to do?"

I didn't answer but stared at him directly.

He got right in my face and said, "Stay by Ryan. That's all I asked for you to do ... and did you do that? Noooo!"

I refused to back down as I shouted back, "Would you rather I do nothing and let Danny get pounded on?"

"This is your problem, Kirin. You do everything on your own, without thinking things out." He raised his hand, clenched his fist, and then spun around and walked away.

I threw my hands up in the air in frustration and did the same.

Robert walked up and tried to calm everyone down. "Okay, okay ... it's in the heat of the battle, so everyone chill. Besides, look at what I have." Robert raised the credits that we had won, which was a significant amount. The guys were busy celebrating, but Tobias once again got under my skin.

I was too upset to care as I walked away, but there was something troubling more than Tobias. I thought, *How'd that one guy take that full hit to the center and not feel it? Did I miss?* I didn't mention it to the other guys, who were too busy celebrating, but it just seemed odd.

"Nothing is more powerful when the many can function as one."—Sifu

Friends—1 Year, 236 Days

I was out by myself again, which would've driven Tobias as well as my parents crazy. I was watching one of the matches, and the amount of credits being exchanged that night was high. I knew we needed more credits to keep the school open for another month. It seemed like a struggle even with our success. We all had finally realized the sacrifices Sifu must've made to keep the school open even though it wasn't profitable.

I was looking for a chance to get in on the action. As they were calling for volunteers for the next match, I was about to step in, when I was grabbed by the arm and dragged in from the side.

"Come on, slow poke. Walk with me," Ripley said.

"What are you doing?" I asked.

She winked at me and said, "Just follow my lead."

The ring leader asked, "Well, what do we have here? It seems we have Whiskey along with her friend. Every guy's dream come true—two girls at the same time."

The crowd laughed, but I didn't appreciate the joke. I saw that Whiskey rolled her eyes and twitched her lips.

"So, what say you? Who wants to go two-on-two with these beautiful girls?"

Ripley looked at me and said, "How many credits do you have on you?"

I said, "A hundred."

Ripley gave me a look and said, "A hundred? Jeez, I'm sure your parents give you more money than that for allowance, Kirin. Fine. Give it to me." She opened her hand and wiggled her fingers, waiting for my donation.

I don't know why, but I just handed over the credits. She walked to the main guy and said to him, "Here's three hundred credits on us."

He said, "Wow, three hundred credits from this beautiful dynamic duo! Who wants—?"

Ripley said, "Three hundred credits, not two-on-two, but two-on-four."

His eyes lit up with surprise. "Did you hear that, fellas? Two versus four with three hundred credits on the line. And to sweeten the deal, whoever enters, I'll double the amount of the winnings."

Ripley walked back to me as the betting went into a frenzy.

I said, "Two-on-four? Are you crazy?"

"Relax, we can both kick ass. Besides, you want the money, right?"

I decided to keep quiet, since I didn't want Ripley to have any idea what was happening with our school. After several minutes passed, four guys were lined up from a distance against us. They were your typical street thugs, who looked like they thought this was easy cash.

The ring leader said, "When you're ready, fight."

The main guy of the group stepped up and began mouthing off. "Whiskey. Well, well, I bet this isn't the first time you've been surrounded by several guys."

"No, but I'm sure this is the first time you've been with a girl." She mouthed off back to them.

His friends started laughing at him and jeering him on. He pointed toward Ripley and said, "I'm gonna finish you quickly."

Ripley replied, "Being this is your first time, I'm surprised you didn't finish already."

He stomped back angrily toward his companions.

I said, "Give me Mr. Big Mouth."

Ripley nodded. "Let's make this quick."

I nodded back.

Mr. Big Mouth came charging in with a flying side kick. I chuckled at the attack and quickly stepped to the side. As he turned around, I made sure he'd have a hard time procreating in the future, so I punched him hard in the groin. He stood there, tearing up as he silently squatted in place and teetered over.

Ripley shouted back at me, "Double tap!"

I said, "What?"

"Hit him again," she said in a condescending voice.

I was just about to walk away, but I ended up spinning around and kicking him one more time in the groin. He was out cold.

I shouted, "Behind you!"

She heard me and thrust an elbow behind her as another chump tried to get the edge. She moved in a circular motion after he leaned forward from the hit. Grabbing his arm, she spun him around like a little rag doll and flipped him into the crowd.

I was busy dealing with two guys quickly and chained several aggressive attacks toward them. I could feel the rush of adrenaline through me, as the hits flowed like music and each one was quickly neutralized.

Ripley shouted, "Kirin, finish him!"

As the two guys lay on the ground behind me, Ripley had a serious joint lock on her opponent. She swung him in my direction. He staggered toward me, out of control. I threw a side kick into his gut so hard he fell to the ground and began to vomit.

Both Ripley and I watched as we were horrified to see what he had just eaten.

Ripley said, "Eww!"

I said, "I don't think I've ever seen that before."

Ripley replied, "I don't think I want to see that ever again."

The crowd cheered in excitement, as we were the last two standing. The rest of our opponents were spread on the floor out cold and in pain. Ripley walked toward the main guy and grabbed the credits from his hands.

"I'll take that," she said. She began counting it as I watched her. She then handed me some credits.

"For you," she said.

She gave me 1,000 credits, and I frowned. "Wait, this is too much! You're not dividing it equally. I only contributed a hundred."

"Seems fair to me to split it in half," she said.

"Wait, what about the extra two hundred credits left over?" I asked.

She tucked away her share of the credits and then grabbed my hand. She took the remaining credits and tossed it in the air. She looked at me and said, "Let's run."

The credits flew in the air as the crowd made a mad dash to collect them. Within seconds, we were out of the crowd's range, and we were laughing with our loot for the night.

"Why'd you do that?"

"You still haven't learned, have you, Kirin?"

"Just coz you won doesn't mean it's safe. You can't trust anyone when you get involved in this kind of life."

I looked at her and said, "Anyone?"

"Almost anyone," she said. She started walking away and said, "So, you coming along or what?"

I thought about it for a second and said, "I'm coming."

Ripley continued walking and said, "Good … you owe me a dinner."

I yelled back, "I bought last time."

She replied, "Pretty sure you can spare a few credits."

"It is only in the darkness when you can truly see who your friends really are."
—Sifu

Worth the Kiss?—1 Year, 273 Days

Danny looked at Carlos and took a swipe at his arm. "Come on, Carlos! Jeez, my grandma can drive faster." He then muttered something in Spanish, which no one understood.

Carlos looked at him funny and barked back, "I asked you if you wanted to drive, and you said no. So, let me do what you didn't want to do. Besides, this is a minivan. How fast do you think this can go?" He checked the back mirror, and I made eye contact with him. I tried to fake a smile, but I knew what was at stake tonight. *Everything*.

Danny said, "Maybe you'd be driving faster if you didn't have a burger in your other hand."

Carlos shouted back, "I told you I was hungry. Besides, this is for sustenance. A guy has to eat to survive, doesn't he?"

Danny smiled and said, "You're surviving for multiple guys?"

I snickered at the joke, hoping for anything to ease the tension. The car ride to the park was tense, and we all remained quiet for most of the ride. Danny had said he found a fight that would cover us for the entire year. We were struggling to keep the school open, and I refused to let it shut down.

"Zzzzzzz."

I peeked to my side and shook my head. Ryan was sound asleep and somehow generating an unbearable sound. I thought, *Jeez, Ryan get your head in the game.*

I asked Danny, "You sure about this? We've never done one so far out of town. And I'm not particularly happy that we're going to the abandoned America is Great Theme Park."

"Trust me on this. I know what I'm doing. Besides, my new girlfriend promised me this would be a cinch for us, especially for our group."

I thought it was strange that she knew about our group. In the back of my mind, two things stuck out: nothing is ever as easy as it seems … and nothing ever went well when Danny said, "Trust me." But, these were desperate times. Even with our success with the fights, we were barely making it each month to keep the school open. Our winning constantly meant lower odds and payout for us, so with every good came a bad.

"All right," I said reluctantly.

Danny replied, "I just hope she doesn't realize that this isn't the A team."

Jake responded, "Hey, I heard that! Besides, I pity the fool." He seemed real tough, as he was playing his kazoo along the ride.

Chris said, "A little respect, please. We all did agree to help you guys out."

Rico responded, "Last I heard, you were the last man on the totem pole of the A team, Danny."

Danny turned around and pointed to him. "You know, if I was leading your group, I'd be the tallest of the midgets."

Rico said, "But, that sounds like you're agreeing with me."

Danny stopped to think about it and said, "Never mind."

I looked around, thinking Danny was right. I didn't want Tobias to know about what we were betting on to secure the school for a year because he'd say it was too reckless. So, other than Danny and Ryan, I'd composed the team with several guys who had less than two years into the art. Jake, Lou, Carlos, Chris, and Rico were the unknown cast that would've been the first to go in a movie.

Carlos asked, "So, how long did it take before she was your new girlfriend and for you to fall in love?"

Danny said, "Quiet, Carlos. When you see her, your jaw is going to drop. She's hot as hell, she's a gamer, and best of all she can fight."

Ryan woke up from his sleep and muttered, "Are you sure we're not talking about your hand?"

I looked toward him and said, "Hmm, you're not the least bit concerned, Ryan?"

Ryan said, "The way I see it, either Danny's dead right, or we're massively screwed."

"So, you're willing to gamble on that?" I asked.

"I'm willing to gamble I can outrun Carlos," he laughed.

"Hey!" Carlos yelled back with food stuffed in his mouth.

I looked at Carlos and asked, "Uh, you have both hands on the sandwich. How are you driving?"

Carlos replied, "With my knees."

"Please get us there in one piece, Carlos." I checked my seatbelt to see if it was secured.

Danny confidently said, "Trust me on this. If our group can win five matches in a row, we take the entire pot … and it's a huge pot of credits that'll have us set for an entire year."

I said, "Yeah, but we're gambling the deed to the school. We've never done that before."

Danny replied, "It'll be worth it. Besides, I think it's a risk that we need to take."

Forty-Five Minutes Later

As we approached the abandoned amusement park, the hair on the back of my neck rose. The place had been unmaintained for the last several years, giving it a creepy atmosphere. It felt just like in a horror movie, but the big difference was that this was for real and we were the cast.

Chris said, "I'll be the first to say it: this is pretty freaky."

Danny said, "You know what's scarier?"

I said, "What?"

Danny replied, "If the toilets aren't working ... did you see how much Carlos ate?"

Ryan shouted, "Yeah, I know. You could've given me some of the sandwich, Carlos."

"Shit!" said Carlos.

"What?" I asked.

Carlos looked concerned. "Do you think the toilets aren't working?"

I rolled my eyes and said, "Guys, we need to focus."

We finally parked the minivan and got out. Danny was leading the group through the eerily quiet park. After several minutes of walking around, we finally saw some activity from afar.

Danny shouted, "There it is! I told yah. This is where the fights are held."

From a distance, we saw a large crowd surrounding a group of fighters in the middle. This was the largest I had ever seen gather, which was unusual. As we approached, it all became familiar, the typical sounds of cheers and swears, the smell of sweat, and the intensity of the crowd. This calmed my fears for the moment, as I sold myself into believing that we could possibly pull this off.

Danny said, "Where's my girl? She said she'd meet us here."

The last guy knocked out his opponent, and the crowd cheered. As we got there, the circle surrounding them strangely opened as the loser was dragged out. In the center, the main ring leader was revving up the crowd. His back was turned to us as Danny led our group closer to the action.

Finally, the ring leader spun around, and my jaw immediately dropped.

Danny pointed at her and then ran in her direction. "There's my girl."

It was Ripley. I thought, *What is she doing here?*

Ripley began running toward us and jumped into Danny's arms. She gave him a big kiss as I watched in disbelief. The rest of the guys howled and cheered him on, but now my fears came back and intensified. Something felt off, but I wasn't sure what to do. Danny was definitely not Ripley's type, but there they were, locking lips.

I heard her mumble, "Hey, lover, so you brought your friends as well as the prize."

Danny said, "Lover?"

Ripley replied, "You win tonight's fight, and you can have what you've been waiting for."

Danny's eyes popped open, and a hint of a drool ran down his mouth. He pulled out the deed to the school and handed it over to Ripley.

Ripley said, "Is that a roll of quarters I'm feeling?"

Carlos shouted, "I'm pretty sure it's two quarters and a dime."

Ryan looked at Carlos and said, "How would you know?"

Carlos shrugged his shoulders.

I began moving toward Ripley and Danny, but she quickly snatched the deed, gave Danny another kiss on the cheek, and ran to the center.

Ripley shouted, "Tonight, we have something very special! The famed Wing Chun group of eight is here to give us a delightful night of entertainment."

I looked at Ripley, who was acting weird. My gut feeling was on overdrive as nothing about this seemed right. I started looking around, realizing that some of the faces in the crowd looked familiar. My senses were tingling that this was all wrong.

Ripley continued, "Many of you might recognize them with their unbeaten record in challenge matches as well as current fights. But I'm here today to give you the opportunity...."

Then someone from the crowd shouted, "That's not them!"

Ripley stopped and then stared at our group. She said, "What do you mean?" as she made her trademark annoyed face.

One husky-looking guy walked up to Ripley and whispered in her ear. Her smile changed to a frown, and I could see that she was angry. She flung her hair and in a model-like walk approached Danny. She got close to him and slapped him on the face.

"What the hell was that for?" said Danny. He held his face in shock.

Ripley yelled, "I thought I told you to bring your group here tonight."

Danny said, "This is our group."

Ripley shouted, "This is not your main group, is it?"

"No, but—"

Ripley slapped him again.

"Woman, you do that again…" Danny threatened as he held his index finger right at her face.

Ripley, with a devilish smile, turned around. Her hair flung like a shampoo commercial as Danny stood there mesmerized. She arched her back and showed off her best asset and said, "Like what you see?"

"Danny!" I shouted.

It was too late. She launched a punch to Danny's stomach as he crumpled to his knees. She was about to walk away, but spun again, gaining momentum to kick Danny square in the face. He sailed through the air, landing with a big thump. I ran to him at once. I could hear her annoying laugh as I came to Danny's side. The rest of the guys huddled around him.

"What the hell are you doing, Ripley?" I said, staring directly at her.

She ignored my question and continued to walk away.

Ripley held up the deed to our school and said, "Everyone, I hold before you the deed to their school. As most of you here know, most of your own schools were shut down because of them. So, I propose a balance of karma tonight. I suggest you take out your revenge on these eight while we shut them down permanently."

I shouted at Ryan, "See if Danny's okay!" I stood up and began to scan the faces surrounding us. I can't believe I didn't recognize it right away, but most of these faces were opponents we had fought in the past.

I stood up and shouted, "You don't think we can stomp a pathetic group of thirty thugs, Ripley? We've beaten these guys before; we can easily beat them again."

"Fuel to the fire, Kirin. I love it." Ripley stared at me and said, "Oh no, Kirin, I'm sure you can handle a group of thirty, as you said. That's why I invited more of my friends to come along." She raised her hands and turned around, laughing as evilly as one could possibly imagine.

Suddenly from all corners of the amusement park, people came charging toward the group. In every direction that I turned, the number of people kept increasing. They stopped short of engaging us and formed a circle around our entire group.

Chris said, "Holy shit!"

I looked around and said, "Everyone—"

Jake said, "Any chance we can make a run for it?"

I looked at Carlos and Ryan. "We could make a run if you have no problem leaving Carlos and Ryan behind."

Ryan said, "Right now I want to leave Danny behind."

I said, "Take a number."

Rico said, "Jeez, guys, remember the Alamo?"

Danny replied, "I think so. Didn't that work out well for the underdog?"

Ryan shouted, "Dammit, Danny! The next time I say, 'can you be any dumber' ... guess what? That's not a challenge."

Danny pleaded his case. "It's not my fault. It's not my fault."

Lou said, "So, what's the plan? There's a ton of guys hell bent on kicking our asses."

Chris asked, "What are we gonna do?"

I was about to take charge and lead us out of this mess. I would've felt more comfortable if our core group was with me, but all I had were Danny and Ryan, and a bunch of rookies in the art.

Think, Kirin. Think!

Suddenly Ryan shouted, "Okay, everyone, be quiet and listen to me!" All the guys turned around, and all eyes focused on him. "We're gonna form a circle. Danny, Kirin, and I will form the outer perimeter. Each one of us will have at least one backup. Carlos and Lou, stand behind Danny. Jake and Rico, watch Kirin's back. And, Chris, get behind me. Danny and Kirin, you'll deal with all the initial attacks. No more than two hits to get the job done. I want you to toss the leftovers to whoever's backing you up. Everyone, be direct and hit fast and hard down the center."

The guys nodded and hurried into position. I didn't say a word, since Ryan was the most senior of our group, but I knew his strategy was not going to work.

I watched as hordes continued to shift in position around us.

"Guys, one more thing. Remember, above all, no matter what, maintain this circle. Once it breaks, we break. Understood?" shouted Ryan.

The guys nodded and stood their ground.

Rico said, "Jeez, now that you mention it, I do recognize some of these guys."

I said, "That's because we kicked their butts and closed their schools."

Jake said, "What about these parkour jumping ones? Are you guys seeing this?"

I saw exactly what Jake was talking about—a different style of fighters that we'd never seen before. They were leaping around acrobatically from places one normally shouldn't be able to. The additional new fighters all wore these eerie masks that looked like they were from the Renaissance times. They were various shapes and sizes, some with horns on top of their heads and elongated noses to cover their faces.

Lou said, "Jeez, as if things can't get any worse...."

Danny said, "Maybe they're capoeira."

Carlos muttered, "Jesus, the mask is freaking me out."

Chris said in a panicky voice, "What do we do about them?"

Ryan shouted, "Doesn't matter! Let them come to you. Don't go chasing them out. The circle, guys. Stay and deal with everything within it."

Just as Ryan finished shouting to our team, our opponents stood still as if they had been given a command.

I looked for Ripley, who had suddenly disappeared. Then on top of the food shack she popped out. She was holding her fist as everyone kept all eyes on her.

Carlos said, "I should be home eating, but instead I'm about to get my ass kicked."

I turned toward Carlos and said, "Focus. And, remember, don't block with your face."

Ryan said, "Shit ... Robert's not here to do the math, but I'm counting at least seventy."

Jake responded, "For an Asian guy, your math sucks. It's closer to a hundred guys."

I shouted at Ripley, "Why are you doing this?"

Ripley responded, "Remember when I told you I'd do anything to keep *my* school alive? Well, I've sealed the deal to make sure that is the case. Besides, Kirin, you honestly didn't think we were friends ... did you?"

I stepped forward and pointed to Ripley. "I'm coming for you, Ripley."

Ripley said, "Nice words, Kirin. But, if I were you, I'd be more concerned about surviving the next couple of minutes."

I didn't say another word. I had to be strong. The guys were looking to me to set the tone.

Ripley shouted, "Punish them first! Let's have a little fun."

I watched as Ripley stood there smugly, commanding everyone from afar. Suddenly, the entire place filled with a hush of silence. She smiled and said calmly, "Attack them ... now!"

Several Minutes Later

It was total bedlam. I was too busy trying to put chaos back into order, and Ryan's plan had no chance of working. A hit here, a kick there, a throw from every direction, wave after wave, it was never-ending.

I shouted out, but wasn't sure anyone could hear me. "This is not working!" I continued to throw everything I had at whoever was close by that wasn't considered a friend. I thought, *It's impossible to maintain this formation.*

I heard Danny shout from a distance. "Kirin's right! We're getting smoked here."

I took a quick peek as several of the guys were down. I finally decided to take charge to keep our group alive.

I screamed, "Danny, Ryan, follow my lead!" I saw Jake was getting pummeled by several guys as I snatched him from harm's way and then threw him at another group that was charging from behind.

Jake screamed, "What are you doing?"

I thought, *Saving your butt.* As he flew into the crowd, I used him as a shield and took out several guys. I made sure I kept him close to me and continued to throw him around, catching our opponents off guard.

I had a split second to see how the other guys were doing, and both Danny and Ryan finally copied my tactic.

I shouted again, "Use them as shields to keep them safe."

I recalled that Sifu once told me that, to protect the ones you love, you shouldn't have them hide behind you, but instead use them as shields. When I first heard it, the strategy sounded totally foreign, but now seeing it in action, at this level, really was surprising.

Jake shouted, "I'm so not enjoying this!"

I replied, "You haven't taken a hit since I started using you, right?"

Jake paused and said, "Sling me away."

All my opponents had that shocked look on their faces when I continued using Jake as a shield. But, that's exactly what I wanted. I followed up each look of surprise with a smash to their faces or any other part of their center that was exposed.

Ten Minutes Later

I looked around; my team was beaten. We were still surrounded. Rico was bruised and battered and was kneeling to catch his breath. He cradled his arm, which appeared to be broken. Danny was tending to both Chris and Lou. It was difficult to tell which one looked worse. I stared at Jake, whose eye was swollen shut. He looked at me and smiled—and then spit out a tooth. Ryan stood on guard, waiting for the next onslaught, and I saw blood drip from his nose. I peeked to my side and saw Carlos sprawled on his back with his eyes closed. I rushed to check on him and asked, "Pluck a duck … Carlos, you okay? You okay?"

He opened his eyes and said, "Is the fight over, Kirin?"

"Where does it hurt?"

He sat up and looked around as he dusted the dirt of his clothes. "I'm actually okay. I'm just exhausted."

I rolled my eyes, clenched my fist, and punched him hard on the arm.

"Ow!"

"Get up … you dumb ass!" I grabbed him by the collar and had him back up on his feet. "Do you understand they're not here to kick our butts? They're here to get rid of us permanently."

Ryan said, "This isn't looking good, is it, Kirin?"

I analyzed our situation. The guys were gassed, and we had several members who were injured and couldn't run. We had no choice but to fight to the very end. There were at least about eighty or so opponents that still surrounded us. I looked to the top of the food shack where Ripley was walking back and forth.

Ripley began clapping, and everyone stared at her. Again, she wanted to be the center of attention. The sight of her made me sick to my stomach.

Ripley yelled. "Bravo, bravo! I do believe I owe you applause for your effort, Kirin."

I stared at her and shouted, "I do believe I owe you this" as I waved the middle finger toward her direction.

Ripley frowned and stared me down. "You know, in the movies, they always give you a way out. It's never quite the same in real life. I figure, why just kick your asses when we can just make up a story that you snuck into the park and had a fatal accident?"

Ripley raised her hand and signaled to all the gang members surrounding us.

I shouted out, "Ryan and Danny! We form a perimeter around the rest of the guys. Carlos, you tend to the wounded." We got into position and were ready to make a final stand.

Danny said, "I'm sorry, guys. I'm sorry for fucking up."

I said, "If we somehow get out of this alive, I'm gonna kick your ass."

Ryan said, "You know what we need right now?"

I looked at him and said, "Please don't say a sandwich."

"Jeez, Kirin." Ryan thought about it and said, "Although, if we are going down, I could use a last meal."

I shook my head. "Ryan...."

He shouted, "No. Seriously. No ... I'm holding out for a hero."

"Ryan, this isn't the movies. You can dream all you want for what you need, but we are definitely on our own."

I clenched my fist as Ripley was about to lower her hand, and the final charge would be on its way. We waited in the silence of the amusement park.

Ripley said, "Goodbye, Kirin. I can't say it's been a pleasure ... although seeing the end of you and your school comes pretty close."

Danny shouted at Ripley, "Ripley, you can consider our relationship over!"

I looked at Danny and rubbed my eyes. He nodded his head as if he'd showed her who was boss.

Ripley giggled. "You know what, Danny? All this was so worth kissing you." She began to make her motion for the attack when she paused and began looking around.

I wondered what was going on, but then suddenly I heard it. The faint sound of music began to approach closer. I wasn't the only one who was trying to figure out where the music was coming from. Everyone was scanning the park to find the source.

As we waited, the song became louder. Suddenly, I saw from afar something I hadn't expected at all. I shook my head at first and then smiled in relief. Standing over the hillside part of the park next to the withered flag, I saw Tobias. He came in with the rest of the gang. In typical Tobias form, he'd decided to bring his own music. He was carrying a vintage boom box as his 1980s music continued to blare out loud.

Ryan said, "So, it's not like the movies. Huh, Kirin?"

Danny said, "Now that's an entrance."

I replied, "I'd be more impressed if he came riding on a fiery steed."

This time, all eyes were focused on Tobias and the rest of the guys—Ken, Doc, Big T, and Robert stood behind him. The music was blaring as Tobias posed and stared at Ripley from a distance.

Ripley began to laugh. "Well, well, so now I guess my luck has turned…. The fab eight are all finally here. I guess the end of your school will officially happen."

Tobias shouted, "You know what, Ripley! You are beautiful."

She smiled and tossed her hair. "Guilty as charged."

Tobias added, "But as hot as you are, I'd never date a crazy bitch like you."

Ripley cringed in anger and said, "Do you think having an extra five people is gonna save your asses?"

Tobias made a motion. One by one, each of the guys pulled out a staff from behind; they were armed with the Wing Chun bo. Each one of them pounded the staff to the ground and held it erect.

Ripley laughed again. "Five guys. Oh, Tobias, you are hilarious! Five guys with five little sticks."

Robert shouted, "Just coz I'm Asian … don't assume my stick is little."

Big T looked around and said, "Well, there's no way she was talking to me."

Ripley said, "Is that the best you can do, Tobias?"

Tobias looked at me from a distance and winked. He then turned to both sides and smiled. "Actually, this is the best I can do." He raised his bo and then led a charge. As the guys immediately followed, a slew of other martial arts groups, the three remaining schools that came to our meeting, followed the guys from behind in the charge.

Ripley screamed, "Kill them all!"

The next ten minutes were just a blur. I was still instructing the guys to carry on with the original plan, even with Tobias and the rest of the guys moving to help us. My biggest concern was making sure I didn't hit anyone from my team. When a battle erupts, pretty much everything goes out the window.

With the huge crowd of fighters, I was looking for one person only. I continued laying out a path of destruction until I knew I could be within reach. I found her from a distance fighting the guys from our side, and then I yelled out her name.

Strangely enough, a path cleared for us to face each other.

"Don't think you can run!" I shouted.

"Who said anything about running?" said Ripley.

"You have something that belongs to me."

Ripley pulled out the deed to the school. "Oh, you mean this little thing? If you don't mind, I'm going to keep it."

I've had enough. That was it. I charged in, gunning for her. I closed the gap between us quickly and went for a punch. She stepped to the side, grabbing my arm as she went for a lock. As she tried to drag me down, I went with the force and simply rolled out of the motion. We ended up staring at each other briefly and then went at it again.

I thought, *Get her to bite first. Don't give it away.*

I moved in and tried to keep my cool. This time, I faked a motion to see how she would react, and she did just that. I got her to bite, and she shifted off to the side, while I stayed neutral. I thought, *Gotcha.*

With her mistake, I landed several blows, and she fell backward and onto the ground. She was in total shock that I had gotten through; she touched her face and saw her own blood.

"Why, you little bitch!" said Ripley.

"Wow ... you have no idea how good that felt." I started walking toward her to get what I wanted back. From the side, I got tackled and found myself on the ground. He got on top of me and tried to smother me. I turned to the side and saw that Ripley was getting up. I knew I couldn't let her go, so I dug my fingers into his eyes.

He rolled off to the ground screaming in pain, but when I stood back up, I crashed back to the ground. "Dammit." I thought I had twisted my ankle; I held my leg and looked at it.

A new sound came from every part of the park—the police. If it wasn't crazy enough, people were running away as cops were beginning to arrest people. Ripley took off as I tried to get back up and immediately fell. Amid the chaos, a hand extended toward me and I looked up.

"Need a hand?" asked Tobias.

I looked up and grabbed for it. "We have to get Ripley. She's got the deed for the school."

Tobias looked around, and I saw Ripley ducking away behind one of the abandoned stores.

"We have to let it go, Kirin. Either we try to get her, or we get arrested."

I screamed. "Let's get her!"

"No, Kirin."

I tried to hobble and move with him, but I was slowing him down. Tobias grabbed me and carried me. He shouted, "Guys, we are leaving!"

I looked around as the rest of the guys somehow heard him. We followed the path of least resistance as more people continued to run away. We hoped the route we picked would lead to our escape.

Tobias shouted, "Doc, open this door! Let's hide in here."

Doc did as he was told, and our group hung out inside the store, staying silent.

I said, "I don't think we're gonna be able to escape. They've surrounded this entire area."

Ken was leaning under the window as a shadow from the outside passed over him.

I looked at Ryan, who was holding his breath.

Danny said, "Where's Big T?"

"Dumb ass, I'm right behind you. Don't you dare say you couldn't see me."

Robert said, "Shh...."

As we hid quietly in the dark, the door slammed open as a flashlight cut through the night. Someone said, "I know someone's in here. Come out now!"

We did as the officer said, and we all stood up.

The figure holding the flashlight was shaking his head. I immediately recognized who it was. He said, "What the heck are you guys doing here?"

"Holy cow! It's Phil."

Phil shouted out to us, "Tobias! Get your group out of here before you get caught. Go through the back, and I'll tell them this area is clear."

Tobias turned around and said, "I owe you one."

Phil replied, "Your math must be off.... Anyway, get out of here; I'll cover you."

Tobias yelled, "Guys, scatter!"

Two Days Later

I didn't believe it when Tobias told me, so I had to go see for myself. I'd had an easier time convincing my mom that I'd sprained my ankle falling at Gwen's house than I did leaving my house that early Sunday morning. I hobbled with my crutches toward the school, and from a distance I could see something hanging on the front of the door. On the glass where Sifu's school sign was, someone had spray painted a giant X through it. It reminded me of the four guys who had tried to vandalize the school. I cringed at the sight, but then focused my attention on what was plastered on the front of the door. It read: "School closed—Notice of abandonment. UFMF school coming soon."

I immediately shut my eyes and began to cry. The pain was crushing as my heart sunk to my stomach. Everything that we had done was for naught. I opened my eyes and wiped the tears from my face, hoping this was only a dream, but the words stayed the same. I stood there for over thirty minutes, staring at those words. My blood was boiling as I read the message again and again.

SECTION 2

Sifu's Journey Entry #11—Ready to Open

The Week of Christmas 2030

"Lucy, I'm home!" shouted Sifu with his terrible impersonation of Ricky Ricardo. He held his luggage in both hands as he entered his old place. The room remained silent, and Sifu's jaw dropped when he looked around his restaurant. "Holy smokes," he stuttered as he began examining the new look of the place.

As he spun in a circle, he said, "How long have I been gone?"

Lance, his friend and confidant, was watching from a distance and finally came within Sifu's view. "You've been gone too long," said Lance as he approached Sifu.

Sifu dropped his luggage, walked toward Lance, and extended his hand out for a shake. The year-long journey had finally come full circle, and Lance shook Sifu's hand firmly and followed it up with a great bear hug, happy to see his friend in one piece.

"So, do you like it?" asked Lance as he gestured for to Sifu to get a better look.

"Like it? That's an understatement. I guess you were busy while I was gone," said Sifu as he continued inspecting the entire place.

"I hope you don't mind the little touches I added to your original concept. I kinda guessed on several of them.... I was gonna ask you overseas, but I wanted to keep it a surprise, and I figured you were too busy perfecting the ramen." Lance stood back and stared at Sifu admiring his work.

"I am really impressed, to say the least. Although I hope you spent some of your time training on all your forms." Sifu raised an eyebrow just to see what Lance had to say.

"Ah, always the teacher." Lance shook his head. "I can't say that I missed your sharp tongue."

"Hmm, you seem to be stalling. You still haven't answered my question."

"Does the sun always rise from the east?" asked Lance.

"Come to think of it, when I was there, I never confirmed that fact," chuckled Sifu. He continued admiring the new look of the place when he asked, "Did you only work on this area?"

"Nope, you were gone for some time, so I thought of every possibility for improving the main floor of the restaurant as well as the kitchen. However, I didn't touch your basement, your sanctuary … well …"

"Hmm…," said Sifu. "If anything, I bet you were afraid to touch my mess."

"Hey, I know there are certain things a guy shouldn't mess with. Your basement is your baby … or better yet, your mess to deal with … but there was one thing I tinkered with," said Lance.

"Fair enough, I'm sure whatever it is, it's for the better. So, show me around."

"Well, follow me. I want you to see for yourself." Lance directed them toward the shelving that led to the secret basement, well hidden from the casual guest.

"Now I didn't want to change your handiwork for opening the basement." He continued fidgeting with a secret locking device. "Sifu, this is only temporary. Can you say something that we can use for the password?"

Sifu blurted out, "Uh, Ramen!"

"Perfect. We can always change it later," said Lance.

"Change what?" asked Sifu.

"Say it again, will you please, Sifu?"

"Uh, okay." He cleared his throat and shouted, "Ramen!" The door slowly opened without Lance touching it, and the basement passage was now accessible.

"Voice command?" chuckled Sifu.

"Is that over-the-top useless?" Lance seemed a bit concerned with the answer.

"Obviously! But, I love it," said Sifu as he shook his head. "Wait one second, Lance."

"What?"

"Open your stance," directed Sifu, and he waited for Lance to do so.

Lance did as he was instructed to do and opened his stance right on the spot. Sifu watched his every motion. Upon seeing Lance's stance, Sifu smiled.

"Why are you smiling?" asked Lance.

"So … you have been practicing," said Sifu. He walked toward Lance and pressed slightly on his chest. "Impressive. I'm liking what I see."

"Okay, what's going on here?" asked Lance.

"What do you mean?"

"I mean, what happened to the real Sifu? I'm not sure I like this new one filled with compliments," joked Lance.

"Hey, I've always been very complimentary," said Sifu.

Lance rolled his eyes and got out of his stance. "Come on and follow me downstairs to the basement," he commented.

Sifu walked downstairs with Lance and saw that Lance had organized the entire basement. "Come over here, Sifu," he instructed. "Check out what I did to your dummy stand."

Sifu walked toward his wooden dummy and he could see the stand had a unique contraption attached to it. Sifu examined it and had the faintest clue as to what Lance had done.

Lance said, "Press the button."

"Okay," said Sifu as he pressed the button. Upon doing so, the dummy began rising. "Holy cow! You made an automatic height adjustment?"

"Yup. Hope you don't mind. I had a hard time using the dummy since it was so low, and I thought it would be easier for the both of us to adjust it," said Lance.

"It's incredible. You should market this and make some money," said Sifu.

Lance laughed and said, "Maybe sell it to the UFMF?"

Sifu pretended to cough as they both stood motionless for a few seconds. That moment of quietness between the two friends quickly became a burst of laughter as they each reacted to the UFMF comment.

"Let's head back upstairs. I want you to show you what I've learned," said Sifu.

The men headed back upstairs, where Sifu began preparing the kitchen to make his ramen meal for Lance.

"Do you need my help?" asked Lance.

"No … I want you to watch everything I do, okay?" said Sifu.

"Sure thing."

Hours passed as Lance watched Sifu's moves diligently. He interrupted with questions every once in a while. He was amazed at how different Sifu looked even in the kitchen.

Sifu finally put the finishing touches on his soup and put the steaming hot bowl of delight in front of Lance. Steam covered his face as Lance leaned over to feel the warmth emitting from the bowl.

"Go ahead; try it," said Sifu, convinced he had duplicated it.

Lance began to stir the broth and scooped it. He blew on it gently several times as he closed his eyes and took a sip of the ramen.

Sifu watched his every move and this time was confident in the outcome. He had learned a lot from Megumi's dad, but the most important lesson echoed in his head.

Lance opened his eyes, didn't say a word, and simply smiled.

Sifu closed his eyes, realizing that the smile was the answer he had been waiting for from Lance.

"Do you understand now what I meant about something missing?" asked Sifu.

"I do." Lance dove in to finish the ramen. A few minutes passed as a single slurp signaled the end of the meal. Lance looked up and stared at Sifu. "So, after you start teaching me how to make it, will we be ready to open up?

Sifu laid his hand on Lance's shoulder. He said, "I just have one more thing I need to square up, and then we can open."

Lance looked up to Sifu and said, "Can I have more?"

CHAPTER 12

Justice for All

The Night Before the Final

Watanabe was speaking over a video intercom with Justice. He seemed pleased with the day's events. "Your work at the weigh-in was most exceptional."

"Thank you, sir," said Justice as he remained stern-faced and unemotional.

"I just want to make sure we are clear on what you are going to do for tomorrow." Watanabe swung around and turned his back to Justice. "Kristen will go over the details with you."

"I'm listening."

Watanabe walked away, but was well within hearing distance. He stood inches from the glass, looking out the window. He waited to hear Kristen's voice break the silence.

Kristen began walking toward the video conference, her heels clicking away, as Justice waited for her instructions. She cleared her throat and began to speak. "Justice, we'd like you to draw out the match as long as possible. Can you do that?"

"Yes. In fact, you can tell me the second you want me to end the fight."

Kristen looked at Justice and said, "Are you sure you can execute it that precisely?"

"The child is no match for me," said Justice.

Watanabe turned around and said, "Justice, don't be so overconfident. She possesses a tenacious fighting spirit."

"Regardless, my skill is beyond hers, sir. I apologize if I sound overconfident."

"Very well."

Watanabe went back to looking outside as Kristen took over the conversation.

"I want you to make her suffer for the entire match, Justice. Only when you are given the signal, then and only then, will you finish her."

"Finish her?"

Kristen said, "Yes."

Watanabe put away his lighter and interrupted again, "Her death will push the uprising over the edge and, with it, force Collins's hand in dealing with it."

"Yes, sir," said Justice.

"Please … the decision still weighs heavily on me, and it wasn't made on a whim, mind you, Justice. But this is a small sacrifice for the sake of the greater good."

Justice bowed and did not respond. The screen flashed for a split second and then blanked out.

Kristen turned toward Watanabe. "Sir?"

"It's late, Kristen. Go home now. Tomorrow's a busy day."

Kristen walked up to Watanabe, pressed her chest to his back, and leaned on his shoulder. She whispered. "I don't want to go home."

Watanabe stared outside and took a deep breath.

The Morning of the Fight

Angelo tiptoed into Kirin's hotel room while she was sound asleep. He leaned over and saw that Bacon's butt was smashed across Kirin's face. He laughed slightly and then cringed at the thought.

He decided to delicately wake up Kirin, who'd had a rough night. She was set for an even greater adventure for the start of the day. He went to the window and quietly raised each shade. With each one being lifted, the room began to brighten as the sun's rays took over.

When the light hit Kirin's face, she remained asleep. Angelo waited several minutes and checked his watch. He began to become impatient, and he tapped his foot.

He muttered, "Come on, Kirin. Wake up already." He paced back and forth, knowing Kirin had to prepare for today's fight.

Ten minutes later, she was still frozen in the same position. He frowned and wondered how she could still be asleep. He was getting frustrated, but he then snatched the covers from her. She moved slightly, so he thought that did the trick, but his moment of happiness ended with her snoring.

"Good lord, what's it gonna take to wake you up?"

He examined the situation and looked at Bacon. "Ah, I have an idea."

He walked over to the other side, and Bacon's butt was still by Kirin's face. "This is for your own good." Angelo leaned over and placed both hands around Bacon's stomach. He slowly began to squeeze, and a foul stench silently began inhabiting the room.

Angelo's face cringed. The smell was unbearable. He held his breath and watched. A few seconds later, Kirin jumped out of the bed and screamed, "Bacon, what the heck?"

When she saw that Angelo was holding his nose, she said, "What are you doing?"

She waited for an answer as Angelo's face started turning red. He finally let out a gasp of air and shouted, "What are you feeding this dog?"

"Dog food, Angelo ... like always." Kirin touched her face and rubbed it in pain. "Ugh, I feel awful."

"Well, it's time to get up. Besides, you've got several appointments this morning, and you need to get ready."

Kirin lay back on her bed and said, "You do know I have a fight tonight." Kirin reached back and put the pillow over her face.

Angelo ran into the bathroom and turned on the shower. He then took off for a minute and returned with a freshly brewed cup of black coffee.

He smiled and waited.

"Coffee," she muttered. She removed the pillow and sat up.

"Just as you like it." He held the cup close to her face as the coffee aroma drifted to her nose.

Kirin was about to reach for it, but Angelo carefully snapped it away.

"What gives?"

"You get the coffee if you promise to shower and get ready ... ASAP."

Kirin pouted for a second, but the smell of the coffee broke her defenses. "Fine! I promise. Now give me my coffee."

Angelo smiled and said, "Okay, you've got," he checked his watch, "nine minutes and thirty-seven seconds to go."

Kirin turned around and grabbed the coffee. She let the heat warm her hands as she took a sip and smiled. "Ouch, my jaw still hurts." She wiggled her mouth to see if it was okay. She gulped the coffee down, kissed Bacon on the head while he still slept, and sprinted to the bathroom.

Angelo was waiting in the living area of their hotel room as Kirin put in her scrunchie and sloppily adjusted her hair. "One minute to spare ... ready as promised."

Angelo check his watched and said, "Good girl. Did you want to eat breakfast? Although..." he looked her over from head to toe, "your definition of ready is not mine."

"Don't start. I got ready like you asked."

Angelo said, "I'm just saying...."

Kirin rolled her eyes and shook her head. "Angelo, I'm not hungry yet ... besides, who's my first appointment with?" She looked around, found her coffee and enjoyed the moment of peace.

He scrolled through his pad, pretending to search for the appointment. But, Angelo already knew who it was. "Uh, Hunter...."

As she heard Hunter's name, she spat out half the coffee on the floor. "Hunter? What? Are you crazy?"

"He said he really needed to speak with you and—"

Knock. Knock. Knock.

Kirin and Angelo turned their heads and stared at the door.

He looked at her and said, "Speak of the devil, he's on time. Heh, heh...."

Angelo was fearful of dealing with Kirin any further and hurried along to answer the door. He shouted, "I'll be right there!"

Angelo pranced away and opened the door. He quickly exchanged greetings with Hunter and directed him to Kirin's presence.

Hunter walked toward Kirin and looked shyly away. Kirin did the same as she gently said, "Hi, Hunter ... it's, um ... good to see you."

"Kirin, before you say anything else ... I wanted to explain something to you in person."

It was difficult for Kirin to stay mad at Hunter. It was her doing for being too busy to talk to him. She finally made eye contact and approached him. She said, "What is it?"

"I swear I wanted to tell you.... I left you several messages and texts, but you never returned them," said Hunter.

"I know. I know. It's my fault."

"No, it's not your fault. I'm just going through school, and you're actually doing something worthwhile, something that impacts the entire world. It's understandable that you never had the time for me."

"It's not that, Hunter. I never meant to ignore you. In fact, I took it for granted that my closest friend would always be there for me ... never realizing that someone else might be able to capture his heart."

Hunter looked down. "Kirin, it's ... complicated. Olivia is really...."

Kirin moved closer and said, "You don't have to say anything. I spoke with her, and she sounds like a wonderful girl." It tore into Kirin to say that, but she continued to spill out her true feelings. "You've always been there for me, and if you tell me you're happy, then I'm happy for you."

"I'm happy," he said as he tried to see Kirin's reaction.

Kirin tried to stay stone-faced, but her feelings for Hunter were easier to see, now that she'd lost him.

Hunter said, "Look, I know you're busy and the timing couldn't be any worse, but I had to tell you that in person."

Kirin leaned forward and touched Hunter on the cheek. Hunter touched her hand, as she kissed him on the cheek. They both bumped their heads gently against one another as Angelo at first watched and then turned away.

Hunter said, "I better go."

He started slowly walking away, and Kirin quietly began to shed a tear. As Hunter was about to exit the room, he turned around and saw that Kirin was crying. He rushed back toward her and gave her a hug. He whispered into Kirin's ear, "You'll always be my first love ... always."

Kirin returned the hug, squeezed, and then broke the bond between the two. She watched as Hunter walked away, and Angelo closed the door behind him.

Angelo pulled out a handkerchief and handed it to Kirin. He stared at his watch and waited until she dried her tears.

"Okay, you've got fifteen minutes before your next appointment. How about some breakfast?"

"I'm not hungry," said Kirin as she walked to the window to see a huge crowd on the street enjoying the weekend's festivities. The crowd saw her from the street and began to cheer.

Ten minutes passed before a knock sounded at the door again.

"This better not be another surprise," said Kirin.

"It's not," said Angelo.

Knock. Knock. Knock.

Angelo opened the door, and this time Quinn stood at the opening. Kirin stared at the entrance and shook her head.

"Seriously?" said Kirin.

Quinn quickly moved forward, using his walking stick to find the path to Kirin. He said, "Come on, Kirin. Please talk to me.... That's all I'm asking from you. I've tried calling you night and day, and all I get is your voicemail."

"Quinn, you couldn't possibly have picked a worse time to come."

"Look, I know the timing's terrible. Can't you cut a blind guy some slack and just tell him the entire story?"

When Kirin didn't respond, Quinn tried again. "Honestly, Kirin ... I just want to know. I have no idea what I said or did wrong.... That night we spent together was more than just a fling ... at least for me."

Angelo clasped his face, as that information shocked him.

Kirin didn't say anything as Quinn's words spun in her head. She finally replied, "Quinn, I care about you ... but I just can't deal with this now.

Technically, you didn't do anything wrong, but working for the UFMF just kinda caught me off guard."

Quinn said, "I still don't get it. You work for the UFMF as well."

"I just can't get into it right now," said Kirin. "I promise, after the fight, one way or another, I'll resolve this issue between us."

Quinn leaned over and said, "Look, Kirin. I care about you. I really do … so please, promise me you'll hear me out after the fight." Quinn leaned forward, but Kirin pulled away. He had a sad look on his face as he turned to leave the room.

Feeling guilty and unsure, Kirin called, "After the fight, I promise."

Quinn mustered up a smile and went on his way.

Kirin gave Angelo a look. "Angelo … no more surprises." As she walked past Angelo, he shuddered in fear. He took a quick peek at his watch and released a deep breath.

Kirin began doing her first form. Her nerves were kicking in. Unlike the first fight, Sifu was not there to help guide her. Angelo, on the other hand, was pacing back and forth, making an attempt to look busy as he continued to take glances at his watch.

Several minutes into the form, she noticed he was still jittery and shuffling about. At first, she ignored him and closed her eyes, but she could feel his tension. Finally, she said, "What's going on?"

Angelo shrieked, "Uh, nothing! Just nervous about the fight."

Kirin kept her eyes closed and took a deep breath. She quieted her mind but knew something was up. "Angelo … what's going—?"

Knock. Knock. Knock.

Kirin's eyes popped open as she stopped what she was doing and headed to the door. Angelo tried to cut her off, but she gave him a stare that made him cower like a bad dog.

"Angelo, you are really pushing your luck. I swear, whoever this is—"

She stopped abruptly as the door opened to reveal Tobias.

As he started to open his mouth, Kirin slammed the door in his face.

She went face to face with Angelo, whose back hugged the wall as he tried to move away from her.

"Look at me, Angelo. Did you know Tobias was coming over? Tell me the truth."

Kirin leaned in closer as Angelo looked away in fear.

"Speak, Angelo!"

Tobias opened the door to see Kirin hovering over Angelo. As soon as he walked in, Kirin lifted her hand and signaled him to stop.

Kirin said, "Angelo!"

Angelo panicked and fell to the ground and began to cry. He opened his eyes and looked back and forth over-dramatically. He finally blurted out, "Yes, I added him on, Kirin. It's not my fault. I swear. It's not my fault. Of the three guys you like, I think Tobias is the hottest."

Upon hearing that, Tobias's eyebrows raised with a look of confusion. He saw Angelo peek in his direction, and he looked away.

"Kirin … give me a chance to talk to you."

"Give you a chance?" Kirin shook her head and looked at Angelo. She said, "I'll deal with you later." She turned her back to Tobias and began to walk away.

Tobias grabbed her by the arm and said, "Just listen to me for a second."

She refused to look at Tobias and said, "Why are you even here, Tobias? Where's your girlfriend-slash-stripper that you love so much?"

"She is not my girlfriend!" yelled Tobias.

"Oh, I'm sorry. Maybe I should rephrase that. How's your whore doing?" snapped Kirin.

"She's not a stripper or a whore. She's a cocktail waitress."

Kirin finally turned around and looked at Tobias. "You're right; that's a more honorable profession."

"Don't be so judgmental, Kirin. You know finding a job in this economy is extremely difficult."

"Wow, Tobias. I didn't know you cared so much about the future of this country. I'm sure you're doing your part to help college girls and single moms during these tough economic times."

"Just stop it, will you? Look, I didn't come here to talk about all this. In fact, I came here because you need me right now."

Kirin's eyes blazed as she said in a sarcastic voice, "I need you right now? You arrogant bastard."

Tobias grabbed Kirin by the other arm and stared her down. "Kirin, will yah shut up for a second and just listen to me? You need me right now because you can't beat Justice—"

"Let go of me! Get out of here, Tobias. Go back to your stripper."

"She's not a stripper. Now will you just listen, Kirin?"

Kirin had had enough. She broke out of Tobias's grip and attempted to push him off his center. He quickly countered, and suddenly they were fighting. They scuffled briefly with one another, exchanging attacks and counters. Kirin pushed through an attack, but Tobias blocked it. She was about to counter again when Tobias shouted, "Enough!"

Her entire body froze. She felt the familiar power—Sifu's power—in the touch. She was about to yell back at Tobias when her face changed. "Pluck a duck," she said in surprise. "You can do it?" She repeated it to herself just to know it was for real. "You can do it."

"That's why I'm here..."Tobias sighed. "I'm here to help you with tonight's fight."

"I, uh ... I didn't know you could do it?"

"If you gave me a second, that's what I planned on telling you."

"Can you do it as well as Sifu?"

Tobias replied, "No one can do it like Sifu, but I can help."

Tobias walked past Kirin and entered the living room of her suite.

"What are you doing?" asked Kirin.

Tobias said, "It's time to train."

The Showdown

Kirin's team was ready to do its march down to the stadium. Tobias and Bryce were standing side by side in front of Kirin. The spectacle of humanity celebrating this event was incredible to see, as the numbers were still unimaginable to those present. Although everyone in Kirin's camp, except Bryce, had experienced the event before, there was something special about this finale.

Tobias turned around and said to Kirin, "Here we go ... again."

Kirin leaned forward and shouted, "Don't think just because of this morning.... This in no way means I've forgiven you."

Tobias rolled his eyes and turned away. He looked over to the side and saw that Bryce was nervous. He poked him in the arm and said, "You okay?"

Bryce was startled and said, "Oh, yeah. I mean, I'm okay. I have just never seen anything like this before."

Tobias said, "This is the big time—250,000 people in one stadium and millions watching around the world. It sure as hell can be overwhelming, but you'll get used to it."

"Yeah ... yeah, that's it." Bryce continued to squirm as he faked a smile and waved to people.

The Fight

As the referee signaled for the match to begin, the crowd's sound was drowned for a moment. Kirin and Justice stared at each other, both standing with no guard, waiting for something. The crowd looked somewhat confused, wondering what was going on. Neither was willing to make the first move. Then a sliver of Kirin's hair blew slightly across her face. She felt it, and Justice saw it. With that little motion, Justice didn't hesitate to begin the charge forward.

The five-minute round was entertaining, as attacks, blocks, and counters were being exchanged like a chess match. Tobias watched, and he could see Sifu's training stamped on the movements of both fighters. Justice was of Sifu's oldest generation of students, while Kirin was of the latest.

Kirin and Justice were locked in a stalemate. Justice smiled at her and said, "It's a shame the old man can't be here to watch you lose."

The words broke Kirin's focus, and she got emotional. It infuriated her, and she lost control. She cleared the line from Justice and invested in a heavy hit. She wanted him to pay so badly for his remarks.

Justice was waiting for this mistake and took full advantage of it. Her over-extended hit exposed her fully and laid open a clear path to her center. Justice took it and immediately connected, sending Kirin flying to the ground in a spiral. As she landed, she looked up to see Justice laughing. The bell rang, signaling the end of the first round as she wiped the blood from her mouth. Kirin slammed her fist on the mat and got back up. She walked back to her corner and spat out some blood.

Tobias said, "Well, that was ladylike."

Kirin looked at him. "Maybe I'll curtsey next time, just before I spit."

Tobias said, "Look, you're doing well out there, except for that … last hit. Don't get impatient."

Kirin said, "Just looking at him pisses me off."

Tobias said, "Well, that's no different than when you look at Robert."

Kirin replied. "It is. Robert's a dick, and this guy … I just want to smash his face in."

Tobias looked at her and said, "And the difference is?"

When Kirin didn't even crack a smile, Tobias sighed. "Anyway, just control your emotion and don't let him bait you. Got it?"

"Yeah. I got it."

As round two began, Kirin and Justice crashed into one another. The intensity picked up as more combos were flying, but mostly catching air. Every so often, a slight error in Kirin's game plan left her exposed just enough that she took some hits. In the first round, she had sustained only one hit, but now the numbers were beginning to increase as Justice was starting to connect more often.

Just like the first round, Justice snaked his way in for another big hit that sent Kirin flying at the end. Kirin picked herself up as the end of the round was signaled. Justice gave her a look, smiled, and then walked back to his corner.

Kirin watched Justice and said, "He's holding back; I can feel it.... In fact, I know it."

Tobias said, "Careful! I told you not to go for the kill."

Kirin said, "He's toying with me. I was open several times, and he didn't take it."

Tobias said, "Stick to the game plan."

Kirin looked at Tobias and said, "And, that's what? To survive?"

Tobias put both hands on her face and said, "Center, target, own it ... you got that?"

Kirin mumbled, "I got it."

Tobias said, "Say it!"

Kirin looked him in the eye and said, "Center, target, own it."

"Good girl ... now keep your cool."

Round three began, and it was clear to everybody that Justice was leading on points. Kirin closed the gap like she always did, but this time Justice stood in his place and then held his hand out. Kirin stopped in her tracks and wondered what he was up to.

Justice said, "I think it's time I demonstrate what you can really do with this art. Now I'll show you the true power, instead of your piddly exhibition last year."

Kirin cracked her neck from side to side. Even though she was losing, she was still geared to fight. There was no backing down for Kirin, as her will fueled her to never stop.

"You know, Justice, I preferred it much more when you didn't speak." After saying those words, she moved in for an attack. Kirin went straight down the center, but Justice didn't even flinch. His center was wide open, as she went for a straight punch down the attack line. She could feel how close her fist was to connecting, as she laid down the hammer to the nail. Just an inch away, she exploded the power of her hit, but Justice blocked her attack with just a pak at the very last second.

Justice said, "This is exploding power." In a flash, he released the point of control and quickly switched hands. With one hand controlling her, the other fist connected to her center. It felt like her insides imploded as she dropped to the ground and could barely look up to see him.

Justice commanded, "Get up!"

It took a minute for her to recover as she got up and tried to sneak an attack on Justice. He was prepared, as the attack didn't fool anyone, even when she tried to flow it into a combination. She tried in vain to chain several attacks together, but after each motion Justice would use her energy and then send it right back to her. He looked at her and said, "This is connecting power." He slapped her across the ring—his way of adding insult to injury.

Kirin found herself laid out on her back, as her face held a bright mark across it. She thought, *Get up, Kirin.* She finally struggled to stand on both feet, when the ring of the bell saved her from further beating. Tobias got into the ring and helped her to the corner. Tobias checked Kirin's face. "Does this hurt?" He touched it gently.

Kirin said, "I hope you're not planning on kissing me."

Tobias shouted, "Kirin, will you be serious?"

Kirin shouted back, "Does it look like I'm not trying?"

Tobias said, "We worked on dealing with this."

Kirin stared at Tobias, "Yeah ... exactly! We worked on it. Just this fricking morning. Well, guess what? Maybe I need a little more practice."

"Just like we practiced," he encouraged. "Come on!"

Kirin said, "I can't counter it. I can't beat him."

Tobias grabbed Kirin by the arms and said, "You *can* counter it. Stop trying to beat him. Control yourself, and you can counter everything that he's doing."

One would think that being beaten for three rounds would cause Kirin to hesitate, but her tenacity showed. With the start of the fourth round, she continued to charge in on Justice. And just like the previous three rounds, the beatings continued. Justice would show her a particular skill, and then afterward beat her down with it.

Justice said, "This is spring power." *Whack!* "This is bounce power." *Bam!*

Kirin was on the floor, trying to catch her breath. She looked badly bruised and beaten. She got up and looked wobbly in her stance.

Justice said, "I'm saving the best for last." He waved his hand toward Kirin to come. "Get up, Kirin! I'm not done with you just yet."

It took all of Kirin's strength to get up. She took a deep breath and stuck to the same game plan. The blood poured down her face as she ignored the cheers of the crowd. She thought, *Let's do this.*

Kirin began running into Justice, trying to see if he would bite on a fake. He didn't. He was patient as he dared Kirin to tag him with an attack. This time, she went for an unusual line down the center which hopefully would catch him off guard, but it didn't. Instead, he smiled, and Kirin felt the surge through her body. Normally she would flow to the next attack, but he aligned himself so perfectly that there was nowhere for her to move. Even though her feet were perfectly balanced, she didn't feel like she could transfer weight from one side to another.

"You know the feeling, don't you, Kirin?" Justice seemed to enjoy the power he had over her. "When you can do the freeze, it turns mortal men into gods." He released her from the control, and she chained several more attacks onto him. Justice would turn on and off his ability like a switch. As she started her attack and pressed harder, Justice would counter her motion, freeze her for that split second, and slap her on the face. With each hit, the crowd winced with her pain. But, just like that, he froze her motion again. "The old man never taught you how to do it—or, more importantly, how to counter it."

Kirin had the look of panic. With this much control, Justice could end it whenever he wanted to. Then she realized what Tobias had taught her. She said to herself, *Mind zero.*

Kirin took a deep breath and began to calm herself down. She began concentrating on her breathing. She need to silence the noise and clear her mind. After eating several hits, Justice continued to stop her motion and give her a smack. She went with the force and tried another hit as she felt herself frozen in place. She struggled to release herself from his control. But then suddenly, an epiphany: she realized that was fighting the force.

Justice smiled, "I can do this all day, and you won't be able to stop me."

Kirin didn't say a word. She focused, relaxed, and concentrated on herself. And for a split second, she finally could move.

Justice was surprised and caught off guard as Kirin broke his freeze. She slipped through to deliver her first hit, which knocked him back. As she moved in, the bell rang and the referee jumped in to stop her charge.

Kirin staggered to her corner as Tobias ran out to help her get seated. Bryce helped by pulling out a seat. Kirin plopped down and showed every sign of exhaustion.

Tobias wiped the blood from Kirin's face and applied pressure to her eye. "You did it. You finally broke his freeze. You're doing good."

Kirin said, "Are you watching the same fight that I'm in? I'm pretty sure I'm still getting my ass kicked."

"Look, you finally broke it."

"New flash: I'm losing right now!" shouted Kirin.

Tobias replied, "It's all set up for you. In the next round, just land that one punch and finish this fight."

Kirin shook her head. "Uh, I think that's what I've been trying to do."

Tobias said, "You can do this. I believe in you. Like I said, you got one more round, and it only takes one hit. There's no doubt you got into his head when you broke his freeze."

Kirin looked at Tobias and shook her head. "I have no idea what the heck I did to break it.... I just did it."

Tobias said, "Just control yourself and play your game, like we did in practice."

Suddenly one of the handlers from Justice's camp began talking to the referee in the center ring. He pointed to Kirin and began shouting at her.

Tobias watched, wondering what was going on. "Hold on a second. Let me see what bullshit is happening now. Bryce, watch over Kirin and give her what she needs." Bryce nodded as Tobias headed to the center of the ring.

Like the fans, the announcers were enjoying the match. Stabler said, "I've never seen anything more entertaining than what I've just laid eyes on for the first four rounds."

Krenzel said, "I swear it's like straight out of the movies."

Linkwater said, "I feel like I'm in my youth again and watching Gung Fu Sundays on TV."

Grandmaster Chang said, "Don't you mean Kung Fu?"

Linkwater gave Grandmaster Chang a look.

Stabler said, "Last year, she proved how tough she could be with the beating she received from Diesel. However, these four rounds have been even worse."

Connor said, "Kirin Rise is gonna need a miracle to win this match. Either she knocks him out, or Justice will be the champion."

As Tobias was busy dealing with the referee, Bryce grabbed Kirin's water. In his hand, he had something that he was fiercely gripping. Bryce struggled with his conscience, but then suddenly envisioned the face of his sick daughter. He closed his eyes and slipped something into her water. Kirin was trying to gather her strength and was too distracted to notice anything.

He took the water bottle and shook it before handing it to Kirin. Bryce said, "Drink up, Kirin. You'll need it."

Kirin drank the water as Bryce watched and waited, just as he had been instructed. The chaos in the center ring killed more than enough time. Bryce waited for that full minute as sweat poured from his head. He said in a crackled voice, "Kirin, look at me."

Kirin did as he asked. He stared into her eyes, noting that her pupils had changed. Bryce leaned forward and whispered in her ear. He quickly looked to see if Tobias was still dealing with the referee.

Bryce said, "If you understand, bow your head."

Kirin bowed her head and remained seated.

Tobias came back and said, "You ready for the last round, Kirin?"

"Yeah, I'm ready."

The referee checked both corners as Kirin and Justice stood up.

Tobias yelled at Kirin. She turned around as Tobias said, "You can do this. . . . You can beat him!"

Kirin nodded and waited for the signal. She stood in a nice relaxed position as she stared down Justice for the final round.

The referee shouted, "Fight!" and the beginning of the end was upon them.

It had been a grueling four rounds, and Kirin had taken an insane beating. She was bloodied and weathered, but as soon as she heard the referee, her instincts kicked in and she closed the gap one last time. This time, it was different. As Justice began his onslaught of attacks, Kirin stayed on the defensive and merely blocked. After a series of impressive dodges, blocks, and counters, an attack slipped through, and Kirin found herself flying through the air.

The crowd roared as she looked up and tried to shake off the hit. Justice did not move in and waited. Kirin thought, *What's wrong with me? I should be attacking.*

Kirin slammed her fist into the mat and stood up. Justice had a smirk on his face as he was ready to continue. After taking a moment to catch her breath, she went in again after him. As soon as she was in striking range, she again stopped short of her attack. The next thing she knew, she was merely blocking his attacks one after another just like before. Eventually another one got through her defense, and she was sent crashing to the ground.

"Uhhh...." She grabbed her ribs and then her face. It really didn't matter because every part of her hurt. *What the heck am I doing? Why won't I throw an attack?*

The referee was hovering over her to see if she would get up. All the while, Justice did not follow up on his attacks even though he had a clear advantage. From a distance, she could hear Tobias yelling.

"For Christ's sake, attack, dammit. Attack!"

Justice turned around as his handler signaled to him. There was but one minute left until the end of the fight. He nodded his head and then focused his attention toward Kirin. It was time; he knew what the order was. He had no hesitation over executing it.

Kirin got up and stood still as Justice began to move in. Millions of eyes were watching as the fight was nearing an end. Kirin did not move and just stood in an open position.

Tobias watched, wondering what was going on. He screamed, "What are you doing?"

Kirin could hear him as his voice echoed through her body. She remained still as Justice went in for the kill.

This time, something greater came over her, as if her will were no longer her own. Kirin watched and knew she should be moving in, but her body was doing the opposite from what her mind told it to do. She felt like she was going to move, but she remained motionless. She thought, *Move, Kirin. Move or else....*

Justice got into range more confidently than ever that this was the end. He knew Kirin would not counter his last attack, as he launched his punch with one intent in mind.

Kirin was frozen on the outside, but shaking desperately on the inside to free herself from this position. Things were flashing in front of her. Were her real parents still alive? Did she doom their fates by going against those who were trying to control her? She desperately needed to know the truth. Millions were relying on her to bring together the country divided between the rich and the poor. She had to help Bryce and not let him bear the burden of such a challenge alone. And, finally the question as to what could possibly happen to her own friends, family, and most importantly Sifu.

It wasn't time. She wasn't prepared to die. She had to fight. She could overcome whatever it was that was holding her back from moving. She screamed loud from within, but no one could hear. The blood and sweat poured from her as she fought a battle from the inside that only she was aware of.

As Justice's fist landed, she felt the impact of the hit and cringed. The pressure felt like a grenade was being set off inside her. He went for the full kill and unleashed everything into her chest. Kirin so desperately wanted to move. In the blink of an eye, and at the very last possible second, she made a slight turn and invested every ounce of her will to fight what was happening.

BANG!

The hit launched her off her feet in a whiplash motion as her tiny frame flew across the ring.

Stabler shouted, "Oh my God, that impact was devastating!"

Tobias watched in horror, and Bryce turned away in shame. Tobias said, "Oh my God! Holy shit!"

Everyone was stunned by what they had seen. The crowd felt Justice's attempt, and the power he unleashed was an eye opener.

The referee looked at Kirin, who appeared to be out cold, if not worse. He quickly stood in front of Justice, putting his hands up and telling him to stop. Justice peered over his shoulder and then saw Kirin's body slightly twitch. He thought, *She should be dead.* Justice shook his head in disgust, angered by his failure. He grabbed the referee and threw him out of the way. This cleared a path to Kirin, who remained unconscious.

He quickly began to close the gap, as he launched himself in the air. The crowd watched in horror. Everyone knew what he was planning on doing. He was going to go for the kill and finish her off. Justice was hanging in the air, waiting to connect and finally finish his job. As he hit the peak of his jump and was about to land on her, something grabbed him from the air and threw his center into a spiral. He felt his entire being going in the opposite direction, away from Kirin. As he landed on the ground, he went with the force and rolled to not take damage. He slid, regaining his center, and looked up to see Tobias.

Tobias stood in a dominant position as he stared down hard at Justice.

"You touch her again, you die!" shouted Tobias. Deep within, he hoped Justice wouldn't listen. This was a golden opportunity for Tobias to unleash the beast.

Bryce came over to check on Kirin as chaos was everywhere. Kirin was still down and unresponsive. Bryce leaned over and whispered in her ear, "I'm so sorry, Kirin. Please, forgive me." He snapped back and tried waving the medical staff to come in.

Meanwhile in the announcers' booth, confusion reigned.

Stabler continued to broadcast. "I'm not sure what's going on. Who is that that just tossed Justice?"

Krenzel replied, "That's Kirin's sidekick ... uh, I mean trainer, Tobias Jackson."

Connor said, "I don't know if anyone's noticing this, but Kirin is down and she doesn't look like she's moving."

Linkwater replied, "This match is over."

Grandmaster Chang replied, "I think she's dead."

Tobias and Justice continued their stare-down.

Tobias said, "Come on! I got something real for you in these hands!"

Justice smiled and in an instant, he decided to move in and close the gap on Tobias.

Tobias returned the smile and spoke in Tagalog. "Patay ka!"

As soon as he saw Justice move in, Tobias rushed forward to meet the clash. Security surrounded the arena as the stadium was erupting into a crazed frenzy.

As both men reached attack range, each waited for the other to initiate the first motion. It was a game of chicken. Each hoped to have the very last bit of advantage and get the other person to reveal his hand first. The question was who would blink first.

Tobias saw that Justice wanted him to initiate, so he did just that in a manner that wouldn't give Justice the upper hand. Asking hands was the closest thing you could label in Wing Chun as a fake—designed as a passive motion for your opponent to deal with and then allowing you to counter his reaction.

As Tobias released his attack, Justice bit on it and revealed his hand first. Justice took an angle and launched a punch that traveled with utter precision, cutting through the air toward Tobias's center. It drew within an inch of hitting the target, as Tobias remained focus to his goal and wanted him to invest it all.

As it touched the outer part of Tobias's shirt, he turned at the last second to counter the attack. As Sifu had taught him, the harder the attack, the closer you want it to come in. Once your opponent commits heavily in his attack, it makes it extremely difficult to counter your motion. That was the training, that was the discipline, to not fear the attack but to keep the focus on the opponent's center, which was the target.

Bang!

The hit connected as Tobias drew first blood. Justice had no time to recover from the shock as Tobias continued attacking and pressed hard. Death was in each attack that he delivered, which kept Justice on the defensive. He was trying to buy some time until he could recover from the first hit. But Tobias was motivated, he wanted payback for Kirin, he wanted more than blood, he wanted justice.

Justice felt Tobias's intent was greater than his so he unleashed the freeze as he smiled at Tobias. His moment of relief quickly dissipated as Tobias countered it with his own. Justice's eyes widened, as he was caught off guard. Sifu always said that only a handful in the world were able to develop this skill. Justice believed he was the last of Sifu's students to have learned it.

Both fighters ended up neutralizing each other, and Tobias said, "Playtime's over."

As he said that, both went for a front kick to the chest and knocked each other down. Justice fell backwards and rubbed his chest for a brief moment. He quickly jumped up from his prone position and geared up to charge in. Tobias rolled on his back and went with the force, his momentum left him in a push up position staring dead at Justice. He ignored the kick to the chest. Tobias did a helicopter spin and was back up on both feet ready to go.

The referee finally got up and stood between both men. Security rushed in to help him forming a barricade between the two.

Once Tobias realized that it was safe to turn his back, he immediately ran toward Kirin and kneeled down beside her. He shouted at Bryce, "How is she?"

"I don't know. I've been waving the medical staff to come down here, and they've taken forever."

Tobias looked her over as he checked her chest and saw it was moving. He thought, *Oh, shit … thank God. She's alive.*

He leaned forward and saw she wasn't responding. He quickly picked the acupressure point above her lip and began to rub it. "Come on.... Come on, Kirin, wake up, dammit."

He glanced up. "Bryce, wave those mother fuckers down. Now!"

When he looked back down at her, Kirin slowly opened up her eyes. Tobias began to shed a tear as he said, "Oh, shit. You're okay."

Kirin tried to smile, but as she began to get up, she grasped her chest. "Ah," she said.

"Don't … don't move." Tobias held her up and hugged her tightly.

Kirin whispered, "I'm sorry."

"You never have to apologize, Kirin. I'm sorry. I'm sorry for being so stupid and selfish."

Kirin cried on Tobias's shoulder.

Suddenly, the medical staff arrived and asked Tobias to move. He kept a watchful eye on everything. As they picked her up and headed back to the locker room, Tobias held her hand throughout.

After the Fight

Watanabe was glued to the screen as he continued to watch the ongoing news.

"How is she?" asked Watanabe with a genuine look of concern.

Kristen replied, "I've got my people checking on her status, but they've rushed her to the hospital."

Watanabe walked away and sighed.

"Sir, I guess Justice missed his mark," said Kristen.

"I have to admit that did surprise me."

"Don't you think there's a bigger concern, sir?"

He chuckled.

"Sir?"

"So, you know why Justice missed the mark?"

"All I know is that something had to happen for him to miss," replied Kristen.

"Good eye. Somehow, someway, she is one of the rare few to fight off the pill, but there are still some questions that need to be answered."

The TV showed a sign that another call was incoming.

Kristen said with a surprised look on her face, "Sir … it's the five."

One Day Later

Back in Chicago, Thorne was having an intense meeting. He finished talking to Watanabe as Bryce was sitting uncomfortably in his seat.

Fawn was by Bryce's side, circling close by.

Thorne said, "My apologies … business, you understand. Would you like a drink, Bryce?"

"No. Not at all. In fact, the sooner I get out of here, the better."

Fawn snapped, "You're being somewhat of an ingrate, don't you think?" Fawn leaned over his shoulder and raised his eyebrows in a smile.

"Get away from me, Fawn. I did what you asked. I don't owe you any longer."

Thorne said, "Bryce, you seem somewhat bitter considering I saved your daughter's life."

"Mr. Thorne, I appreciate you doing that … but—"

Thorne interrupted, "It's the price to pay, and I think saving your daughter's life was worth it. Don't you agree?"

Bryce squirmed in his chair. Inside, he felt like a monster. Saving one life to sacrifice another. He'd betrayed Kirin's trust. He hung his head down low, as his decision came with a heavy heart.

Fawn grabbed him by the shoulders and said, "Don't be so judgmental, Bryce." He leaned in and whispered, "In the end, you were the one who compromised his own morals."

Thorne looked away as the conversation with Watanabe had him wondering. He knew well enough that something was off, and he felt he was being kept in the dark.

▲ ▲ ▲

At the Hospital

Roughly a week had passed since Kirin's fight in the Dome. Controversy always seemed to surround her, as the discussions and debates were never-ending. The buzz still hadn't faded, and new talk had already surfaced regarding the upcoming season. Last year's fight brought record numbers for the UFMF, but they were dwarfed compared to the battle between her and Justice.

Today, Kirin was finally going to be released from the hospital. She had recovered from her injuries, but inside she was still hurting. She had been fortunate enough to dodge death by the blink of an eye. As she stared through the window from her bed, it began to rain outside.

Knock. Knock.

"Come in," said Kirin.

The door creaked open, and a hand reached around from the other side. Tobias finally peeked through to reveal himself.

"It's me," he said cautiously.

Kirin looked away, ashamed of the loss as she stared out the window.

Tobias walked in and held a bouquet of flowers behind his back. They were, of course, Kirin's favorite, tulips. As he approached her bedside, he stayed silent and placed the flowers by her stand.

"So, the doctors said you can go home today," said Tobias.

Kirin still didn't answer, as her eyes were glazed with tears ready to fall.

Tobias, who always remained strong, saw that Kirin was hurting inside. He got on his knees and grabbed her hand. He said in a most vulnerable voice, "Please, Kirin, I'm asking you to forgive me. I can't change the past, but it's killing me that the two of us aren't right." Afterward, he laid his head down on her bed and fell silent.

Kirin listened to Tobias's words and placed her other hand on his head.

She leaned forward and cringed slightly, as she felt a slight pain in her chest. She said, "I'm not mad at you anymore. Besides, how can I stay angry when you're the one who saved me?"

Tobias lifted his head and looked up to Kirin. "It seems I've been doing that ever since we met."

Kirin suddenly recalled all the times Tobias had done just that. Inside, she was grateful to have such a friend.

"What about us?" asked Tobias as he continued to hold her hand and leaned closer.

Kirin said, "You sure are direct, aren't you?"

Tobias tilted his head and said, "It's the Wing Chun way."

Kirin had so much on her mind the last week that she hadn't given a thought to love. She looked deep into Tobias's eyes and asked, "Well, what do you want to happen between the two of us?'

Tobias grinned and leaned forward. He placed his hands on her face and slowly caressed Kirin's check. He moved in, wanting to answer her question with a kiss. Kirin closed her eyes, and Tobias was just inches from the touch—

Knock. Knock.

"Can I come in?" It was Angelo, waiting behind the door for confirmation.

Kirin pulled back, and Tobias rolled his eyes and pinched the bridge of his nose. He thought, *Karma.*

"Come in," said Kirin.

Angelo quietly tiptoed in. He smiled, showing his brightly polished white teeth that were perfectly aligned.

Kirin laughed as she looked at Angelo. It was refreshing to see him be himself. "Will you quit it? I'm okay…. Please, just come in normally … or … you know what I mean."

Angelo changed his demeanor as he stood straight up and then from behind his back pulled out some goodies. "Oh, my," he said as he saw Tobias, "I'm sorry. I hope I didn't interrupt anything."

In a sarcastic voice, Tobias said, "Oh no, your timing is perfect, as always."

Angelo ignored Tobias's comment and said, "Look what I have for you." He waved in pride toward a fresh cup of coffee along with an assortment of pastries.

"I'm not hungry."

He put on a sad face and said, "What?" He set the assortment to the side and rushed to feel her head. "Are you sure you should be going home? Maybe you're not ready yet."

Kirin slapped his hand away. "Will you cut that out? I'm fine."

Angelo said, "I don't know. The Kirin I know would never turn down freshly brewed coffee. Anyway, I've got your car ready to go to the airport. I've postponed all your appointments for another week. It's nothing but rest for you. Rest, rest, and more rest. Doctor's orders, you know."

Kirin sighed as Angelo continued to talk. She ignored him. She felt lost in her thoughts as her own battles remained. This time, there was no celebration, but merely relief. She had survived the Dome and could finally go home. She was still not quite sure what had happened, as the events of that night were merely a blur. However, she knew one thing. She needed to see Sifu immediately.

Kirin asked, "What day is today?"

Angelo smiled. "Why, it's the day before Christmas—perfect timing, if you ask me."

Kirin was in a daze as Angelo's words snapped her back to reality. She looked up to him and said, "Seriously?"

Angelo nodded and said, "It definitely is … just say the word, and I'm ready to take you home."

"I'm not going home."

"What?" Angelo spun in a circle, confused by Kirin's words. "You're not going home?"

"Nope, I have to go see Sifu."

Angelo staggered to get the words out. "Uh, it's Christmas Eve, Kirin. It's not like a hotel where you can come and go as you please."

Kirin stared Angelo down. "Angelo, this is the one time I'm going to use my celebrity status. I don't care what you have to do. I need to see Sifu, and I need you figure out how to do that ASAP."

Angelo paused and thought about it. He said, "This is why you pay me to be your assistant—to do that which no one else can do. Very well then … let me make a couple calls while you get ready to go." With that, Angelo snapped his fingers and walked out of the room.

Kirin stared at Tobias, as he let out a little sigh and pulled away. The moment had passed.

Five Hours Later Back in Chicago

Kirin turned to Angelo and said, "Thanks for doing this for me. You're the best."

Angelo said, "Please don't say that. Now you're going to make me cry." He began waving his hands to dry his tears.

"Now if you don't mind just waiting here, I'd like to see Sifu by myself."

Angelo nodded and said, "Sure thing. Anyway, I have a ton of work to do, so take as long as you'd like." He then leaned forward and whispered in her ear, "Good luck. Just follow the line to booth nine. He'll be there."

Kirin took a deep breath and nodded as she watched Angelo walk away. Her heart was racing as she didn't know what to say. She had been through so much, both emotionally and physically. As she looked up from a distance, she could see the outline of a figure resembling Sifu. At first, she was hesitant to move any faster, but as his image became even clearer, she yearned to finally see him again. When Sifu was in plain sight, Kirin immediately teared up and began running toward him.

Kirin slowed down until she stopped just a few feet from him. Sifu was sitting in a chair behind the glass. He looked to be in good spirits as he smiled. Sifu stood up and placed his hand against the glass. Kirin forced a smile and approached the glass. She lowered her head at first but then slowly extended her arm as they matched hands with one another. It didn't matter that there was an inch of glass separating the two; both Kirin and Sifu felt one another.

Sifu stared directly at her as the bruises on her face were quite prominent. She was ashamed of her loss. Kirin stared away from Sifu's directness, but that did not last long. This was the first time she had been able to lay eyes upon him, and she fought her ego and pride to finally look at him.

"You look terrible," said Sifu in a strangely comforting voice.

Kirin chuckled slightly, as she thought Sifu was going to tell her his usual line.

"For a moment, you had me worried," replied Kirin.

"Why's that?" Sifu scratched his head.

"I thought you were going to tell me 'not bad, not bad.'" She winced from the bruise on her face. She quickly smiled, trying to hide the pain she felt.

Sifu stared even closer as he tried to examine Kirin's face. He had a look of concern, but tried to lighten the mood. "What did I tell you about blocking with your face?"

Kirin tried to crack a smile, but her lips trembled as she hung her head in shame. Her voice cracked as she said, "Sifu...."

"What is it, Kirin?"

She stood silent and then finally blurted, "I'm sorry.... I'm sorry I failed you.... I'm sorry I lost."

Sifu shook his head.

At first Kirin thought he was disappointed, and she began to cry in shame.

"One should never apologize for losing, Kirin." Sifu leaned lower trying to make eye contact with her. "Kirin, look at me."

Kirin began to shake as she found it difficult to follow his request. Sifu did not utter another word, and waited until Kirin did as he had asked. A few seconds seemed to linger forever, as she tilted her head to face him. However, she still was unable to make direct eye contact with him.

"Kirin ... please. Look at me."

Kirin bit her lip. With sheepish eyes, she finally looked at Sifu.

In a stern yet empathic voice, he said, "Apologize to me only if you plan to quit."

Sifu's words squeezed her heart as she began to wipe the tears from her face.

"I don't know what happened. I honestly don't remember what happened toward the end."

Sifu looked cautiously around before speaking another word. He nudged forward and whispered, "Trust should be earned, Kirin, and not just given."

"What do you mean?"

"I'll speak of it later. You could say the walls have ears."

With a confused puppy dog look, Kirin tilted her head, wondering what it could be. Sifu was being more cryptic than usual.

"But I'm glad you're okay. I was truly worried."

"How could you be so worried about me? You're the one who's stuck in prison. This is no way for you to spend your Christmas," said Kirin.

"Not everything is as it seems, Kirin. Remember you said choice is an illusion? Freedom is no different." Sifu said it with such assurance that it puzzled Kirin.

"I don't understand, Sifu."

"Four walls appear to be captivity. Do they not?"

"Of course, Sifu. You can't do what you want to do." Kirin was convinced by her own words.

"Yet, look around and see the people around you. Have they not created their own prisons and their own limitations? As for yourself, are you not fighting against those who have control over these people? In the end, the greatest lesson I can teach you is the control of your own self. Be able to do that, and you can set yourself free."

"I don't know how you do it, Sifu," said Kirin.

Sifu smiled. "I don't have all the answers, Kirin. To believe that would mean just the opposite. However, I do know I'm gonna have a good Christmas."

"Why's that, Sifu?"

"Coz you're here, silly, but most importantly, you're safe."

Kirin's eyes welled up again. The tears forced themselves uncontrollably down her face. She whimpered and said, "I guess you and I are gonna have a merry little Christmas."

With those last words uttered by Kirin, Sifu said, "Have yourself a merry little Christmas, Kirin." They both leaned forward head to head as the glass separated them from each other.

"The change we want, begins with the revolution within."—*Sifu*

THE END

SECTION 1

Short Stories #12—Ping, Hunter, Sifu & Gwen

<u>Death Drug—332 Days</u>

P ing was recently appointed the head of the east side gang of Chicago. He was young and ambitious, and he didn't care what he had to do to get to the top. The power and the glory were just too intoxicating to turn down, even if right and wrong were as clear as day. The last several months, he had been busy dispensing drugs given to him by Fawn. Fawn had wanted to see the results and effects of these drugs on live subjects. Inside his warehouse, where his other side business took place, he was on the phone chatting with a fellow associate.

Suddenly, one of his henchmen came crashing through the door.

"Mr. Ping! Mr. Ping!" he shouted.

He quietly ended his phone call and raised his hand.

"What is it?"

The henchman rested his hands on his knees and tried to catch his breath. He looked back and noticed the door was still open.

Ping said, "Zhang, go catch your breath before you do anything else."

"Yes … boss … yes. I need to tell you something privately," said Zhang as he looked to Ping's bodyguard who was also in the room.

Ping signaled to his single bodyguard to leave the room. He walked out and shut the door behind him.

"Now, speak!" He poured himself a drink and then lit up a cigarette.

"Well, you know that one school that we've been trying to shut down?" panted Zhang.

Ping took a puff and said, "Last time I checked there were several schools we still have to shut down."

Zhang gasped for air one single time and said, "The Wing Chun school. The one with that Sifu Kwan guy who's been a thorn up the UFMF's ass."

Ping shook his head as he immediately recalled who Zhang was talking about. "Ah, yes. How could I possibly forget that? He's actually number one on my list."

"Well, I gave a test drug to one of our men. Just like you said … you know, to scare the old man while he's in his car."

"Good, maybe he got the hint," said Ping as he took another puff of his cigarette.

"It's not good. I don't know what happened. He was supposed to just scare the old man while he was driving, but I think we got a bad batch or he had a bad reaction to the drug he took."

"So, what went wrong?" asked Ping.

Zhang shook his head. "What went wrong? The dude flipped out and rammed his car head on into another car."

"Perfect, problem solved," said Ping as he didn't even flinch at the news from Zhang.

"Boss, it's not that. You said we were supposed to report any issues with the drugs."

"Yeah, so, what's the problem?"

"Problem is … Kwan wasn't in the car. Instead, his wife and three kids were in it."

Ping finally put out his cigarette and then sat up in his chair.

"Fuck," said Ping. "It's been rare, but we've had a couple test subjects go bat fuck crazy from it. You sure you gave him the right drug?"

"Positive, boss. He was one of our regulars who'd done several jobs for us before. I figure I'd go with our most dependable guy."

Ping slammed both fists into the table and swore again. "Dammit, Zhang. You had one job to do, and you fuck it up like that?"

"It's not my fault, boss! Do we still need to report this incident to Fawn?"

Ping thought about it and said, "Yes. Every pill given to us is marked, and they want direct test results for anything that happened, regardless of success or failure."

Zhang said, "Can't we just tell them something else?"

Ping said, "You think I'm a piece of shit. If it ever comes back we hid this from the UFMF, it'll come back to bite me in the ass. I've worked too damn hard to get where I am." Ping stood up and began to pace the room. "If there's one thing I know, it's impossible to cover your tracks. So, let's follow orders and give Fawn exactly what he wanted."

Zhang said, "What do you want me to do?"

Ping asked, "So, what happened to the family? What about our driver?"

Zhang said, "I got people scoping out to see what happened to Kwan's family, but definitely our guy is dead. At the very least, I know the kids are toast."

Ping said, "A casualty of doing business, I suppose."

Zhang said, "Don't we need to get a hold of his body? I mean, we can't just let them run a tox screen on him. Shit, if they find something, then this will really go public."

Ping listened but didn't panic. He looked at Zhang without speaking a word.

Zhang asked, "Sir, give me an order. I'll do whatever you need me to do."

Ping approached his henchman and said, "Here's exactly what I want you to do—and, Zhang, make sure you follow this to the T. First, take three of your men or however many you need, and go down to the morgue."

Zhang said, "So you want us to beat them before they examine him?"

Ping thought about it. "Actually, it doesn't matter. Let them run the test on him. That way, we save money on the results. That info can be forwarded to Fawn."

Zhang said, "Good thinking, boss … and then afterward?"

"So afterward, regardless of what the result is, get that info for us and silence whoever knows by whatever means necessary."

Zhang said, "What about the police? I'm sure they'll be around there."

Ping said, "What about them? Dumb ass foot patrols will look at this as a simple intoxication case. It'll blow over fast."

"Got it, boss. What about the old man?"

Ping said, "If his family is dead, that should break anyone … but just in case, I've been working on a plan to get the deed to his school, one way or another."

Zhang said, "What is it, boss?"

Ping said, "Let's just say a perfect trap to get all those schools we need to take over, to fall one by one."

Bad Timing—297 Days

Weeks of preparation had finally come down to this single moment. Hunter had gathered the school band and a handful of students from the chorus and dance club. He also enlisted the services of the science club, to help him out with some of the pyrotechnics. In his mind, he had envisioned the perfect and most elaborate way to ask Kirin to the prom. The amount of time and effort he invested would all be worth it, if only she said that three-letter word: Yes.

It was just nearing sunset as he watched Kirin's house from afar. Inside, he felt kind of bad for spying on Kirin, but he had to know exactly what her pattern was to make sure he pulled this off.

Hunter had everyone already in position. The band of about thirty was already nestled together hiding on the other side of Kirin's fence by her neighbor's house. It was a sight to see: teenage students all dressed up in full uniform, crouching with their instruments by the bushes. Along the side of the road, the chorus and the dance club were tucked away behind the cars, ready to begin the show.

Hunter made one final check, as he called on his cell phone.

He said, "Hey, Chang, are you guys all set?"

Chang replied, "Give us five more minutes, Hunter."

In a nervous voice, he checked his phone and the time and asked, "Five more?"

Chang replied, "Uh, yeah. It's the fireworks. I think the last thing you want to do is burn down the neighborhood."

Hunter shook his head and replied, "You've got a good point." He realized he really didn't have much of a choice and said, "Text me once you're ready. Oh … Chang, launch the fireworks once Kirin swings her window open."

Chang said, "Relax, that's the easiest part."

Hunter began to pace back and forth. He was nervous and wanted everything to be perfect. He knew everyone was waiting on him to give the signal. It was nearing 7:00 pm, and Kirin would normally be hitting her room just about this time. He thought, *Come on, Chang … text me already.*

He was staring at his phone when a simple message popped up from Chang: "GTG."

"Finally!" he shouted in excitement. With that, he sent a mass text to everyone there to wait for the lights in Kirin's room to turn on.

Everyone was watching and waiting as a few minutes passed and still no lights came from her room. Hunter thought, *That's odd; she's like clockwork. She always goes to her room around this time.*

The minutes passed as Hunter felt a knot grow in his stomach. He hung his head, mumbling, "Jeez, what else can go wrong?"

Suddenly, he got a text from one of the students that said, "The lights are on."

Hunter's head sprang up as he looked to see that Kirin's lights were on. He saw a shadow from behind the curtain pass by as he texted back to everyone. Hunter thought, *And so it begins.*

Everyone waited and knew exactly what to do. First, the band lined up in marching formation and began playing a song. It was loud but well in sync as the leader of the group led them in formation toward Kirin's house. Once they got into their final position, the next group would begin their job.

The chorus group gathered in front of Kirin's lawn and began belting out their vocals. They lined up in two rows, all wearing their robes, as their voices carried throughout the neighborhood. It made for such a nice harmony, as it blended smoothly with the band. As Hunter waited for his turn, the group of dancers spun in front of Kirin's lawn. There they were, paired up together, doing a combination of different styles of dances. For the next several minutes, one would think a live Broadway show had somehow gotten lost and ended up in the wrong location.

As the introduction of song and dance ended, Hunter walked in with several of the actors as they were lip syncing a scene. For the next ten minutes, the blood, sweat, and tears they had poured into practice was all coming together. Every so often, Hunter would glance upward to the window as the shadow behind the curtains continued to wait there.

Finally, the end was nearing, as everything led to this single moment. As the chorus group finally stopped singing and the music ended, Hunter walked to Kirin's window and paused for a moment to gather his breath. All eyes were on him, as everything had come off just as he had planned.

He smiled at the work and effort that was put into it. Everything was going just right.

He looked up and yelled at the top of his lungs. "Kirin Rise, will you go to prom with me?"

The shadow behind the curtain didn't respond right away. A bead of sweat from Hunter's head dripped down his face. He swallowed and waited. His eyes widened as the curtain stretched apart and the window finally flew open. Kyle looked down on Hunter, smiled, and sang at the top of his lungs, "She's … not … heerrreee!"

Hunter's face froze in shock. He couldn't believe what had just happened. Suddenly, fireworks began to explode above, blanketing the sky. No one knew what to do, as Hunter wasn't the only one caught off guard. He stood there, shaking his head, realizing that his elaborate plan had failed to secure the most important thing.

Coffee, Anyone?—Mid-September 2033

Billy came knocking at the back of Sifu's restaurant.

Knock. Knock.

He waited patiently as the door swung open. There, the two stood facing one another. Sifu carried a surprised look on his face, and Billy stood carrying a box of pizza.

Billy said, "Extra hot, just like you wanted." He looked around and then gave a wink.

"Mmm … how'd you know? I love pizza." Sifu grabbed the box and gave Billy some extra credits. He made sure he kept the conversation to a minimum.

Sifu brought the box inside and laid it on the counter. Sifu thought, *Pretty heavy, it must be deep dish.* Sifu lifted the top cover. Inside was a brand new laptop computer along with a set of instructions. Sifu said, "Well, this is gonna be an interesting day."

Thirty Minutes Later

Sifu sat in a coffee shop and pulled out his computer. On a little sheet of paper, he followed the instructions that were written down. There were several steps to follow with a list of what to do—and what not to do. He opened the screen and logged on. Within seconds, a chat popped up.

He looked at his screen name: Yummyramen. The name made him chuckle. He pulled out his glasses and then saw a new name pop up, Hellonwheels.

A timer popped up, marking thirty minutes, and it began to count down.

Hellonwheels: Let's get right to business. We've got thirty minutes before this line is no longer secure.

Yummyramen: Why the code names?

Hellonwheels: I thought you'd appreciate the undercover stuff.

Yummyramen: I do, and all this looks pretty cool … but damn expensive. lol

Hellonwheels: I'm pretty sure you can afford it.

Yummyramen: I see someone's been digging around.

Hellonwheels: Sorry. I was curious.

Yummyramen: Np. I'd be disappointed if you didn't question how I was able to pay for all this.

Hellonwheels: Sorry, I'm always digging. It's in my nature.

Yummyramen: Anyway, did my information pay off?

Hellonwheels: If it was the lottery, you could say it matched all six.

Yummyramen: I guess you can say I know what that feels like.

Hellonwheels: Lol … uh, yeah.…

Yummyramen: So, who's playing the puppeteer?

Hellonwheels: I got it confirmed he's in the UFMF, but he's the highest of the high, and he makes Thorne look like the chauffeur.

Yummyramen: There's always someone higher.…

Hellonwheels: I don't think there's anything higher.

Yummyramen: So, he's a one percenter?

Hellonwheels: I'm not sure even sure how to label him. But from my digging he's like .01%

Yummyramen: Hmm. Got a name?

Hellonwheels: Youshiro Watanabe. He hasn't been sighted in years, but piecing together all they're doing is going to be difficult. I'm getting bits and pieces to a huge puzzle.

Yummyramen: All highs come with a price. You don't become the largest corporation in the world by simply promoting fights.

Hellonwheels: No, you don't. By the way, I wanted to thank you. I guess you're fighting strategy on attack and defense works with everything.

Yummyramen: Universal common sense. It's unstoppable, but curious how you are using it.

Hellonwheels: The rule of thumb is anything can be hacked. If you forget that, you're screwed. A lot of times, we like to create a false sense of security and think that we can protect ourselves from everything … when, in fact, that way of thinking leaves us most vulnerable. For example, as secure as the encryption code is on these computers, technically there's always a way to trace. Just like karma, you can't cheat it, but you can do the next best thing and make it extremely difficult to detect and follow.

Yummyramen: Impressive. By the way, my apologies.

Hellonwheels: Regarding…?

Yummyramen: The waiting list.

Hellonwheels: Was that for motivation?

Yummyramen: Yes.

Hellonwheels: Well, it worked. I pinpointed that bastard, and he's going down after we are all done.

Yummyramen: Karma?

Hellonwheels: I'm willing to burn it, when I'm done with him. He won't even exist digitally.

Yummyramen: How are we on time?

Hellonwheels: We're good still, but we got some huge hurdles.

Yummyramen: I thought anything could be hacked.

Hellonwheels: It can, but the real juicy stuff is going be a pain. Their setup is surprisingly simple. Let me explain it without being too technical. They have a door; we need the key. That is going to be difficult, but let's say we do get that key, we literally have to be physically there to unlock the goodies.

Yummyramen: Be there?

Hellonwheels: Yup, can't hack it from a distance. Best way to explain how they have things setup is to think of a one-way street. Things can go out from their place, but in order to access anything of importance … you literally have to be there.

Yummyramen: There being?

Hellonwheels: The UFMF headquarters in NY.

Yummyramen: So going back to stage one, which is the first hurdle, how do we deal with that?

Hellonwheels: The prize they've buried is so big.... Care to take a guess?

Yummyramen: I'm afraid to ask.

Hellonwheels: Prison.

Yummyramen: So, what do you suggest? Visiting hours.

Hellonwheels: Hear me out. The only way you're gonna get and confirm the information you want is to go to the source.

Yummyramen: It sounds like you are suggesting that I get arrested.

Hellonwheels: That's exactly what I'm telling you to do.

Yummyramen: So, how exactly do I get arrested and placed in the same prison as the source?

Hellonwheels: Leave that to me. They've been tailing you forever and trying to find something on you. I already talked to your lawyer. Seems like your little gamble on last year's fight would be illegal if you were to be tied to Kirin's camp. Then it would lead you right where we need to be.

Yummyramen: How are you gonna get me associated with something Kirin never signed?

Hellonwheels: Easy. That same bastard that took me down from the waiting list. I hacked into his computer already and used his login to place the signature on it. Besides, the UFMF has been spying on you for some time. They just needed something on you.

Yummyramen: Since when?

Hellonwheels: Even before the Jabbiano incident, they've been keeping an eye on you. Looking for you to slip up.

Yummyramen: They sound paranoid.

Hellonwheels: The UFMF is beyond paranoid, so much so they spy on everyone. They have like a reverse search engine. If you enquire anything about them, they'll know. They copied what the government has been doing to citizens for years, but juiced it up to the max.

Yummyramen: You sure you can pull this off?

Hellonwheels: Everything's digital, and always remember anything can be hacked. I can make sure step by step you get into the right prison, the same holding block, and when the time comes, also get you out.

Yummyramen: You positive about this?

Hellonwheels: Like I said … it's your art's strategy being implemented.

Yummyramen: How so?

Hellonwheels: The problem with security is that they always look for a way to block things out. But that just creates a false sense of security. Just like it would be impossible to make something so perfect that you couldn't get hit. I always use this same strategy to get through all my hacks.

Yummyramen: I see your BFF has rubbed off on you.

Hellonwheels: Exactly. The best defense isn't preventing access to your system. It's allowing them to get into it and then you can see who or what is trying to get in and beat them to the punch.

Yummyramen: It's almost as if you're baiting them in.

Hellonwheels: How's this sound so far?

Yummyramen: I'll make sure I don't drop a bar of soap. Tell me more of this key in prison.

For the remaining fifteen minutes, Sifu and Gwen went over the game plan. All the details were laid out, and Sifu realized what needed to be done.

Hellonwheels: I think it's time we both log off. I'll be speaking to you again.

Yummyramen: So, should I call you?

Hellonwheels: Use your phone, but remember: it's hacked; can't let them know anything's unusual. I've got another way we can communicate.

Yummyramen: Sounds expensive.

Hellonwheels: Lol. It won't be … for you.

Both Sifu and Gwen closed their laptops, miles apart from one another, as the plan had been set.

As Gwen looked up across the coffee table, Sage smiled back. "You're all done?"

"On the contrary, my very cute boyfriend. In fact, you could say, it's just the beginning."

"I just find you so attractive when you have that glimmer in your eye," said Sage.

"I have a feeling, before all this is over, you and I are gonna have one heck of a story to tell our kids."

Sage smiled and said, "I'd like that."

Gwen said, "I'm surprised. . . . You didn't even blink when I mentioned the possibility of both commitment and kids."

Sage said, "You always said I was brilliant, didn't you?"

Gwen nodded and said, "I did."

Sage said, "Well, it doesn't take a genius to know when you've found someone special."

Gwen smiled, and then quickly her mood changed.

Sage asked, "Did I say something wrong?"

"No. It's not that, but the mention of kids and family. While I was digging through the parts of the server on the UFMF, there was a file I happened to see on Sifu's family."

"Holy crap," said Sage. "What did you find?"

"I couldn't hack into it," said Gwen.

"What? Something even you couldn't get through?"

"It's not that simple. I can hack into it, but they're using a proximity sensor to access this special file. That means you literally have to be within the vicinity to be able to check it out," said Gwen.

"Wow. If that's the case, it must be something extremely important."

"Tell me about it. I didn't have the heart to tell Sifu about it, but I'm sure it ties into everything," said Gwen.

SECTION 2

Sifu Journey Entry #12—A Letter to Megumi

Christmas Day 2030

With all that Sifu had overcome, there was still one thing that continued to stab at him. This unfinished business haunted him every waking second and, until completed, would not give him peace. Since the funeral, Sifu had been unable to go back and visit the graves. The pain was unbearable, as he was constantly riddled with guilt and confusion. This was a tall task for anyone, but the emotional turmoil that felt unresolved was taking its toll on Sifu.

He told Lance that he had one thing he had to do before he was ready to open their business adventure together. It was early Sunday morning, and a light snow was falling upon Chicago this Christmas morning.

Sifu had spent a restless night knowing what his main goal was for the day. He left his apartment, and the chilly air immediately hit his face. He exhaled, and the frost from his breath created steam. He thought, *I can do this. I have to do this. It's been far too long.*

The cemetery was lodged in the heart of the city, only a few blocks from where he taught. He had taken a cab and asked to be dropped off a block away from the entrance. Since Sifu's return to Chicago over a year and a half ago, he had kept a low profile. Only Mike and Phil, his former students, had known of his return, and Sifu had asked them to keep it quiet. He was not quite ready to deal with all his past, just yet.

He stepped out of the cab and looked around before proceeding. Sifu was all bundled up in winter gear, which made it perfect since he didn't have to put extra work into disguising himself.

Sifu began walking toward the location of the graves. He was halfway there when he suddenly stopped. A figure stood some distance away, but he immediately recognized the individual. It was Kirin.

He hid behind one of the standing memorials and leaned against the wall.

Sifu thought, *What's she doing here?*

He rounded the corner, inching his way just enough to see what Kirin was doing. There, she was, busy tending to the graves. She had placed a flower on each one and made sure the fresh snow didn't cover their names. Sifu noticed that a small tree had been planted near the graves.

"I wonder if she was the one who put it there?" Sifu whispered to himself.

He leaned against the wall and began to tear up. He thought, *I can't believe she's been taking the time to take care of the graves.* He took another peek, and Kirin was still there. He felt both sad and guilty that he had left her on her own, but he had needed time on his own to find the strength to continue after such a tragedy.

After several minutes, Sifu pulled out the paper from his coat. He had so badly wanted to read it during the funeral, but he hadn't had the strength to endure the pain of the moment.

His goal was to go visit the graves and read it in front of his family. He needed that closure; he needed to say what he wanted to say. That would have to wait for another time, as he decided to simply look at it. The cold air no longer bothered him, and he took one last look to see if Kirin was still there. She turned around quickly as Sifu ducked back into the corner. He wondered, *Can she feel my presence?*

Sifu waited several minutes. His nerves at the prospect of seeing his family's graves had subsided. He decided instead to read it where he stood. This was the first time he had looked at it since he had written it. The message read:

> As people, we expect an answer to all our questions. It burns within us for closure to ensue. I cannot describe the pain. I cannot tell you of the loss. However, I did not want my final words to my wife and children to be about sadness. Instead, I wanted to speak of the love my wife and I shared, because that is the one thing I'm sure she would want me to do.
>
> My Dearest Megumi,
>
> You love because love is who you are. In the same way a river that tumbles over a cliff does not know it is a waterfall. You do as you were meant to do, never fully realizing the significance of your own purpose, but at the same time trusting in the flow of the universe.

Megumi, you brought life to my world. Until I met you, I had no idea what it was to love. The one thing I never questioned was my dedication to my art, and to me that was love. But, the very first day I met you at the restaurant, as I gazed into your eyes and saw into your soul, was the day that changed my life forever and redefined its meaning.

Love is a sacrifice; I learned that from you. It is the unquestionable surrender of one's soul to someone, without the desire for anything in return— only to trust the will of the force, that energies match, and continue to grow beyond the physical and without limitation and to become everlasting.
You let me be me. What more can anyone ask for?

Sifu's hands began to shake, and several tears pelted his piece of paper. The pain he would have to endure for another day, as the universe was not yet prepared to allow him to heal. He looked back to the grave to see if Kirin was still there. She had finally left, and the snow continued to fall. His chance to finish his task was at hand. Instead, Sifu took his letter and folded it back up neatly into his pocket. As the snow hit, he began walking away from the graves and back to the exit.

About the Author

Ed Cruz is an expert in the martial art of Wing Chun Gung Fu. He has been studying and practicing it for thirty-nine years and teaching it for eighteen. His Kirin Rise series uses the real martial arts philosophy as the basis for a dystopian YA thriller.

Cruz was trained in various martial arts for eleven years, but Wing Chun Gung Fu and its effective approach caught his attention. He met with Augustine Fong, a Wing Chun Gung Fu master, and has since devoted his life to mastering the art. Cruz is now an expert and has been publishing articles about Wing Chun Gung Fu for eighteen years.

Cruz was born in Manilla in the Philippines but immigrated to the United States at the age of three. His family resettled in Chicago, Illinois, and it has been his home ever since.

67461862R00270

Made in the USA
Lexington, KY
13 September 2017